Bridle Path
Press

Through the Channel

a novel

Melissa Westemeier

Through the Channel is a work of fiction. Names, characters, places, and incidents are the products of the author's imagination or are used fictitiously. Any resemblance to actual events, locales, or persons, living or dead, is entirely coincidental.

For information or permission contact:

Bridle Path Press, LLC
8419 Stevenson Road
Baltimore, MD 21208

www.bridlepathpress.com

Direct orders to the above address.

Printed in the United States of America.
First Edition.
ISBN: 978-1-7321630-6-5

Library of Congress Control Number: 2019957271

Book Design by Elizabeth Ryan Cole
Cover Design by Mitch Miskoviak

Bridle Path
Press

For Travis, Brent and Gregory—with great love and hope that you each find your purpose and place in this life

Through the Channel

ONE

June 1988

"**H**I, CALLER, YOU'RE ON the air with Garden Talk."

Mona Butterfield leaned forward in her seat and took a deep breath to calm her nerves. A steep climb had brought her to this moment and she felt both terrified and excited. Garden Talk! She'd listened faithfully to the public radio program for three years now, ever since she propagated her Grandma Butterfield's seeds and started what had become a thriving greenhouse business. Her farm market stand, "Dirty Girl Veggies," had become a staple for local customers, including a few restaurants. Local bait shop salesman and marketing guru Maw Cooper had helpfully provided the provocative name and logo of a cucumber resting alongside two tomatoes. Mona sold bushels of fresh vegetables May through October at the weekly market and during the winter months provided several local restaurants with fresh greens grown out of the greenhouses she and her dad had built behind the milking barn on their dairy farm.

The journey had not been an easy one. For starters, she'd had to convince her dad to take her on as a partner in the farming business, instead of her older brother Sean, who was now using his chemistry degree at a pharmaceutical company, researching cancer treatments. Then she'd fumbled her way through learning how to grow for profit, eventually taking a handful of classes at a technical college in nearby Northport. Applying her memorization skills to learning botany instead of drink orders, Mona studied propagation, soil, accounting and marketing while serving drinks and burgers at the Bassville Pub. She'd nurtured her greenhouse business against all odds and finally poured her last pitcher of beer in February. Now she was full throttle farming.

The biggest sacrifice, however, had been letting go of her boyfriend Jake Paulick. That memory still wrenched at her heart.

He'd netted his dream job as a project manager for a construction job, which normally wouldn't split up a couple, except for the fact that the job was in Atlanta, Georgia. Her family farm business was in Bassville, Wisconsin. Twenty-four hours of highway driving separated them, and so did their vision of a future. When he'd asked her to marry him and join him in Atlanta, she couldn't say yes. She'd wanted to, but to give up all she'd worked for to move to a strange place? It was too much to leave behind.

Chickenshit. That's what her best friend Jenny Bender had called her.

She and Jake had tried, briefly, to pretend her rejection of a marriage proposal and a long-distance relationship didn't matter in the six months until he moved. Of course they mattered, though, and finally the phone calls and letters between them diminished a year after he'd left. He'd started a new life; the reality sunk in every time he talked about people she'd never meet and places she'd never go. They found less and less common ground when they talked—and their conversations had dwindled to once a month. Mona had begun to wonder if she was holding out too much and whether it was time to move on since she'd turned twenty-six. She spent her spare time going to the same old places with her old friends: Jenny Bender, her best friend since elementary school; Scotty Trayson, the son of her parents' best friends; and Judi Linski, a welcome addition to their small town when she'd bought the Bassville Hotel five years ago with her mother.

Three years since Jake's proposal had made her a different person. A couple of weeks ago, the production manager for Wisconsin Public Radio's Ideas Network had called, asking if she'd be a guest on Garden Talk, a call-in radio program about all things related to gardening. Mona Butterfield was on the air! She was perched on a swivel desk chair across from the show's host, snugged in between two tall filing cabinets, a desk which overflowed with papers and a bulletin board covered with *Far Side* comics and directions on where to go in case of an emergency.

"Hi, I'm Jayne from Freedom. Last summer my tomatoes turned brown and spotty on the vine. Was that blight? How can I prevent that from happening again?"

The show's host, a pleasant man in horn-rimmed glasses named Larry invited Mona to answer the caller's questions. She leaned a fist's distance from the microphone on her side of the desk and suggested changing the placement of the tomatoes and growing them on a mound. "Tomatoes don't like wet feet," she explained. "And marigolds can be a good friend, so plant a few nearby."

The show continued in this vein. Larry and Mona bantered with each other about peppers and pumpkins and suddenly the hour was up.

In the hallway outside the cramped studio office, Larry shook her hand. "You did great, Mona," he enthused. "Can you come back again? People love guests on the show and I think it's important to have younger people. Show folks that gardening's for everyone, not just us old fogeys."

"I'd love that, Larry." Mona pulled one of her business cards out of her purse and handed it to him. "Call me and we can set it up. This was fun."

Driving west towards Bassville, Mona reflected on the afternoon's success. She'd made it, she thought. Business owner, town council member and now a radio personality. Maybe she'd do for her greenhouse what Maw had done for his bait shop. It just stunk that she was doing it alone. Running her business alone meant working fifty to sixty hours every week, and Mona was physically spent. But sore muscles aside, she wanted to tell someone—Jake, really—about her day. She wanted to have someone cheering for her little victories and encouraging her, the way he had done. The space between them wasn't just miles anymore. She knew that it expanded beyond what they could reasonably reach across. It made sense to her to break it off, but her decision still haunted her, especially in moments like this. She dreamed about him at night, his strong arms wrapped around her body, his lips on her cheek. The alarm would wake her up and desperation and longing would flood her mind when she'd open her eyes to the empty pillow beside her head. It was like grasping for water with her fists, reaching for his touch in her dreams and waking up alone in her house in Bassville.

It was late afternoon and the sun had dropped enough that she had to pull down her visor to see the road ahead of her. The glint of the Wissipaw River, which ran through the town, appeared between the trees as she crested the hill. The town, straddling both sides of the river and connected by a bridge, came into view. To her right was the faded billboard advertising Bassville as the "White Bass Capital of the Western Hemisphere," the cartoon image of a fisherman reeling in a giant fish luring tourists to pull over. Mona drove over the bridge and could see Jake's little blue cottage on the shore.

Jake had come home for Christmas last year. He'd called her and she'd gone to his parents' place since he was renting out his cottage while he was living in Atlanta. They'd acted like they were on a first date. Hesitating and too polite, they'd made small talk. Naturally, all of his family and their friends wanted to spend time with him, too, so she'd had to share his attention. His visit was too short to reconnect and get their groove back. At the airport when she'd said goodbye, he had paused. If he'd have asked her again to marry him, she would have said yes in that moment. Instead he'd kissed her and told her to be good before lifting his duffel bag to his shoulder and disappearing down the corridor leading to his plane. That was six months ago and they'd only spoken by phone a few times since.

Mona turned the dial on her car radio. She needed a happy song to take her mind off Jake. But every song brought him to mind and by the time she turned off the highway towards her family's farm, she'd turned off the music and listened instead to the steady churn of her tires on the highway.

A bulldozer and a digger sat silently on the edge of the field. Plastic flags fluttered from their stakes, marking the lot lines for the future subdivision. A few farms bordered the field, two barns visible beyond their cropland and pastures. A blacktopped road edged with cement curbing snaked through the field. Three huge holes had already been dug, the basements poured. Two men in hardhats and work boots leaned against the side of a pickup truck, studying a clipboard. Further into the subdivision stood the first two houses, one a two-story Cape Cod and the other a low-slung ranch. Mona drove past the scene and stared. What kind of people were moving to Bassville? She'd seen one of the new families at the gas station a few weeks ago, but the other was a mystery. It seemed unlikely that anyone her age would be moving into the new houses. She continued along the county highway to her parents' place. She needed to check in with her dad before heading home for the night. They had a forty-pound order of greens to fill tomorrow and he'd been in charge of harvesting it.

A few minutes later her tires crunched across the gravel driveway and she pulled in next to her parents' two-story white farmhouse. Mona waved at her mom while she passed the house on her way to the greenhouses behind the barn. Her mom raised a yellow-gloved hand in greeting and called to her through the kitchen window. "Staying for supper?"

"If you don't mind. I haven't had time to go grocery shopping and I think the only thing to eat at my house is a box of Pop-Tarts."

"I heard you on the radio on my way home from work today. You were wonderful!"

"Thanks, Mom!"

The air inside the greenhouse was humid despite the open vents and the doors. Mona inspected the soil's moisture levels and spot-checked beneath a few leaves, her busy fingers pruning back a few suckers while she made her way through the flats of plants. All looked good, she thought before turning towards the milk barn where her father finished his evening chores.

"Hey, Dad!" Mona called, treading carefully between a couple fresh piles of cow poop.

"You're back just in time," Loyal Butterfield replied. He stepped out of a stall and reached for a pitchfork. "Here, you can pitch in." A smiled creased his craggy features.

Mona groaned and grabbed it from him. Dad's jokes were the worst.

6

"Just the far stalls. I'm done here," Loyal said. He pulled the mesh John Deere ball cap off his grey hair and ran his other hand over his sweaty forehead. His T-shirt was wet beneath the arms and in a long vee down his front.

"It's only May and this warm. What will summer feel like?"

"Worse," Loyal said.

"You get those greens ready?"

"Packed in bags in the fridge, just like you asked."

"Thank you."

She helped her dad finish up in the barn and returned with him to the house.

In the kitchen, June Butterfield bent over the oven and slid out a casserole that steamed up a savory aroma. June carried the pan to the kitchen table and set it on a potholder. "Wash up," June told them. "Dinner's ready."

After quickly bowing her head to say grace with her family, Mona scooped some fruit salad onto her plate while her father portioned out the main dish. "How was work today?" she asked her mom.

"Quiet, and I can't complain about that."

June had taken a part-time position at a women's shelter since starting as a volunteer two years ago. Now she was responsible for administering the office and raising donations.

"Did you hear the latest news here?" Loyal asked June.

"What's that?"

Loyal set down his fork. "One of the new families in that subdivision has been hassling Gene and Dottie to mow the fields around their house. As you might imagine, they've sprung up thick with weeds since no one's planted them in the last year. Gene told me the lady threatened to sue them."

"But it's not their problem!" Mona exclaimed. "Didn't they sell the land to someone else? The developer should be responsible for mowing."

7

"It's just like I predicted," Loyal said with a wry expression. "City people like the idea of country living until they actually live in the country. Then they want the country to turn into a city, complete with mowed lawns and a McDonalds on every corner."

"I'm sure they didn't know any better about Gene and Dottie." June emptied the rest of the fruit salad onto Loyal's plate before reaching back to set the dish on the counter. "The sign does have their name on it, 'Traysons Acres.' But those fields are pretty bad, you can see the thistles from the highway, they spread everywhere."

"It's got to feel so weird for them to see those houses going up where they once had their fields," Mona said. She knew it bothered Gene and Dottie's son, Scotty, because lately he asked her questions about their farm that he'd never brought up before. Like he was trying to prove he hadn't forgotten how to farm even though he didn't work on one anymore.

"I wonder what they'll do," June said. "Dottie seems like she's at her wits end just keeping house. Angie's a junior now, hardly needs her mother anymore. Do you suppose they'll retire to Florida and live by a golf course?"

Loyal laughed at the suggestion. "Gene would hate living close to neighbors like that. No, he won't turn full-time golfer. I wish he'd kept a few breeding cattle just to keep himself busy, though."

"Speaking of busy, how's the dining room coming?" Mona asked her mother. June was turning the space into a home office with a sofa. She'd sold the big table and hutch earlier that spring and stripped the space down to baseboards and carpet.

"I picked out a border yesterday and I want you to see it. Your dad drew the line at new carpet, but paint and new furniture will make a big difference."

Loyal waved his wife and daughter out of the kitchen. "You already put in a full day working at the women's shelter. I'll get the dishes, you go show your project off to Mona."

"Look at this man! Doing supper dishes—who says people can't change?" June leaned over to peck her husband's cheek.

Mona grinned at them while thinking that was exactly the problem *and* the blessing sometimes. People did change.

TWO

Maw cooper cursed loudly as a stack of mailing envelopes slid to the floor like dominoes. There was no fighting gravitational pull while the pile shifted and fell. Besides, Maw was elbow deep in a cardboard box full of can coolers and matchboxes he'd had printed up with the store's logo: Maw's Bait and Tackle: Home of the Pitbull Minnow. The logo curved below a cartoon sketch of a whiskered and fierce-looking minnow clamping razor sharp teeth onto the tail of a walleye.

The spring fishing run had boosted sales of T-shirts and other branded merchandise. The actual bait sales weren't that great, but neither was the weather. An unusually cold and sloppy spring had lured only the most dedicated fishermen out to the Wissipaw River. Everyone else stayed hunkered down in the taverns and resorts, hunched over their beers and burgers and complaining until the season ended. Now the heat of late May had cooled fishing on the river. As more boats and the newly popular jet skis churned up wake, the fishermen retreated to more remote spots on the river or gave up weekend fishing altogether.

Never one to miss an opportunity, however, Maw decided he'd try cashing in on this new pleasure boating crowd. He craved fame and fortune ever since a Chicago-area disc jockey had called for a fishing report one morning in 1984. Maw had thrown him a line of bullshit which had led to TV appearances and he'd been trying to duplicate his fifteen minutes of fame ever since. Boaters were assholes, but they came through town wanting to spend, spend, spend. He'd watched the Shanskis evolve the Bassville Pub from a burgers-and-beer bar for locals and fishermen to more of a party vibe.

Pub owner Steve Shanski now wore a T-shirt with tropical flowers bordering a new logo with a distinctly nautical theme. His wife, a tall, chain-smoking woman with a penchant for wearing dangly earrings, had coiled ropes around the base of the barstools and a new Budweiser sign with a lighthouse took the spot of the old Pabst Blue Ribbon sign behind the bar. Their menu now included gyros and baskets of deep-fried cauliflower and mushrooms. And for a spot of fun, the locals would poke Steve about the margarita specials. That was Arlyce's idea and twice Maw had seen his friend explode with frustration over blender drinks. Both times he'd ripped the blender cord out of the electrical socket and walked it to the end of the pier where he chucked it into the Wissipaw River. "Stupid margaritas. Why can't these assholes just drink beer like normal people?" Steve had fumed when he stormed back behind the bar. And both times he had come back to work the next day to find a brand-new blender plugged in next to the ice machine.

Ever since Mona quit bartending, Steve had cycled through a series of college kids who just never seemed to clue in or keep up. The latest was a thin, brown-eyed boy named Tyler—or was it Trevor?—no

11

matter, he'd be gone next season anyway. None of the new kids would shake dice to see who'd pay for a drink or demonstrate any sense of humor in dealing with the regular customers like the compulsively gambling Spade or the barrel-sized Dohill brothers.

"Maybe bringing in boaters isn't such a good idea," Maw mused aloud. The bearded middle-aged man looked down at the neon green and pink can coolers and shrugged. Unless he could figure out some consumable thing to sell boaters, he'd be a one-stop kind of deal for them. How much of a headache could that create?

He'd just finished stocking the beer cooler when the front door swung open and in flounced Jenny Bender, a petite and fiery party girl, carrying a purse the size of a tackle box. "Maw! I've got a bone to pick with you!"

Maw greeted her with a toothy smile. "Jenny, baby. You look fantastic. Are you doing something new with your hair?"

"Don't you try and sweet talk me, buddy." She dug around in her giant purse and pulled out the advertising circular Maw had printed up for the season. "What's the deal with this?" she demanded, poking at the flyer with a long red-painted fingernail. Today the twenty-six-year-old curvaceous woman wore a halter top with denim shorts, showing a lot of her tanned skin.

Maw bent forward to look more closely at the glossy brochure in her hand. A line of young women wearing swimsuits posed in front of a bass boat and beneath the picture ran the caption, "Maw's Bait and Tackle—Home of Maw's Specialty Minnows and Bassville's Bikini Fishing Team." It looked exactly like the one he'd ordered. He frowned and shrugged. "What about it?"

"Seriously?" Jenny's voice rose to a higher pitch and she stabbed her fingernail against his chest. "You let Sheila take center stage and practically cropped me out of the photo."

Maw squinted at the image. Jenny's body had been cut in half by

12

the edge of the picture. Ed Lyons, a local wedding and graduation photographer, had directed the girls in a series of shots involving the boat, minnow tanks and the front of the store. Since the front of Maw's store looked like shit, they'd settled on the pose by the boat. He hadn't noticed that the final brochure chopped Jenny's size two body in half. He took the brochure out of Jenny's hands and held it in front of his face.

"Oh, Jenny." Maw groaned. Hell hath no fury like Jenny Bender when she was mad. How to appease her? She loved Beau Longwell and attention; while he couldn't deliver Beau, he could give Jenny extra attention. "I'm sorry. I didn't even notice. I can make it up to you."

Jenny crossed her arms and leaned back against the bait shop counter. "This better be good."

"How about I give you extra months in this year's calendar. I usually give each girl her own month and then fill in the rest of the year with group shots, but I can feature you for three months instead."

"I want the cover."

"What?"

"Three months and the cover. Think about it, Maw. I'm a finalist in the national Coppertone Tan Contest, so it makes sense to have me in there more than the other girls anyway."

Maw briefly considered the rest of his Bikini Fishing Team, five local girls who were generally easygoing and down for the party when he needed them to show up. He'd placate the others if he needed to down the road; all five of them combined gave him less trouble than Jenny. "Fine."

"Don't screw me over again, Maw." Jenny headed for the door.

"What's got her panties in a twist?" Maw grumbled aloud when the door slammed shut behind her. He looked over the inside panel of the brochure where it listed the tour times of the minnow laboratory and Maw wondered whether he should tear it down and try something different. He'd built the space when Dave LaMay, the morning DJ on Chicago's most popular radio station, had landed him a gig doing a documentary. Maw had contrived a scheme to portray himself as a sort of minnow scientist, genetically breeding specialty minnows in his on-site laboratory. The film director called his bluff and actually used his footage of Maw and the shop in a TV series about scams and hoaxes. They'd featured him alongside a *Ripley's Believe It or Not* museum in the Wisconsin Dells and some of the sideshow acts from a circus. He'd tried to make the best of the publicity by charging admission to see "behind the scenes" of his minnow business. Every Saturday last summer he'd stationed one of his kids at the hall leading to the back rooms of his bait shop where he'd kitted out his minnow lab. But much like a hot August day on Pigeon Lake, nobody took the bait. Not even a nibble. Maybe he'd overpriced the experience at three bucks a ticket, but even offering "free admission" with a purchase of five dozen minnows and a T-shirt hadn't garnered much interest.

It was time to come up with a new plan.

The construction foreman for Traysons Acres tipped his hardhat back from his forehead and glared. Last night he'd left the worksite clean, he knew it. He was fastidious in his habits. Every nail swept up, every lock turned, every plank stacked. He'd signed a contract a year ago to begin building five houses and a strip mall on the former farmland. Three months ago, the first foundations had been poured. There had been nothing but trouble since he'd pulled up behind the semi-trailer hauling in the digging equipment. Flat tires, torn tarps, missing tools—he'd even arrived one morning to find a freshly poured basement filled to the brim with water. He didn't even know how such a thing was possible. It took three days to pump it dry.

This particular property, 259 Angie Lane, had been completely dismantled. Last night the garage and half of the main floor had been framed. Today every single board lay horizontally in stacks along the perimeter of the property. Atop the lumber were the colored flags that were meticulously placed to indicate where water pipes and electrical lines should get trenched in.

The foreman spat on the muddy ground and turned around to look at his work crew. They leaned against the two pickup trucks sipping coffee out of Styrofoam cups and smoking.

"Call Diggers Hotline," the foreman told one of his workers. "There's a pay phone at the gas station in Bassville. The rest of you start framing. Since it's your second go with this, it should take half the time, right?"

It took a lot to make him lose his temper, but this came close. He scooped up his clipboard from the front seat of his truck and read through his notes. Trusses would get delivered today. If Diggers Hotline could mark the utility lines by Friday, they would stay on schedule. He sighed and adjusted his hard hat over his bald head. As long as rain held off and the vandalism stopped, his crew could get the house built by the end of August.

THREE

Mona entered the bassville Pub and waved at Steve, who stood behind the bar wiping down the rail bottles.

"Hey, I've got a great job opportunity for you," he said. The husky, balding bar owner gestured to the metal trough of ice and the soda gun. "You could start tonight." Steve and Arlyce Shanski had owned the Pub for fifteen years and the biggest headache they had outside of the long hours was finding good help. Mona had been their best bartender—easy with the customers and willing to pitch in as dishwasher, waitress or cook when needed.

She laughed and pulled up a stool next to Jenny and Sheila Faulk, a good-natured sports fanatic they'd chummed with since middle school. "Thanks, but no thanks."

"Long weekend hours and shitty pay guaranteed," Steve told her. He folded the bar rag and crossed his arms.

"I already have long hours. Jenny," Mona nudged her best friend since childhood. "You could do it!"

Jenny scrunched up her nose and tapped her long nails on the edge of her wine glass. "I'd break a nail. No way." Jenny worked at a women's clothing store at the mall in Northport where she nurtured her huge love of fashion shopping. Tonight, she wore a denim miniskirt and a GUESS tank top. Her tan arms glittered with gold bracelets and rings.

Sheila laughed and leaned forward. "Judi's coming, right?" she asked Mona. Sheila was a cheerful strawberry blonde with big teeth and brown eyes. She was a year older than her friends and worked as a dental assistant in Northport. Tonight, she'd swapped out her scrubs for khaki shorts and a faded Milwaukee Brewers T-shirt.

"I'm surprised she's not here by now," Mona said. Judi Linski handled the cooking and cleaning for the guests at the Bassville Hotel. Mona thought Judi had class—she was well-read and thoughtful, but never acted snobby about hanging with the Bassville locals. She'd gotten engaged to Will Donne, the manager for Dave LaMay, the crazy DJ from Chicago who'd made Maw world famous. Judi and Will were getting married in a few weeks and Mona dreaded saying goodbye to her.

"No boys tonight?" Steve asked them.

"Hell, no," Sheila declared. "I'm sick of them. Spade always wants to gamble on everything and Scotty's been a crab for ages. Don't even get me started on Beau."

Jenny nodded her head, her ponytail bobbed with the movement. "If I find him tonight … "

Mona cut her off. "You won't. *Girls'* night out. No boys."

"Where you going?" Steve asked them. "And what'll you have?" he asked Mona.

"Beer. We're going to Sawdust City. There's a band playing."

The tables by the windows were taken by dinner customers so the girls decided to stay at the bar and chat up Steve until Judi arrived. Mona was halfway through her glass of Bud Light when someone tapped her on the shoulder. She spun around on her bar stool to see a woman who looked to be in her mid-thirties with a sharp nose and frosted blonde curls. "I heard you're Mona Butterfield," the woman said. Mona nodded and wondered what she wanted. Maybe she'd heard her program on the radio?

"Arlyce over there told me you're on the town council. Is that right?"

"I am … "

"I'm Tammy Parker, we moved into Traysons Acres a few months ago."

"Welcome to Bassville," Mona said.

"We've been having some problems and my husband suggested that taking them to the town would be the best way to handle them."

Mona felt very aware of her friends and Steve listening in on this conversation. *I bet this is about the weeds in her field.* She recalled what her dad had told her at dinner last night. "Go on." She glanced over the woman's shoulder and saw the rest of her family eating a large pizza—a wide-eyed man with a moustache and baseball cap, with a girl and boy who looked like they were still in elementary school.

"For starters, our mail."

Mona held up a hand. "That's not something we have any control over. The post office is federal government, not local."

"Well, I'm going to tell you about it anyway. Some days it comes at noon, some days at nine in the morning and sometimes we don't get it until almost dinnertime."

"Listen, Mrs.—"

"Call me Tammy. It's very inconvenient not to know when to expect it. Then there are the empty lots in the subdivision. Everything's overgrown with weeds already, it's making a mess of our newly seeded lawn when it blows in and the farmer up the road keeps making a stink of things with a manure spreader."

Thank God I only drank half a beer so far, Mona thought. She closed her eyes and inhaled before responding. "Our next meeting is in two weeks. Monday night at six-thirty. You're welcome to attend and share your concerns during the open session, but I don't know what we can do to help you. A farmer's got every right to spread his manure on his fields, and part of country living is farms nearby. The cows have been there for a hundred years. As far as the weeds go—"

Tammy cut her off. "I've read the county statutes. Property owners are required to destroy invasive weeds—and I quote—'before the plants mature to the bloom or flower stage.' And if they don't cut them, the county will, and charge the property owner. The law covers everything, including dandelions."

Shit. "Have you talked to the developer about this? I think they're technically the property owner."

"I have. The Traysons are refusing to mow anything."

"Tell you what, I'll talk to Dottie and Gene. I'm sure it won't be any trouble to get a tractor out there and mow things down. But I really think you need to call the developer because they might own the property."

"Who are Dottie and Gene?" Tammy put her hands on her hips. "The Traysons?"

"Yes."

"Yeah, I've tried getting in touch with them. They're completely unreasonable. He said it's not his problem and new lawns always have lots of weeds. Who is he to give me lawn care advice?"

"Well, he's actually a farmer, so he knows quite a bit about plants. But that's not the point. Maybe if I try talking to him … "

"You said Monday June 15th, right? Six-thirty? I'll be there. Too late to do anything about the mess in our yard, but maybe we can make life better for the next people to move in." Tammy turned on her heel and walked back to her family's table, her flip-flops slapping against the soles of her feet.

"Holy shit!" Jenny squealed. "Bug crawl up your ass much, lady?"

"Shhh!" Mona hushed her friends and glanced at the woman who was sitting at her table now and talking heatedly to her husband. "Don't be so loud."

"Who does she think she is?" Sheila asked. "And what do you expect when you move out to the country? Of course there's dandelions and cow shit."

Steve gave Mona a sympathetic look. "Glad I'm not on the town council. Good luck with that, Mona."

"I'm going to need more than luck." She leaned on her elbows and felt her cheeks burning with anger. "What nerve! My dad said this would happen. He was against that subdivision from the start, said there's no way city people and country people could coexist and it looks like he's right. And another thing, I thought the Traysons actually sold their property to the developers. It wouldn't be their responsibility anyway."

"They're going about this all wrong," Steve mused. "They could probably get the whole thing mowed for a case of beer if they asked nicely."

Sheila nudged Mona's arm with her elbow. "Forget her. We've got big plans for fun tonight. That old nag probably just needed to blow off some steam. A lot of people are like that, just want to complain and once they dump it on somebody else, they're good to go."

"I hope you're right," Mona told her. She'd definitely have to clarify who owned Traysons Acres. She could've sworn the developers were legally responsible for the property. And even if they weren't, how could anyone expect country fields not to have weeds growing in them anyway? She bitched about the mail, too … maybe Sheila was right. Maybe this lady was just a complainer and everyone in Bassville would do well to avoid her.

20

FOUR

Tom ogden parked his family station wagon on the gravel road along the freshly poured concrete curbing and turned off the engine. He turned to his wife and handed her the keys. "Ready to see our new home?"

She grinned back at him and flipped up the collar of her polo shirt. "Let's roll."

Their two sons tumbled out of the back seat and began scavenging the piles of dirt and mud-packed earth for rocks to chuck. Todd was seven, a freckle-faced ball of energy who loved assembling train sets and blocks. Robbie was nine and permanently affixed to his skateboard.

"Careful, you two!" Kelly called after them. She smoothed the pleats of her plaid Bermuda shorts and jingled the keys. "Let's check it out." She led the way up the concrete step to the front door of the split level ranch house with slate blue siding. "When did the builder say they'd have the shutters hung? I think burgundy will really pop against the slate blue."

"The shutters will be installed later. Those are just finishing details we can work around after we move in," Tom told his wife.

Kelly turned the key in the deadbolt and opened the door. Their rubber soles sounded loud against wood floors. The footsteps echoed down freshly drywalled hallways leading to the upper and lower levels. "I can picture this with blue floral wallpaper and navy wainscoting. Or maybe I'll stencil it."

Tom slung his arm round his wife's neck. "Whatever you do, I'm sure it'll look great."

"Oh. My. Gawd." Kelly pointed towards the patio doors that led to the backyard.

"What?"

"Is that—is that a FENCE?"

Tom dropped his arm and headed for the patio door, dust-coated from construction. He swiped his palm across the glass and looked through. "That's an electric fence," he muttered.

"Electric?" Kelly repeated, her jaw slack.

"Seems pretty close," Tom said through gritted teeth and he jerked the door open. "Hey, boys!"

Their sons paused mid-run. The older son had a softball-sized rock balanced in his left hand, ready to chuck over the fence.

"You stay away from that fence! You'll get hurt!"

"Tom, what will happen to them if they touch it?" Kelly asked.

"Just a bad jolt, nothing permanent, but it'll be unpleasant."

"Pee on it!" the younger son was telling his brother. "I heard you can pee on these fences and it's cool!"

"Don't you dare!" Kelly yelled. She turned to face her husband. "That fence wasn't there the last time we came. Is it even legal to put a fence by our property like that? I think it might even be on our property."

Tom strode across the field for a closer look. He located a stake and a single flag marking the west corner of their lot. The electric fence wire ran exactly six inches from it. This farmer, whoever he was, had measured with precision. Devious precision. Tom wiped sweat off his wide and receding hairline with the back of his hand and cursed.

"What the hell?" Kelly prodded. "How is this even safe? Or legal!"

"Maybe we end up putting up fencing sooner than planned," he told her. "At least along the back of our lot." He shrugged. "I'll come to town next week and talk to someone in the village office about it. It might be a mistake."

"Yeah, right." Kelly's sarcastic tone matched the angry expression on her face "Some farmer 'accidentally' set up an electric fence and didn't notice the three houses being built right alongside of it." She gestured angrily toward the framed structures going up on either side of their lot. "Think they know about this?"

"Doubt it," Tom twisted his mouth while studying the fresh mounds of dirt at the base of the fence's posts. "This looks pretty fresh."

The loud slap of a stream of water hitting the ground caused the Ogdens to look up with startled faces. A black and white cow had appeared and was answering nature's call ten feet from where they stood.

"EWWW!" the boys ran towards it for a closer look.

"Don't!" Kelly yelled.

A sharp snap sounded and both boys jumped back upon connecting with the fence.

"Are you okay?" Kelly rushed to where they stood gasping with laughter and rubbing their hands.

They shook their arms and legs. "That was so weird!"

"It felt like getting vibrated. But really hard."

"Don't touch that fence again. Do you hear me?" Kelly pointed to the cow. "Stupid animal has more sense than you two."

Tom put his arm around his wife's shoulder and kissed the top of her head. "You wanted country living."

"Shut up, Tom."

FIVE

FRIDAY MORNING MONA STOOD astride her mountain bike and watched the bulldozer grind its way slowly back and forth against the berm of willow trees at the creek's edge. The vacant barn and shed nearby would be next, she knew, and it made her feel hollow inside. She'd heard about the vandalism at the building site, but today the wood-framed structure looked like a house in progress was supposed to. Soon the walls of a house would surround another new family in Bassville.

Four years had passed since the Traysons got zoning permits changed to develop their family farm. At first it seemed like nothing would change, but in the past year everything steamrolled ahead. Gene and Dottie hadn't moved, of course, but the cornfields around them gradually flattened and packed into empty lots, plotted out with wooden stakes topped by fluttering plastic flags. A road curved through the former field, separated into two directions where it circled back onto itself. The large white sign at the edge of the county highway announced "Traysons Acres! Lots Available!" Beneath were pictures of families standing outside ranch-style homes with shiny cars parked in driveways.

The tradeoff had been money for their daughter Angie's bone marrow transplant. While the farm got plowed under, Angie's leukemia stayed in remission and she was undistinguishable from her eleventh-grade peers, skinny legs in pegged blue jeans and high ponytail.

All the undulation of the fields, formerly spotted by cows, had been graded flat. The barbed wire fencing, corn stalks, even the huge pond were gone. The main barn and a few outbuildings near the house stood empty. When a developer offered him a small fortune for the property, Gene had auctioned off the barn's contents. By the end of the day most of the farm had been loaded up and carted away. Mona's dad bought a trailer, half of the heifers and a plow.

It had been strange to watch Gene and Dottie transform from humble dairy farmers to wealthy retirees. Mona had grown up alongside their family as her parents were best friends with the Traysons. She and Scotty had clocked hours of free time together over the years. Mona had heard Loyal talk about how Gene didn't know what to do with himself. He drifted restlessly between house to barn and back again with nothing but time on his hands and no way to spend it. Dottie still kept house like before. Her life hadn't changed much other than having Gene under foot more often. As long as Scotty and Angie lived under their roof, her life had purpose.

Like his father, Scotty was caught between worlds. He loved the farm and he was sorry his family sold it. At the time, he was mastering the carpentry trade. After his former partner skipped town following the suspicious death of his girlfriend, Scotty kept contracting himself out to whoever needed an extra hand. He hung ceilings, drywall and windows. He installed carpet, wiring and pipes. When the farm chores disappeared, Scotty picked up side jobs landscaping and roofing in the summer. He helped Mona's dad and a few other farmers bale hay and plant when they needed an extra hand.

A movement caught her eye and Mona saw Scotty walk across the yard and head into the main barn. He had been part of her world her entire life, her earliest memories included playing with him while their parents visited. Side by side they'd worked on 4-H projects, went trick-or-treating, and learned to drive. Just the person she needed to talk to. She knew she could read through old files in the town's office, but it would be easier just to ask him if they retained any responsibility for the land. She navigated her way down the slope towards the barn and hopped off her bike. Mona propped it against the side of the barn and followed him inside. She watched Scotty slowly pass through the stalls, adjusting the remaining equipment hanging on hooks and kicking at the few pieces of hay strewn on the ground. The empty barn depressed her. The place felt like a broken dream, abandoned and sad. His footsteps echoed through the rafters and startled the starlings nested there. The old boards creaked gently in the wind. You'd never hear that over the noise of the cows.

The center of the barn's floor was worn down from years of heavy traffic. A narrow trench traced the path of so many hooves and feet that had crossed from stall to field and back again.

Scotty looked forlorn. Mona hesitated to interrupt his meditations. But it was way too late for second thoughts.

"Hey!" she called out and he turned to watch her jog the length of the vacant building.

"Hey." He bowed his head and scratched the back of his neck. His skin was white where his T-shirt sleeve pulled back a little. Tall and lanky, Scotty had inherited his mother's curly hair and wide blue eyes.

"You've got a farmer's tan." Mona pointed to his arm.

"Funny. I'm not a farmer."

"It's sad in here, isn't it?"

They looked around. Scotty nodded. "If I could go back in time, I'd do everything differently."

"How's that?" She'd thought the same thing thousands of times—about Jake. But she didn't know what she could've done to change the course of their lives. "What would you do different?"

Scotty took a deep breath and exhaled slowly. "I guess I don't know." He seemed to choose his words carefully. "I know I can't control how Angie got sick, but maybe if I had stepped up and helped more my folks wouldn't have sold the whole place off. I didn't know. I just worked and fished and hunted and screwed around with The Pole and while I was busy doing that, this ... " He spread his arms open above his head to indicate all of it. "This slipped away. I didn't even think I wanted it, but now it's too late."

"Maybe not," Mona said. She had no idea, really.

"Are you crazy? All that's left is a big empty barn. What good is an empty barn? And starting the whole thing from scratch is out of the question."

"How come?"

He frowned. "Money. Obviously."

"But didn't you make a killing when you sold some of the lots?"

"We sold the farm for three thousand an acre. The developer has it priced at twenty thousand an acre now."

"Oh."

"Once it's gone, you can't get a farm back."

"Wait, did you sell *all* of it? You don't own *any* of the land anymore?"

"Just the ten acres here with the house and the barns. Developer owns the rest of it."

So she was right. And she'd let that nasty Tammy lady know it, too. "I'm sorry."

Scotty nodded and headed for the door.

Mona watched him walk outside and head into the house. She knew he wasn't mad at her, he was mad at himself. She pedaled away feeling bad she'd interrupted him. Between Jake leaving for Atlanta, Judi heading to Chicago to get married and Scotty in the dumps, Mona realized how lonely she'd become.

Maw blew his nose into his handkerchief before taking his pocketknife to the box on the counter. He dreaded the moment before him. It had seemed like a genius idea when he'd first hatched it: mail order bait. All winter and spring he'd successfully shipped hundreds of packages across the Midwest. Grubs, worms, leeches, crawlers left his shop in cardboard boxes. He suspected people ordered them because of the novelty of his shop, the clever branding he'd devised. No matter, he'd shrugged. Money was money and fame was fame. He'd mail marked-up invertebrates as far away as people wanted—so long as they'd pay.

Then the weather turned hot. Live bait survived cool temperatures just fine, but once the thermometer reached eighty degrees, everything died. Upon receiving dead bait in the mail, angry customers would return the rotting carcasses with demands for refunds.

Maw slit the tape across the top of the box and pried back the cardboard. He lifted out the Styrofoam container of grubs and peeled open the plastic lid to reveal the curled-up corpses of grubs. Dead bait. Maw read the enclosed note with an exasperated sigh. Time and labor aside, the returns were expensive. He had to eat the cost of the bait and packaging, and shipping both ways. Reaching into a cooler for a fresh can of Mountain Dew, Maw grimly accepted the reality of his situation. He couldn't control the weather, so this deal was a bust. He had to walk away before he lost his shirt.

How to keep the engine of success working, though? He leaned his forearms on the counter and tugged at his beard with stubby fingers. Tearing out the minnow lab and expanding his shop into those back rooms could be a possibility. He surveyed the room. Only two walls were load bearing, the rest could go. Extra space for what, though? Maw cast his thoughts and gaze along the racks of T-shirts and lures and poles.

SIX

A WEEK BEFORE HER WEDDING, Jenny and Mona decided to throw Judi a bachelorette party—Bassville style. Saturday night Mona, Jenny and Sheila guided Judi across the parking lot of the Luau Lounge, stumbling in their high heels while navigating the gravelly surface. Judi was wearing packages of condoms safety-pinned to an oversized black lace nightie that covered her shorts and T-shirt. A white veil bobbed crookedly from her auburn curls and she clutched a bouquet of yellow plastic flowers in her fist. The other three women wore ruffled and ridiculous bridesmaid's dresses and floppy hats.

"Here comes the bride!" Jenny sang while pushing open the door.

Beau waved from behind the bar and the girls worked their way to an open spot. The customers greeted them with curious and amused expressions.

"What'll it be, ladies?" he asked while wiping his hands dry with a towel. His hair was slicked back and his button-down shirt was open at the collar to reveal two gold chains shining against his tanned skin.

Sheila slammed down the penis-shaped plastic bottle they'd been forcing Judi to drink from all night long. "Fill her up, Beau." She unscrewed the top and passed it to him.

"What are you having, beautiful?" Beau asked Judi with a wink. Jenny shot him a dirty look, but Mona grabbed her shoulder and muttered in her ear. "It's her bachelorette party. Seriously, Jenny."

"Malibu and Coke. Diet Coke." Judi pulled at the veil that had caught in her mouth. "I am so glad I'm not wearing one of these on my actual wedding day."

"When's the big day again?" Beau asked her.

"Next Friday," she said. "We're flying out west to Vegas and getting married by Elvis."

Beau's forehead wrinkled with confusion. "I thought he died."

Jenny reached across the bar to punch his shoulder. "No, dummy. Not the real Elvis. An Elvis impersonator."

"Like getting married by Santa Claus then," Beau said to Judi. "Will your union be legal in all fifty states?"

"Yeah, but classier." Judi took her penis bottle back from Beau and put the straw in her mouth for a drink.

Mona and Sheila bent over laughing. "It never gets old watching her do that," Sheila hiccupped.

"I'll bet," Beau said. He winked at Judi who blushed.

"This is seriously humiliating," Judi told Jenny.

Mona and Sheila burst out laughing again while Beau ignored his other customers and waited for them to pull themselves together.

"Just beer," Mona wheezed.

Sheila nodded and Jenny peeled a ten-dollar bill off the wad of drinking money they had pooled together for the night. "Whiskey sour."

"Not sweet?" Beau asked Jenny.

"I'm sweet enough on my own," she told him and turned around to survey the crowd. A lot of boaters, not too many people from town here tonight. She waved to a group she recognized and nudged Judi. "What do you suppose Will's up to? Did Dave plan a bachelor party for him?"

"Oh God, I hope not."

"How come?"

"Dave LaMay's the worst kind of pig. No, Will's going golfing with his brothers and a few friends. His plans sounded pretty low key."

"Isn't that one of the new families over there?" Jenny asked. She pointed at a couple sitting at a table in the dining room. "I think they're the ones building that house over at Traysons.'"

The girls stared at the man and woman, who were wearing matching red t-shirts with Bucky Badger emblazoned on their chests. Their sons were blowing bubbles through their straws into their kiddie cocktails.

"Did you talk to them, Beau? What are they like?" Mona asked. She hoped they weren't as crazy as Tammy.

Beau shrugged and kept drying a glass with a towel that matched the white of his button-down shirt and teeth. "Seem nice enough."

"Did you learn anything about them?" Mona pressed.

"Yeah." Beau put the glass on the shelf beneath the bar and flipped the towel over his shoulder before leaning forward. The gold chains around his neck swung back and forth and he beckoned Mona closer with the crook of his index finger.

Mona bent lower to listen.

"The adults drink light beer, the kids drink soda and they ordered chicken for dinner. I really like that black lace bra you're wearing."

Mona jerked upright, her hand pressed against the top of her blouse. "Asshole."

Beau laughed at her. "You're too easy."

A few hours and three stops later, the girls ended their night around a table at the Riverside Bar. Rosie, the owner, sat with her feet propped on a barstool nearby and worked over a crossword puzzle in the newspaper while the girls drank their way through the last pitcher of the night. Mona watched Rosie fish the pen from her beehive hairdo and write an answer on the page. Mona's brain was fogged with alcohol and she knew she was slurring her words.

"Our last Death March with you," Sheila was saying to Judi.

Judi's veil had disappeared somewhere between the Luau Lounge and Grumpy's, and the black nightie had lost its condoms, though a few holes marked where they'd once been pinned to the sheer fabric. Judi leaned her head on Sheila's shoulder. "I'm going to miss you all so much."

"We'll come visit you in Chicago!" Jenny promised.

"No. You won't. People always say they'll visit, but they don't." Judi's eyes looked teary.

"Don't be like that." Mona reached over and clutched at Judi's hand. "We're friends. Never forget that. Plus, you'll come visit us." Mona sat up straighter, pleased by the sudden revelation penetrating her foggy brain. "Your mom lives here! You'll come back."

Judi smiled. "I will, won't I? I will come back."

Rosie pushed her stool back with a loud scrape across the floor. "That's it, ladies. Lights out, time for bed. You know I don't need Joe the Cop hassling me for staying open after bar time." She began removing the glasses from their table.

"Rosie, you're going to miss Judi, aren't you?" Sheila asked.

"She has to leave before I can miss her." Rosie snagged their ashtray and now the table stood empty. Her face softened for a moment. "But I will. Good luck to you, honey. You're a good girl."

Judi wrapped her arms around Rosie and after she finished hugging her, began hugging everyone else. The girls stumbled out the front door of Riverside Bar and down the block. Sheila and Jenny turned left towards the Pub. At the front door of the Hotel, Mona took a deep breath of the cool night air and tried not to cry. "I'm going to miss you so much."

Judi pulled her in for a bear hug. "Me, too," she said against Mona's hair. "You've been the best friend. I wish you could move to Chicago with me."

"I wish you could stay." Mona pushed her away and started down the sidewalk towards home.

"I'll see you before I leave!" Judi called to her. Mona turned around and waved before continuing home. The streets were empty and dark; the only sound was a dog barking in the distance. She was glad to be alone because the purple bridesmaid dress made her look obnoxious—she looked crazy when she was with her friends but being dressed up together had been fun. Mona tried to remember the last time she'd gotten so very drunk. It had been a long time, she decided. Maybe New Year's Eve last year? She tripped on block of concrete pushed up by a tree root and caught her balance by grabbing hold of a picket fence. Okay, she thought, pausing to catch her breath. Move slower. She heard a plane passing overhead looked up at the starry sky.

Somewhere Jake was doing something. She tried to imagine him sleeping or sitting at a bar with his new friends in Georgia. Maybe he was still at work. No, that was stupid, it was early morning in Atlanta. The vast night sky and her irrational brain were deeply—so deeply—affected by beer and tequila shots. Two more blocks before she was home.

She concentrated on moving forward and listening. Tree leaves rustled and in the distance a truck or car moved down the highway. The gentle slap of the river hit the seawall of the house next to her as her feet clipped across the cement. One house had a light on and through the window, Mona saw that someone was watching a movie on their TV. *Caddyshack.* It would be nice to get home and sit on her couch and watch a movie, she thought.

She was nearly home. A little further. Tears dripped down her cheeks while she thought about Jake and how they were really over. But maybe they weren't. She could call him. She *would* call him. Why hadn't she thought of this sooner? Just call him and tell him she missed him and they'd work it out.

On her front porch she fumbled for her keys and opened the door. She kicked off her shoes, walked across the room to the couch and lay down. She'd close her eyes for a few seconds, she decided. Then she'd call Jake.

SEVEN

Maw had just finished dipping minnows when the bait shop's phone rang. He wiped his wet hands across the thighs of his jeans while walking from the minnow tanks in the back of the shop to the front counter. He grabbed the receiver on the sixth ring. "Maw's Bait and Tackle."

"Hey, hey, hey. How my favorite fisherman?" a smooth low voice crooned into Maw's ear.

"Well, what do you know today, Dave LaMay? How's it shaking in the Windy City?"

"Rocking and rolling. You know how it is. Hey—Ozzy! Get off the desk! Leave Samantha Fox alone!" Dave made some random moaning sounds before returning to the phone. "What's the word on the water?"

"Copacetic, baby. The water's calm, the fish are abundant and my Belligerent Minnows are bringing them in faster than the fishermen can handle. Heck, I just saw a guy with a bucket of my minnows sitting in his boat and three fat perch jumped out of the water right into the bait bucket."

"That sounds too good to be true."

"It might be. You'll have to trust me. The fish are jumpin' and the rods are pumpin'. If you catch one too small, dump him. Plenty more will bite, it's a beautiful sight."

"Listen to you, Maw," Dave chuckled. "You sound like a rap god."

His compliment hit him like a spotlight. Maw's lips spread into a wide grin. A rap god. He liked the sound of that. If the Chicago Bears could turn out a rap hit, why couldn't he? He knew a plethora of words; his vocabulary, quick wit and natural charisma were the right ingredients for rap. Why not?

"Dave, I can't believe this never came up before, but I *am* a rap god. A minnow-breedin', bottom feedin', song-bleedin' rap god. It's my secret passion. I've written a stack of songs. Do you want to hear them?" He'd listened to those idiotic football players recite the lines against the synthesized beat. That's all rap was, speak-singing rhymes against a rhythm. He could come up with better lyrics if he put his mind to it—and probably deliver them better, too.

"I'd like nothing better. Can you rap me a fishing report next week when I call you?"

"Every word of it. I'll just have my homeboy Dob drop me a beat and we'll have her ready for you." Maw reached under the counter for a pad of paper and pencil. "You coming up to fish this summer?"

"I'm thinking about it. You know my manager's getting married in a week. Most guys go to Bassville to catch fish, but Will went up there and caught him a lady. He didn't invite me along on the honeymoon, so maybe I'll take my vacation up your way."

"Me and the Bikini Fishing Team would be honored to party with you, Dave."

"And the fish are really biting?"

"If you didn't know better, you'd think it was feeding time in a tank full of piranhas."

Dave's laughter filled Maw's ear. "Sounds good to me. I'll call you next week for that rappin' report."

After he hung up, Maw stared at his notepad. Inspiration came from the strangest places. He'd just needed to be patient, but now he had the big idea. *Okay smart ass. You talked a big game, now write one.* How did one write a rap song? One word at a time. He began listing words that showed up in a fishing report. Temperature, water level, depth, bait. All he had to do was pick words that rhymed. How difficult could that possibly be?

"My name is Maw, I have one flaw, I drink my beer using a straw." Maw experimented with different rhythms while he continued his morning chores around the shop. "If you like minnows with really fast fins, look no further, Pugnacious always wins." He straightened a display of spinners and kept muttering to himself. "Passive-aggressive has really sharp teeth … what rhymes with teeth? Seethe? Beneath? Bequeath?"

He would write a series of songs and then cut an album. And then he could make a music video! The Bikini Fishing Team could back up on the vocals and add a little sex appeal. He'd seen enough MTV to understand the formula. "My name is Maw, guess what I saw? A bunch of fish in the Wissipaw." Dave would give him airtime on his radio station. "Floatin' downstream with my rod and reel, a dollar a dozen's a pretty good deal, an afternoon fishin' followed by a free meal … " He stalled out. "Kneel? Feel? Creel?"

He'd get there, it might just take a little practice. Maw Cooper, rap god and bait salesman. Why not? It worked out for Weird Al, and he wasn't even original.

Otto Zimm, Bassville's most dedicated fisherman, had eased his boat, *Reel Good Dreams*, into the perfect fishing spot. Tucked into Cooper's Bayou, about thirty feet from the riverbank, he dropped anchor and situated his tackle box and rods. Rex, his faithful black lab, paced from one end of the boat to the other, tongue hanging out and tail wagging. By the time Otto got the hooks baited and cast his line in the Wissipaw, Rex had curled into a pile of fur and lounged in a sunny spot on the boat's floor. Otto tipped his fishing hat back from his forehead and sat down with a grunt. At fifty-eight, he'd gained a little weight around his midsection and his skin was spotted with age. The lines on his face had come from the sun, not laughter. Otto was a resolute grump.

The sunshine glimmered off the water's surface, small ripples from the current making it tricky to keep an eye on his bobber, but Otto was an old pro. Tiny flies swarmed just above the water, tempting the fish below. The river's current made the pole tug gently in his hand and felt as comfortable to him as holding a baseball or moving the stick shift in his truck. He didn't have to think, one of his favorite things about fishing. He just had to sit and enjoy the experience.

Birds sang overhead and Otto caught sight of a hawk perched on the branch of a maple tree. The hawk sat still among the rustling leaves and Otto watched for the moment when it would dive towards the ground in pursuit of a mouse or rabbit. He never got bored out on the water. There was so much to pay attention to. The people who thought moving fast was the way to enjoy the river missed everything important.

Off in the distance, Otto could hear the steady hum of motorboats. The lake would be packed on a Saturday like this, people zipping around on water skis and jet skis, kicking up a huge wake and making a racket. A person couldn't fish in that environment, couldn't relax at all with all that activity. And on a sunny day the fish never bit well, so it suited him fine to quietly drift into this shady dead-end spot. Nothing would bother him back here. He'd been working overtime at the paper mill in Northport and looked forward to this day on the water. The lawn was mowed, he'd unclogged the kitchen sink for his wife and now he was free to pursue his own happiness for the rest of the day.

A dragonfly droned past his left ear and he watched it glide past Rex's nose and land on the edge of the boat. Its iridescent green wings twitched. Tiny waves lapped at the side of the boat. Rex napped. A strong tug at the end of his line brought Otto to his feet.

"That didn't take long," he muttered to himself while jerking the pole skyward and starting to reel in the first catch of the day. The rod made a buzzing sound while he cranked the line in and after a minute, he caught sight of a silver figure fighting just below the surface of the water. "That's it! Come on!" he encouraged it.

A flurry of splashing water welcomed the crappie into Otto's waiting fishing net. Rex rose to his feet and stretched. The dog examined the fish with his greying muzzle. "She's a big one. First one's a keeper today. When does that ever happen, buddy?" Otto reached down to scratch Rex's ears.

Rex licked at the water puddling beneath the net and wagged his tail. He trotted from one end of the boat to the other before returning to his previous spot. He circled twice and lay down with his head on his paws.

Otto tossed the fish into the cooler he'd filled with ice and rebaited his hook. At this rate, he was in for a very satisfying day. Later he'd get home and fry up his catch. His wife would make some potatoes and coleslaw and they'd eat like kings. He slowly dropped the line into the water and had settled back onto the cushioned seat when two jet skis came zooming around the bend toward his boat. He flew to his feet and shouted at the teenaged drivers who waved back at him. "Go back!" Otto waved his arms and yelled louder. One of the drivers skidded his jet ski to the left and sent a stream of water in his direction. The spray landed perfectly across his boat and left a dark line on his shirt sleeve.

Fury welled up in Otto's chest. These new personal watercrafts had started appearing on the river two summers ago—the aquatic equivalent of motorcycles except the people who rode on them didn't follow any boating protocols. Even the most inexperienced boater knew to stay in certain areas and avoid getting too close to others. All boats passed to the right of buoys and kept a respectful distance from docks and shorelines. But not the jet ski riders. They screamed between and around larger boats, recklessly zipped close to the shoreline and docks and made a real racket. Their main purpose, from what Otto had observed, seemed to involve driving in circles so the riders could enjoy the thrill of bouncing themselves silly in their own wake. He'd never seen anything like this, never imagined the quiet peace of his fishing spot would be disturbed by morons who could gun their engines into every nook and cranny the Wissipaw had to offer. It was one thing for these fools to wreak havoc on the lakes—although Otto hated that, too—but it was a different deal when they came back into the bayous specifically marked as no-wake areas.

"Goddamn idiots!" he raged. He pulled his line up out of the water and rested it on the floor of the boat. Then he reached for the key in the boat's ignition. Cooper's Bayou was a dead end. Those kids would have to come back the way they went in and Otto would be waiting for them. He started the boat and motored to a narrow spot between the banks and shut it off. Sure enough, a moment later he heard the whine of the jet skis coming closer. They rounded the bend at top speed. The first kid swerved left to avoid crashing into *Reel*

Good Dreams and ended up straight in the path of his buddy.

In slow motion the second driver hit the first broadside and flew over his head and into the bank. The first jet ski tipped sideways and the rider slid into the water. Otto watched in horror as the kid slowly bobbed to the surface, kept afloat by his life jacket. Blood trickled in a steady stream down the left side of his still face. The other kid wound up buried in the branches of a fallen tree lodged on the edge of the shore. He screamed obscenities while flailing his arms to get free. Otto could barely see him through the leaves, but he could tell where he was from the way the branches moved. The kid's machine was still running, louder now that it was upside down and ashore, miraculously suspended above the rider's body.

"Shut it off!" Otto yelled at him. He steered the boat toward the kid in the water. "Hold on, I'm coming!" he called.

The kid in the water didn't move and until he drew closer. Otto imagined he was dead. How could you survive getting run down by one of those crazy machines? Had it hit him? Tore him up? Thank God he was wearing a life jacket, or he'd be drowned and there was no telling how they'd find the body. Otto carefully pulled up alongside the kid and saw his lashes flutter. Still alive but unconscious. Thank God.

Otto leaned over and grabbed the lifejacket, dragging him close to the boat so he could get leverage to pull the kid out of the water. "Easy there, son," Otto muttered. He hitched the kid beneath his armpits and slid him over the side of the boat. The boy's lanky arms and legs flopped limply on the floor. Water mixed with blood turned a pale red color. Otto knelt and felt for a pulse. It was strong. The kid's breathing sounded shallow, but steady. He searched for the source of the blood and found the deep gash along the left side of the kid's head. Half of his ear had been shorn off—how was the injury not worse? How had it gotten cut?

Reaching beneath one of the seat cushions, Otto dug out a clean rag and pressed it against the kid's head. He turned him on his side and boosted him up with a spare lifejacket to apply pressure on the ear. Then Otto stood and yelled again at the kid stuck in the tree. "I said, turn it off!"

A minute later the engine stopped and the silence almost deafened him. Rex pawed at the front of the boat and Otto steered towards the wreckage on the shore. "Can you get out of there?" he asked.

"I'm fucking stuck!" The voice sounded high pitched and frantic.

"Are you hurt?"

"I'm stuck."

"Okay. Hang on."

Otto surveyed his options. He couldn't pull closer to the tree. He'd risk getting wedged in there himself. He couldn't pull along to the shoreline for at least a hundred yards because of the fallen trees and branches blocking access. He looked towards the mouth of the bayou. "Listen, I'm going to drop anchor a few yards from here and then I'll climb on shore. I'll walk over and try and help you."

So much for a quiet day of fishing, he groused to himself while looking for a reasonably flat spot on the riverbank to make his approach.

It took Otto almost a half hour to park his boat, climb on shore and pick his way through the thick underbrush to reach the kid in the tree. Otto dulled his best fishing knife hacking away at branches. The kid had somehow landed beneath the tree; Otto guessed the force and weight of the jet ski propelled him there. All the way back to his boat the kid bitched while he limped behind Otto. His bare feet got torn up by the pinecones and sharp branches littering the forest floor. His long arms and legs were covered in scratches. He'd lost his Ray Bans (this seemed to bug him most of all) and he finally stopped talking when he climbed in *Reel Good Dreams* and saw his friend.

"Christ. Is he gonna be okay?" He bent over and turned his friend's head to face him.

"Don't!" Otto barked. "Keep the pressure on that wound. I don't know how bad he is."

"Shit. Shit shit shit. My dad is gonna freak."

"Is he your brother?"

"No. Mikey's my friend. My dad is gonna be so pissed."

Otto refrained from commenting. He untied his boat from the log where he'd secured it and used an oar to shove off to the center of the bayou.

"Mikey, hey, Mikey. Man, you're gonna be okay, all right?"

Otto started the engine and headed away from Cooper's Bayou feeling his guts churn like the water beneath him. So far the kid hadn't blamed him for what happened, but Otto knew he'd caused the accident. Why did he do it?

Because he wanted a little peace and quiet. He'd deliberately picked a spot off the main waterway to enjoy his day off work. He lived on this river, the Wissipaw belonged more to him than it did to these weekend visitors. Obviously these two kids had no sense; they'd driven back into a bayou where nothing but a johnboat or a canoe could navigate. They were careless and reckless with powerful machines and—Otto knew he'd hurt them.

What had he intended? To slow them down, yes, but also to get back at them for disrupting his solitude. He'd wanted to make them feel like he had when they'd sprayed his boat and screamed past.

He hadn't meant for them to end up like this.

"Can you go any faster?" the kid was asking him.

"I'm doing my best, son."

The first dock out of Cooper's Bayou and a quarter mile up the Wissipaw River belonged to Pine Acres Resort. Otto tied off and instructed his passengers not to move, not that one showed any sign of hearing him. The kid with the head wound hadn't even opened his eyes. Otto ran to the resort's main office, a sturdy log cabin with a porch running along the front of the building. He leapt up the steps and banged through the screen door. "I need to use your phone," he said too loudly to the startled teenaged girl behind the counter. She dropped the magazine she'd been reading and pushed the black telephone across the counter towards him.

"Local calls are a quarter. Long distance you have to use a card."

Otto's eyebrows furrowed while he dug into his pocket and pulled out a quarter. "You got a number for emergency?"

"What's wrong?"

"Got a hurt kid in my boat. He was in an accident."

She stood and pulled a thumbtack from the bulletin board on the wall behind her. She handed Otto a list of emergency numbers which he studied for a second before opting for "Ambulance."

Forty more minutes passed before the kid got moved out of Otto's boat. Campers left their lawn chairs and gathered on the dock and riverbank to watch the drama unfold. The two paramedics praised him for applying pressure on the wound and leaving him on his back. "Always best to keep a victim still. Sometimes you can cause more harm moving them. Spinal injuries can be very serious," one told him.

"I did move him, though," Otto argued. "I lifted him out of the water."

"Well, you had to do that or he might have drowned. I'm only saying it was smart to leave him in the boat."

The other kid sat beside the stretcher in the back of the ambulance. He now looked like *he* was in shock. His mouth hung half open and he stared at his bare feet.

"Is he gonna be okay?" Otto asked, pointing to kid on the stretcher with his thumb.

"He's stable. That's all we can say right now."

Otto left his contact information with the ambulance driver and watched them drive away, the siren announcing their journey past the campsites and down the gravel road toward Northport. The paramedic had cautioned Otto that a spine injury was a possibility, but it could just as easily be a concussion and contusion, which would heal in no time.

He stood on the end of the dock beside *Reel Good Dreams* and watched the campers return to their lawn chairs. After a moment he lowered himself into his boat and reached for Rex. The dog licked his hand and whimpered. "It'll be all right, pal," Otto mumbled, massaging the dog's silky ears and neck before opening the fish cooler and tossing his catch of the day overboard.

EIGHT

THIRSTY. THAT WAS MONA'S first thought as she woke up. Her mouth felt stuffed with dryness. She opened her eyes and immediately closed them against the piercing pain in her head. She felt as though she'd fallen off the hayloft and landed on her back. Every single muscle in her body hurt like a bruise. She reached slowly to rub her temples and a loud crash made her ears ring.

It took a moment to realize that the ring wasn't her ears but the sound of her phone landing on the floor beside the couch where she'd fallen asleep. Mona opened her eyes in panic and stared at the white painted ceiling. *Did I call Jake?* She racked her brain to remember. *Oh geez. I hope I didn't.* The humiliation of drunk calling an ex-boyfriend was something she could live without. Mona turned over and looked at the phone. The receiver was knocked off and the busy signal droned. She replaced it in the holder and sat up. She could call him and ask, but that would be stupid because then he'd know she'd meant to call him. No. She'd just have to pretend she hadn't.

She also hoped to hell that Jenny and Sheila felt as lousy as she did right now. But not Judi. Judi deserved to feel happy.

Another piercing ache shot behind her eyes and nausea swept over her. How stupid to get carried away like that last night. Leaning back, Mona covered her face with her hands. She had to get over to the farm and load up for the roadside stand. If only she could call her parents and have them do it for her, just lay back on the couch and wait for the poison to ebb out of her system. She groaned. Then loud knocking on her front door made her flinch.

Squeezing her eyes shut, then opening them and focusing on the ten feet across the room from couch to door, she inhaled deeply. Who could be here on a Saturday morning? She shuffled to the door and unlocked it.

There stood Scotty, good 'ol Scotty with a huge grin on his face. He held up a can of Pepsi and a bottle of Tylenol. "Heard you went on a bender last night. You look kinda green around the gills."

"Come in," Mona turned around and headed back to the couch. He followed her.

"I'd suggest biting the dog that bit you, but maybe not." Scotty grabbed a glass out of the drain rack in her kitchen and cracked open the can. The hissing sound made Mona feel a tiny bit of relief. She knew the combination of a cold drink infused with caffeine and the Tylenol would take the edge off her hangover.

"How did you hear?" she croaked.

Scotty handed her the glass, tiny bubbles fizzing to the surface, and she drank half of it in three gulps. "Well, last night when you called me you sounded pretty messed up. I couldn't understand everything you were trying to tell me, but I did make out that you needed me." He shrugged. "Told you I'd be here first thing in the morning. Here I am."

I called Scotty? Thank God I called him instead of Jake. "Thank you."

He sat across from her and shook his head, acting like he was disappointed. "You oughta know better, young lady. Didn't six years tending bar teach you a damn thing?"

Mona smiled weakly.

"I ran into Beau at the gas station this morning. He told me you girls were on a mission last night. Sorry I didn't see you. Spade and I went to Sawdust City to shoot darts." Scotty paused to open the Tylenol bottle and shake three white tablets in her palm. "It won't be the same when Judi leaves. She gives our group a little class."

"I'm going to miss her," Mona agreed. She swallowed the Tylenol and started to lie down again.

"Uh-uh, you have a farm stand to open, missy. Get up."

"I can't."

"Up." Scotty glanced at the wall clock that hung above Mona's kitchen sink. "You've ten minutes to get ready and then we'll get over to your dad's. Between the two of us, it'll take half as much time."

Mona jumped in the shower and was rinsing shampoo out of her hair when it again occurred to her how lucky she was she'd called Scotty instead. *He's able to show up.*

The morning business was brisk and Mona worked through the throbbing in her head while she weighed produce and made change for a steady run of customers. By one o'clock Scotty was loading the last of the empty crates into the back of his truck and he slammed the hatch closed.

Mona climbed in beside him. "Can I buy you lunch for helping me out?"

"I never say no to free food. Where do you want to go?"

"I really want a Pub burger."

He laughed at her. "You can take the girl out of the country, but you can't take the country out of the girl. To the Pub."

They rode in silence down the highway and Mona gazed out the window at the greening fields. She caught a glimpse of two deer at the edge of stand of birch trees and watched a red-tailed hawk dive bomb from the top of a telephone post to the ground, probably in pursuit of a mouse. "It was really nice of you to come over. Thanks again for the soda and drugs."

Scotty shrugged. "No big deal."

"What were you going to do today?" she asked.

"Probably nothing. It's too hot to fish, I'm between odd jobs and there's no farm." Bitterness crept into Scotty's voice. "I'd probably end up parked at the end of the bar watching NASCAR and shaking dice."

"Hey," she reached over and put her hand on his arm. She tried to think of something to say to make him feel better. He was really hurting more than she'd thought. "I'm glad your schedule was open today."

"Yeah?"

"Would you be interested in making this a regular thing? No pressure or anything, but you were a huge help. Dad's way too busy—" Mona hated mentioning her father, a man doing the work she now understood that Scotty missed. "Anyway," she corrected her course, "I could make it worth your while if you wanted to partner up on Saturdays. That farm market's a lot of work."

Scotty frowned. "I don't need the money. I've got plenty of income."

"I know you don't need another job! But I hardly expect you to give up running the river with Beau or NASCAR every Saturday for nothing." His dignity was a fragile thing. She started to realize that in a strange way he might need her more than she needed him.

"Lunch. And gas money. That's it, all right?"

"Deal. But next week you get to pick where we eat. That's only fair."

"Deal."

They continued down the highway towards Bassville, each lost in their own thoughts.

After a greasy burger and fries and another Pepsi, Mona felt almost human again. Steve's new bartender, a lanky college-aged kid, stood stoically behind the bar, too unsure of himself to make conversation. The bar was empty, and all the lunch customers were outside on the deck, so Scotty and Mona had the entire place to themselves.

"Geez," Scotty wiped ketchup from the edge of his lip. "T.C.'s up north for another week. No Spade, no Dohill brothers. Where is everybody?"

Arlyce came over and slapped their bill between their drinks. "What are you two up to today?" The skinny waitress had tied her greying hair into a ponytail and tucked a yellow plastic flower behind her ear in an attempt to look tropical.

"Just got done at the farm market, then I'm going back to bed," Mona said.

"Heard you girls had a good time last night," Arlyce dug into her apron pocket and pulled out a pack of cigarettes. "Got pretty rowdy." She cocked an eyebrow at Mona.

"Who did you hear this from? And for Pete's sake, we didn't even do anything bad. Is this town so boring that you have nothing else to talk about?"

Arlyce shrugged and flicked her lighter twice before it caught flame. "Guess not," she mumbled. "Saw Rosie at the grocery store. She told me she had to kick you out of her place. Said next time she sees you coming, she's setting up a barricade to keep you out."

"We tried a different order," Mona admitted. Usually their Death

March, which was a stop at each bar along Main Street, started at the Pub and ended at Grumpy's.

"I'm sure she really appreciated the gesture." Arlyce tore a few pages off her order pad and handed them to the bartender. "Deliver these to those tables out on the deck, will you?" She pointed out the window. "Pizza, burgers and combo basket, just drinks." When the bartender walked away she turned back to Mona and Scotty. "You didn't answer my question."

"Don't know," Scotty said. "I might track down Beau maybe."

"Wow. Youth really *is* wasted on the young." Arlyce scrunched up her face at them in disgust and walked back to the kitchen.

"I feel terrible about myself now," Scotty said.

"Don't." Mona left money on the bar and pushed back her stool. "Arlyce has a knack for making everyone feel terrible. She's always crabby. Just think of her life. Four kids and Steve and she's trapped in this place. She's jealous of us."

They walked outside into the bright sunshine and Mona squinted while her eyes adjusted from the dimly lit bar. A siren wailed in the distance. "Well, something's happening somewhere today," she said to Scotty.

"Guess so. Want me to take you to the farm or your house?" he asked.

"Farm. We gotta get those crates out of your truck." *And then I can lie down in my old bedroom and sleep*, Mona thought. The idea of acting like a kid again, waking up to her mom making supper, sounded very appealing.

Otto scanned the Bassville Pub looking for a local on the deck overlooking the river. He didn't know any of these people except Arlyce, who was scowling at a table of two couples wearing bathing suits while she wrote down their order. He tied off his boat on the dock and whistled to Rex. Steve would give the poor dog a dish of water, then he'd round up somebody to help sort out the jet skis back in the bayou.

The new bartender was getting a tutorial about how to shake dice from Spade. Nobody else was hanging around inside the bar on a hot sunny day. The cool air felt good on Otto's arms and face, and he took a seat at the bar. "Pepsi for me and can you get Rex a dish of water?"

While the bartender filled his drink order, Otto turned to Spade. "I was hoping to find Scotty or Dale, but you'll do."

"I bet you say that to all the guys," Spade quipped. He was a short wiry man with red hair and thick glasses. A bachelor with a gambling addiction, he worked at a mill in Northport and spent all his spare time and money hanging around Bassville's bars. "What's the problem?"

Otto explained the situation, leaving out how he'd maneuvered his boat to a new location in his desire for revenge, but emphasizing the need to retrieve the jet skis. "I doubt those kids would be able to remember where they left them for one thing. And for another, those machines are expensive."

"Where do you want to tow them?" Spade asked.

"I figured we'd just bring them to the marina. That's probably where they buy their gas, so the guys there might even know who the owners are and have an idea of how to reach them."

Spade nodded and rolled the dice out of the dice cup. "Pair of twos!" He rubbed his hands together and grinned. "I win!"

The bartender pushed a five-dollar bill across the bar at Spade and sighed. "I guess I can spare my *one customer* to help you out."

"Hey! It's my decision whether I help him or not. You're not in charge of me." Spade was busy folding his winnings into his thick leather wallet and getting ready to leave. "But yes, Otto," he said benevolently. "I will help you."

For a guy who was born and raised next to the Wissipaw, Spade never looked comfortable on the river. He sat next to Otto wearing a bright orange life jacket and clenching his fists in his lap. "How much farther did you say it was?" he yelled over the sound of the motor and the air rushing past.

"Almost there. About five more minutes." While they careened towards the bayou Otto thought about the two kids. He hoped the kid on the stretcher had woken up by now. *Did they have to make a police report? Would I get blamed for the accident? It was their fault for speeding, but still ...*

They flew past the wooded edge of the river and came up on Pine Acres Resort. Otto slowed down while he hit the bend and waved at two men he recognized who were leaving the dock in their bass boats. He speeded up on a straight stretch of river that was bordered by farm fields on his left and county highway on the right. Another minute and they'd reach Cooper's Bayou. The pleasure boaters had begun packing it up for the day, and Otto and Spade passed several boats heading down the river in the opposite direction. Otto guessed they were grabbing early dinners or even loading their boats onto trailers at the landing now.

The farm fields became a berm of willows and then a thick growth of pine, birch and maple trees. He turned into the bayou and they drifted towards the spot where Otto pointed out the first jet ski, upside-down on a fallen tree.

Spade took off his glasses and wiped them on the edge of his T-shirt. "How the hell are we going to get that down?"

"That's why I asked Arlyce for the axe."

Taking the same path as he had earlier, Otto led Spade from the boat to the shore and along the river's edge to the tree. He tossed a length of rope to Spade. "I know you don't want to get wet, so my plan is to tie it up, cut her loose, then drag it back to the boat."

Spade nodded.

"If I fall in, you're gonna have to help fish me out."

"I thought that's why you brought the dog," Spade said.

"No, I bring him for company."

Otto gingerly tested the trunk. The tree still had green leaves, so he knew it wasn't rotten, but he worried about how stable it was. Stupid, he knew, since a kid and a jet ski had been tossed into its branches without budging it loose. He grasped a thicker, sturdy-looking branch and held onto it while he side-stepped his way down the trunk towards the blue and white striped machine.

When he reached the jet ski, he examined it closely and tried to decide the sturdiest part where he could tie the rope. The handles looked easiest to break, so he looped the rope around the neck a couple of times. He looked down at Spade. The man was many things but definitely not athletic. He wouldn't risk asking Spade to toss him the other end of the rope. Pausing to slap at a deer fly taking a chunk of flesh out of his right shoulder, Otto crawled towards him.

"Here." He handed the end of the rope to Spade. "Hold on and don't let go." He picked up the axe he'd laid on the ground and climbed back to the jet ski. Chopping it loose would go pretty fast. He wished he'd gone home for a chainsaw. Each time he drew back the axe he felt the branches shift beneath him and he had to stop and regain his balance. Eventually the jet ski was tilting towards the river. Otto braced himself against the trunk of the tree and kicked at it. The machine seesawed back and forth. The trunk swayed slightly and he dug his fingers into the ridges of bark. Otto tried again, hoping the momentum would give it more force. The fourth shove did the trick. The ski teetered and slid into the water with a mighty splash. And, he noted with satisfaction, it landed right-side up.

Hefting the axe over his shoulder, he side-stepped back to Spade. "Let's drag it in."

The men returned to *Reel Good Dreams* with Rex trotting behind them. Spade had to stop several times to work his way over snags of logs and trees, but they eventually climbed on board with the jet ski's rope in tow.

"One down, one to go," Otto announced and started the engine. Spade pulled the jet ski closer, knotted the rope to a sternboard cleat and coiled the end neatly on the floor of the boat. Otto nodded his approval at Spade's work.

They churned up the bayou and Otto saw the white plastic bulk caught in the edge of some reeds. That was a relief, he thought. It would be no trouble to hook that thing and drag it out.

Shadows had grown long by the time Otto and Spade slowly dragged the skis to the marina. Otto had lashed rope around the two skis and cushioned a couple of bumpers between them to prevent any damage. The key from the treed jet ski was still in the ignition and Otto had successfully turned it on. The men had scoured the reeds and the riverbank for the other key. Usually people kept them on a floatable key ring. Otto knew the drivers also tethered their keys to their wrists, so maybe it was still attached to the kid in the ambulance. He hadn't noticed anything on his wrist, but so much of the afternoon was a blur in his memory. He wondered how the kid was doing, if they'd brought him home yet.

Otto finally broke the silence when they reached the marina. "I probably owe you dinner for helping me out."

Spade shook his head. "I wasn't doing much, anyway."

"Maybe the Pub owes *me* dinner for taking you off their hands," he joked.

Spade gestured towards the jet skis behind the boat. "So, we just leave them here and head back, right?"

"That's the plan. You can wait here." Otto expertly steered them into a slip, working the throttle to slow and stop *Reel Good Dreams* alongside the dock. He jumped out, tied them off and headed into the marina's office. A moment later he returned with a teenaged boy wearing a tank top and bright blue swim trunks.

"Oh yeah, I've seen these two before," the kid said after taking a look at the jet skis. "Guy that owns them has a cottage over on the lake. They're from Milwaukee."

"Can we leave them here? Will you let him know?"

The kid shrugged. "Sure. I mean, I don't know how to reach the guy and my boss is gone for the night, but he probably can. I'm sure we've got a service order on file for one of these—" he pointed at the jet skis. "Or maybe his boat. They've got a pontoon boat, too."

Otto unlashed the two machines and the kid helped him guide them to the front of the dock near the office. He took his bumpers and one of the ropes and told the kid if there was a problem, to call him at home. He smiled at Spade. "Let's go."

"Fine by me," Spade said.

Rex lifted his head and raised one eyebrow.

"Home," Otto told the dog.

After depositing Spade back at the Pub, Otto got his boat onto the trailer he'd parked at the public boat landing and returned home. His wife met him at the door, hands on hips and scowl on face. "Where have you been?"

She never fussed. Thirty years of marriage were peaceful because Otto followed his father's advice: Happy wife, happy life. He never went fishing until she was content—hinges oiled, gutters cleaned, windows washed—whatever chore list she produced, Otto finished his assignment and the payoff was freedom to fish. She'd never met him at the door mad before.

"Had quite an adventure today," he explained cautiously.

"That's what I heard." She glanced at a slip of paper in her hand. "Some man named Mr. Pierce has called three times wanting to talk to you. What happened, Otto?"

After removing his shoes and pouring a scoop of kibble into Rex's bowl, Otto led her to the living room couch and told her about his day.

She exhaled, relief relaxing the tightness on her face. "He wants you to call him back at this number." She passed the slip of paper to Otto. "His son's all right. A concussion, some stitches. He's concerned about the jet skis and your boat." She looked up at him inquisitively.

"My boat's fine. Spade helped me haul the jet skis to the marina. I'll call him and tell him."

"Are you hungry?"

"No. Just tired."

"It's too late to make you a proper supper. I'll make you a snack."

"I didn't catch any fish anyway," he told her. Otto followed her into the kitchen and lifted the phone receiver off the wall. If the man was worried about the jet skis, that meant the boy really was okay. *Thank God*, he thought and dialed the number his wife had written down.

Otto felt relief when Mr. Pierce began their conversation by thanking him for bringing his son to get help. He told Otto that the boys hadn't owned the jet skis very long and seemed apologetic for the trouble they'd caused. Leaning his head against the door jamb, Otto sighed. By moving his boat, he was trying to teach the boys a lesson about being safe. He'd wanted them to slow down. Hearing how inexperienced they were pricked his guilty conscience. *But how can you let them ride so fast in such dangerous waters?* Otto wanted to ask the man. Instead he told Mr. Pierce he was happy to hear the boys were okay and told him where to find the watercrafts.

When he'd hung up, his wife handed him a plate with a sandwich and orange slices. "I'm proud of you, honey. You really were a good Samaritan to those people." She patted his arm.

Otto grunted and took a bite. Ham and cheese loaf on white with mustard. His wife knew him well, but she didn't know all the facts, and neither did Mr. Pierce. He knew he was lucky those boys didn't have a clue that he'd moved to that bend in the bayou. They had no idea he'd deliberately caused their accident. Now he looked like a hero, bringing them to safety and rescuing their watercrafts. The bigger issue lingered, though. Some folks didn't know how to share the river. Maybe, Otto considered while he chewed his sandwich, this tragic accident could change things.

NINE

Monday afternoon Maw was working on finding a clever rhyme for "bobber" when three customers walked into his shop. A dad with two kids getting their fishing supplies. Maw introduced himself and quickly learned that they needed more than just a couple dozen crawlers.

Kitting out a new fisherman was one of the best parts of owning a bait shop. He got to teach them everything he knew and give advice on how to spend their money. Maw instructed his customers on casting and selected reels and poles for them to try. "Have you gone fishing on the Wissipaw before?" he asked the man. His two kids were messing around elbow deep in the minnow tanks after Maw demonstrated how to use a small dip net to catch them.

"I did as a kid, but that was years ago," the man explained. "We just moved here a month ago and finally are settled in. Been promising to take them since we bought the lot over in Traysons Acres last year."

"Welcome to town, neighbor!" Maw's grin grew wider. "What's your name?"

"Rawley Parker. This is Miles and Hannah."

"You build the ranch or the two-story house over there?"

"The two-story."

"Bassville's a great place to live, you'll love it here."

"We do so far. A couple hiccups along the way, of course, but you expect that."

"Do you have a boat or plan to fish off the shore?"

"We haven't got a boat yet, so what do you suggest?"

If they had a boat, they'd be using it. Maw scratched his beard and pretended to think. They didn't have a boat so he could take them out himself. He'd get to fish and charge money while acting as their guide. On a Monday the shop was usually slow, so he could easily leave it. "It's been hot this summer, so the fish are hanging out in the deeper waters. Hard to reach those spots if you stick to shore."

The kids' faces fell and Maw's forehead wrinkled with concern. "No, don't worry. If you want, I can take you out myself and give you a guided tour of the river." He glanced at Rawley. "It costs a little, but worth the price. You'll know a lot if we spend a few hours out there together. Then the next time you'll be able to go on your own."

He watched Rawley begin the mental calculations and interrupted quickly to close the sale. "I guarantee you'll end the day with fish in your cooler, ready to bring home for supper. And what tastes better than pan-fried fish on a summer night?"

"Dad! Can we? In a boat?" The kids pleaded.

Maw shrugged helplessly at Rawley. "It's not that big a deal. I can get one of my kids to take over here for me. My boat's ready to go."

Even more fun than kitting out a new fisherman, Maw reflected while he called over the shop's intercom to the house, was getting paid to go fishing for the afternoon.

The kids' joyful expressions were priceless. Maw pointed that out to Rawley while he opened up the throttle and they raced down the middle of the Wissipaw, his boat gliding across the water at top speed. "If you're ever in the market for a boat," he shouted over the wind and motor, "I can help you get a good deal. There's always somebody in Bassville selling used stuff so they can upgrade. You name it, you can find it used—boats, trucks, snowmobiles!"

Rawley nodded and Maw watched the man relax into his seat. He seemed like a nice guy. An accounts manager for an insurance company, he'd said, a little white collar, but genuinely interested in learning about the river. He'd explained that he and his wife were new to the area from a Milwaukee suburb. He'd taken a new job in Northport to get out of the stress of commuting to the city. Housing was more expensive in Milwaukee, and he and his wife, Tammy, thought a smaller school and town would be safer and cheaper for raising their family. "A half-hour commute on a country highway is nothing compared to forty-five minutes stuck in city traffic," he'd told Maw.

Maw assured him that Bassville's school system was top notch, crime was almost unheard of. He didn't mention The Pole, of course, but that wouldn't've affected them anyway. That situation was strictly personal and nobody had seen or heard from The Pole since he disappeared three years ago. Living near the water offered all kinds of opportunities for fun.

They passed Pine Acres Resort and Maw pointed out a popular sandbar where two boats had dropped anchor on this early summer afternoon. "Great spot for swimming. The water's only a couple feet deep there." They headed towards the Luau Lounge and Gala Resort.

"We camped there a few summers ago," Rawley said while pointing to Gala.

"Good place, great people run it. We're heading up to Partridge Point. The pan fish bite like mad over there and the kids will love it."

Two hours later the Parker children were sated with laughter, fish and joy. They cracked open a couple of sodas Maw had thoughtfully tossed in the cooler and began retelling their catch of the day stories. Maw tied a hook to Rawley's line and showed him how to store the rod properly. "You always want to leave some slack, don't let the end bend down." Maw hooked the line to one of the guides and gently reeled in the slack, leaving about an inch of loose line. "Just like this."

Rawley and his children followed his instructions with the remaining rods and lay them in the bottom of the boat. Then Maw gestured to the captain's seat. "Want to take us back?"

Rawley's face lit up with excitement, looking like a kid himself. "Really?"

"You're a local, you have to know the water like one."

Maw sat back and gave occasional directions while Rawley steered the boat up the river towards the dock. Maw peppered the group with stories along the way. "You see that cut right there?" He pointed to a spot where a tributary of the river bent back upon itself and disappeared behind a stand of reeds. "Best duck hunting in the fall. One time I was back there with my buddy Dob, you'll love him when you meet him. Anyway, we'd gotten up really early and were all set up in our blind. Dob was a little under the weather from the previous night and had fallen asleep when all of a sudden ... "

Back in the bait shop Maw beamed at the generous tip Rawley tucked in his hand after they'd settled up the charges for the day.

"Thanks. I mean it. This day was really special for all of us." Rawley tousled his son's hair and nodded toward the Styrofoam cooler of fish they were bringing home.

"I'm glad you moved here, Rawley. I think you're a great addition to Bassville," Maw told him.

"Glad you think so. I don't think everybody in Bassville is excited to have new neighbors."

"How's that?"

"There's been some vandalism on the other building sites in our subdivision. The head guy came around the other day asking us to keep an eye out and let them know if we notice any unusual traffic or activity, especially at night."

"What kind of vandalism?"

"Flag markers removed, basements flooded, framework dismantled. He told us they're behind schedule on the third house, but one is ready for the new owners to move in. Anyway, we're pretty sure it's locals messing things up because who on earth would be out by us in the middle of the night?"

"That's true. I'll keep my ears open and let you know if I hear anything." Maw couldn't think of too many people who'd mess around like that, but one name sprung to mind.

Rawley lowered his voice. His kids were listening to Maw's youngest, who leaned behind the counter, playing the wise sage. Maw's son was telling the two which teachers to avoid at school and about the Bassville Bobcats' odds of making the playoffs in football this fall. "It hasn't been easy on the kids, leaving their friends and their neighborhood. I thought they'd love being in the country, but they're really lonely out there by themselves. Guess I hadn't figured on being the first family in the subdivision with no one else around. There's another family going to move in before school starts, but I haven't seen them yet. Today's the first time they've looked happy since we got here."

The two men looked over at Rawley's son and daughter.

"You know, you can bring them and their bikes into town and leave them here on a weekday. My kid would be glad to shepherd them around. Teach them the lay of the land, so to speak."

"I'll have to talk about that with my wife. She's pretty protective. She never let them cross the street on their bikes until last year."

"It's a standing offer, friend."

Rawley nodded his gratitude before rounding up his kids and leaving.

"What did you think of them?" Maw asked his son.

"They're okay." He shrugged. "Kind of sucks that they live so far out in the country. I'd hate that. They don't even have cable out there. There's nothing on regular TV."

Maw absently rubbed his son's mop of hair and then glanced at the clock. "Almost supper time. Go help your mom."

Rawley seemed like a good guy. A little awkward and uptight, but he'd loosen up after he got comfortable. He'd be a good fit for Bassville once he relaxed. Maw decided he'd help make that happen.

TEN

Mona lay on her stomach across Judi's bed watching her pack. She'd leave tomorrow morning for Chicago, where she and Will would board a plane to Vegas. Then she'd return to her new home—an apartment in West Town, Chicago. The room's contents had been mostly boxed up and loaded into the back of Judi's car. All that remained was a small pile of clothes and some cosmetics. "Are you scared?" Mona asked.

"Of what?" Judi held up a long-sleeved pinstriped shirt and considered it before refolding it and placing it in her suitcase.

"Getting married. Spending every day with Will."

Judi sat next to her on the bed and pulled her jewelry box onto her lap. "Not at all." She sighed and pulled out a cluster of necklaces and started to unknot the chains. "I'm looking forward to it, actually."

"Won't you get bored?"

"Doubt it. Chicago has everything—museums, restaurants, parks.

Once I'm settled in, I plan to find a job."

"Do you really want to work in a hotel again?" Mona rolled onto her back.

"Hotel work is my fallback option. I'd like to see if I can get into one of the art museums."

"Sue's going to be lost without you."

"My mom will be fine once she's done being stubborn."

Sue still hadn't hired anyone to replace Judi. Judi had interviewed applicants and offered to train them but refused to hire her replacement. She insisted that since her mother would have to work with them, not Judi, it really didn't matter what she thought.

"Betchya Snuffy would clean up nice if you'd help him," Mona snickered. Snuffy was the bartender at Grumpy's who slept every night on their pool table. Mona, along with many other locals, took care of the homeless man. "And he could move into your room!"

Judi giggled at the suggestion. "I'd rather have Beau in here. But then we'd have bigger problems. Imagine him in action working at a *hotel*!"

Mona laughed louder. "He's already such a player—it would be too convenient for him to work here."

Judi made her voice deeper in an imitation of Beau Longwell hitting on a woman. "Hey baby, looks like we put you in room seven. That's funny, you're a ten in my book."

"Baby, I'll take you to back to seven, then straight to heaven." Mona said.

"Love your outfit—but it would look better on the floor by my bed!"

Tears seeped down Mona's cheeks. She was going to miss her friend.

Then Judi sat up. "What about Scotty?"

Mona frowned. "What do you mean?" She propped her head on her hands.

"Well, you mentioned he's pretty bored now that the farm's gone. Maybe he'd like working here."

"No. Definitely not. Scotty's an outdoors kind of guy. He'd hate being cooped up inside."

Judi raised her eyebrows at Mona and shrugged. "It's not my call. But can you do me a favor?"

"Anything."

"Look out for Mom, okay? Let me know if she seems over her head with this place. I'm afraid she's going to get overwhelmed without me around."

Mona put her arm around Judi's shoulder. "I've got her back. Don't worry."

Judi slid a gift-wrapped package from beneath her bed and handed it to Mona. "This is for you."

"You don't have to give me a present! You're the one getting married and moving away."

"You gave me that picture frame and that terrific window box. The minute I get settled in, I'm figuring out how to cook with fresh herbs."

Mona toyed with the yellow bow on the box. "Well, it's not necessary." She flipped the box over and tore apart the paper. She studied the glossy cover of the book. *Monet: The Triumph of Impressionism.*

"It's a coffee table book of his art." Judi opened it and pointed to the painting depicted inside. It was a bridge over water with flowers. "His work is at the Art Institute of Chicago. I want you to come down and see it. I gave it to you for two reasons. The first one is corny, but he painted a lot of water scenes and they're really beautiful, just like the Wissipaw. The second reason, well, he's an impressionist. At a distance you get a big view of things, but as you look closer, you see how each part is distinct, more textured, the artist playing with the light."

Mona nodded. She knew about Monet and impressionist art from high school.

"It's like Bassville," Judi continued. "When I first got here, I got one view of the place. It's pretty backwards and quirky, kind of run down. But then I got to know you better—and other people, too—and my view of things changed." Judi put her hand on Mona's knee. "I'm really going to miss you, Mona. You're a great friend and you helped me see this place as more than just safe spot to get my mom situated. You helped make it feel like home."

Mona's eyes filled with tears and she hugged Judi. She'd keep the book on her coffee table and read it. "I'll definitely come to Chicago and see you. And Monet."

When she left the Hotel later that evening, she called over to Sue, who working at the front desk. "See ya, Sue!"

Sue looked over the top of her glasses and waved at her. "Don't be a stranger, Mona."

Mona paused by the wood paneled walls and admired the old black and white photographs depicting the white bass run on the Wissipaw River. She took in the four chairs and low table situated by the desk, the rack of brochures advertising local attractions. Without Judi, she'd have no reason really to stop at the Hotel, but she'd promised to keep an eye on Sue. She'd have to insist on coming here for drinks with her friends more often. The Hotel bar was quiet, so they never stopped in regularly, but they'd have to start.

ELEVEN

DOTTIE TRAYSON ASKED GENE to order her a brandy Old-Fashioned before perching on a barstool in the corner of the Bassville Pub. By five on a Friday the place had filled up with people dropping in on their way home from work and people heading out for dinner and drinks. She watched Steve and Arlyce bustle between tables carrying glasses of beer, burger baskets and pizzas. Maw held court across from where Dottie sat, shaking dice and spinning tales with the Dohills, the Traysons, Beau and Spade. It was his turn to buy a round and he was just about to give the sign to Steve—raising his index finger and making a circle was the universally accepted signal—when the door opened and in walked the Parkers.

"Rawley! You old son of a bitch, how's it going?" Maw roared his welcome and shouted across to Steve, "Catch these fine people on me, too."

Dottie and the rest of the crowd leaned forward curiously to look at Rawley and Tammy, both dressed in Northport date night attire, which was a step up from Bassville's weekend wear. Rawley who wore khaki pants and a polo shirt, stuck out in a crowd of jeans and shorts and T-shirts. Tammy wore a denim skirt and blouse, looking quite dressed up next to Dottie in her Bermuda shorts and bright yellow tourist T-shirt from her and Gene's winter trip to Jamaica.

Maw slung his arm around Rawley's shoulder and dragged him into the circle of locals. "This here's Rawley Parker. He and his family just moved here a couple months ago. They built the two-story over in that new subdivision."

Rawley raised his hand and said hello. "My wife," he added, "Tammy."

Tammy smiled and nodded to the group, who greeted her in return.

"What are you two drinking tonight?"

"I'll have a Coors light, what'll you have sweetie?" Rawley asked his wife.

"Malibu and diet," she told him.

Maw grinned at Tammy and reached for his wallet. "Your kids sure had a great time fishing the other day. Bet you ate like kings that night, all those pan fish."

Tammy gave him a funny look before saying, "We put them in the freezer for later."

Jaws dropped. Dale spoke up first, his low voice a rumble. "You put fresh caught fish in the *freezer*?" He sounded incredulous.

"Yeah," Tammy said. "For later."

"You helped clean them, right?" Dale asked Maw, just to be certain.

"I did! Of course I did." Maw sounded offended by Dale's question. "Taught the kids how to scale them and deboned them and everything." Maw turned to Tammy. "How come you didn't fry them up right away?"

She shook her head and scrunched up her nose. "Have you *smelled* raw fish? It's disgusting. And it takes forever to get the smell out of the house."

The men laughed. "Raw fish doesn't smell until it goes bad," Spade said. "Even I know that."

Tammy flushed. "Well, I think it's terrible and I didn't have time to mess around with figuring out how to make it when I'd already made beef stroganoff for supper. In fact, it was waiting on the table when you came home, Rawley."

"Wait a minute!" Dob's deep voice took on a teasing note. "Have you ever cooked food that didn't come from the grocery store?"

The woman shook her head and crossed her arms. "I've lived in a city my whole life. I don't have anything against people hunting or fishing, but this is the first time I ever had something come to me straight out of nature or whatever." She shuffled her feet.

"The cow for your beef stroganoff came out of nature," Gene chuckled.

"It's okay," Maw told Tammy. "But just so you know, fish doesn't smell, unless like Spade said, it goes bad. Freezing it takes a little of the flavor out, but it's okay. You really don't need to freeze food before you cook it."

"Think about it, Tammy," her husband piped up. "How did the Indians do it? They didn't have freezers."

While she nursed her Old-Fashioned, Dottie examined the woman. She felt a little sorry for how the guys were ribbing her and her husband now acting like a know-it-all, but that didn't change the fact that she'd called their number four times demanding Gene come over and mow the fields around their subdivision. Lady had some nerve, Dottie thought. If Arlyce weren't so busy waiting tables right now, she'd love to point her out. Arlyce would know the perfect way to confront her, too. She was confident that way, and never backed down from giving somebody a piece of her mind.

The conversation shifted to fishing and Maw continued making introductions around the circle. Dottie braced herself to shake hands with Tammy, while feeling self-conscious about her appearance. A round woman with short curly brown hair, Dottie had a shelf-like bosom and viewed clothing as a particular challenge and necessity. If you were what the advertisements called "queen-sized," fashion wasn't much of an option. Even after they sold the farm and paid Angie's medical bills, Dottie didn't find pleasure in shopping for clothes because when you were shaped like a beach ball, the "full figured" options all looked the same: draping and floral.

Dottie and Gene had plenty in the bank, but their life hadn't changed other than to take a trip every year to someplace exotic. Dottie took another sip of her cocktail and waited for the inevitable moment when Tammy would walk over to her and want to start talking. She glanced towards the kitchen. Maybe she could make her escape back there.

"So, I suppose you know all about cooking fresh game," Tammy said by way of starting a conversation. The woman sat on the empty bar stool beside Dottie and stirred her drink with a straw. "Nobody in my family fishes or hunts. You just go into the butcher shop and tell them exactly what you want. It's easy, they cut and wrap up whatever—you want four pork chops? They give you four. Two pounds of skirt steak, they cut it right there for you. There's a butcher in Bassville, right? Or do I have to go to Northport every week for shopping?"

Dottie smiled and nodded. Would she recognize her voice from the phone when they'd spoke? "There's no trick to fish. Except maybe keeping an eye on not drying it out because fish isn't fatty like pork or beef. I usually cook up fish with butter. Bud's Supermarket has a good meat selection. And Bud can cut to order if you need him to."

Tammy shook her head. "I just always got my meat from the grocer. I don't even know how to tell it apart without the label on the package. Meat all looks the same to me, the butcher could probably sell me a butt roast and how would I know it's not a pot roast? Meat's meat."

"Fish is easy, especially if you grill it. And everything's good with butter."

"Do you fish, too?"

"Not really. I'm a committed knitter."

"I never learned to do that. But I can crochet. My grandma taught me. I used to crochet doll blankets when I was a little girl. And of course we all made those afghans with the squares, you know … "

While Tammy chattered on Dottie's mind raced thinking for something interesting to say. "So you have two children? How old are they?"

"Hannah is ten and Miles is twelve. Hannah's my reader, she's always got her nose in a book. Miles is always go-go-go. Kid never sits still. We waited to move until his baseball season was over, and he can't wait to start football and meet some boys his age."

"Ten and twelve are fun ages. Was it hard for them to move?"

"Very. We had a lot of tears on moving day. We resorted to full-scale bribery by promising them a boat. Have you looked at how expensive boats are? Some of them cost almost as much as a new house! And my friend told me the repairs never end. She says 'Boat means Bring On Another Thousand.' We're still looking for one, but so far the closest they've been to the water was when Rawley took them fishing."

"There's always somebody selling a boat around here. I bet you'll get a good deal. And I know you can rent a slip at the marina, which is really convenient."

"A slip?" Tammy asked.

"It's like your own permanent dock space. The marina has a parking lot and you can just drive up, get on your boat and enjoy the water. Sure beats packing it onto a trailer every time you want to get on the water. I have no idea why folks like Otto do that, as much as he fishes. But he's cheap, so there you go."

"Tell me how a trailer works."

"Well, you know a boat trailer is just a wagon for hauling your boat behind your truck."

"We haven't got a truck. We have two cars. I told Rawley if we're moving out to the country, we should buy a truck just for getting through snow, but he's so stubborn. I couldn't drive a truck, they're so big, I've only ever driven cars. And I can't drive stick shift."

"Oh. Well, you pull the trailer to a boat landing—there's one just on the other side of the Pub's parking lot, below the bridge there. It's a bit of a pain, you have to back it in, keep it straight, lots of fussing with steering it backwards, but then you can leave your truck and trailer in the parking lot while you use your boat." Dottie paused to thank Steve for the refill on her drink. "This boat landing is free, some of the others charge a fee. But it's still cheaper than renting a slip."

"I have a lot to learn." Tammy sighed.

"You moved here from Milwaukee, right?" Dottie asked, knowing the woman wouldn't come up for air for at least three minutes. Tammy could talk paint off a wall.

"Brookfield, actually. Living up here is our dream—we wanted to live in the country where we'd have privacy, fresh air and space for the kids to run around. Turns out I hate it so far. The house is nice, brand new, of course. We have privacy, so much that I'm bored out of my mind. As for fresh air—ha! I have to keep the windows closed because of the smell of cow manure blowing in."

"But you have space," Dottie reminded her.

"We have space. There's only one other family moving in soon in Traysons Acres and I still haven't met them yet."

Dottie thought it was strange to hear her name referenced like that, but she knew this woman had no idea who she was. Now the question was should she bring it up? No, she decided. "I've seen that other family out for supper the other weekend. Their kids are around the same ages as yours."

Arlyce sashayed past, balancing a round drinks tray on her right hand. "I need a round of margaritas and two taps of Bud Light for that big table on the deck, hon," she said to Steve. She set down the tray, dug into her apron pocket and retrieved her pack of cigarettes. She shook one loose and lit it, her stressed expression relaxing when she inhaled. "All the kids are out to play tonight," she told Dottie.

"This is as busy as I've ever seen it on a Friday in summer," Dottie agreed.

"We've got Maw's kid in the kitchen making pizzas and washing dishes, but I could use another set of hands. You sure Angie doesn't want to work this summer?"

"Next year," Dottie told her. "She's only sixteen. I told you, she's able to babysit."

Arlyce grunted and took another drag. "I was waiting tables when I was her age." She stubbed out the cigarette and flipped through her order pad. She jotted down a few numbers and made a circular motion to Steve to hurry him along. "Just once I'd love to trade places with him. Look at him, just jawing with the customers and pulling taps."

Steve returned with Arlyce's new drink order and set the glasses on the tray. "There you go."

"If you can get away from behind the bar for a couple minutes, there's some tables that need to get cleared off."

Arlyce returned to the deck and Tammy watched her leave. "I

could never work in a restaurant. It looks hard. Having to remember people's orders, on your feet all day, come home smelling like food. I worked in a clothing store and as a receptionist."

"Did you like it?" Dottie asked.

"I went to college for fashion merchandizing. Worked as a store manager until the kids were born. Now I'm a stay-at-home mom. You have no idea how busy life is with two kids. We are just go, go, go between activities and errands and, of course, Rawley doesn't do *anything* to help run the household."

Dottie understood. She'd helped run the farm and raised two of her own, but she just nodded and turned to Gene. "Are we going to order soon?"

"Sure. Let me catch these guys a round and then we'll head to the dining room."

"About time, you rich son of a bitch." Dale gave Gene a hearty slap on the shoulder. "Been waiting for you to catch a round ever since you sold your farm, Trayson."

As Dottie sensed the woman next to her freeze, she slowly turned back her. "The fish is excellent here, so's the pizza."

Tammy's eyes narrowed as she made the connection. "I've called you. Trayson? That's your name? You're the people who own the subdivision, that's your name on the sign."

"We've talked four times," Dottie said in a resigned voice.

"There are thistles almost two feet tall in that lot next to us now. Do you have any idea how big they're going to grow? I've seen them. Bull thistles grow up to twelve feet tall. They'll be everywhere, too. We've spent a thousand dollars on this lawn and the last thing I want is to worry about is my kids stepping on something sharp with bare feet. And the other weeds! Everything you're letting grow is taking over the entire field."

"I imagine they are," Dottie said. Her pudgy hand gripped her glass. She tried not to think about throwing it at Tammy's perfectly made up face.

"Someone needs to mow them. Our yard is full of dandelions. Dandelions, then thistles, then Lord only knows what's next." Tammy's voice was cold.

Dottie clenched the glass in her hand, trying to keep her hand from trembling. "You heard Dale. We sold the property. It's not our responsibility."

"Well, it must be *somebody's*. Your name's on the sign. Don't you have any pride in that?"

"The title isn't in our name. Call the developer." Dottie stood. "Or better yet, buy a weed whacker and take care of it yourself." She reached for Gene's elbow. "I'll be in the dining room. Come back when you've settled up here."

The men had fallen silent while they overheard the exchange between the women. Dale broke the tension. "You need something mowed? Alois Schmidt has a tractor and nothing but time until he's cutting hay in a couple weeks." He smiled at Tammy. "I can give you his number."

Tammy's fury simmered beneath the surface while she answered him in clipped tones. "Somebody is responsible for mowing the empty lots around us. It's the law. All of those weeds have gone to seed and are blowing into our new lawn. Do any of you have a clue how difficult it is to get a lawn going?"

Rawley put his arm around his wife's shoulder. "Honey, we can talk about this later. These men don't care about growing grass."

The woman shrugged off her husband's affectionate gesture. "I'm sure they don't care because they have nice lawns already."

"You'd have thistles anyway," Maw said, trying to help. "It's part of country life. You can't stop nature from blowing stuff around. Heck, Steve here can barely see in the spring, his eyes get so swollen from pollen."

Tammy shot her husband a dirty look. "You know the kids have allergies, Rawley."

"Nobody ever died from allergies," Steve volunteered. "You have a better chance of dying in a car accident than dying from allergies."

"Well." Tammy slung her purse onto her shoulder and stood. "I feel so much better now knowing that." She turned to her husband. "I'm ready to go."

He held up his can. "I just got a full beer."

"Tough nuts." She strode towards the door.

The men watched closely. What happened next would establish the kind of man Rawley was. Would he cave into his wife and walk out leaving a full can of beer on the bar? That would make him weak. Would he dig in his heels and leave when good and ready? That would earn their admiration. Would he split the difference, drink half the beer and be out the door within five minutes? That would be wisest.

Rawley shifted his weight from foot to foot looking uncomfortable while he decided. He shook his head and gave the men a sheepish smile. "Women. You know how they can be."

"Nope!" Spade piped up cheerfully. "I have no idea. If you keep the relationship strictly professional, they can't drive you up a wall."

"Spade here's a confirmed bachelor. Swears by it," Maw explained.

"You wouldn't necessarily guess it by looking at him," Dob said, "but he's probably the smartest man in town."

"Scotty's still single," Gene said. "He's pretty smart."

"Not by choice, I'll wager," Dob told him.

"You're a smart man," Rawley said to Spade. "I, on the other hand … " He shrugged, then took a long swallow of his beer before setting the can on the bar. "Gentlemen, I'll catch you next time." Rawley left the Pub, aware he was under scrutiny. He could prove his manhood another time, but he had to spend the whole weekend with Tammy, who could nurse a grudge like no one's business.

"Shit!" Maw exploded as soon as the door swung shut behind him. "That one's gonna need a lot of training."

"Happy wife, happy life," Dob quipped.

"And where's your wife right now?" Dale asked his brother.

"With yours, probably bitching about how terrible we are." His laugh was deep and infectious.

"And mine is waiting for me in the dining room." Gene left with a raised hand, both in farewell and resistance to the comments his friends were making.

"And mine looks like she needs another round," Steve said and moved to the end of the bar where the new blender sat ready for action.

TWELVE

SATURDAY MORNING MONA ARRIVED at the farm with two travel mugs filled with coffee. Her good mood plummeted when she didn't see Scotty's truck beside the greenhouse. *Well, we hadn't made a formal agreement,* she thought. She left the mugs on the potting bench beside the door and started preparing the crates for the farmers market. She felt foolish thinking he'd be waiting for her, ready to volunteer his Saturday to help her sell vegetables. Who was she kidding? He didn't need the money or the work. He had plenty to keep busy working for the Dohills and side jobs he'd picked up on his own. He totally deserved to sleep in on a day off and go troll the river with Beau if he wanted to. And she could probably use the extra coffee anyway, she'd need the energy.

Her dad had helped harvest and sort root vegetables, peas, beans and cucumbers yesterday. The greens, however, had to wait until that morning to get picked. They were popular with customers, but also very fragile. The longer she could leave them attached to their stems, the better they looked. Mona started snipping and filling plastic bags with red lettuce, arugula, spinach and chard. In the barn she'd plugged in a large refrigerator discovered at a scratch and dent sale to store the peppers, cucumbers, peas and beans. Market day was a lot of work, but it was the best way to sell her vegetables until she had enough restaurants lined up for a delivery business.

She laid the last of the bags of lettuce in a Styrofoam cooler and was headed for the door when she heard tires crunching the gravel in the driveway. She felt her heart jump and realized just how much disappointment she'd felt. Pushing the door open with her elbow, she greeted Scotty with a huge grin.

"I bought you a coffee—it's on the bench over there."

"Thanks." Scotty's hair was damp beneath his ball cap, the curls darker and laying on his tanned neck. He smelled like soap. He took the cooler from Mona's arms. "Do we want to use my truck again? It worked pretty well last time."

"If you're cool with it," Mona said. The pleasure of seeing him was ridiculous. She must be that desperate for help, she decided.

The hours flew by as they set up the stand and handled the early sales of the day. A steady stream of regulars hit the farmers market at eight o'clock each week, with the more casual shoppers arriving around nine. By ten they worked at a relaxed pace, Scotty weighing potatoes and talking with an elderly man while Mona made change for a family with young children in a wagon. The mother, a woman Mona's age with a tie-dyed sundress and braided hair, was talking up a storm while selecting beans and carrots. "My husband and I had a crazy dream to run a farm together. It's cool you two are doing it."

Mona glanced over her shoulder to see if Scotty had heard her. He was adding a few potatoes to the bag to make weight. She decided to go along with the woman's assumption; it would take too long to explain the situation anyway. "Do you have my card? I can make boxes ahead of time if you're interested in ordering. Then everything's weighed out and packaged and you just pick them up." Mona pulled one of her business cards off the stack by the metal change box and handed it to the young mother. "My contact information is right there."

"Thanks! You two have a great day," the woman said while pulling the wagon towards the next booth where an overall-wearing hippie named Fred sold jars of pickled vegetables.

Scotty waved off the elderly gentleman and wiped his hands on his jeans. Mona thought he hadn't heard the woman's comment until he said, "If we're in this together, you're going to need to change the name. I'm thinking Scotty and Mona's Veggie Stand."

"You're hilarious. I just didn't want to have a whole conversation about the farm's history," Mona said. "That's all."

He raised his eyebrows, but let it go.

Later, when the market was winding down and he'd gone to buy them a couple of lemonades from Al's Fresh-Squeezed Fruit, a few stands over from their spot, Mona found herself wondering what she'd rename the business *if* her situation changed. *But that's a big if.* Besides, she had a great name and the Dirty Girl Veggies logo looked cool.

That afternoon she rode into Bassville feeling content and rich, even after paying Scotty the agreed-upon gas and lunch for his help. Another very successful day. She was only left with a couple pounds of potatoes and two bags of carrots. Her ledgers were meticulous. Jake had encouraged her to write everything down and pay attention to discrepancies and patterns. Save every receipt. Make notes about how much time and space it took to grow things (time is money) and what sold and what didn't. This helped her determine price points and volume. He'd given her so much good advice when she was getting started.

"What are you doing with the rest of your day?" Scotty asked, interrupting her thoughts.

"I think I'll pop in on my grandparents. I haven't seen them in a few days. Maybe I'll order a pizza from the Pub and bring it to them."

"I saw them a couple mornings ago at the Pub having breakfast. Your grandpa's a piece of work."

"That's true, but why this time?"

"You know how he's nearly deaf—well, sometimes I think he pretends he's worse than he really is. Spade was doing the Shake of the Day with Steve and up they roll, Frank pushing Nancy in her wheelchair. Your grandpa says, 'Thank you, young man. It's nice of you to buy us breakfast.' He leaves the bill right next to Spade and starts pushing Nancy out the door."

"He did not!"

"He did! And I swear he winked at me when I held the door for him. He knew exactly what he was doing."

"I can't believe it." Mona thought about her grandpa, a frail and stooped man who cared for his wife since she'd suffered a stroke. They lived in an apartment on Main Street, their life confined to that block where Frank pushed Nancy to breakfast at the Pub and sometimes a burger at Riverside Bar and to church. Mona's mom took care of their weekly errands to the grocery store, haircuts and doctor appointments.

"My dad was laughing—he told us after Frank and Nancy left the bar that he remembers the shit your grandpa used to pull back when they owned Riverside Bar. He used to jack up the prices when the fishermen came to town—called it the Illinois Surcharge. Honest to God, he'd charge locals one price for a beer and the out of town guys a different price. And he used to make prank calls to the other bars. Once he called Steve—this was right when he was pretty new to tending bar, and your grandpa knew it was busy because it was suppertime. He called Steve and asked for Jerry Ford. Of course Steve yells for the guy across the bar. He yells over and over, 'I'm looking for Jerry Ford. Is Jerry Ford here?' My dad was sitting at the bar that day and told him, 'Steve, the President isn't in your bar today.' Yeah, your grandpa's a funny guy."

Mona laughed. "I guess I remember hearing some stories."

"People always said Nancy was the crazy one, but Frank's just as nuts. They're a pair all right. Peas in a pod."

"You want to come?" Mona asked.

"To your grandparents'?"

"Yeah. Just for an hour or so. Feed them pizza, make sure they're doing all right—unless you have plans … " Mona trailed off.

"Sure. I'll come along. I get a kick out of those two."

"The pizza's on me."

"Of course it is. You think I do stuff for free?" Scotty asked.

And there it was again, Mona noticed. A vague feeling of disappointment when he said that. Somehow, she had expected Scotty to do stuff with her—*for her*—for some other reason. She scowled at her reflection in his side view mirror. What the hell was wrong with her today? She was probably off her feed because she missed Judi, that's all. Judi, who was by now married and enjoying her honeymoon in Las Vegas. Her friend had definitely hit the jackpot, and Mona felt glad and a little jealous at the same time.

THIRTEEN

KELLY OGDEN ARRIVED AT their new house, which had the chemical aroma of fresh paint and new carpet, and surveyed the bare rooms. She set down a box of cleaning supplies, rags, detergents and rubber gloves. It would take all morning, but she'd feel better about moving in once every speck of construction dust was wiped away. Tightening the bandana on her hair, she decided to work her way from left to right, the bedrooms and bathrooms first. Kelly was anxious to get started since they were a month behind the move-in date the builder had initially promised. Hiccups at the job site kept occurring—the newly poured basement had flooded, though Kelly didn't recall it raining much. But perhaps they hit an underground spring. And then there were other phone calls insisting everything was under control, but delays were happening of one sort or another. Sick of living in limbo with half their possessions in boxes and storage, Kelly was ready to get unpacked and settled.

An hour later she was examining the carpet burn on her knees from crawling around the perimeter of each room to wipe down baseboards. While she considered whether to rummage in her car's first aid kit for a bandage, somebody knocked on the front door.

Kelly opened it to a woman with frosted blonde hair and what looked like a permanent furrow between her eyebrows. Despite her cheerful smile, the woman looked ... intense. "Hello?"

"Hi!" The woman shouldered her way past Kelly towards the kitchen and set the casserole dish she carried on the counter. She turned back to Kelly and put out her hand. "I'm Tammy Parker. Your new neighbor. Well, actually, you're *my* new neighbor since I moved her first."

Kelly wiped her hand off on her shorts and returned the handshake. "I'm Kelly. Ogden."

"We moved here a month ago from Milwaukee. My husband works for State Farm Insurance. We have two children, a boy and a girl, and soon we'll have a dog, but we're waiting for the lawn to get established first. Have you ever tried having a dog without a lawn? Don't. It's an absolute mess. But the weeds won't give up and the stupid farmer or developer or someone can't be bothered to mow *their* fields, so it's taking forever to grow grass. It's like a battle for every inch of land out here in the country. I feel like a complete pioneer when I wake up and see the weeds and the rocks and the mud—I have to drag the sprinklers around the yard to try and water it. Have you ever lost a flip flop in the mud? This happens to me almost every day. So I brought you a casserole. I hope your family likes turkey tetrazzini. There's no Welcome Wagon, trust me, I know. No one came to visit when we moved out here, so I figured I'd do you one better than what we got on moving day."

The woman stopped to take a breath and Kelly broke in. "Thank you." Tammy's energy was overwhelming. But maybe Kelly just felt tired from cleaning all morning. Plus, moving was emotionally draining, too.

"I've been trying to petition the town to enforce their laws, either mow the fields around us or hold someone responsible for doing it. Now that you're moved in, you can help me wear them down."

Kelly's eyes widened. That sounded like exactly the last thing she wanted to do after moving in. She kept this thought to herself, however, and instead said, "Well, I can't wait for our kids to meet each other. I know mine will be glad for people their age. We're leaving a wonderful neighborhood and this will make it easier."

Tammy moved the casserole to the refrigerator and turned back to Kelly. "Bake it at 350 for forty-five minutes. You can serve it with a tossed salad, maybe some beans or fresh fruit."

"I am sure we'll enjoy it very much. Thank you." Kelly started for the door to give her new neighbor a hint to leave. She didn't want to be rude, but she was so worn out and not feeling like talking to anyone.

"I didn't think your house would ever get finished, what with all the excitement on the job site. Rawley and I couldn't believe that one morning when we woke up to see the other house had completely disappeared!"

"What are you talking about?"

"Craziest thing—we'd walked over the night before—we did the same when yours was being built. They'd been framing it and we like to walk around and figure out which room is which and where the windows will look out and so forth. So we'd walked around that night, gone home and the next morning Rawley's looking out the window and says the house disappeared! It looked like somebody had taken every piece of lumber apart and stacked it on the edge of the lot."

It was irritating to think of people walking through their house, even though it wasn't built yet. It was even more horrifying to think that someone had taken an entire frame down in the middle of the night—but why? And had anyone tried to sabotage their house? "Do you think the builder did it? Maybe they'd made a mistake."

"No way," Tammy shook her head. "I watched him make a dozen or so phone calls and then when they did get back to work the whole place looked the same. He came by and asked us to keep an eye out for suspicious activity. That's how I knew it was no accident."

Kelly was speechless.

"So, you gonna give me the grand tour? Ours is two stories. You have the bedrooms down the hall?" Tammy was already walking through the living room and Kelly realized she would lose the battle with this woman. She had a moment—seconds, really—to establish boundaries and prevent her from invading her time and her space. It might seem rude, but polite didn't work on people like Tammy Parker. She gulped back all of her hesitation and raised her voice.

"Please don't."

Tammy paused and turned around.

Kelly shrugged apologetically. "I really prefer to finish cleaning before we show anyone around. It's probably the Dutch in me, but that's how I am." She reached up and gently grasped Tammy's elbow. "Thank you again for the visit. I will invite you over for a nice chat once we're all settled."

Tammy, who had rarely been shown a door or a line to leave uncrossed, silently obeyed.

Kelly shut the door and sunk to the floor. When she was finished crying from exhaustion and frustration, she wiped her eyes and inhaled deeply. It would be a new start in a lot of ways, living in Bassville. She didn't want to make enemies, but she had a strong feeling that without trying she'd already done so.

FOURTEEN

OTTO WAS TIGHTENING BOLTS on his boat trailer parked in his driveway when his wife called him into the house to answer a phone call. He wiped his fingers across a rag in his back pocket and headed inside, wondering who would call him on a Monday night—right before the monthly town council meeting.

"Hello?"

"Otto Zimm? This is Jay Hodge, attorney-at-law."

Otto gulped. He had expected a phone call, a court summons, something to happen after the incident on the river. "Yes?" His mouth grew dry and his breath felt shallow in his chest.

"I heard you were involved in an accident last weekend involving two personal watercrafts on the Wissipaw River."

Otto answered in the affirmative. He opened a drawer to find a pad of paper and a pen to write down whatever this man would charge him with.

"The traffic on the river has exploded in the last few years, due in large part to pleasure boaters. There has been increasing conflict with motorboats ripping through the river at a fast rate, endangering the safety of those living on the river and peacefully enjoying it, don't you agree?"

Otto agreed, naturally, and his shoulders relaxed. This man didn't sound like he was against him.

"I own a small cottage, a little ways up the river from Bassville. I spend most weekends there with my family, my kids and grandkids. We fish a little, the kids like to swim off the dock and float on inner tubes. But lately the crazy speedboats have gotten out of hand. A group of us have banded together to try and change the no-wake rules on the river. We're calling it 'No Wake: Take Back the Lake.' We heard about your situation with the boys on the jet skis, and I think this is exactly the sort of story that will get attention. What happened was terrible, but it could have easily been a bigger tragedy. Those young men are lucky to walk away from that accident."

"You said you're a lawyer," Otto said.

"I am. And I'm a property owner on the Wissipaw."

"So why are you calling me?"

"I want you to share your story, Otto. We're creating an advertisement for television and some promotional material to get the word out. We're appealing to the local and county governments to support the change to make a permanent no-wake zone from south of the public boat landing through town and put no-wake buoys in the major bayous."

"Well, that would be really helpful," Otto said. He rarely went past Bassville on his boat, but he saw no reason why anyone needed to go through that stretch of water full throttle.

"We're meeting this Thursday at five o'clock at the Bassville Town Hall. Anyone interested is welcome to come. Bring your friends. If you can make it to the meeting, we'll record you telling your story. It's got great appeal. Really drives home how dangerous the river is when people go too fast. Those boys could've been killed."

Otto agreed again, although he knew nothing at all would have happened that day if he'd just stayed in his original spot. But the idea of slowing down the traffic! And possibly discouraging the boaters from coming through Bassville entirely … if they made the river no wake from the boat landing all the way through town, it would take people a half hour to get through. And if it took more time for people to get where they wanted to go, they might decide it wasn't worth the hassle and stay away. The more Otto thought about it, the more excited he became. Otto finished his phone conversation and walked into the living room where his wife stood at the ironing board while watching the news on TV.

"Honey, you won't believe who was on the phone just now."

Mona noted on the minutes that the monthly town council meeting started on time while Dale Dohill read through last month's minutes and asked for a motion to approve them. Otto, Dale, Gene Trayson, Loyal and Mona shuffled their papers and settled into their metal folding chairs. Mona tapped her pen nervously on her notebook while they ran over the treasurer's report. Tammy Parker was sitting in the front row in the nearly empty room. She was revved up if her appearance was any indication. She wore a skirt and blazer with high heels that looked out of place among the rest of the locals, who were wearing polo shirts and blue jeans or work pants. Tammy held a leather briefcase that Mona suspected held copies of the county law on weed control. Her hands were knotted in a fist on her lap and she stared straight ahead at the council members, paying attention to every detail while they went over the business at hand.

The June meeting was typically pretty short. They had to approve a couple of license requests, including a temporary liquor permit for the firemen's chicken barbeque, and listen to an update on a road construction project north of town. Finally, they came to the public comment portion of the night.

"The floor is now open for public comment," Loyal said as though he had no idea the one extra person in the room was there for that very reason. "Does anyone want to speak?"

Tammy raised her hand.

"Can you state your name and address for the record, please," Loyal told her.

"Tammy Parker, 1363 Angie Court, Bassville. I'm here about the weed infestation over in Traysons Acres. The vacant lots in the subdivision are completely overgrown with noxious weeds like bull thistles and dandelions. According to this county statute," Tammy pulled a sheaf of papers out of her leather briefcase and passed them to the council members, "the property owner is responsible for mowing. We've planted grass and all of these weeds have gone to seed and made our new lawn a mess. Now, I'm not going to sue for damages, but I want whoever's responsible to take care of mowing down the weeds out there."

The council members made a show of reading her handout thoughtfully while she fell silent. After a moment, Dale cleared his throat. "Do you know who the property owner is?" He tilted his head toward Gene and raised his eyebrows. Mona caught the twinkle in his eye and stifled a smile.

"Well, I thought it was the Traysons," Tammy nodded to acknowledge Gene at the front table, "but I have since learned the developer is the owner now."

"That's correct." Dale nodded to Loyal. "Can you look up the contact information for the Nelson Land Trust, LLC?" He turned back to Tammy. "That's who you want to talk to. They're the owners."

"But I've called them and gotten nowhere!" Tammy's voice rose with frustration. "The Traysons say it's not their responsibility, and the Nelson Land Trust office just takes my messages and won't do anything."

Loyal looked up from the papers Tammy had handed them. "According to this document, we can publish a notice on behalf of the town. It needs to be sent by registered or certified mail. How long do we want to give them?"

Otto shrugged. "Two weeks?"

"That sounds reasonable," Dale said. "Figure it'll take a couple days to get the notice drawn up and sent, then gives them at least a week to comply or not. They might need to hire it out, but either way they have a little window for weather and whatnot."

"Two weeks?" Tammy asked in a sharp voice.

Loyal kept reading, "And they have the right to request a hearing. If they do, we'd have to hear them at next month's meeting. Otherwise if they don't comply, we can go ahead after two weeks and hire somebody to mow the fields and then send Nelson the bill."

"So what you're telling me," Tammy said slowly, "is that those weeds might not get mowed for at least a month."

"Could be," Loyal said with a shrug.

"This is outrageous! Do you have any idea what it's like living out there surrounded by that mess?"

Mona's lips twitched but she kept her thoughts to herself. She knew exactly how that 'mess' looked when the Parkers bought their lot a year ago. Those fields were blooming with alfalfa and thistles, dandelions and worm-seed wallflower. How did weeds in the country come as a surprise to her?

"Well, Mrs. Parker," Gene said, "controlling nature is a difficult thing under any circumstances. If it makes you feel better, people in town battle dandelions and thistles, too."

"What happens if I hire somebody to mow? Can I make the Nelson company pay for it?" Tammy crossed her arms and tilted her head back.

"No," Mona spoke up. "I mean, you could try, but there's no guarantee. Your best bet is to go through the proper channels like you are right now."

"Unbelievable." Tammy pursed her lips and snapped her briefcase shut.

"So, you want us to go ahead and publish a notice?" Gene asked.

"Yes. And I'll be back next month to follow up. There are laws for a reason, if anyone here cares."

The council members looked at each other with quizzical expressions and finally Dale said, "Does anyone else care to add to the public comment portion of our meeting?"

Aside from the scrape of a chair, the room was silent. Otto cleared his throat while Tammy headed for the door. "I guess it's not a complaint or anything, but I had a phone call tonight about a group that's calling themselves 'No Wake: Take Back the Lake.' They want to extend the no-wake area through town just past the public boat landing."

"I was afraid something like this might happen," Loyal said to Otto. "When do they plan to petition the council?"

"I'm not sure, but they're having a meeting later this week to discuss how to move ahead."

"Who's involved?" Gene asked.

"A lawyer from Northport. Not sure who else."

"A lawyer?" Dale laughed. "That makes me think of an old joke."

"Well, if they want the river no wake through town, then they'll end up here because that's our decision," Loyal said.

"I didn't know that," Otto said, surprised.

"State statute, all waterways are under local control. If they wanted a different part of the river slowed down, say over by Gala Resort, that's not in the town's boundaries, so the county would have to make the call there."

"Huh," Otto mused.

"Smart of them to go straight to a council member," Mona said.

"The guy called me because of the accident with those jet skis," Otto explained.

"Makes sense. I also wondered when this would come up. River's gotten busier over the last few years. This will ruffle feathers, that's for sure," Dale said.

"How come?" Otto asked. "It makes sense to slow people down before somebody gets really hurt out there."

"But how many local businesses are gonna want it?" Dale asked him. "You have to think about it from their perspective. They added a no-wake zone by Clearwater and about dried up their business. Takes people too long now to drive through, adds at least a half hour to their trip, so they skip going there. I imagine it's only a matter of time before the powerboats create their own alliance to fight against the speed limits."

"Why did they pass the no-wake rule, then?" Mona wanted to know.

"Depends on who you ask. Some thought the no-wake zone was caving to pressure from homeowners living on the water who didn't like their docks and shorelines getting beat up from the wake. Others blame the fishermen," Dale cut a glance at Otto, "who add to the congestion by dropping anchor right in the center of the channel."

"Hey!" Otto protested. "I was in Cooper's Bayou when this accident happened. I wasn't nowhere near the boat traffic." He looked over to Loyal for support.

"No one's saying you were, you're smart about where to fish. But let's face it, a lot of fishermen don't like to play nice with the boaters. Sometimes they play dirty."

Otto's face grew red and he scowled.

Dale continued, "If we don't want a fracas on our hands, we need to proceed with caution, that's all I'm saying. Our businesses need the river traffic, from the Pub to Maw to Gala and the rest. We risk hurting them by making it unfriendly."

"But we have to make it safe, too," Loyal said.

"So let's study it," Gene suggested. He placed his hands on the table and met Otto's gaze. "Let's start counting boats and how many violations the wardens see in this stretch of the river."

Otto rolled his eyes. More warden traffic was never the answer in his opinion, but he kept that thought to himself. "It's those damn jet skis and Sea-Doos and what-have-yous causing most of the trouble. Plus every other boat's dragging an inner tube behind it."

"Well, let's get our facts first," Gene flipped his ballpoint pen over to click it shut. "We shouldn't make any decision without the facts, so I'll contact Joe and we'll get some patrol boats out there in the next couple of weekends and get a read on the situation."

"Who's going to follow up with the Nelson weed problem?" Mona asked.

"You are, since you brought it up," Dale told her. "Anyone else for the public comment?" He watched the wall clock count off ten seconds before asking for a motion to adjourn.

"Weeds and water skis," Mona muttered to her dad on their way through the parking lot. "If these are the big issues our town faces, I shouldn't complain."

"Small problems," Loyal agreed. "And if you deal with small problems, they don't become big problems."

"I hope that's true," Mona said. She glanced up at the dark sky above and inhaled the sharp scent of ozone. Puffs of cottonwood seed drifted overhead like snowflakes. The wind had switched directions since the meeting started and she turned towards it so her hair didn't blow across her face. "Well, we need the rain."

FIFTEEN

THE PUB WAS BUZZING the next morning with opinions about the no-wake rule when Scotty stopped by to get his thermos filled with coffee before heading to a job site with the Dohills. Maw proclaimed it "a death sentence for every business on the river," and Steve agreed. Scotty offered his view that it was a person's right to decide what happened to their property, but the river didn't belong to anybody, so what right did a person have to make rules on it.

"But you gotta have some rules," Gene said to his son. "Even yielding to traffic on the left is a rule."

"That's just common sense," Scotty argued.

"Well that's the trouble with people," Arlyce announced while refilling coffee mugs. "Most of 'em don't have a lick of common sense, which is why you gotta have rules. Without rules, how do you keep the idiots in line?"

"She's right," Loyal agreed. "And the problem with more people is you have to have more rules."

"They're not bad people," Maw said and placed his hand over his coffee mug. "No thanks, Arlyce. I have to get back to the shop." He turned to Loyal. "I took Rawley and his kids out fishing last week. He's a really nice guy if you get to know him. I think it's good to have new people move here."

"We should've never sold that land, Dad," Scotty said. "We opened a whole can of worms."

"Or a can of thistle and dandelion seeds, to hear Tammy Parker tell it," Gene joked. "But I was glad to tell Dottie what happened when I got home last night. She and Tammy didn't exactly get off to a great start."

"That woman has to be crazy," Arlyce declared. Scotty knew Arlyce couldn't comprehend anyone not loving one of her best friends. "Dottie's got the biggest heart around." She took Scotty's dollar and handed him his full thermos.

"Her husband's a good guy," Maw protested.

"She's not crazy." Loyal stood and stretched. "She's just mad and she doesn't understand country living. I warned you this would happen. Wait until the tractors clog up the roads this fall when we harvest. I'm just thankful they didn't move in until we were done planting. And it's just a matter of time before somebody bitches about the way manure smells."

"The subdivision's upwind of your farm," Gene reminded him.

"We're all downwind from someone."

Back at home where he'd obediently crawled into the closet beneath the stairs, Maw scratched his head with the tip of his Bic ballpoint pen and exhaled. He'd spent all morning working on song lyrics and had gotten nowhere. He glanced at the pile of bills and orders he needed to get to and reached across the floor to pull them closer. His family locked him in a closet one morning a month so he'd actually get his paperwork finished. The imprisonment probably seemed medieval to an outsider, but the system worked. His wife, Peg, understood how easily distracted her husband was, and the second time the electricity and cable TV service got cut off after Maw ignored the business end of things was a convincer. As a consequence, once each month Maw willingly ducked his head and entered the cupboard beneath the stairs in his house. A small desk, chair, office supplies and all of the paperwork awaited him.

"I'll get these done and work on the second verse," he announced to the walls. "Let's see … " he pursed his lips and studied the electric bill. Then he scrawled his signature on a check, filled in the amounts and account numbers and slid it into an envelope. He repeated the routine with cable, insurance and was halfway through updating tax records when his mind wandered back to the commercial.

After some digging, Maw discovered a recording studio in Milwaukee where he could cut a rap album. He planned to release a music video starring himself, of course, backed up by the Bikini Fishing Team, and with some editing the video could double as a commercial for the shop. A couple of high school kids from the AV Club had signed on to give him a beat and synthesized melody using computers. He'd written three songs so far, but none were the right song for a commercial spot. He tried again with a first line he liked after crossing out two words.

> You're itchin' for fishin' on the old Wissipaw
> Nobody can outfit your tackle box like Maw
> I've got worms that will squirm
> Catch your walleye in a flash
> My cantankerous minnow will kick your fish's ass!
> Bluegill, catfish, muskie and sucker

Smallmouth, flathead, crappie for supper!
But the fish you'll land as fast as you can cast
Is the Wissipaw River's world-famous white bass.

"Ha! That'll work!" He banged his fist against the door and hollered for Peg to release him.

She opened the door a crack and peered in. "Hand them over." Peg reached out her hand and her dimples creased her cheeks when she smiled at her husband. Her grey-streaked hair curled over her forehead, brushing the frame of her eyeglasses. Peg had inherited the solid build, practical thrift and excellent posture of her Dutch ancestors.

Maw handed her a small stack of envelopes.

"And receipts."

He passed her a fistful of bill statements and receipts for her to file.

"Go in peace." She kissed his cheek. "Lunch is on the table."

"I'm ready for the big time, Peg," Maw told her while he stiffly crawled out from the closet. "Listen to this." He slapped his hands on the table to give the rhythm before he started rapping.

Before he finished the first verse she was laughing, by the second verse she was waving her hand for him to stop. "How do you come up with this stuff?" she asked him when he finished.

"Can you picture it, Peg?" Maw held his palms out. "We'll have the lights turned way down in the shop, so it's like a backdrop. I'll wear a T-shirt with the logo and a bunch of gold chains and sunglasses, maybe a hat with the bill sideways. The girls can be backup dancers, maybe I'll give them a little bit of singing, like an echo effect. Some strobe lights and crazy camera angles, we'll look cool!"

"You'll look like something, all right." Peg lifted a potato chip off his plate and thoughtfully munched on it. "Guess extra attention can't hurt. What's this gonna cost us?"

"Well, you gotta spend money to make money."

"So you keep telling me." Peg leaned back and crossed her arms. Her mouth twitched, whether in amusement or in an effort to bite back criticism, Maw couldn't tell.

"It's gonna be a huge hit, babe." Maw wiped the crust of his sandwich across his plate to capture the bits of potato chip before stuffing it in his mouth. "White guy from Wisconsin who can bust a rhyme? The world's been waiting for this. They just didn't know it yet."

"I have no doubt the world's not ready for a song that rhymes 'current' and 'belligerent' and 'spawn' and 'gone.'"

"The words just flow out of me. Must be all of those Word of the Day calendars. I've stored up vocabulary at a vociferous rate."

"Indeed." Peg stood and removed Maw's empty plate from the table. "Do me a favor, honey. Don't spend more than we'll make on this, okay?" She knew her advice was futile, but you never knew when it might seep into his thick skull.

"Won't cost hardly anything. My talent is free," Maw assured her. "I'll be out in the shop if you need me."

The wind had picked up, slapping waves against the shoreline. The boats lined up along the docks bounced and strained against their ropes. Up and down the river jet skis zoomed, their whine echoing into the bayous and culverts. Scotty arched his back and wiped his forehead while he watched the scene below from his perch on the Hotel's deck. Sue had asked him to repair a few loose boards and build a gate across the steps to the dock below. Occasionally he had to fix things he'd built with a man named Adam Lewsciewski, commonly known as The Pole. Seeing his old friend's handiwork would remind him of the time they'd spent together working and joking around. The Dohills were fun guys, but they kept a big crew of workers, so it wasn't the same as working with only one other person. When you worked close with a partner you got to where you didn't even need to talk, you just knew exactly where to hold your balance of a board, where to stop nailing in a row of shingles, how to avoid knocking into corners while carrying heavy things.

It had been six years since he and The Pole had built the structure, and it had stood up really well. The floorboards were just as flush and level as the day they'd screwed them in. Scotty ran his hand over the stained and treated planks. They'd done good work together. Sometimes he really missed his old friend. After Joanne, The Pole's girlfriend, had been found in the Wissipaw mysteriously drowned, speculation had run wild. Half the town believed The Pole had been responsible for her death, the violent act of a jealous man. The other half chalked it up to an unfortunate accident. But when Adam had left town right after the funeral, everyone agreed it made him look guilty. He'd never resurfaced. Scotty would always ask people he met from the northern part of Wisconsin if they knew a large Polack named Adam, a man with a dark beard and skill with a compound-miter saw. So far nobody had. His disappearance was as mysterious as Joanne's death.

Scotty picked up odd jobs because he had the time, but he really wanted his own gig. There wasn't enough work for a single guy—that's why the partnership with The Pole had worked. Together they could do bigger projects that took too long for one person to handle. And as for one-person jobs, well, most guys in town could do those on their own and didn't need to hire them out. Looking back, he knew he should've stayed farming. Every day when he woke up in his parents' house, a twenty-six-year-old man still sleeping in a twin bed across the hall from his little sister, he felt like a failure. He had to strike out on his own. It wasn't a question of money, he had plenty of that. It was a question of where to go. Although lately he knew exactly where he wanted to go on Saturdays. He'd silently worshipped Mona since they were kids and watched from the sidelines while she fell head over heels for fun-loving and crazy T.C. before taking up with Jake. Scotty couldn't compete with a guy who was homecoming king and stud quarterback. No, Mona was definitely out of his league. He accepted that. He'd settle for her friendship and helping her out at her farm stand, though, even if a guy like him never stood a chance with her.

An engine rumbled closer, the noise pulling his attention back to the traffic on the river below the deck where he worked. It was harder to relax on the river anymore. The jet skis had taken over and annoyed the hell out of everybody. What was the point of them? They just went fast. And were loud. A person couldn't fish off of one. No one seemed to ride them to get anywhere. They just rode around in circles, bouncing on their own wake like maniacs. And now Otto had even seen one back in the bayous where the big boats never went.

Yes, Scotty thought, bending over to measure another piece of oak to support a railing, those jet skis wrecked everything that was nice and peaceful about living on the river.

Mona hurried across the Pub's parking lot, guilty about showing up late for the meeting to plan the annual chicken barbeque fundraiser for the volunteer fire department. Cutting through the kitchen, she said hello to the kid working the grill and squeaked around the corner into the dining room. "Sorry I'm late," she announced to the women sitting around a table covered with a bright yellow tablecloth. She waved at her grandparents who were having a late lunch at their favorite spot by a window. Escaping the wind that had picked up, Mona imagined.

"You're fine, we were just catching up on important stuff," her mother told her.

"Pull up a chair," Dottie said. "June was giving us self-defense tips on how to stay safe in a parking garage. You weave your keys through your fingers to use as a weapon. Did you know that?"

"You want something to drink?" Arlyce asked. "Coffee or soda?"

"I'm good," Mona said. She opened her notebook and clicked her ballpoint pen.

"This year's goal is five thousand," Peg said. She passed around a spreadsheet. "Obviously we're not in a position to buy a new truck yet."

Mona studied the spreadsheet while running numbers in her head. She'd gotten good at spreadsheets while running her business. "This looks like the same profit margin as last year's event."

Peg nodded. "Prices haven't changed, so we kept everything the same." She took off her glasses to rub the lenses clean with the edge of her T-shirt.

"Seems like the only way to get more money is to get more people to show up. The numbers have been steady for four years now." Dottie sipped her coffee and continued. "Not sure how we change that problem. Each town has their Sunday for this event, we lock the dates down so's not to conflict with the others. We can't hold our chicken barbeque on any other day."

"It is a standard tradition," June agreed.

"Hello?"

The women turned around towards the voice in the door. There stood Tammy Parker with her two children. "We came by for a soda?"

The woman sounded strangely hesitant. Normally she wore her confidence like a top hat.

Arlyce stood and nodded at the kids. "Out running the river today?"

"We went for a bike ride through town," the girl told them.

"What'll you have?" Arlyce asked.

Tammy answered while tapping each child on the head to indicate the choices, "Root beer, 7UP and I'll have a diet whatever." She walked over to the table and pulled up a chair nearby. "Is it okay if we sit in here?"

"Mom? Can we have money for the pool table?"

Tammy looked at Arlyce. "Is that okay?"

Arlyce shrugged. "That's what it's there for."

Mona watched Tammy dole out quarters from her pocket. The kids followed Arlyce through to the bar and Tammy pushed her hair back from her forehead. "It sure is windy, but it's the first day it hasn't been blazing hot. Are you ladies having lunch?"

"We're planning this year's chicken barbeque," June told her. "It's a fundraiser for the fire department."

Tammy perked up and scooted her chair closer to the group. "That sounds fun. What's your target?"

The women looked at her quizzically.

"Your goal," she clarified. "How much you want to make off it."

"Ah," Peg nodded. "Five thousand."

"For what?" Tammy asked.

"We're saving up for a new fire truck. They cost about fifty-thousand, so this is a start."

Tammy's eager gaze dropped while she considered this information. Finally she murmured, "It will take you ten years."

Mona nodded.

"That's crazy. Sorry if that sounds rude, but it will take you forever to hit your goal at that rate." Tammy reached over to grab June's copy of the spreadsheet and started reading it. "You charge seven dollars a plate. I pay eight for a chicken dinner at a restaurant, plus tip and drinks. Start by charging more for your chicken. And what's this per pound price? Where do you get that?"

"That's the price Bud charges us for the chicken," Dottie explained.

"All the other fire departments charge seven a plate," Peg added.

"This skinless and cut up?" Tammy asked Dottie, pointing to the chicken price with her finger.

"Yes," Dottie said. "I thought you didn't know anything about meat."

"I don't know anything about *fish*, but I know the difference between skinless and boneless and whole chickens. That's on the labels," Tammy explained. "What else do you sell besides chicken?"

"Drinks," Peg said. "We sell soda and beer by the can. And there's a raffle. The barbeque starts at eleven, so right when people get out of church, and it goes until we run out."

"Says you served about 714 people last year."

June nodded. "That's right. People come from all around. It's kind of a thing in the summer, everyone hops from town to town for different chicken barbeque each weekend."

"They fry it in peanut oil, that's what makes it taste so good," Mona added.

"You get a lot of volunteers?" Tammy asked.

"Tons," Peg said. "Every guy on the fire department plus their whole family."

Tammy nodded and tapped her finger on her chin, contemplating the information she'd gleaned. "Okay, let's shoot for ten."

The other women exchanged a look of concern mixed with curiosity. "Ten what?" Mona asked.

"Ten thousand. You can't wait a decade for a new fire truck. And here's what you're gonna do," Tammy continued, flipping over the spreadsheet and picking up Arlyce's pen. "First, you raise the price per plate. Seven's a steal. Let's bump it up to eight-fifty. Then we're gonna negotiate a better price on the chicken. If your guy can't come down, then you find somebody who will. We'll put the kids to work cutting it up, that's a huge savings right there."

"I guess we could have our kids prep chicken," Arlyce said. "It's an easy enough job."

"And you have to sell something besides beer and soda." Tammy turned to Arlyce. "A lot of people don't like beer, especially women. You need to offer a sweet option. Maybe consider wine coolers."

"You have a lot of ideas about this," Arlyce remarked. She pulled her pack of cigarettes out of her apron packet and tapped them gently against her palm.

Tammy shrugged her shoulders and kept running her index finger down the columns of numbers on the spreadsheet. "I used to work in retail. I managed a store. Promotional work was my main job."

Mona watched Tammy take over the planning and nobody, not even Arlyce, raised an objection. She jotted calculations in the margins and pushed back from the table, grinning with satisfaction. "There you go! Ten thousand-five hundred." Tammy pointed at June. "You make sure every piece of advertising includes the goal of a new fire truck. People spend more when they know what you're raising the money for." Tammy turned to Peg, "You've got the chicken bid under control?"

Peg nodded. Her husband was a force to be reckoned with. She now knew the female version of Maw and it was both disconcerting and incredible. This stranger had sat down and completely redid twenty-six years of fundraising tradition. And the kicker was Peg knew her ideas were good. They probably *would* clear ten thousand.

"And this raffle business. No crap prizes. No one wants to buy a ticket for junk. Go fifty-fifty or get some really good prizes donated, like Packer tickets or something. It's a tax write-off for businesses, so hit them up for decent stuff." Tammy glanced at her watch. "I have to get my kids home and make supper. When's our next meeting?"

"Shit!" Nancy exclaimed from the table where she and Frank had been eavesdropping.

Tammy whirled around and glared at the elderly couple. "What did you say?"

Nancy tilted her head back and laughed. "Shit."

"Are you trying to be funny?"

Mona felt sorry for Tammy, who obviously didn't know that was all Nancy could say. Frank had half-risen from his seat when June spoke up. "That's my mother. She had a stroke. She can only say three words and shit's one of them."

"Oh. Okay then." Tammy gave the couple a brisk nod.

"Next Tuesday, two o'clock, right here," Arlyce told her.

"Got it. See you all then!" Tammy bustled out to the bar area and gathered her children. In the dining room a stunned silence hung over the women. Finally, Arlyce spoke.

"Looks like there's a new sheriff in town."

Laughter trickled around the room while they shifted in their seats.

"Who knows? Maybe her ideas are nuts, but maybe they'll work. Look at Maw," Peg pointed out.

"We always said new people living in town would bring change," June said.

"That's not just change." Arlyce slid a cigarette out of the pack at her elbow. "She's a force of nature."

Mona privately agreed.

Later when Mona was at the farm thinning carrots in the field, she reflected on how efficiently Tammy Parker planned the fire department's event—and how she managed to take it over and in doing so, became central to the Ladies' Auxiliary Club. *Did she know they were meeting*, she wondered. *There's no way she could, but she definitely took opportunity by the short hairs and worked it to her advantage. She's assertive, but she wants to pitch in. Not a bad quality for a new neighbor.* She'd give good money to be in the room when her mom dished about it later with Arlyce and Dottie at their weekly knitting group.

"Yoo-hoo!" a high-pitched voice called across the field. Mona sat back on her heels and brushed the dirt off her hands while she watched her best friend since elementary school pick her way across the field, holding her hair back from her face as the wind blew it around. Jenny Bender's stiletto heels sank in the muddy surface and she finally stopped and yelled for Mona to come over. Mona sighed, feeling a little disappointed that Jenny's lurching high step was halted, and jogged over, her worn sneaker treads giving her no issues while she passed between rows of potatoes and beans.

"You're out of your natural habitat," Mona greeted her.

"Well, you're never home and don't answer your phone." Jenny tried wiping a clod of mud off her shoe against a pumpkin leaf. "We're planning a boating party after the barbeque. You in?"

Mona put her hands on her hips. "I have to work it. You know that."

"We're going to get a regatta together and float up to Clearwater for the rest of the day. Can't you get someone to cover for you? It's gonna be so much fun."

"I can't, Jenny." Mona closed her eyes and shook her head. "It's part of being on the council. They expect me to help out."

"You used to be a lot more fun before you got all adult-y," Jenny pouted.

Mona had nothing to say to that, so she reached to pluck a tall pigweed that was growing by her feet.

Jenny nodded and pointed at the rows of vegetables growing around their feet. "This is still working out for you, huh."

"Wouldn't want to be anywhere else on a day like this." Mona tilted her head back. The sun felt hot on her face but the breeze kept the bugs away today. "You don't get to experience different seasons in a mall."

"Hey, we put up different decorations! And you get great deals in a mall. I have a cute new bikini for the fourth, looks like an American flag. Very sexy and patriotic. Maw might take some pictures of me holding sparklers for his next calendar when I wear it that day."

"Yeah, a bunch of old fishermen looking at pictures of you wearing a bikini. That's not creepy at all."

"When you say it like that, it sounds gross."

"It *is* gross, Jenny."

"Maw's making a rap video. He's using the Bikini Fishing Team in it. I'll be on TV."

Mona smirked. "That's actually not the craziest thing I've ever heard of. If anyone can rap, I bet Maw can."

"He's cutting an entire album."

"Only Maw could take bait to that level."

"You done yet?" Jenny gestured to the rows of vegetables.

"I'm never done. Why?"

"I'm bored. Let's go grab a drink at the Pub or something. Those new margaritas Steve makes are delicious. Plus it's fun watching him get all pissed off when you order them."

Mona felt bad telling her no. It seemed like she was always telling Jenny no lately. "I'm sorry, I'm filthy and I've got to get this stuff done before Saturday. Rain check?"

"Your loss, lady." Jenny began her lurching high step back towards where she'd parked her car by the barn. She stopped suddenly and turned around. "We're trying to get the new people to come, too."

"The Parkers?"

"Yeah, Maw invited them."

Well, that would be an interesting twist to the party, Mona thought. She wondered about the other new family. Would they come, too?

She'd only seen them at the Luau Lounge that one night, hadn't heard whether they were as pushy as Tammy. Maybe it would be 'the more, the merrier.' She hoped so.

After Peg left and Frank steered Nancy back to their apartment down the street, the Stitch n' Bitch group sat around a table at the Pub, talking faster than they were knitting.

"Have you ever seen anything like it?" Arlyce paused to take a drag off her cigarette. "Just sits herself right down and starts running the show."

"Well, we sort of let her," June pointed out.

"That's not normal," Dottie said. "Normally people hang out on the sidelines and learn how things work before jumping in to steer the ship."

"Mixing a few metaphors there," June said. She grinned at her friend. "But she had good ideas. Who knows? Maybe fresh blood is what the event needs. Changing things up can't hurt."

"It might," Arlyce said darkly. "What happens when one of our kids slices their hand open while cutting apart whole chickens?"

June burst out laughing. "I'm sorry, but really? Your kids fillet fish for money every spring. They set traps and catch wild animals. I saw Hunter shooting at fish off the end of the dock last week while his brothers were swimming not even ten feet away. You're suddenly worried they'll cut themselves while doing food prep?"

"Do you have any idea how slippery a raw chicken is?" Arlyce snapped back.

"Um, yes. Yes, I do. You might recall that you're talking to a farmer's wife. We used to butcher them ourselves when we kept hens."

"I'm honestly surprised you don't have your kids doing some food prep here at the Pub," Dottie remarked. She counted stitches across her pink plastic knitting needle, mouthing the numbers while she moved her fingers down the row.

"Those monsters? No way. Not yet." Arlyce stubbed out her cigarette and scowled. "Though Hunter *is* fourteen now, plenty old enough to do dishes and stock the bar. How have I let him get away with not working this summer?"

Dottie chuckled. "Same way I let Angie get away without having a job yet. I want to keep my baby young as long as I can."

"That's an interesting thing for you to say," June said. "Isn't Scotty still living at home?"

"He is," Dottie said. "Funny, but I never think of him in the same way as Angie." She flipped her project around to purl across the row.

"Well, he wasn't sick," Arlyce pointed out.

"Yes, and he's always worked. He helped out on the farm from little on, but when Angie got sick, we had hired help by then. But I don't look at Scotty as living at home. I mean, he does, but he's hardly ever there. He sleeps there, but that's really it."

"Do you do his laundry? Make him meals?" June wanted to know.

Dottie pursed her lips and thought. "I wash his bedding, that's it. He feeds himself, sometimes he's home for supper, but we don't really count on him. Now I'm wondering, what does that boy do for meals?"

"I feed him most of the time, I imagine," Arlyce said, laughing. "He's like Peter Pan, a boy who never grew up."

"But he has," Dottie argued. "He started working full time right after high school and has always had at least two jobs between farm work and construction. He pays for his own insurance, truck and toys. We never buy him anything. Basically the only thing he hasn't done is buy his own house, but what's the point? There isn't much property to rent in Bassville and if he bought a house he'd have to mow the lawn and so forth. Maybe he's smart just to sleep in his old bedroom at our place for now."

"Could be," Arlyce agreed. "It's not like that one gives you any trouble. Still, he's getting kind of old. Don't you worry that he'll turn out like Spade?"

"A gambling addict?" Dottie said. "Maybe that's his dirty secret." She didn't think so, but it troubled her to realize her twenty-six-year-old son was still living the same way as when he was eighteen. Didn't people usually move on and move out by now? She was married and a mother by age twenty-two. What was that kid still doing at home?

"Or worse," June said and leaned forward conspiratorially. "He could end up like Beau."

"Lord, no! Stop!" Dottie chuckled. "He's just a late bloomer. I'm sure someday he'll move out."

"But when?" Arlyce kept pressing. "And I'm not talking about Scotty now," she laid her hand on Dottie's arm to placate her. "I'm talking in general. What makes a kid move out? We all married young and that sealed the deal, so to speak. What about the single kids?"

"Mona moved out pretty young," June said. "I think it was in response breaking up with T.C. when he moved to Alaska for that fishing job. But she bought that house when she was twenty-one."

"Girls mature faster than boys, too," Dottie added. "Maybe Scotty's on pace if you factor that in."

"On pace for what?" Steve walked into the dining room holding a large box.

"We're talking about Scotty and when he'll move out of Dottie's house," Arlyce told her husband. "What's that?"

"Pickled asparagus. Some guy dropped them off. He's trying to sell them, wants us to put them in our Bloody Marys instead of pickles." Steve set the box down and lifted out a jar. "Want to try one? They're not bad."

"No thanks," June told him.

"Scotty'll move out someday," Steve told Dottie. "You just make it

116

too easy for him to stay."

"You guys talk like it's a problem," Dottie protested. "We don't mind him at all. He's easy. He does stuff around the house if I ask, it's not a big deal to feed him when he's home—you know that as well as I do, June. In fact, how come nobody's bugging you about Mona practically moving back home?"

"Mona moved back home?" Steve asked. He twisted the lid off a jar and a sour vinegar odor emerged. He plucked out a limp stalk of asparagus and dropped it into his mouth.

"No," June said. "She didn't. She's around a lot because she's using the property for her business, but she still has her house."

"Why's Scotty gotta move?" Steve asked Dottie.

"He doesn't. I don't even know how we got on this topic," Dottie wound her yarn up and stuffed it in her bag. "I thought we were talking about the chicken barbeque."

"We were," June agreed. She sensed Dottie's growing annoyance and didn't want her leaving upset. "I do think Tammy has some good ideas. It's worth trying some of them."

"She's pushy," Arlyce declared.

"You're one to talk," Steve said. "Sure you don't want any asparagus?" He bit off the end of another one and held out the open jar.

Arlyce waved him out of the room and reached across to grab Dottie's crochet hook. "Dropped a stitch. This pattern's a bear." She gestured to the knitting book on the table open to a pattern for a hooded cardigan. "I'm only saying it's pretty presumptive of her to muscle in the way she did."

June tapped the table with her knitting needle thoughtfully. "Aren't we a funny bunch? New ideas for the barbeque irritate us, but we want Scotty to change his life. Guess we only like change when it suits us."

SIXTEEN

THURSDAY MORNING KELLY OGDEN woke up to a loud rumbling sound and opened the blinds of her brand-new master bedroom. She expected to see the morning sun glowing across the open fields and the berm of trees alongside the creek a quarter mile away. Instead she shielded her eyes from the glare of the morning sun reflecting off the metallic surface of three large tractors. There was a narrow gap between the machines at the end of her driveway, but most of the road was completely blocked.

Kelly dodged past the chaos of unpacked boxes stacked in the middle of the bedroom floor. She pulled on her bathrobe and paused at her front door to dig her feet into flip flops before stomping to the end of her driveway.

"What's all this?" she asked the teenaged boy who was climbing onto the seat of the largest tractor, parked beside her mailbox. "Why are these machines parked in front of my house?"

The kid looked at her with sleepy eyes from beneath the brim of his faded blue baseball cap. "Cuttin' hay," he drawled. The toes of his work boots were rubbed down to the steel.

"What?" Kelly looked over her shoulder where a loud noise had started up.

"WE'RE CUTTIN' HAY," the boy repeated in a louder, slower voice. Then he shifted the tractor into gear and Kelly watched the huge tires roll to the edge of her newly planted yard before turning into the field, dragging a disc mower behind it.

The loud growl of farm equipment made her cover her ears and the air filled with tiny particles of grass sent flying by the massive blades' rotation. Kelly stormed back inside and started slamming windows shut. Her to-do list was two pages long, she didn't need to clean the house again on top of everything else involved with settling into their new home. Through the back patio door, she watched the tractor inch past the property line. The boy driving waved at a man who stood beside a large wagon. She noted that a section of the electric fencing had been removed in order to get the tractors on the field. She also noted No Trespassing signs had been nailed to the fence posts.

Her sons were sprawled on their bellies watching TV in the living room and she told them she'd have breakfast ready soon. Then Kelly poured herself a cup of coffee from the carafe her husband always prepared before he left for work and stood at the patio door glaring outside.

Obviously this farmer wanted to harass them. He was angry about the development, but it wasn't Kelly's fault they bought a lot and built a house here. Heck, they hadn't even finished unpacking their stuff or met any neighbors yet. As far as she knew, they hadn't done a thing to disturb this guy, and they stayed within their property boundaries.

More to the point, Kelly really wanted to stay. She liked her new house. She liked the peace and quiet, the idea of her kids having the kinds of adventures she remembered from her childhood on the outskirts of a small town. She and her siblings and the neighborhood children could build a fort, catch fireflies in jars, see the stars at night. Sure, they had made a compromise moving away from the city. Things like bike rides to get ice cream or go to the library were inconvenient now. The kids weren't close to a bunch of friends like they had been, but the tradeoff was that they didn't have any annoying friends, either. Kelly didn't have to play referee and make snacks for a dozen sweaty bodies every afternoon. Plus there was always that one kid who never took the hint to leave at dinner time. No, Kelly didn't miss the suffocating closeness that came from living in a city neighborhood.

Her stubborn streak ran deep and she didn't care how stubborn this farmer was, she wasn't going anywhere. She would not stay locked in her house while he tortured them with his electric fencing and big tractors. She was ill-equipped to fight fire with fire, however.

"Mom? Can we go outside and watch the tractors?" Her youngest climbed onto a kitchen stool and swung his tanned legs back and forth. "Please?"

She stared at him for a moment, thinking hard. Then answered, "Yes, Robbie. After you eat breakfast."

Kelly was stubborn, but also an optimist. She could fight back, but not in the way this crotchety old man expected.

It was noon on the dot when the tractors quit. Kelly watched from the kitchen window as the kid and an older man climbed down from their seats and walked across the fields towards her house. She waited for them.

The kids lay on their stomachs watching TV and eating hot dogs, long ago bored by the monotony of farm machinery chewing up row after row, back and forth, back and forth. "Boys, I'll be outside for a little while."

Kelly lifted the tray holding two tall glasses of lemonade and a plate of homemade snickerdoodle cookies. Using fire to fight fire ended up burning everything out of control. Her approach was different and, based on her experience, bound to work. She eased open the front door and carefully stepped outside while balancing the tray. She greeted the two at the edge of her yard. "Hi!" she called out to them in a cheerful voice. "Boy, that looks like hard, hot work on a day like today. I brought you something."

The men approached after exchanging a suspicious glance with one another. The older man was about her age, Kelly realized as he drew closer and could see his face more clearly. Tall, lean and ruddy-cheeked with dark brown eyes. He wore worn jeans and a faded Def Leppard T-shirt. The younger boy didn't look anything like him with clear blue eyes and black hair. Probably not father and son.

She lifted the tray towards them. "Help yourself."

The boy waited for the older man to accept the gift before he took the second glass and gulped it down without taking a breath. "Thanks," he gasped when he came up for air.

Kelly smiled pleasantly and nodded towards the cookies. "My mother's recipe. Hope you like cinnamon. I'm Kelly Ogden, by the way. Your neighbor."

"Ezra Pike," the man muttered. "Thanks."

"Do you own this field or do you just work it?" Kelly asked.

"Both. My farm borders this housing development."

"I see. Strictly dairy or cash crop, too?"

He raised his eyebrows in surprise at her knowledge about farming but didn't comment on it. "Dairy. Everything we grow goes into the cows."

Kelly nodded and then waited. If raising two sons had taught her anything, it had taught her patience. Of containing her actions until it was time to act.

"Thanks for the cold drink." He placed the glass back on her tray and slapped the boy on the shoulder. "Time to get back for lunch."

The boy handed Kelly his empty glass with a nod and followed the man to the pickup truck parked behind the farm equipment on the road. She watched them leave and then returned to the cool dim interior of her house. This would take some time, she thought. But Kelly Ogden had plenty of time to spare.

Maw struck a series of poses for the photographer beneath the bridge, the concrete base tagged with graffiti chalked onto the surface by his kids. "White Bass Running" and images of fierce fish with jagged teeth were scrawled onto the pocked grey wall. Maw wore a hat with his shop's logo and a T-shirt. Chains hung around his neck and three crankbait lures dangled from one of the chains like pendants. He crossed his arms high on his chest with his hands tucked beneath his armpits and stood sideways. Then he made peace signs with his fingers.

"Is that supposed to be some sort of gang symbol?" Peg asked him.

Ed Lyons, the local guy who specialized in senior portraits and family photographs, kept dropping to his knee to get crazy angles on Maw. "Looking good, Maw," he encouraged. "Try not smiling now."

Maw's huge grin closed into a smug expression and he turned to the other side. "Gangster tough, baby. You think I'm sexy?" he asked Peg.

Peg laughed. "I think you're an idiot."

"This album cover," Maw paused to lean forward and let the crankbait lures swing away from his chest, "will look tough. What do you think, Ed? We going with the black and white?"

"I think so," Ed replied. "Unless the graffiti fades out too much. That's why I'm taking rolls of color, too."

Maw's daughter, Katie, stood up from her lawn chair. "This is taking forever," she complained to her mother. "It's supposed to be *my* photo shoot, not his."

Peg patted her shoulder and fluffed at the girl's hair. "I know, I know. But it's cheaper to add this to your senior picture package than if your dad did this separately."

The girl tugged at the deep vee of her sweater and rolled her eyes. "I don't want a single fishing anything in my pictures, Mr. Lyons. No water, no minnows, no bridge, no boats."

Ed cranked the film reel on his camera. "How do you feel about a rustic barn door?"

"That would be all right."

"See, sweetie? Nobody's going to know your crazy father was anywhere near your senior photo shoot. And Ed's got that nice gazebo in his yard, too. Plenty of fish-free options."

At that moment two boys in a johnboat plowed past going half-speed and kicking up a powerful wake. "Katie! Katie!" The boys called and waved.

"Dad!" Katie Cooper looked near to tears while her father started jabbing at the air with his fists. "I mean it—stop!"

"Ed, are we about finished?" Peg murmured to the photographer.

Ed Lyons knew placating an ornery teenaged girl was tougher than stroking Maw's ego, so he replaced the lens cap on his camera and nodded. "Okay, Maw. We've got two rolls. I'll drop off the proofs next week. Katie my dear, it's your turn to shine."

"Shine like my golden shiners, darling," Maw teased his daughter, who scowled at him. "I'm kidding, don't cry."

Peg firmly grasped her daughter by the shoulders and steered her towards their Buick. "Back to your studio, Ed?"

"I'll follow you over."

Maw untangled himself from his jewelry while he slid into the back seat behind his daughter and wife. "Drop me at the shop on the way over?" he asked them.

"Drop him off the bridge," Katie muttered.

"Katie," Peg warned and glanced at her husband in the rearview mirror. "Yes, enough rap star fantasy for the day. You need to get back to work."

"Kiddo, when your dad's a famous rap star, you'll be begging me to hang out with you. Maybe if you're lucky you can come along to the Grammys with me."

"Is he seriously still talking?"

"I think my next album will be dedicated to the teenaged ingrate. *Watch her eyes roll and hear that awful whine, that teenaged girl is giving us a sign.*"

The Coopers' Buick kicked up gravel while Peg accelerated out of the boat landing parking lot. Peg wanted to ditch both of them and sit in silence with a Diet Pepsi. And a shot of whiskey, she thought while glancing at the Pub. She should've left these two at the landing with Ed and hung out there instead.

Scotty slammed shut the tailgate on the back of his truck and waved at the Dohills before leaving the job site at a medical clinic in Northport. It always felt satisfying to wrap up another big project. The office space they'd renovated with new ceiling tiles and lighting looked fresh and brand new. Plus, Scotty learned a few things along the way. In this case he mastered a few electrical tasks like wiring electrical panels and drawing schematics for rewiring motor control. Before he'd packed up his toolbox to leave, he had inhaled the mildly

124

chemical smell of new carpet and paint and wondered if he'd ever be the top dog on a job like this one.

Did he want to be? Not really. Scotty knew he wasn't a leader. He liked getting his marching orders and then being left to put his head down and get things done without anybody breathing down his neck. The Dohills trusted him, which made it easy to work for their crew. It wasn't fun like with The Pole, though, joking around and sneaking out early to go fish or something.

He had at least five hours of daylight left, so Scotty decided to make the most of it. He swung by Maw's to grab bait and drove to the dock where he kept his boat tied up. Soon he was quietly drifting along the shore near Thornside Cut, a shady bank where the Wissipaw's outside stream flowed towards a marsh. Dragonflies swooped across the water's surface and tiny ripples fanned out from the red and white bobber he'd dropped into the water. Scotty had wadded his sweaty T-shirt into a ball behind the base of his neck and tipped the brim of his cap low on his forehead to block the sun. Anyone driving past would think he was sound asleep.

The riverbank hummed with life. Insects and birds, frogs and the occasional squirrel rustled and chirped. The Wissipaw sounded like a quiet breeze flowing against the tall grasses growing along the shoreline. Leaves rattled in the trees and bushes. Beneath the water's surface Scotty could see sleek minnows darting and a fat, lazy catfish drifting in the river's chilly current.

The muscles in Scotty's neck and shoulders relaxed while nature's peace took hold of his mind. Here in the quiet, solitary joy of his boat he could ponder small questions, like should he use a live minnow or a lure, and large questions, like should he stay living at his parents' place. Today he reflected on how long he wanted to work for the Dohills. Most of his friends were anxious to be their own boss. They boasted of plans to open garages or small businesses. Scotty didn't really want to call the shots for other people, but he didn't necessarily want to be at the mercy of somebody else, either.

That's what made farming such a great gig, he thought. You were your own boss, but you weren't ordering employees around. Too bad milk prices were in the tank and land prices were sky high. After his parents sold their farm, there was no way he could ask them to front money to buy a new one. That would be insulting, even though they hadn't moved on to any other kind of life. No, his parents were at loose ends since selling off the lot. His father puttered around aimlessly, sometimes helping a neighbor out with planting or harvesting, but otherwise he had nothing to do outside of golf league and town meetings. And his mother! Without a child to nurse to health and both kids grown older, she had no household to manage. He'd actually caught them sitting together at the kitchen table a few times just staring at the wall.

Could he ask his dad to partner with him on a small outfit? He'd heard there were a couple farms about to hit the market a few towns over, nothing special, places with around fifty head. What would that cost? The farming schedule appealed to him now—up early to milk, chores, afternoon free, back to milk later. Before, he liked hopping from job to job, the freedom to go fish any day he chose, head north to snowmobile for a long weekend or cut out early for a Friday beer. Was that what it meant to finally grow up? To want stability and sameness? How boring! But farming wasn't boring, that he knew. It was challenging each new season; the weather, nature, animals, markets always changed. Farmers were more adventurous than most other people. The only thing that didn't change was their location.

As good as it felt to survey a completed job site, construction work didn't make him feel happy the way the farm did. And, he felt a tentative tug on the end of the line and sat up slowly to see what took the bait, he could still go fishing if he owned a farm.

SEVENTEEN

Otto pushed his black-framed reading glasses up his nose. He read the script again like the cameraman asked, slower and adding frequent pauses. "I've fished the Wissipaw my whole life and always enjoyed the peace and quiet of the river. Recently, an accident wrecked my love … " He slapped the paper down on this thigh and sighed. "This makes me sound like an idiot."

Jay Hodge held up his hand, a tan hand decorated with a heavy gold signet ring. His silver hair was gelled into place and his polo shirt looked as though it had been ironed. "That's all right," he told the camera man. He turned to Otto. "Let's try something else. Why don't you just talk like you're telling me what happened over a beer."

"That's what I told you when we started," Otto said. "I said, 'Why do I have to read a script? Why can't I just tell you what happened?' We'd be done by now if you'd just listen to me."

Jay Hodge's nostrils flared when he inhaled. He composed himself before speaking in a soft voice. "Tell your story, Otto." He nodded to the cameraman.

Otto leaned back, satisfied that they were finally taking his advice. He folded his hands and gazed into the camera. "I'm Otto Zimm and I grew up fishing and hunting on the Wissipaw River. It's the most peaceful place you can imagine, best place in the world to relax and catch your supper. Folks have safely coexisted on the river for years, fishing, enjoying nature, swimming. Then a few years ago people showed up with their jet skis. Not sure if you've ever seen one of these things, but they look like a motorcycle on water. Only thing they're good for is going fast and that's exactly what they do.

"From what I understand, jet skis aren't really regulated. Drivers don't need a license and the way they're built, these things can get back in shallow waters where boats don't go. They're loud, destructive and invasive. People who drive them don't think about anybody but themselves."

Jay Hodge leaned forward and asked, "Can you talk about what happened to you a couple weeks ago?"

"Sure," Otto squared his shoulders. "I was fishing back in Cooper's Bayou, a pretty quiet part of the river, probably only ten feet in the deepest part. It turns into marsh when you don't expect it, so people only go back with flat bottomed boats, a johnboat or a canoe, unless they know what they're doing. I had set anchor near the opening of the bayou so's I could fish. Along come two boys on jet skis, racing right past me. The second one kicks up a huge stream of water and they buzz around the bend. I knew when they went back there they'd have to turn around. Nobody belongs back there, too swampy, it's all cattails and marsh grass growing about five-six feet high. Well, sure enough, a couple minutes later they come back through the bayou, still going top speed.

"These kids aren't from around here, they don't know the river, they think every bend looks the same, all trees and grass, right? So they come around the bend, flying at top speed, and about hit my boat! The first kid flips right over, lands upside-down in the water. The second drives right over the top of his friend's watercraft and heads straight for the branches of an upturned tree on the shoreline. He ends up caught in the branches, his jet ski's suspended above him, engine still wide open and making a hell of a racket.

"Of course my first concern was the kid in the water." Otto shook his head at the memory. "Luckily he was wearing a life jacket and floating face up. I motored over and pulled him into my boat. Made sure he was breathing and put pressure on his head. He had a big gash right by his ear. I placed a towel on that.

"Then I had to go down the river a ways to find a good spot to climb on shore. Took me a while to cut the other kid loose, all I had was a fishing knife handy. I got the kid off the branches where he was pinned. Then I brought them both to Pine Acres Resort where I called an ambulance and got them first aid."

"It's lucky you weren't hurt," Jay told Otto.

"Yep. Hate to think if they'd crashed into the side of my boat. Had my dog with me. Don't know any of us would've made it if they'd hit my boat."

"What happened after the ambulance?"

"I went back with a buddy and we cut the other jet ski loose and towed both of them to the marina."

"What do you think these young men learned from this experience?" Jay baited Otto like a pro, which he was after years of prosecuting criminals in a courtroom.

"Well, I hope they learned to slow down," Otto scratched at the back of his neck. "I hope they think about others and act more carefully next time they get on the water."

"If you could change one law about the river, what would it be, Otto?"

"Ban those jet skis." Otto's lips pulled into a frown. "No, it's not just the jet skis. It's everyone going too fast when the river's busy. People need to slow down. For safety. And to keep the fish from swimming away."

Jay stood, shook Otto's hand and gave him a brochure advertising the next No Wake meeting date. "I hope you'll show up. We need as many people as we can get to help support this change. A no-wake rule will make a difference." He walked Otto to the door while the cameraman packed up his gear. "Your testimony will bring attention to this cause. Plus, you're local, which makes a big difference in Bassville."

Otto stopped at the edge of Jay's driveway and looked down the sloping lawn towards the river. The wind had died down and the light on the end of Jay's dock showed the river's surface was calm. Otto didn't care much for these rich fellas moving in and pushing everyone around, but it suited him fine if they were on the same side of things.

On his way home, Scotty swung by Mona's house. Her front porch light was on and he could see the flicker of the TV set against the living room wall. He knocked twice before she opened the door, barefoot with damp hair. She smelled like flowers.

"Hey, come in," she invited.

"Brought you something," he said and handed her the plastic cool whip container.

"Store brand nondairy whip topping? My favorite!" she gushed.

"Open it, smartass."

She peeled back the lid and her eyes widened. "Nice."

"Found a patch while I was fishing tonight." He sat on the couch and watched her take a raspberry and pop it into her mouth.

"Thought if you wanted we could pick it tomorrow or the next day. Tons of them. You could sell them at your stand."

"Sell them?"

"Yeah, you know, with your vegetables."

"I didn't grow them," she pointed out.

"Well, duh. That's obvious."

"I only sell what I grow."

"How does it matter? Don't see the difference. You pick it, still counts, right?"

"It feels wrong. Where did you find them?"

"In the woods past the Luau Lounge. I was fishing the cut out there." Scotty shrugged, trying to hide how annoyed he felt. Didn't she know he was trying to be helpful? "Anyone can go pick them back there. Figured it would be easy money. And your customers would like them."

"It's part of my deal that all my produce is grown without pesticides and stuff," Mona said. She ate another berry.

"Well, they're growing in a patch by the river, so probably not sprayed by anyone. Look, it's no big deal, I just thought you'd like the idea." He got up to leave.

"It just feels wrong if I didn't plant them."

"You wouldn't plant an orchard every year, or a berry patch. But whatever, it's your deal."

"Scotty," Mona followed him to the door, "I just never thought about selling scavenged food before. I guess it's not wrong."

"Don't know why it would be," he muttered.

She wrapped her fingers around his forearm and he tried to ignore the small electric buzz when she touched him. It was Mona, for crying out loud. Mona who he'd grown up playing with in the sandbox at his parents' place, Mona who copied his math homework in eighth grade, Mona who'd snuck out with him in the middle of the night to break curfew in high school. Mona. Just Mona. He had to get over how he felt about her.

"I'm sorry. Don't be mad. Let's do it." She shrugged and smiled. "We'll label them 'wild' or 'handpicked' so it's not dishonest, and if nobody buys them we can say we tried anyway. When do you want to pick them?"

"Don't care. You call it." He still felt irritated by her reaction.

"When do you get off work tomorrow?"

"Around four."

"I'll meet you at the Luau Lounge about four-thirty. I'll bring the bug spray, you bring the buckets."

"It's a date."

Walking to his truck, Scotty mentally scolded himself for those last words. *It's a date?* Geez. He was helping a friend. That's all. Helping a friend.

EIGHTEEN

Maw held up the two photos he was considering for his rap album cover when Peg walked in the bait shop Friday morning. "I have a great smile in this one, but I look thinner in this one." He showed them to Peg who pressed her lips together while she compared them.

"This one," she said, pointing to the one where Maw looked thinner. "Your smile looks the same in both, I don't know what you're talking about."

"You're the boss."

"Ha. But if that's true, then you need to hop to it and change the oil in the Buick before you head to town later. I'm afraid the engine's going to burn out."

"All cars smell that way when it's hot out," Maw said. He pulled at his beard and decided on the other picture for the cover. "I need to get to the studio and meet with the sound mixer."

"I always hate to ask this, but what's it going to cost?"

Maw reached over to pull Peg close. "You have to spend money to make money."

"You have to make money."

"It'll be fine."

"How much, Maw?" She pushed him away and occupied herself with hanging packages of lures in correct order on their display case. "How much?" she repeated.

"The sound mixer charges twenty an hour."

"That's one part of it. How many hours?"

Maw shrugged. "I never cut a rap album before. Maybe three?" He was guessing. He was also hiding a lot of overhead costs from his wife and becoming a little nervous about it. Who knew producing music was so expensive? The layout of the cover, the photography (even though he'd rolled that in with his daughter's senior pictures), the recording and now the studio guy in Milwaukee said something about mixing as part of the deal. The receipts were stuffed behind the radio in the bait shop, but the credit card bill would show up in the mail next week. He'd definitely have to intercept that. "Can I change the oil tonight?"

"It's gonna cost way more when your engine burns out halfway to Milwaukee."

Maw glanced at the clock and exhaled his submission to her. "Watch the shop, I'll do it right now." He slammed the door harder than necessary on his way out to the garage where he located a filter and oil and the drain pan he used for the job. His mind worked over the numbers while he propped open the hood. The total production costs were still adding up. So far, he'd have to sell five hundred and six tapes to break even.

The optimistic part of Maw's brain reminded him that he'd make a lot of money as a rap god. He could go on tour! Hit the nightly talk show circuit on TV. Maybe even get on David Letterman! Yes, his imagination and potential had no limit, even if Peg's patience did.

At the Pub, Arlyce climbed up on a bar stool and turned off the TV set. "What's he thinking? No wake will kill us!" Her hands shook with anger and she steadied herself before descending to the floor and storming back to the kitchen to grab the order for a table on the deck.

She'd been getting drinks from Steve when she glanced up and saw Otto's face on the TV screen. She'd assumed he was talking about fishing because what else did he ever talk about? Steve noticed him, too, and told Arlyce to turn up the volume. They'd watched together with growing concern while Otto shared his story about the jet ski crash on the river and made his case for changing the wake rules through Bassville. Two other people said their piece on the issue and the news reporter interviewed another man who claimed to be the president of No Wake: Take Back the Lake. "It's about safety. Safety and preserving this beautiful river for generations to come."

"Oh, barf!" Arlyce said. "I know him. That's the guy who used to drive that cigarette boat through here at top speed years ago. Now he's old and has a pontoon boat with a bunch of grandkids. So typical! He wants no rules when it suits him and wants to change the rules when it doesn't." She climbed back up on a bar stool to turn off the TV.

"No wake through Bassville would mean traffic would turn around down by Catfish Landing," Steve mused. He opened two cans of Pepsi instead of Diet Pepsi and put them on a tray for Arlyce before scooping ice into glasses. "But maybe not. The boat landing here brings a lot of traffic."

When Arlyce returned from the kitchen she grabbed the tray from her husband and carried it out to the deck and back again. "Pepsi. Not Diet."

"Sorry." He switched out the cans. "We'll be fine."

"We'll fight that bozo—all of those bozos." Arlyce was practically growling, she was so mad. "No wake, are they crazy? Do they have any idea how much traffic we get from people passing through? Boaters spend big."

"Bigger than the summertime fishermen, that's for sure," Steve agreed. "Those are all local. The boaters do like their premium beers and blender drinks, goddamn them."

"And they eat. Not a lot, but they order a lot, eat a little, pay for it all and throw the rest away."

Arlyce was right, boaters tended to order a lot—combo baskets, appetizers, burgers and pizzas. Each person would order their own thing. But eating for them was more of a social event than an actual activity. The heat, combined with sitting around all day and the heightened body consciousness that came from wearing a swimsuit, resulted in small appetites. So they'd order huge amounts of food, pick at it, then drive away with piles of half-eaten burgers, barely touched French fries and slices of pizza sitting on the deck tables. It didn't matter to Arlyce since it was paid for. It annoyed the cook, though, to see food go to waste like that, but he had to learn to put it in perspective, Arlyce argued.

The seagulls loved the boaters, because their departure meant a feast. They'd aggressively float down from the roof of the Pub, their beady eyes alert for open access to food. Within seconds they'd be pecking at the remains, wings spread wide to protect their turf from other birds—and the waitresses who would frantically try to shoo them away while they cleared tables.

The other customers always enjoyed the show, entertained by the contest of man versus nature, plus all wildlife was exciting to people from the city. They delighted in the seagulls, tried to lure them over with spare fries and bits of hamburger buns. Children named the gulls and women took photographs of them. This only made Arlyce madder. "Don't they know the diseases birds carry? Lice and God knows what else. They're rats with wings! They fly from here to the dump and back again—disgusting!"

The tourists' fascination with the seagulls confounded the locals. Even Spade and Beau were heard to remark on it. "Do we go to Northport and take pictures of robins and earthworms?" Spade had asked one day while sitting at the bar looking at the frenzy taking place on the other side of the window.

"If we did, they'd think we were as stupid as we think they are right now. Come on, Spade. Let's feed some rice to one of those gulls and give the kids a real show!"

"Don't, Beau," Steve said, laughing because it would be funny, but also offensive to his customers. "Please don't."

"You people don't know how to have fun," Spade groused. "I bet the kids would love it."

"Like fireworks, only a little messier," Beau agreed.

Arlyce returned from the deck after delivering the correct drink order and resumed venting to her husband about how dumb and harmful and crazy a no-wake rule would be. "I know the traffic gets busy, but for crying out loud! Get a patrol boat out there on the weekends. That's the only time it's bad anyway." She pointed outside where two boats passed each other, waving in that friendly way boaters did when encountering floating vessels. Steve wondered why people in cars or on motorcycles didn't do this. If you were to make generalizations about people based on their behavior, then the waving put boaters a little higher on the scale.

"And what's this nonsense about property damage? The whole town has a seawall protecting it from the wake. Only time we need people to slow down is in the spring when it floods." Arlyce slammed her tray down on the bar and headed to the kitchen.

Mona waited for Loyal to slide the pallet farther down the row of beans they were picking. Then he plunked down the five-gallon bucket he was using as a seat and adjusted himself to start combing through another section of plants. He held back the flat leaves and exposed the plant's clusters of beans. Mona had similarly situated herself across from her father, one row over and was efficiently snapping the beans from their stems and tossing them into her own flat box.

"I have to hand it to you," Loyal said and swatted at a mosquito humming around his right ear, "these filet beans are really good."

Masai Filet French Beans. He remembered reading the label on the seed packet with skepticism. The only beans he ever recalled people planting were Kentucky Wonder. People either planted a pole bean or a bush bean, none of this French bean nonsense. He'd asked Mona about it and she'd explained how this bean was smaller, more tender and better for harvesting.

"Your regular beans produce for about two weeks and then they're done. These will produce until first frost, so instead of a huge bumper crop for a limited period of time, we'll get a steady harvest for months. Or so I've read."

"Well, you were right, too, Dad," Mona said from where she perched on her own five-gallon bucket, bent double to gather fistfuls of beans. She arched her back for a stretch and reached her tanned arms towards the sky. "Beans are a pain in the butt. Very labor intensive. I should've listened to you. I was just so anxious to have a lot of different things to bring to market, but I don't know it's worth the trouble."

"Listen to you!" Loyal exclaimed. "Are you saying your old dad was right about something?"

"I say that all the time and you know it." Mona scooted her own pallet farther down her row. "You did warn me. But I keep forgetting to ask, is this worse or better than milking cows?"

Loyal chuckled. "Well, one nice thing about beans is you can take care of them any time. Cows have to keep to a schedule. Beans are more forgiving if you show up at six in the morning or three in the afternoon. But the back-breaking end of it sure feels the same."

They worked in silence for a while and Loyal wondered again if selling off the cows would be a wise idea. He'd gone over the books and even with milk prices in the tank, vegetables didn't bring in the same amount of money. They'd have to grow more volume to make that—and to do that they'd have to get more help. As it stood, he and Mona put in long days in the fields. But would the exchange of time be even without the herd? He couldn't say.

Of course, they could hire somebody—some teenager for the summer to pick and sit at the produce stand. He'd always hired extra help when they chopped hay; why should the manpower be that much different for vegetables?

What Loyal wanted was a tried and tested model of this kind of farm. He only knew dairy and cattle. He had no script to follow for vegetables. What kind of profits could a person expect from vegetables? And what kind of balance of overhead? Mona was keeping track of things pretty well. Loyal had to give her credit. Jake had given her good business advice and she had a method for figuring out what to charge for things based on the time and effort required to grow them.

As if reading his thoughts, Mona spoke up. "If we'd planted traditional beans instead of these heritage filet-style, we'd have to plant new rows every week or two. This kind's nice because it's once and done."

A small flock of finches fluttered past, their yellow and black bodies moving like bullets before they landed on the branches of a birch tree growing on the edge of the field. The air was still and Loyal appreciated that this kind of farming did smell better than cows, too. Maybe Mona was onto something. He had to give her more trust and time.

"Mom said Sean was almost finished with the patent work on his project," Mona said.

Loyal grunted. He still carried a grudge about his oldest, buried in his work at a pharmaceutical laboratory on the East Coast. He was proud of Sean but carried disappointment that he'd left the farm. Why couldn't he just switch his expectations of his kids? It made sense, it should be easy, but Loyal couldn't get past it—not entirely.

"Just think, someday we'll hear about a person using his blood pressure medication and know it was Sean that saved their life. It's pretty amazing when you think about it." Mona's voice always reflected her admiration of her older brother. "He's so smart."

"You are, too."

"You just say that because you're my dad."

"Not true." Loyal slid further down his row and calculated how many more times he'd have to repeat the move until he reached the end and could stand up and walk away from the beans for another week. "You thought of planting beans in a better way."

"No, I read about how other people did it and copied it. These are old beans, people just forgot about them when the seed companies gave them hybrids that produced more, faster."

"You're on the town council," Loyal continued his list of his daughter's accomplishments.

"So's Otto. So was Maw. That's not exactly a measure of intelligence."

"You're building your own business from scratch. This takes brains and guts."

140

Mona laughed. "The whole package then. Speaking of the town council, do you have any new thoughts on this No Wake stuff?"

"My first reaction is that Otto's right. The river has become more dangerous with those jet skis racing around. They go too fast, they're loud and the people driving them don't seem to show much sense about safety or sharing the space with others. Damn nuisance, he's got a point."

"Okay. That's your first reaction. What's your second?"

"Well, it's a person's right to be an idiot, even if I don't agree with them. So I have a hard time banning something just because I personally don't like it. Though I wish we could keep those skis out of the river."

"But a no-wake rule's not banning the jet skis, it's just banning the speed they go."

"And as a result, the speed any other boat can go and there's the problem."

"You really think it'll cut into business at the Pub and Riverside and the Hotel?"

Loyal nodded and paused to crack his knuckles before grasping another handful of beans from their stems. "People are in a hurry nowadays, they don't want to take their time, even when they're relaxing. If it takes too long to putter up the river to Bassville, then they'll skip the trip and that means fewer customers. If we make the full stretch of town no wake, it'll take about thirty minutes to drive through. Trouble is, the widest, straightest part of the river runs through town."

"It would make sense to put the no-wake buoys where it's narrow and twisty—like at the entrance of all of the bayous."

"Exactly."

"So maybe what we need to do is suggest that instead of a blanket rule through town."

"Except the people Otto's backing are homeowners along this stretch of river, so they won't want to change their mind."

"Those rich people from out of town? Who cares what they want?"

"As property owners they get as much of a say about how things go," Loyal shrugged. "It's fair, I guess."

"But they don't live here. That's goofy. They only use the river a few weeks out of the year and then disappear. They're part of the problem, too. They want it quiet on the weekends when they want to use the river but could care less what happens the rest of the time."

"True."

"So maybe the rule should go into effect on weekends only, when the traffic's heavier. Let people go full throttle the rest of the time. That might be a compromise the town could live with. I mean, safety's got to be a concern," Mona added. "Except I hate the idea of catering to just a few rich people who aren't really part of our town at the expense of people like Steve and Arlyce and Sue."

"I totally agree."

"And I think we can agree that Otto's sort of a pain in the ass," Mona said. "He only cares about himself."

"Most people do," Loyal said. He picked up his flat of beans and appreciated the weight of it in his hands. "About ten pounds here."

"We have to dig out the potatoes and onions next."

"You're a slave driver," Loyal groused. "And I don't know who 'we' is. I still have to take care of the dairy side of this operation."

"Fine. Can you leave them in the fridge? And take these with you, too?" Mona handed her father her flat and grabbed the handles of her wheelbarrow. "If you get bored you know where to find me."

Loyal smiled and carried the week's bean harvest back to the barn. There was comfort in the ritual of taking care of cattle. Maybe he'd eventually find ritual in the vegetables, too.

Mona checked her watch. Four-forty. Scotty was late. She sat on the hood of her car in the corner of the Luau Lounge parking lot watching the road. Nothing but the sound of birds and some crickets and frogs. Maybe he forgot. Probably, Mona thought and decided in five minutes she'd head home. It didn't bother her that she'd sprayed herself down with OFF!—that was part of daily life in the farming business. But she was ready to pick berries and didn't have a single container to set them in. What a wasted trip.

Unless … she eyeballed the dumpster behind the supply shed at the back of the parking lot. If the Luau Lounge was anything like the Pub, there'd be boxes, flats from cans of beer and soda or from the kitchen. Pocketing her keys, she decided not to waste the trip. It would be light for hours; why not pick the berries anyway. She had a pretty good idea of where they grew based on Scotty's description, at the edge of a grassy meadow before a small grove of trees beside a bend in the river. Maybe a quarter-mile hike. Mona jogged across the gravel lot toward the hulking rusted garbage dumpster.

The sour, rotting smell of garbage made her eyes water as she boosted herself on the edge to look inside. Almost empty. The truck must have come through yesterday. Stuck in the far corner was a short stack of cardboard flats probably dumped in last night, perfect for berry picking since Scotty and his ice cream buckets were nowhere to be found. Mona had pulled on a pair of old jeans to protect her legs from the prickly brambles—they'd keep her skin from burning on the hot metal. She hefted herself over the edge of the dumpster and landed with a dull thud accented by a squishing sound. "Ew!" Mona looked down at her feet and discovered the source of the slippery mess—someone's discarded burger and potato salad. "Gross."

Two careful steps later she squatted in the corner of the dumpster to pry the boxes loose. She tossed them over the side and too late discovered she didn't have a foothold to get out as she had getting in. The inside of the bin was smooth metal, a five-foot barricade. There was only one garbage bag tossed into the massive dumpster—the Luau Lounge probably only had their trash collected every couple of weeks, Mona figured. She reached up to pull herself up and discovered that her arms were as pathetically weak as when she always failed the Presidential Fitness Test in school. She never could master even a single pull up, and not even now when it mattered.

Taking a shallow breath—the dumpster STUNK from inside— Mona pushed back her panic. Eventually someone would pass by. Her parents would notice she was missing by tomorrow morning when she didn't show up on the farm. Maybe the cook would drop in this evening for some prep work in the kitchen before the Luau Lounge opened for the week. Why did they decide to close Monday *and* Tuesday? She could yell—if someone was fishing nearby, they might hear her. She peered over the edge of her prison, the river and road were both empty.

"Help!" She hollered, as loud as she could. "Help! I'm stuck!"

A half hour passed while she yelled intermittently and all she got for her trouble was a sore throat and the start of a headache. Why was it a person never felt thirsty until they knew they couldn't get a drink? Or have to pee the minute they knew they couldn't use the bathroom? This made her think of T.C. and how he'd gotten in-school suspension when they were in high school. Why? She tried to remember. He'd been busted for a senior prank, that's it. They'd wired a radio to the sound system in the school's auditorium, connecting it directly to the speakers. The school used the auditorium for study hall and for a week, until the batteries gave out, the auditorium blasted rock music and the DJ's commentary on weather and sports. How had T.C. been caught? Mona couldn't recall, but she did remember he complained that they only gave him three bathroom breaks for

144

the day, which seemed like plenty until you thought about it and then it seemed insufficient.

She didn't have to pee yet, but she would eventually. "I'll have to pop a squat in the corner. But at least I have privacy."

Her head jerked up at the sound of gravel crunching. Tires crossed the parking lot and stopped. An engine turned off and a moment later a car door slammed. "Help!" she called to Scotty.

"Mona?" He spun in a quick circle, looking around the parking lot for her.

"In here! I'm in the dumpster!"

His footsteps grew nearer and his voice echoed on the other side of the steel wall. "What are you doing in there?"

"You didn't come and I didn't want to waste my trip for the berries, so I came in here for these stupid boxes. I didn't have anything to hold the raspberries." Mona felt like crying with relief.

"Okay, sit tight. You can't climb out?" His mouth twitched at the edges.

"No! Where were you?"

"Got stuck at the job site and then there was an accident on the highway that tied up traffic. Semi overturned by Sunset Curve. It was single lane for a mile both directions. Listen," Scotty furrowed his brow, trying not to grin. "Just wanted to see what we've got to work with. Okay. I'll be right back."

"You're not leaving?" Mona couldn't control the high pitch in her voice.

"No, I'm getting some rope. Hang tight. I always keep some for fishing."

A minute later a length of rope fell down the inside wall of the dumpster and Mona grabbed it. "Can you pull yourself over?" Scotty asked.

"I'll try." Mona grasped the coarse fibers and tried to pull herself up. Squeezing her thighs around the rope, she pulled herself up about five inches before losing her grip.

"How's it coming?" Scotty's voice sounded strained.

"Not so good." She jumped down and the rope flew out of sight. She watched Scotty take a few stumbling steps and fall.

"You could've warned me before you let go. Okay, plan B."

"What's that?"

"I'll go pick the berries and head back to town to call the fire department. They've got a ladder truck and can get you out."

"Scott Trayson! You are not funny!"

"I'm teasing. Tie the rope around your waist. Double knot it. I'll pull you up." The rope flopped over the side again. "Let me know when you're ready. And use your feet to brace against the side and walk up."

Mona looped the end of the rope around her waist and knotted it a few times so it would pull tight. "Okay," she called when she was ready.

The rope pulled taut and Scotty called back, "Start walking up the side!"

Mona leaned back and placed one sneaker at knee-height, then the other, suspending herself at a diagonal against the wall.

"Walk!" Scotty yelled.

She took a tentative step, then another. Her weight was holding but with every inch her fear grew that Scotty would slip or lose hold of the rope and she'd end up landing hard on the dumpster's floor. Her breathing grew faster and her palms began to sweat. With each movement upwards the balance between her upper and lower body would shift, gravity threatening to pull her ass-over-teakettle, and she'd lean forward, quadriceps shaking with effort while Scotty pulled her stable. After a few cautious steps her waist was level with the lip of the dumpster. Scotty had the end of the rope tied around his own waist, then over his shoulder and he was walking away from her, body tilted forward and straining with her weight.

"I'm almost out!" she called to him.

"Grab the edge of the dumpster and pull your belly over it. Then I'll help you down." He steadily turned and grasped the slack of the rope while she pulled one leg over the top of the six-inch wide wall of steel. She leaned her chest against the edge and breathed deep. Fresh air never smelled so good. Scotty trotted back towards her and reached up. "Okay, I've got you now." He spoke to her like he might a startled heifer, his voice soothing and musical.

Mona pulled her other leg over, supported by Scotty's hands on her back, and released her grip. For a moment he held her suspended a few inches above the ground, his wiry arms encircling her torso, his body pressed against hers. He smelled like sawdust and sweat. She noticed flecks of dust clung to his eyelashes and eyebrows.

He let her drop to the ground and busied himself with the rope. "You all right then?"

"Yes. Thanks. Pride is sufficiently wounded, but I'm good." Flustered suddenly, she turned away.

"How long were you in there?" Scotty asked.

Mona glanced at her wrist while untying the knotted rope. "About thirty minutes," she muttered sheepishly.

"Pretty traumatic, huh?" Scotty's voice held the edge of teasing. Mona knew she'd have to just give into his ribbing, there was no way around it.

"It was. I don't think I'll ever be able to look at a garbage dumpster the same way. I probably should get some counseling."

Scotty coiled the rope around his elbow and the heel of his palm. "Still want to use those boxes?" He kicked at the boxes Mona had tossed over.

"You brought buckets, right?"

"I did."

Mona flung the boxes back into the dumpster and started towards her car and his truck, her shoulders squared and posture perfect. "Let's get going then."

"Hey, I'm not the one holding up the show by dumpster diving."

"Shut up." She reached into the front seat of her car and pulled out a can of OFF! to toss to him.

He caught it and sprayed his arms, back and neck before returning it to her. Then he pulled a stack of plastic ice cream buckets from the front seat of his truck. "I'll lead the way. In case I need to fend off raccoons or a wild bear."

"Are you implying something?" Mona asked while she fell in step behind him. A triangle of sweat darkened the back of his shirt between his shoulder blades.

"Not at all." He handed a bucket to her.

They reached edge of the trees and Mona saw how loaded the bushes were with fruit. "Hand me a couple more buckets." She set them below where she picked to catch any ripe fruit that fell as she moved the branches aside.

"Sun ripened doesn't really apply to berries, does it?" Scotty mused. "The fattest ones always grow beneath the leaves." He was bent over, looking upside-down while he picked.

"You're right. And these are incredible. I can't believe nobody else grabs these."

"They might, look at them all. What a great spot." The berry patch did stretch across almost thirty feet of the tree line along the edge of a pretty meadow. Yellow and white flowers bobbed gracefully in a light breeze and Mona could see butterflies fluttering above the blossoms.

"I have some small containers to put them in back at the farm. Figure we'd sell them by the pint or quart."

"What did you decide to call them? Scavenger berries?"

"Very funny. Wild berries, if you must know."

"You want me to help you Saturday?"

Mona glanced over at him, surprised he was asking. "Of course. I mean, if you're free."

"Well, my mom has chores for me, but she doesn't want me taking out the trash."

"Goddamn it, Scotty!" Mona good naturedly chucked an empty bucket at his head and he ducked before it hit him. The plastic bucket rolled harmlessly beneath the berry thicket.

"She's always going on about how I have to take it out before it smells bad." He could barely talk, his chest heaved with laughter.

"Go on then. Get it over with."

He took a deep breath and exploded before calming down enough to whisper, "If you don't take out the trash, we'll get bugs. Or mice."

Mona shook her head and pressed her lips against her own smile. Finally, she gave into the giggles. "It'll be a while before I live this down, won't it?"

"You seem like you're down in the dumps."

"All right."

"When I'm with you I feel like I'm scraping the barrel."

"Got any more?" Mona crossed her arms.

"One more—garbage in, garbage out."

"Are we good now?" She raised her eyebrows.

"White trash." He held up his arm to defend against another bucket. "Okay, I'm done."

The phone was ringing as Mona entered the front door of her house. She hurried to the kitchen counter to set down her purse and pick up the receiver. Dial tone. Rats! She hated missing a call and her answering machine had eaten the tape last week. She kept forgetting to replace it. Whoever it was would have to call back. She was halfway to the bathroom when the ringing started again.

"Hello?"

"Mona?"

Jake. They hadn't talked in months and while Mona thought she'd be numb enough by now to hear his voice without a strong reaction, her breath caught in her throat. "Hi."

"How's it going?"

She knew this wasn't a social call, not after the way they'd left the last conversation over a month ago. He'd sounded distracted while they briefly discussed the weather and her planting schedule before hanging up. That chapter had closed. Unless he was coming back? Yet she didn't feel as excited as she'd hoped. Plus his voice sounded hesitant. "Okay. Busy this time of year with the business, you know. What's up with you?"

"I've got something I wanted to tell you in person before you found out from someone else."

He had a new girlfriend. He'd gotten someone pregnant. He was moving back. Her mind ran ahead.

"I took a new position with a new company, here in Atlanta. It's a great opportunity, Mon. I'll get to run all kinds of projects, the chance of a lifetime. You know how they're hosting the Summer Olympics here in 1996?"

Mona's brain shut down while he talked on. He didn't need to tell her the details, it was clear in the excitement in his voice. He wasn't coming home. Not now, probably not ever. "We'll be building stadiums, all of the venues for the games including the pools and the diving areas. We're working on sidewalks and transportation systems, coordinating with hotel construction and public parks—it's like making an entire city from scratch!"

"Amazing," Mona murmured.

Jake kept talking as though she hadn't spoken, mentioning gigantic dollar amounts and names of corporations involved. "We're creating something bigger than a paper mill. Sports stadiums are modern-day castles, Mona. For generations to come people will see what I helped make. I'm literally getting to build *history*."

"That's what you've always wanted."

"So I've decided to put the house up for sale. I found a great condo here."

"Wow. That's terrific." She tried to put more enthusiasm in her voice. "What an incredible opportunity. You have to do it. And everyone in Bassville will get to see your work on TV in a few years. Not too many people can say that!"

"I knew you'd understand. This is the big time, Mona. I can't believe it's going to happen."

The hum of long distance filled the silence between them.

"Well, I'm happy for you," Mona finally said. "You deserve all of this success. You've worked hard and you have good ideas."

"Thank you." He cleared his throat. "I know you need to stay there. Guess timing and location aren't on our side. It's not like there's anyone else. Hell, I haven't got time for any*thing* else but work for the next five years."

"No, I suppose not. But I'll always love you, Jake," she blurted out the last.

"I'll always love you, too."

After they hung up, Mona sat for a very long time at her kitchen table deep in thought. So it was really over. She knew it was coming, and it struck her as fitting that something as big and important as the Olympics should pull them apart. How can you fight that? You can't. So you move on.

An hour later Jenny met Mona at the Riverside Bar because Mona couldn't bear to face the crowd of regulars at the Pub. "To the final nail in that coffin." Jenny raised her beer to Mona.

"Wow. You have such a sensitive way with words," Mona told her.

"Well, we saw it coming. He wasn't staying and you weren't leaving, so what?"

"Who's 'we?'"

Jenny shrugged. "Me, Sheila, Judi, Beau, Scotty ... " She kept ticking off names on her fingers.

"Geez. I feel pretty stupid thinking I was the last to know," Mona muttered.

"Shut up. Now you move on. There's a new bar opening up this weekend in Northport called Club La Loca. The dance floor will be full of guys. We'll check it out."

"That sounds awful."

"So what then? You gonna meet Mr. Right at your vegetable stand? Because let me tell you how many single guys are buying veggies on a Saturday morning."

"Actually, there are a few."

"And they're like sixty, right?" Jenny asked and jabbed an elbow in Mona's ribs.

"They are," Mona admitted and laughed. "But they buy in bulk. For canning and stuff."

"Oh, honey." Jenny fidgeted with the charms on her bracelet. "You won't find a guy around here, so you'll have to expand your horizons a little."

"Maybe I'm okay by myself."

"Sure you are." She patted Mona's hand.

"Why not? I own my own business, my car, my house. Well, I make payments on the last two anyway. What do I need a man for?"

"Hmmm… " Jenny cocked an eyebrow and smirked.

Mona punched Jenny on her shoulder. "You are so dirty."

"Well, they do make *that* more fun than a solo act."

"Jenny!"

The door to the bar swung open and Beau walked in, followed by Spade and Scotty. "I heard Jake's going for the gold."

"Jesus, Beau. You're a real prick, you know that?" Jenny glared at him.

"Am a prick, have a prick, whatever. You know you like it." Beau wrapped his arms around Jenny's waist. "Any way you want it, baby."

She shrugged him off. "It's about Mona tonight."

"We can all make you feel better together," Beau told Mona with a wink.

"You're such a pervert," Jenny said to Beau. "Sorry about him."

"So Jake's going to be in the big leagues, huh?" Scotty asked. He motioned to Rosie to get everyone a drink and reached for his wallet. "That's pretty cool for him. Imagine, planning an Olympics. Some guy from little old Bassville helping with that."

"It is unbelievable," Mona agreed.

Spade pushed two quarters into the pool table and the balls came crashing into the slot. "Speaking of games and competition, who's down for a game? I'll rack them."

"Nice of you to bring him along," Jenny told Beau.

"Hey, you called and said come over. We were all sitting just fine at the Pub. You could've come over there."

"I didn't want to—because, you know."

"Know what?"

Jenny glanced at Mona and then whispered in Beau's ear. He frowned and gave her a disgusted face before joining Spade at the pool table and placing a five-dollar bill on its edge. "Okay buddy, let's go."

Spade rubbed his hands and grinned before taking his own wallet out of the pocket of his worn out Levi's. "I knew you'd help keep things interesting." His bright eyes gleamed behind his thick glasses. "Best of three?"

"What? You're gonna keep me up all night," Rosie complained from the end of the bar where she sat working on a crossword puzzle and nursing a whiskey and water. She gestured with her hand to the clock. "Don't you kids have to work in the morning?"

"Aren't you happy you get to work tonight?" Spade asked. "Isn't that how you make money—by having people actually come in and drink?"

"Nobody likes a smart aleck," Rosie told him and leaned on her beefy elbows to scrawl in another answer.

"I thought nobody liked a dumbass," Spade said to Beau.

"You're screwed either way, man." Beau chalked the tip of a cue stick and called over to Scotty. "You in? Pairs?"

"Naw, I'm good. You two play for now." He sat next to Jenny and Mona. "I'll play the winner. What brings you two pretty ladies to a place like this on a Friday night?"

"Sure isn't the crowd," Jenny said, pointedly looking around the empty bar.

"I like it here," Mona said. "It's peaceful. And old. I must've been born in the wrong era, I always like the old things."

"Nothing wrong with that," Scotty told her.

"There is if you never try anything new," Jenny said.

"But if you know something's good and you like it, what's the point of switching it up?" Scotty asked. He sipped his beer thoughtfully. "Take this, for instance." He lifted his shell of Bud Light and the amber liquid glowed in the light. "I know I like this beer, why would I walk into a place and ask for something I never had before—like a wine cooler? That's crazy, I want my old reliable drink. I know exactly how it will taste, how many I can drink before I get stupid and start betting too much money on a pool game or dice, what it costs per glass or twelve-pack. There's benefits to going with tried and tested."

"See, Jenny?" Mona tapped her glass against Scotty's. "Truer words never spoken."

"He's honest, but I don't think he's all that smart," Jenny said.

"There are worse things than dumb and honest," Scotty agreed. He ducked his head after giving Mona a sideways look.

"I'm glad you're always on my side," Mona said. "Both of you." She reached around Jenny's slender shoulders and gave her a squeeze. "Thanks for being here when I need you every time."

"What are friends for?" Jenny asked. "Now let's plug some money in that juke box. We gotta keep Rosie awake."

NINETEEN

Mona was waiting for Scotty when he arrived at the farm Saturday morning. She jogged across the yard to meet him, holding out a wrapped package topped with a green bow.

"For me? It's not my birthday."

"Yes, for you, and no, it's something else."

He frowned slightly but took it from her and slid his fingers beneath the fold to open it. "What's the occasion then?"

Mona beamed and waited for him to finish unwrapping. The paper fluttered to the ground and he held the T-shirt up by the sleeves. "Hey, that's pretty official!" The front of the shirt was printed with the Dirty Girl Veggies logo.

"Look at the back," Mona urged.

He flipped it around and read aloud, "Scotty—Picker and Seller." "An official job title!"

"I love it," he declared and handed it to her while he untucked his own T-shirt and pulled it up over his head. "Thanks." He reached for the new shirt and after he got it on, he turned in a slow circle with his arms held out for her to admire.

"Looks good."

"This is probably a bad time to give you my two weeks' notice," Scotty joked.

"Very funny. Nope. You've got the uniform now, so there's no backing out."

"Thank you."

They walked toward the barn where the produce crates were stacked and waiting to be loaded to the truck bed. "Scotty, I've been wondering … "

"Yes?"

"Well, I know you've got plenty of work with the Dohills, but I was wondering if you'd be interested in more of a partnership situation."

"How do you mean?"

Mona stopped in the doorway to the barn and turned to look at him. "If you came on board—even part time—we could expand this operation. You don't have to answer me right now, just think about it. My dad's started talking about getting a person to help him out with the dairy end and I think you'd be perfect. You love cows and farming, and I could use help with the produce side of things. I thought about a high school kid, but the season's really April through October, and if I add another greenhouse it could be longer than that. It would be the best of both worlds having you here, you know the milking side and can pitch in with my part."

Scotty rubbed his hand across his jaw and squinted towards the sun. "Aw, Mona. I don't know. I can't really see working for someone else. I want to have my say about things."

Her heart sank and she scuffed her foot across the dirt. "I understand. I just thought you'd be the perfect match." She glanced up in time to watch a strange expression flit across his face before he reached for the crates to load into the truck. *I read him all wrong*, she thought. *I really thought he'd jump at this opportunity.*

"I'm happy to keep helping you on Saturdays, though. At least until something better comes along." He winked at her.

I have to start looking somewhere else for my right-hand man ... or woman. She'd been so convinced it was Scotty, it never occurred to her he'd say no to her. He never said no to her.

The Pub's parking lot was full by lunchtime on Saturday and while Arlyce and Steve took care of their customers, Tammy and June handled the BBQ pit crew. Seven kids crouched over huge plastic tubs of raw chicken, peeling the fatty skin back to rip off the legs, wings and thighs. At a plastic covered picnic table nearby, Gene and Dottie wielded butcher knives and made expert cuts before loading the carcasses to the bins. A few other volunteers hauled boxes of whole chickens from cooler to picnic table, then lugged the bins to where the children further dismembered them. The birds were still partly frozen which added to the list of complaints coming from the children.

"My hands are numb!" Hunter whined.

"If I can't move my fingers, then the knife will slip and cut my hands open and I might die!" Trapper chimed in.

June crossed her arms and looked down at them, trying to stifle a grin. "This is coming from the same children who refuse to zip up winter coats when it's below zero? The same children who fillet thousands of white bass every spring?"

"That's different," Hunter argued. "We get *paid* for that work."

"If your house catches on fire and the fire department has good equipment to put it out and keep your family safe, why I'd call that pretty good payment," Tammy said. She set down a bucket of soapy water. "Take five—wash your hands and then I have popsicles for you guys."

"Popsicles," Trapper muttered. "I'm not a little kid."

June and Tammy bent to grab the handles of one of the finished tubs. "These feel heavier as the day progresses," June remarked.

The two women staggered back to the cooler, carrying it between them. "We have to be done soon, right?" Tammy called over to the Traysons.

"Just a couple more boxes to go!" Gene called. His face was turning red from the sun.

"Can we go swimming when we're done, Mom?"

"Swimming!" Tammy exclaimed.

"Yeah, in the river."

"Please." Her daughter chimed in.

"There's a good spot a couple blocks from here," Hunter told Tammy. "Just past the church. You go through an empty lot and it's like your own private beach."

"I don't know if that's safe," Tammy said.

"We go there all the time. It's not that deep—not for a little ways, anyhow."

"When my kids were younger, we used to bring them to swim there," June told Tammy. "The bottom's mucky, but it is pretty shallow. They really don't need suits, they can just splash around in their shorts and T-shirts," June added.

Tammy hesitated. "If you want, I can go down there with you," June offered. "There's a shady spot to sit and I think these kids have earned a treat."

"Okay," Tammy agreed. She clapped her hands and called out, "Who's ready for freezer treats?"

"I am!" Gene answered. "Just drop it down the back of my shirt, all right?"

A couple walked past the work crew on their way up to the deck. "Can you believe they use *children* here?" the woman asked her husband. "Is that even *legal*?"

"They're not working!" Tammy yelled after her. "They're not even getting paid!"

"Somehow," June said, "I don't think that makes the point you want."

Tammy laughed.

The Saturday farmers market in Northport was extra busy with the balmy weather and addition of live music. A jazz combo played at one end of the street and lifted everyone's spirits. Mona noticed it when their first customer of the day, a usually stoic older woman whose sunglasses remained in place over her grim expression no matter the weather, smiled and started chatting them up. "Berries! Why, I haven't had raspberries in ages. My grandmother used to grow them in a patch behind the garage."

"Try one," Scotty encouraged and handed her a few. He ignored the way Mona glared at him. She hated giving away anything for free, but a free sample usually led to a sale.

The woman's smile grew wider and she nodded with pleasure at the taste. "I'll take two quarts. Will you have more next week? I'll be back for a gallon so I can make jam."

"You bet!" Scotty said. "Anything else today?"

Transaction complete, he gave Mona a satisfied high five. "Wild berries. Who knew they'd be such a hit?"

"Pretty smug, aren't you?"

"You talking trash to me?"

"Shut up." She turned to pull the rest of the berries out of a cooler. They would sell out before the morning was half over. It was busy, but she wanted to scout the other stalls to discover whether other people sold berries and how they priced them. "Can you handle this alone for a few minutes?"

"Sure." Scotty reached for a plastic bag and snapped it open while greeting a new customer. Mona started down the aisle between the stalls, taking note of who was selling what.

Honey, homemade quilts and potholders, carved wooden toys, jewelry, vegetables, flowers. A Hmong woman sat behind a mountain of vegetables, all scrubbed and beautifully displayed. Mona wondered if the effort was worth it. She never did more than brush the dirt off the carrots and other root vegetables, but she had to admit the vibrant colors did look attractive. She watched while a family approached the stand and whipped out cloth shopping bags. They were clearly regulars and bought in volume with three kids to feed. Most of Mona's customers were older people, a few families and couples. Maybe cleaning the produce made it more appealing.

Crossing the street, she strolled past the rest of the stalls, some selling prepared food and drinks, others selling the same sorts of vegetables she offered. She paused to buy two cups of hand-squeezed lemonade before continuing her lap around the stalls. One other stand sold a variety of berries. She had to admit Scotty's idea was genius, based on the evidence.

"We berry picking again this week?" he asked when she returned.

He looked cheerful and Mona realized something else: helping her at the farm stand made him happy. "Looks that way," she told him and handed him a lemonade. They were down to two pints of berries and it wasn't even ten-thirty.

"Thank you, Scotty," he said before gulping down half the lemonade.

"Thank you, Scotty," she repeated.

"You are the smartest guy I know," Scotty said.

"You are the smartest guy I know."

"Probably should pick on Thursday again, closer to market day," he observed.

Mona nodded. She wondered how difficult it was to make jam. And how many other unpicked berry patches were around Bassville. Should she plant her own canes and maybe explore blueberries and strawberries?

"Stay away from the garbage," Scotty teased, "but you should keep the buckets just in case I can't make it."

"Why wouldn't you show up?" she asked, startled by the realization that he might not come help her.

"You never know with the Dohills. One day I'm done by four, the next I work until seven. Every day's different."

"Oh. Okay." It bothered her to think he might not be there. It bothered her to be bothered by that. "Can you get more beans from the cooler?"

"It's gonna cost you more than a lemonade. I'm going to need to be fed at least once today."

"If all I have to do is feed and water you to keep you working hard, you'll turn out to be a good deal." The way he grinned at her made her insides melt and she started to count the change in the cash box to break their eye contact. *When have I ever needed to avoid looking him in the eye? Geez.*

It was two by the time they'd finished prepping the chicken and nobody had lopped off a finger or died from heat exhaustion. Tammy and June followed the kids down the block, watching them race faster when they reached the corner of the church. By the time the ladies reached the vacant lot, the kids had stripped off their shoes and were wading into the water.

"You're sure this is safe?" Tammy jogged to the water's edge and looked at the brown water. "I can't see the bottom. The shore just drops off into the muck." Her children stood in water up to their knees but the Shanski kids were already chin-deep.

"Oh, those boys always just go for it. It's only about waist deep," June assured her. "Trapper! Stand up so Mrs. Parker can see how deep the water is!"

The younger Shanski son complied and Tammy was relieved to see the river only reached his waist. She still yelled a warning to her own children not to stray too far from shore.

"Have a seat." June patted the grass next to where she had settled down to watch. "There's a nice breeze here. That parking lot was hot with the sun bouncing off the asphalt."

Tammy sat down while never taking her eyes off her kids.

"I bet they'll be happy when school starts," June said.

"They could definitely use a little structure in their day. At first it wasn't so terrible, but now it's really hot and we're trapped inside with no yard to play in—just a big mud pit all around. A mud pit with thistles. At least they've gotten friendly with the Ogden kids."

"Have you thought about getting a boat? Even a little rowboat or canoe would be nice for the kids. Make it easier to get on the water. You could take the kids to the sandbars to swim."

"Rawley's talked about it nonstop since he took the kids fishing a couple weeks ago." Tammy sighed. "We definitely need to do something. I thought they'd be able to ride their bikes, but we live too far from town and it's all highway traffic. It's not very safe."

"Mom!"

Tammy leapt up at the sound of her son's voice. She sprinted to the water where her daughter sat sobbing, clutching her foot.

"It hurts! Mumma, it hurts!"

Blood gushed from the bottom of her daughter's foot. "What happened, Hannah?" she asked, squatting and reaching for her daughter. Murky water swirled around her feet and ankles.

"I stepped on a seashell."

"Oh dear," June had joined them and knelt to examine the wound—a three-inch long slice right on the tender part near the girl's arch. "It was probably a clamshell. They break apart and can be very sharp."

"I wanna go home!" her daughter wailed.

"Okay, okay. Can you walk on it?"

Her daughter shook her head, tears streamed down her cheeks, smeared with dirt and grime. Tammy turned and patted her shoulders. "Climb on. I'll carry you."

Her daughter clambered onto her back and Tammy tried not to think about bloodstains on her khaki shorts. "Grab her shoes, Miles," she ordered her son.

"Do we hafta go?" he complained. "She ruins everything."

"NOW!" Tammy's voice cracked and even the Shanski kids stopped splashing to watch. Her son slowly untied one sneaker and stuffed his foot into it. Hannah wiped her snotty nose against her mother's shirt and watched him expertly push their parent to her limit of patience. Tammy stared at Miles until she felt something on her thigh and she looked down to see blood trickling steadily from her daughter's foot, down her leg, drip from her knee to the ground. "ARGH!"

A sharp stinging pain bit into her left arm. Startled, Tammy jerked her right hand loose to smack a large horsefly. Her daughter fell to the ground with a shriek.

"Damn it!" She craned her neck to see a huge welt appearing on the back of her arm. The thing had to have *teeth* to bite her like that. "My God!" Tammy wanted to cry in frustration, but her audience now included June, all of the Shanski children, and an elderly couple out with their dog. "You can walk," she snarled to her daughter.

"I think she might need stitches," June said. She picked up a stray sock from the grass—one of the boys had tossed it aside. "Let's wrap it up to at least get the bleeding to slow down." June tied the grubby knee-high sports sock around the girl's foot. "Tsk. You'll be okay. Water always makes the bleeding look worse than it really is."

"Fine. Climb back on," Tammy said through gritted teeth. Her arm throbbed with pain, worse than any bee sting she'd ever experienced. Staggering under her daughter's weight, Tammy marched towards the Pub, her son and June trailing behind. Eventually she asked about the Shanski kids.

"They're fine. They go down there all the time."

"That river's a menace."

Ignoring Arlyce's curious stare when they returned to the Pub, Tammy grabbed her purse from the kitchen counter and stalked through the back door. She loaded her children into the car and drove home, muttering outraged curses the entire time.

"Let's get you cleaned up and then we'll get to a doctor," Tammy told her children.

While the water ran in the upstairs bathroom, Tammy called the nearest clinic. "Clinic hours are from eight to five, Monday through Friday. If this is an emergency, please dial … " She slammed down the phone and leaned her forehead against the cool surface of her countertop. "This fucking day could get any worse … " her voice trailed off when the heard the screams.

Taking the stairs two at a time, Tammy flew to the bathroom and burst through the door. Her daughter sat on the toilet seat with her knees pulled up to her chin. Miles was in the tub rubbing his toes with a washcloth.

"What's wrong?" she gasped.

"The worms won't come off," her son said. His eyes were huge with fear and Tammy bent closer. Three glistening black globs adhered to his feet. Tammy reached for the washcloth and scrubbed hard. The globs stretched out but stayed stuck to his feet. "I think they're leeches," he explained.

Tammy reached out her index finger and thumb to grasp one firmly and pull. The worm-like creature stretched into a thin line and snapped free from her grip. Tammy tried again. "Ouch!" her son yelped.

"Okay, let me try one more time. This day is a disaster," she grumbled. Her repeated attempts at pulling the leeches free failed and as a last resort Tammy tried to use the edge of her fingernail to scrape the bloodsucker off his skin. The leech squirmed free and Miles jumped to his feet, sloshing water out of the bathtub.

"Hold still!"

"Don't let it touch me!" her daughter squealed.

"Grab it!"

"No! Don't touch it!" Tammy raised her hands and her kids stood still while they watched the wormlike creature settle to the bottom of the bathtub. "You," she pointed to her daughter. "Get in the tub and try to rinse off some of the blood." Her daughter obeyed, resting her bloody foot on the edge of the tub. "Don't move," Tammy told her son. She warily tried to scrape the other two leeches free without success. "Okay, step out onto the bathmat."

Tammy pulled the stopper out and watched the single leech swirl in a few lazy circles before disappearing down the drain. She sank to the floor. Her head ached, the bite on her arm was a tender welt and she could only hope the ER would toss in leech extraction for free after stitching up Hannah's foot. With the luck they were having, tetanus boosters were probably on the ticket as well. Good thing Rawley was coming home tonight from his business trip because she couldn't take any more country living.

Maw had his mixtape ready for tomorrow's chicken barbeque. For years he'd been the official emcee of the event, using a loudspeaker to play music and encourage the crowd to spend their money. Rawley's wife had suggested getting a band for some live music, which was a good idea, but at such short notice they couldn't find anyone available. But definitely an idea for next year.

He'd spent hours on lyrics and planned to bust some live raps in between songs at the picnic, get some early exposure for his music career. Bassville was mostly a hard rock or country music crowd, but they'd indulge him. Plus it would give him a chance to practice his new material.

"Maw!" He jerked around. He hadn't heard the door open. Jay Hodge approached the counter with a wide grin and outstretched hand.

"Hey-hey, Jay!" Maw gripped the man's hand firmly and slapped him on the shoulder. "What brings you here today? Need some minnows for the grandkids? Gonna take the ol' pontoon out for some afternoon fun?"

"Another time, my friend. This visit is business." Jay set a long cardboard tube on the counter and tapped it. "I'm wondering if I could hang some promotional material here at your store."

Before Maw could respond Jay continued, "I see you have posters for garage sales, the fireman's chicken barbeque, a benefit for the Barlow family—terrible tragedy about their father, by the way. Whitetails Unlimited, Ducks Unlimited, Trout Unlimited—not a lot of creativity with these conservation clubs and their names, is there? Ah, Pheasants Forever. Who doesn't appreciate a little alliteration, am I right? Pheasants Forever." Jay sighed and pointed to bulletin board on the other side of the store. "And you've got a truck for sale, snowmobile for sale, Poker Run. So I'm asking, Maw, can you hang one more poster?"

In Maw's experience the harder the sell job, the harder the sale, so he took his time answering. He suspected he wouldn't like whatever Jay Hodge carried in that tube. But part of running a small business like his meant using diplomacy, so he smiled and said, "Well, Jay, let's take a look at what you've got there."

Jay took the plastic cover off one end of the tube and slid out a roll of poster paper. "Now I know your business depends on river traffic, so before you jump to any conclusions, I want you to hear me out."

Maw stifled a groan. It was no-wake business. He'd heard this group was getting organized to change the no-wake rules and starting to get attention. Sure, the river got crazy sometimes, but mostly on the weekends and mostly because of boaters. The fishermen didn't drive each other nuts out there. They drove fast to get from one spot to another, but then they spent most of the time on the water sitting still. It was the damn boaters and their need for constant movement to entertain themselves that made the river a circus starting Memorial Day weekend. In his view, there was a big difference between using a boat to do something—like fish—and just using a boat to drive around.

With a flourish Jay unfurled the poster and held it up for Maw to admire. The glossy advertisement featured huge yellow text reading "No Wake: Take Back the Lake" diagonally across an image of an overcrowded channel with angry people raising fists at a speedboat moving through and kicking up a huge wake in their midst. The lower left corner gave meeting dates and locations and phone numbers with encouragement to "take a stand and reclaim nature's peace and quiet."

"Well." Maw tugged at his beard and pretended to examine the poster more carefully.

"I'm trying to get these hung up all around the area and I'd like to put a couple up here in your store."

168

The difference between slowing traffic on the river for three months of summer weekends when the boaters acted bananas and instituting a permanent no wake was huge in Maw's mind. It would be a lot easier if people would just apply a little common sense. And he did think once the novelty of the jet ski wore off, people would see less of them. The trouble with saying no to Jay hanging his poster meant he was taking a side against him, which he wasn't—not entirely. But his bait shop thrived on business brought in by the river and if people didn't come through because driving slow would take more time, it would hurt him—and the others in Bassville who depended on the river traffic in the summer months.

If he agreed to hang the poster, he risked the wrath of people like the Shanskis and all the resort owners on the east side of Bassville. He had to live with those folks. But he'd keep the peace with Jay Hodge, a man whom Maw suspected made a formidable enemy when crossed.

"Who did the artwork for you?" Maw asked, stalling for time while he weighed his options. "These are really professional grade."

"A gal I know in Northport. She did some work for some of my clients. Her place is called Picture This. She handles promotional materials like brochures and so forth. So, how many can I leave behind for you to hang up?" Jay asked. He'd begun to thumb through the stack.

Leave behind to hang up. Maw saw his escape route with those words. "How about three, that sound all right? I've got to check the filters on my minnow tanks and I'll get them up on the walls later. Those Pit Bull Minnows don't breed or feed themselves!" Maw laughed heartily and reached across to accept three posters and make a show of rolling them up carefully and placing them behind the counter.

"All right then. I appreciate your support. I know from talking to fishermen that a lot of us want to change the rules on the river."

"Who've you talked to?" Maw asked.

"Otto Zimm actually did a piece on the news the other day for us. Did you happen to catch his interview?" Jay said.

Otto. Figured. In Otto's world the perfect river was one he fished alone. Maw forced a huge smile and nodded. "Well, Otto really does love to fish and he has a special spot in his heart for the river." The best lie to tell was the truth.

"I'll see you soon, Maw. Got to finish making my rounds today." Jay gave him a mock salute and left.

The trouble, Maw thought, with letting everyone and their dog hang posters up in his shop was that everyone and their dog wanted to hang posters up in his shop. But a curse can also be a blessing. He hung the first no-wake poster very carefully—and strategically covered it up with a poster for a Poker Run on the Rat River and a snowmobile T.C. Barlow was trying to sell. The other two posters were similarly placed on the walls around the shop and Maw felt satisfied that he'd placated Jay Hodge while not taking a position that would piss off his clientele or neighbors.

While he loaded the sound equipment for Sunday's chicken barbeque, he wondered how a guy like Otto Zimm connected with a guy like Jay Hodge. One was as straight-laced and singularly minded as they came, the other was more slippery than a ribbon leech coated in algae. Any union between those two knuckleheads would lead to trouble for somebody.

It was after supper when Tammy and her children returned from their trip to the hospital. The kids clambered out of the back seat clutching their McDonalds milkshakes. Tammy held a bottle of white zinfandel and jar of ointment for Hannah's foot. She'd drunk half the wine by the time Rawley strolled through the door carrying his suitcase. "Honey, I'm home!"

"Here." Tammy lifted her head off the couch cushion and gave him a glassy stare.

"Where are the kids?" her husband asked.

"Bed. We've had a helluva day." She raised her wine glass to him. "Cheers."

He kicked off his shoes and walked across the carpet towards her, brow creased with concern. "Everything okay?"

"Don worry," Tammy slurred. "S'all good now."

"What happened to your arm?" He pulled back the ice pack she'd propped against it.

"Deer fly bit me. Or a horse fly. Some fly with teeth, anyhow. An' leeches bit Miles. And Hannah stepped on a clam shell. Bassville fucking sucks." Tammy closed her eyes and sighed deeply.

"Did this all happen today?" Rawley asked. "When we talked on the phone last night everything was fine. You were going to help with the fireman's picnic."

"Yeah." Tammy gulped the rest of her glass of wine and poured a refill. "And then." She pointed at him and nodded. "And then."

"And then what?" Rawley gently took the glass from her hand. "May I?"

"Then the river attacked us. So we had to go to the hospital. And now we're here. An' I'm not goin' *anywhere* ever. Never."

Rawley pulled an afghan over his wife and tucked it in around her arms. "I'm going to say goodnight to the kids. You relax."

"Mmmhm." Tammy closed her eyes.

"I don't know that I've ever seen you drink alone before. It must have been a rough day."

"There were leeches," Tammy murmured. "And so much blood."

Rawley patted her shoulder and headed upstairs.

TWENTY

Sunday morning promised to be hot, sunny and muggy. Perfect weather for boating and swimming, terrible weather for working at the barbeque. The savory aroma of peanut oil reached June's nose before she got out of the car. Across the parking lot large white tents were already in place, picnic tables were lined up in rows and beside a bright red fire engine stood four men in shorts and T-shirts. She unloaded the six cherry and raspberry pies she'd made for the event and carried the stack towards them.

"Over here!" Tammy's voice echoed across from beneath one of the tents. June headed towards her.

Tammy wore a patriotic T-shirt embellished with sparkling stars and stripes. Her hair was pulled back with a glittering clip and her sandal straps matched the red, white and blue theme. No one else had arrived on the scene yet and Tammy was unpacking boxes of Styrofoam containers.

"What are you doing?" June asked. They always left the boxes by the chicken. The firefighters dropped the chicken from the barbeque onto trays, volunteers loaded the to-go containers and they then traveled to a tent where a roll, coleslaw and pie were added.

"Getting ready." Tammy checked her watch. "Where's everyone else?"

"Probably at church. So usually the firefighters load up the chicken and runners bring the boxes to us to finish off."

"That's silly," Tammy declared. "You have to wait for the chicken to cook, right? So it makes more sense to prep the boxes and finish with the chicken at the end, then send them on their way."

June considered her idea. The coleslaw and pie might suffer a little in the heat. "How many do you want to prepare in advance?"

"I figure if we stay twenty boxes ahead of the chicken guys, we should be good. The pick-up station can go to that side of them." Tammy pointed to a card table she'd already set up beside the fire engine. A huge hand-drawn poster advertised the fundraising goal, designed like a thermometer to illustrate how much they had "raised" to buy the engine to "beat the heat."

"Clever sign," June remarked.

"The kids helped me make it. There's a marker to add to the temperature as the day goes on. I think it will help get people excited to spend money if they see how much they're raising collectively."

"Everyone okay after yesterday's adventure? Did your daughter need stitches?"

"We're all battle-scarred after yesterday," Tammy said and grimaced. She pulled up the sleeve of her shirt to show June the still-inflamed deer fly bite.

"Yikes." June winced sympathetically.

"I brought the kids home to clean up before going to the ER in Northport. Miles had three leeches stuck to his feet—I got one off by myself. Did you know you can just dump some salt on them and they'll detach? I learned that from the nurse. And Hannah ended up with seven stitches. She's better today, but she'll need to keep that foot covered for a week so it doesn't get infected. I told Rawley we need to get a swimming pool. Those above-ground ones are pretty nice. No more river for this family."

"I'm sorry it was such an awful day."

"We survived. The good news is we have all that chicken prepped for today and we're going to make a haul on this fundraiser."

Arlyce came around the corner dragging the red wagon she used for grocery shopping. "Slaw's ready!" she hollered. "Steve'll be by later with the beer kegs."

"The cooler's right there," Tammy said.

Arlyce paused by them, wiping her forehead and giving Tammy a puzzled look. "It should go on the other side of the chicken. Unless you're serving right to left?"

"No, same service, but we'll prep the boxes with the sides before adding the chicken. I think it'll be more efficient that way."

Arlyce rolled her eyes. "What's the difference? You gotta add pie, slaw and a roll. It goes in first or last, but it takes the same amount of time to pack a box."

"If you prepack everything but the chicken, then people are only waiting for the chicken. They'll get served faster this way. And I was thinking … "

"You were thinking what?" Arlyce interrupted her. "We shouldn't be changing up stuff at the last minute. It's going to confuse people."

June felt bad for Tammy, who was obviously trying to be helpful. Arlyce, bless her, could be a bear. "Let's listen. What's your idea, Tammy?"

"If we have a separate station for drinks then people might buy more. When people have to stand in the same line to buy drinks as chicken, the line might get long and move slow, and people might figure it's not worth it. If we sell beer and soda at a different spot, we'll end up selling more." Tammy talked fast as if sensing Arlyce was ready to shut her down at any second.

"That's actually a good idea," June said. "What do you think, Arlyce?"

"How you going to man it?" Arlyce crossed her arms. "Do you have a second cash box? A second set of volunteers to sell the drinks?" Arlyce's scowl deepened.

"I think it will only take two people. I'm sure we can spare two people from the food tent," Tammy said.

Arlyce began ticking off the volunteer spots and the people who were working. "Cash box, Peg and Shelly Dohill. Food tent, June, Dottie and me. Emcee, Maw. Raffle tickets, Steve, Dob and Dale."

"There you go! Have Dob sell drinks. We don't need three people selling raffle tickets." Tammy reached in her canvas bag and pulled out a marker. "We'll make another sign for the other table."

Tammy nearly took a step back while Arlyce laid into her about volume and manpower. "We can't spare raffle ticket people! You have no idea how busy they are! You've never worked this before!"

"Okay. How about my neighbors then?"

June had to admit she'd nearly forgotten about the other new people in town. Tammy was such a force, already involved with the barbeque. She'd only seen the other new couple in town once, having dinner with their kids. She knew nothing about them other than which house they lived in—the ranch in the subdivision. "That's an idea. Do you have their number?"

"I do!" Tammy dug in the canvas bag again and pulled her purse free. She rummaged around a moment and brandished a small address book. "I keep a spare for my purse," she explained. Her competence was breathtaking.

"Let's get to a phone then," Arlyce said. She took defeat gracefully … sometimes. Leading the way back to the Pub, Arlyce gestured to the wall phone near the pizza ovens in the kitchen. Tammy picked up the greasy receiver with her fingertips and dialed. Arlyce offered them coffee while they waited.

"No thanks, I can't do caffeine."

"Why am I not surprised," Arlyce said and poured a cup for herself and June.

"Kelly? It's Tammy, your new neighbor. Hope you're not busy today because I have the most amazing opportunity for you—and your husband. Bassville needs people to volunteer for their annual chicken barbeque and it's a great way for you two to meet people from town!"

While Tammy sold Kelly on helping out, Arlyce helped herself to a cigarette break. "Gotta hand it to her, she doesn't sit around and let moss grow beneath her seat."

"Some of her ideas are pretty great," June said. "Did you check out the sign she made with the thermometer? I honestly think we will make more money this year."

"Weather plays a role, too," Arlyce said. "Don't give Tammy too much credit for the day's success. It's sunny and breezy today."

"You and your forecasts. How many weathermen do you follow on the radio and TV?"

"All of 'em. And they're almost always right except that Tom Mahoney. He's wrong half of the time and I tell you, if I was wrong as much as he is, I don't know how I'd keep my job."

"Seems like there's some wiggle room with weather forecasts. What makes them 'wrong?' Does the temperature need to be on the dot or do they get a couple degrees either way?"

"Exactly," Arlyce said. "That's what I'd like to know."

Tammy hung up the phone and raised both fists in the air

triumphantly. "Both of them will work. See? All you have to do is ask and people will come around. Now let's go make ten thousand dollars!"

Mona's skin was slick from head to toe. Chicken grease and sweat made her feel positively disgusting. Her bra was soaked through, the back of her underpants clung to her waist, and her hair was matted to her scalp. She reached for another gallon of coleslaw and started scooping portions into plastic cups.

"Mona!" T.C. waved to her from the line where he stood with their group of friends. "How long are you working? We're heading to the sandbar after this!"

Mona shook her head. "Back from up north? I'm here all day. Have fun."

As a member of the town board, she was expected to help. She had donated cabbage and carrots for the coleslaw, too, and her logo was printed on the brochures for the event. Owning a business and being an adult was a great gig in theory, but in practice it meant missing out on having fun while the party roared on around her. Not unlike tending bar, she reflected. Only she got paid for tending bar. Volunteering her time only made her feel good about helping others.

"What time is it?" June asked Dottie. Mona listened for her answer.

"One-thirty."

By the time she finished serving food and cleaned up, her friends would be long gone. A fly buzzed near Mona's ear and darted away while she swatted at it. At least they'd exceeded last year's profits, she saw when she glanced over at the sign Tammy had made. The red line up the thermometer had passed the $5,000 mark an hour ago and the crowd kept coming.

Her dad stood beside one of the fryers with Gene. Certain families always came out in force to put in their time. That's how it usually worked. A handful did the work while the majority played and went about their daily life without putting in a single hour of time helping their community. People like Jenny, Mona thought. And Spade. They never worked the polls or chicken barbeques or ushered at church. Why did she have to come from a family who always stepped up instead of one that never volunteered? Her mother's cheerful voice reached her ears and Mona watched her compliment a little girl on her new sandals as she counted out change. "Now you put these coins in your pocket so you don't drop them. Then I'll hand you your boxes, honey."

Her parents worked so hard. Her resentment made her feel bad. Still, it was a good thing Jenny was getting her chicken to go because the more Mona thought about it, the madder she got and the less she wanted to talk to her.

Kelly's eardrums ached, if such a thing was actually possible. She'd agreed to help at the barbeque event when Tammy called her. Of course she should pitch in around her new community. Here was an ideal opportunity dropped in her lap like a gift. It was short-term and easy, the best kind of volunteer gig in her opinion. All she had to do was sell beer and soda. Tom was supposed to sell with her, except he got roped into following a barrel-chested man around the picnic ground selling raffle tickets. The barrel-chested man was a few years older and seemed to know everyone. He had a deep mellow voice and laughed often. She'd never seen anyone with a head and neck so large, almost like a giant. Tom looked like an elf walking behind him with an ice cream bucket full of money from the ticket sales. From her perch at the beverage tent, she could see Tom's bald spot and ears glowing bright red from sunburn. In their haste to leave the house, she'd neglected to rub a zinc stick across his nose, ears and head. Not that he'd let her, of course. Men were too macho to accept safety measure like wearing seatbelts or sunscreen. Well, it served him right if he suffered then.

Near her seat a portly bearded guy played music and made announcements over a loudspeaker. He cut in between songs with lively commentary about the fire department and performed a short rap song. Kelly thought his voice sounded familiar, but she couldn't remember where she'd heard it before.

Kelly wore sunscreen, comfortable shoes and a pasted-on smile. Meeting new people was uncomfortable. She was an introvert by nature and not inclined to hang out in crowds. But she also understood the rules of being new in town. Tammy had greeted her with a hug and a barrage of information—and she'd barely stopped talking to her since. She'd told Kelly everything she knew about fundraising, the fire department and the various people working. Kelly had reached maximum capacity for keeping names and relationships straight a while ago, so she'd quit trying and occasionally contributed a nod or mumbled "oh" to the conversation.

"Looks like they're low on chicken, I have to run over and grab more from the coolers. Okay, so fifty cents for soda, a dollar for beer. Wine coolers are two dollars. There's a roll of quarters under here if you run low on change. You know where everything is?"

Kelly bit back a sarcastic reply. She'd been working for over an hour, only an idiot could fail to keep things straight. "Got it. No problem."

"Okay, I'll be back as soon as I can. Lucky there's a lull right now!" Tammy hustled across the grass towards the tent where a group of people prepared chicken for the grills. Kelly sat down on the folding chair provided for her and gazed at the people milling around between tables. A child had dropped his plate and the mother was trying to salvage what she could by plucking pieces of grass from his drumstick. The coleslaw was a lost cause, as was the slice of pie that oozed filling beside their feet.

One table was full of younger people who'd come through her line earlier ordering a lot of beer. The cans were stacked in pyramids on both ends of the table and their laughter never stopped. Kelly wondered why the one girl who looked their age was stuck working in the food tent. Maybe she was one of those unpopular girls no one liked, or perhaps she was shy. Kelly studied the girl, whose brown hair clung damply to her forehead, and who was filling plastic cups with an ice cream scoop. She looked like a nice person, not weird or stuck up. She smiled pleasantly at two older women across the table from where she stood and waved at a skinny red-headed man with thick glasses.

What she'd seen of Bassville today impressed her. The people were cheerful and nice, maybe prone to drinking too much, but it *was* Sunday afternoon and the beer sales were for a good cause. Interesting to note she had not seen the farmer or the kid who had cut hay by her house. Maybe they weren't the socializing type. She could believe it if their other behavior were any indication.

"Good afternoon, young lady." A very tan older man wearing a brightly colored Hawaiian shirt unbuttoned to the center of his very hairy chest smiled at Kelly in an aggressive manner.

"Hi! What can I get you?"

"First, let's see you smile," he urged her.

Kelly obliged with a forced smile that showed no teeth.

"That's better. We'll have three light beers and three piña colada wine coolers." He set a glossy trifold brochure on the table and pushed it across to her. "Have you read one of these yet?"

Confident that a guy buying beer wasn't giving her a religious tract, Kelly shook her head while she pulled his drink order out of the coolers and wiped the water off each bottle with a towel.

"I'm guessing you're local, so this topic should interest you. Do you have children?"

"Two sons. That will be nine dollars."

"Keep the change." The man handed her a ten-dollar bill. "I have grandchildren and their safety is so important to me. There's a group of us working to make the water safer for everyone playing on it—boaters, floaters, tubers and fishermen. The brochure explains how you can get involved."

"Okay. Thanks." She watched the man head towards a table where two other older men and three older women, all equally tan, sat baking in the sun. Kelly flipped open the brochure and had started to read the bulleted arguments for an extended no-wake zone when a younger voice made her look up.

"Can I please get three light beers, a Coke and a 7-Up."

Kelly turned around to see a lanky kid wearing a baseball cap. He didn't look old enough to buy beer, not with the baby-faced dimples and big blue eyes. But she'd seen him with the group of people at the picnic table stacking their empty cans, and they certainly seemed old enough. Besides, she suspected policing underage drinkers would not go down well in Bassville. "Four dollars, please," she told him and dug around in the coolers for the cans.

He slapped a five-dollar bill on the table and said, "Keep it."

"Thank you."

He cocked his head and studied her more closely. "You're one of the new families, aren't you?"

"Kelly Ogden." She held out her hand.

The kid awkwardly shook it and Kelly realized that Bassville was not a handshaking kind of place. "My family used to own that land," he told her. His voice had a hard edge to it.

"You're a Trayson?"

"I'm Scotty. You like living there? It's a pretty spot where you built."

"I do—it is. The farmer next to us doesn't like us there, though."

"Not surprised. Selling it wasn't a popular decision. I wish we hadn't."

He was so matter of fact that Kelly wasn't offended by the remark. "I bet."

"You meet my mom and dad yet?"

"I don't think so," Kelly tried to recall who she'd been introduced to so far.

"Dad's grilling chicken, the shorter bigger guy. Mom's in the food tent, also shorter and bigger."

"And you're tall and thin. I wouldn't have put you together with them."

Scotty's eyes crinkled at the edges when he smiled. "Recessive skinny, tall genes from my mom's side. I also got her curly hair."

"Well, it's nice to meet you." She tried to think of something else to say but he quickly grabbed his cans and returned to his table, doling out the drinks to his friends. Kelly decided meeting people one-on-one wasn't too awful, especially without Tammy standing beside her running every conversational transaction. She started organizing the cash box while she waited for her to return, flipping the bills to face the same direction, president-side up. She knew from her years working at the bank that the tellers appreciated counting money that was sorted properly.

"Everything going okay, honey?" Tom greeted her with a kiss on the cheek. "Our shift is almost over. I'm starving and that chicken smells good."

"It does. Where are the kids?"

"Last I saw them they were headed to the boat landing to chuck rocks in the water."

Kelly tried not to think of them slipping, falling and drowning in the Wissipaw's strong current. Or discovering leeches clinging to their feet, as Tammy had explained was an additional hazard of playing in the water. "Meet anyone interesting?"

"Dob Dohill's a contractor and he helped with the electrical and plumbing for our house. Dohill, do you remember the name? And I met Maw, the bait shop guy from TV with those minnow ads. He's the one announcing, kind of playing DJ up there."

"TV! That's where I've seen him!" Kelly snapped her fingers.

"And I met Gene, the farmer whose field we bought; and Loyal, another farmer. I wasn't too excited about leaving our house on a Sunday but now I'm glad I did."

"Me, too," Kelly told him. "When Tammy gets back I'll find the kids."

"I'm sure they're fine." Tom patted her hand. "They'll turn up once they get hungry."

"I can't believe they haven't been hounding us for sodas."

"Because they're busy having fun."

She watched him resume his post by the giant's side. Rumbling in the distance drew her attention to the road and a line of motorcycles streamed into the parking lot. The people would just keep coming, like the aroma of frying chicken drew them in across the miles.

The day ended with the thermometer filled in all the way with red marker. Arlyce had to hand it to Tammy, she had some good ideas, though the weather probably played a bigger factor in their success. Dale Dohill won the big raffle prize, no shock there since Dohills were always lucky with that sort of thing, and he donated it back to the fire department. Thanks to Dale, the next two winners did the same, knowing they'd look greedy pocketing their winnings after his generosity. She sat in the dining room of the Pub with her feet elevated on the chair next to her and stared out at the water, slick and black beneath the night sky. The silence was lovely after the crazy day.

"Can I get you something to drink?" Steve asked. He carried Victoria on his hip. She was too big for that at five, but she was daddy's girl and their youngest, so Arlyce bit her tongue.

"Peppermint on the rocks. Join me?"

Steve nodded. "Come help daddy pour the drinks," he said to his daughter. They returned a few minutes later, Victoria carrying a tray with both hands bearing both glasses.

"Thank you. Have you worked here long? You're very good at this." Arlyce took her drink.

"Thank you, Mommy!" Victoria said, pleased by the compliment.

"Signs off?"

"All locked down and dark," Steve told her. "Not real busy today with the barbeque." He sighed and sat beside her. "I'm ready for a vacation."

"Two more months."

"Let's go sooner. I'll ask Mona if she could run the place for a couple of days—during the week." Steve talked faster so Arlyce couldn't object. "Maybe Monday, Tuesday, Wednesday. We pack up and go to the Wisconsin Dells or something. When's the last time we did anything like that as a family?"

"But the bar! It's our busiest time."

"Three days—*weekdays*. We could do it! We deserve it," Steve insisted.

Arlyce lit a cigarette and thought. It was nuts. But weekdays were slower. "What if we just closed?"

"See? I like your thinking. We'd have fun. Take the kids to play mini golf, go to a water park, ride the duck boats … be refreshed for the last push before Labor Day … "

"Let me think about it."

Steve knew when to force the issue and when to sit back and wait for his wife to come around. This was the time to wait, so he sipped his drink and reached for her hand. Victoria slid onto his lap and nestled her head into the crook of his neck. Through the open window they could hear the soft cry of an owl and a sudden splash of a fish jumping out of the river.

"It was a good haul today. We made a lot of money with that barbeque." Ice cubes tinkled against the side of Arlyce's glass when she lifted it. "That Tammy had some helpful ideas."

"I thought you said she drove you nuts."

"She does, she did. She's bossy." Arlyce sighed. "But I'm bossy, too. We might be oil and water but I can appreciate success."

"That thermometer sign was awfully clever."

"The Ladies' Guild usually goes out for drinks to celebrate and hash over the barbeque. Guess I'll have to invite her."

"Seems reasonable. I mean, she did contribute a lot."

"That's the thing, she's new in town and made herself part of town. Our job is to stand aside and make room for the new people. I always bitch when people don't step up and help, so when someone does, I ought to be more appreciative."

"What about the other new lady—what's her name?" Steve rubbed small circles on his daughter's back. Her breathing had slowed.

"Kelly. She's quiet but seems okay. Not a raging bull like Tammy, but she did show up to help when Tammy called her. So did her husband. Can always use people like that."

"Invite her, too," Steve said.

"I will." Arlyce squeezed his hand. "Change is hard. Maybe it's good, too."

"Give them a chance."

"I will. *We* will," she amended and tilted her head to rest it on his shoulder. For all the change it was nice to appreciate what didn't— her steady husband and this place with the view of the Wissipaw River and the peace and quiet.

TWENTY-ONE

MAW STOOD IN FRONT of the full-length mirror in the bathroom and practiced his dance moves. He decided it didn't matter how out of shape he looked if he could move smoothly. It was one thing to be a fat man who was a bad dancer—people would make fun of that. He'd have to be good, then he'd be an impressive fat man. His belly loomed over the front of his jeans and he tried a couple new steps. The lawnmower was easy, he'd pulled the crank on engines his whole life. The sprinkler was fun—plus having his hands up by his head drew attention away from his waistline. But the one where you picked up your foot behind you and sort of hopped around? That move needed work.

A new song started on the radio plugged into the wall behind the sink, and Maw bounced on his toes until he connected with the rhythm. Then he kicked up his foot and reached back to grab it. It took a half second for him to miss, lose his balance and crash to the floor with his left leg twisted awkwardly beneath him. He jerked back his head and hit the porcelain toilet bowl. In agony, he screamed a string of curse words.

"Are you okay?" His son's muffled voice came through the floorboards from the kitchen below.

"I'm fine!" Maw yelled. Except he knew he wasn't. The shooting pain and the cracking noise he'd heard—or did he feel it?—when he landed was bad. Maw rested his head back against the cool base of the toilet and inhaled deeply before trying to move. His right leg was fine, but as soon as he shifted his weight to the left he howled again. "Shit!" he roared.

A tentative knock at the bathroom door. "Dad?"

"Probably gonna need an ambulance," Maw called. He lay flat on the linoleum floor and closed his eyes, taking another long breath before speaking again. "Come in."

His youngest son opened the door slowly and switched off the radio. "That's not natural," he said, pointing at Maw's left leg. The foot drooped inward while Maw's knee bent out.

Maw grimaced. "That's why you need to call an ambulance."

"Nine-one-one?"

"Wait. It's cheaper to get me there ourselves. Your mom's going to kill me."

His son shrugged. "If she actually killed you every time you said she was going to, you'd have been dead a thousand times by now."

"Tell you what," Maw commanded through gritted teeth, "Call Steve Shanski and tell him to grab whoever's in the bar with him and get over here. They can drive me to the hospital. That way we only have to pay the doctor's bill."

Half an hour later Beau and Steve had helped lift Maw from the bathroom floor and settle him into the back seat of Beau's car. Beau slammed his driver's side door shut and grinned at Maw in the rearview mirror. "Northport Community Hospital?"

"Step on it," Maw groaned. The door handle jabbed painfully into his right shoulder and he shifted over to get more comfortable.

"Do I get a bigger tip if I get you there faster?" Beau gunned the engine and peeled out of the gravel parking lot. He waved cheerfully at Steve who had grabbed Maw's car to return to the Pub. They'd swap vehicles later.

"I got a tip for you—"

Beau raised his hand. "Say no more, Maw." He executed a rolling stop, glanced both ways and sped east on the highway. After several miles Beau cleared his throat. "I'm guessing this might put a damper on your music video."

Maw closed his eyes. *Shit.* All of that money he'd spent. Could he delay the shoot until he could walk again? Or would he be a rap god perched on a stool? "I'm not going to worry about it until we see an X-ray," he said.

Monday afternoon Kelly's doorbell rang. "Yoo hoo! Anybody home?"

"Coming!" Kelly called. She came around the corner carrying a laundry basket of clean towels and bumped the door open with her hip. "Good morning, neighbor."

"Are you all recovered from yesterday?" Tammy said. "Wasn't it terrific? I could hardly move this morning when I rolled over and tried to get out of bed. On my feet all day hustling like that, it was like when I worked retail over the holiday season. But holy smokes! They made over ten thousand dollars!" Tammy plumped herself onto the couch and waved her hand by her face. "It's so hot. Don't you have air conditioning?"

"We do, but I hate to use it when it's not muggy. Tom's in an office all day and likes coming home to fresh air."

Tammy nodded. "I totally understand. And thankfully our friendly neighborhood farmer isn't busy spreading manure today, so we can enjoy a little fresh air. So, what did you think about yesterday? Did you have fun? Did you meet anybody interesting? Are you glad you helped out? I was so happy you were able to. That Arlyce, she was really giving me the stink-eye about selling the drinks separate from the chicken—obviously we made a lot of money doing it my way, but it couldn't have worked out without you pitching in. Thank you."

It felt good to be appreciated and Kelly found herself again reassessing her motor-mouth neighbor. "Would you like something to drink? Tea or lemonade?"

"I'd love a lemonade." Tammy stood and followed Kelly back to the kitchen and leaned on the counter. "Are you all unpacked? Were you going to hang anything on your wall over there? I think a huge picture would look great in that space, unless you worry about the sun fading it with that patio door nearby. Have you ever had an Arnold Palmer?"

"What's that?"

"Iced tea and lemonade mixed. They're named for the golfer, Arnold Palmer? Super yummy. You should try it."

"Would you like me to make that?" Kelly gestured to the open refrigerator where a pitcher of iced tea stood beside a pitcher of lemonade.

Tammy clapped her hands together. "Yes! Boy, this is a real treat!"

Kelly smiled while she poured the two drinks and then gestured to the patio outside. "I just wiped the chairs off this morning. Let's sit out there."

"That fence. I'm telling you, once I get these thistles and weeds taken care of—which will be soon, I promise you—we're taking on that farmer and his stupid fences and his cow poop. Oh! I forgot to ask—did a policeman stop by your place yet? One came to ask me questions about that new house being built. There's been damage pretty much every week to the property. Stakes being pulled up, basement flooded, all kinds of trouble. Asked if we'd seen anything and to keep an eye out for trouble. Did they talk to you?"

"Yes," Kelly nodded. "We haven't seen anything. It's so quiet here, I feel like we'd notice a car or people moving around—especially with the windows open at night."

"My kids decided they're going to have a stake-out tonight. They plan to sleep in a tent in the front yard and spy on the property." Tammy rolled her eyes. "They watch a lot of movies and cop shows on TV. I suppose they'll be safe if they stay in the yard. I wonder if it's that crazy farmer causing all the trouble. Seems like he's got an axe to grind, doesn't he?"

"Tell you what," Kelly settled back on the plastic chaise lounge and took a sip. The Arnold Palmer really did taste good, Tammy was right about that. "Let me handle the farmer. You've done so much." She could only imagine how her pushy neighbor would butt heads with that stubborn farmer. Tammy would bungle it up for certain. Better for her to deal with Ezra.

"Well, you let me know if you need a hand with him. Meanwhile, I'm going to the town board meeting tonight to make sure somebody mows these weed-infested fields. Oh!" Tammy kicked her feet back and forth and waved her hands. "I forgot to tell you! We've been invited to a celebration dinner Friday night. Apparently the chicken barbeque committee goes out to dinner to celebrate a job well done every year. Arlyce called me this morning and she asked me to invite you, too. Five o'clock Friday night at the Pine Tree Supper Club."

Kelly was startled and pleased by the invitation. It had been a lonely month. She could count on her fingers the people she'd interacted with outside of the barbeque and that included Ezra.

Mona was scrounging around in her purse for a pen when Gene called the council meeting to order, silencing the small crowd that had gathered in the town hall that evening. She knew why Tammy was there but supposed the rest had shown up on account of the No Wake business. A few yard signs had popped up around town expressing both views on the matter—professionally printed signs that read "Safety First—No Wake" and hand-painted boards that read "All speeds welcome" and "No Wake = No Bassville Business." The issue promised to be as contentious as she'd expected.

They started with the Pledge of Allegiance, moved on to approving last month's minutes and a couple of contracts. After a zoning question and committee reports, it was time for Tammy.

"We've had no response from Nelson Land Trust on the public notice," Loyal said. He tapped his pen on his copy of the notice and nodded to Tammy. "Our next move is to hire out the job. We can contract with Alois Schmidt at the cost of seven dollars an hour to mow the property and bill Nelson Land Trust."

"When will he do it?" Tammy blurted out.

Loyal looked over at Mona and Gene, then turned to Dale and Otto. "Can we get them there this week?"

"Don't see why not," Otto said. "He's not cutting hay for a few weeks. Ought to be able to get it done by Thursday latest."

"Thank you," Tammy said, leaning back with relief and satisfaction. "Do we have to go through this process every time or are we once-and-done now?"

"I suppose we can bill the trust for maintaining the property from here on out since we've given them the opportunity to mow it," Gene said. "But I bet they take over once they get the first bill in the mail. They'd be better off hiring someone themselves."

"Whatever they do, as long as those weeds get under control,"

Tammy said.

"Motion to contract mowing to Alois Schmidt over at Traysons Acres?" Loyal asked.

"I move," Mona said.

"Second," Otto said.

"All in favor?" The meeting continued in monotone until the last order of business.

Jay Hodge confidently walked to the front of the room, passing out glossy brochures filled with graphs and charts. The man spared no expense on making his case, Mona thought. She opened the brochure and skimmed over the bullet points. Environmental hazards, safety, pollution, noise, shoreline erosion, he covered all of the possible arguments. He started making his case, sounding like a TV lawyer from *L.A. Law* with his inflection and stories about generations of people coming to Bassville, wanting to enjoy the river and do so in peace. Did the others recognize him as the former owner of a cigarette boat with twin Mercury Marine engines? He used to race down the river with his wife, a completely obnoxious couple in her view.

She remembered the couple and their boat. At the time there were only four of them on the river, usually traveling in what she and Arlyce called the "Baja Regatta." Fast and loud, they'd open up the throttle, going 50 mph through the wide stretch by Bassville. The first time she'd seen them, she'd been impressed at their speed. It was breathtaking to watch the long, sleek machines skim the surface and disappear around the bend, the roar of their engines echoing down the river long after they'd left it. But only the first time. Since then, she'd seen them hog dock space, crowding out smaller pontoons and speed boats. And she'd seen Jay Hodge act like a Grade-A asshole.

Tanned and accessorized with gold chains around his neck and heavy rings, the middle-aged man would sit on the deck at the Pub with his wife and friends. They'd order ridiculous things that took forever to prepare—special-order cocktails that always required the blender. He'd impatiently complain about how slow their service was, comparing their experience to restaurants in Milwaukee. Well, Mona would think, then stay there and don't come here. They'd tip pretty well, but Mona always got the impression that the tip was more to impress their friends, not really an act of generosity. Steve always fawned over these boaters, probably thinking they'd return again and again with others, but it was only the four couples, each in their own boat. They never rode together, which Mona thought odd. Why have such a huge boat and ride with only one other person? To show off, she figured. They weren't unlike those couples who cruised around in their Corvettes.

A few years ago, the Hodges bought a cottage down the river from Bassville near Root Bend, a spot where the river turned hard and was marked by several old maples half-uprooted, their massive underground tendrils on display beside the shore. The Hodges traded in their huge boat for a pontoon boat and now frequented the sandbars with a half dozen grandchildren. The couple had gone from fast and loud to slow and quiet, and evidently expected everyone else to fall in line as it suited them. They were, in Mona's view, the definition of arrogance.

Jay started talking, slow and with dramatic flair, reaching out his hands to gesture key points. He extolled the beauty and peace of the river, unfortunately disrupted by speedboats and the huge, destructive wake kicked up by inconsiderate boaters. He passed the blame to fishermen in their haste to compete in tournaments, young people who only wanted to feel the wind in their hair, kids who didn't appreciate the consequence of their actions. Otto's story was referenced with great detail. Jay carried on about shoreline erosion and the way docks suffered damage. Mona crossed her arms and narrowed her eyes at him. Did he recognize her as his bartender from years ago? Did he really think nobody remembered how he used to behave exactly the way he criticized others of acting now?

When he finished, the board members sat silently for a moment, digesting his performance. Finally, Loyal thanked Jay for sharing and opened the floor for further comment. Naturally Otto inserted his views, which were predictably pro-slow, as Mona coined it in her head. Maw spoke up on behalf of keeping things as they were, concerned about the toll reduced traffic would take on business owners. Gene agreed with him—at least as far as personal freedom was concerned. Fewer laws and rules were always better in a farmer's view.

Mona listened to all of these ideas and jotted a few notes so she could keep the main points straight. She understood both sides, the curse and blessing she possessed. Life would be much simpler if she could take one side or the other as quickly as others did. But that's what her dad said made her a good member of the council, her willingness to take in all the information and make a decision based on considering all of the facts. Mona was never impulsive.

When everyone had said their piece, Loyal suggested they table the conversation until the next meeting since it was almost nine o'clock. "Procedurally, we'd have to complete an application, post a public notice, have a hearing and conduct an investigation of the site. This'll take a while, so I suggest everyone sit tight while we work out a timeline. Table for next meeting? Can I have a motion?"

Mona moved, Dale seconded and then Mona moved to adjourn.

Fifteen minutes later the lights were out, the door was locked and Mona stood talking with her father in the parking lot. "I half-expected you to suggest the town vote on the wake law," Loyal teased her.

Mona grinned. Her first board meeting had been humiliating;

she'd suggested the town vote on whether to allow the Traysons to rezone their property from agricultural to residential and commercial. She'd learned pretty quickly that part of being on the board meant making the tough calls and expecting people to end up angry—at least for a little while—if things didn't go their way. "Sounds like there's already a process for doing this and it doesn't involve a town-wide referendum."

"And knowing how you operate, I imagine you haven't got the foggiest idea about which way you'll vote yet."

Mona laughed. "You know me, Dad. I have to figure all the angles first."

"That's my girl. You've come a long way."

Mona felt the glow of pride when her dad complemented her. It wasn't Loyal's style to gush and his praise was rare. "Thanks."

"I saw you did pretty well selling berries last week," Loyal remarked.

"It was Scotty's idea. I've been trying to work out how I might grow some at the farm."

"Invasive as hell, just so you know. You start a berry patch and they'll end up all over the place. What happens is the birds eat them, then shit out the seeds and you get volunteer canes everywhere."

"Even where we till? Seems like that would keep things in check," Mona said.

"Do your research, that's all I'll tell you. But if I were you, I'd just stick to picking where you find them now. Then you don't have to fuss with them. "

"I know, but I like having control. Even though it is nice getting away for a weekly hike in the woods." Mona felt excited at the prospect of planting her own, however. Adding fruit would make her business special, give more variety and draw more customers. But she'd have to keep an eye on how much work it would involve. "That Jay Hodge is an ass," she said suddenly.

Loyal's expression didn't change but he gave a slight nod. "I agree, but why do you think so?"

Mona told her dad about how she knew him from her bartending days. "It's so hypocritical, wanting to barrel down the river in a big boat one day, but as soon as you want things quiet and slow then all the rules should change—and just for you, of course."

"But that's most people," Loyal said reasonably. "Everybody looks out for themselves first."

"You don't. Mom doesn't." Mona said. "All right, Maw does."

"Maw." Loyal chuckled. "He's a breed of his own."

"Gonna be a rap star from what I heard from Jenny."

"A rap star?"

"It's a music style. The words rhyme a lot and they're spoken more than sung. Kind of a rock beat, but a little faster."

"Never heard of it." Loyal shrugged and reached for his truck's door handle.

Mona knew her father wouldn't care so she quit trying to explain. "I'll see you tomorrow. Good night, Dad." She climbed on her bike and waved before pedaling home.

TWENTY-TWO

Rᴇx ʟᴀʏ ᴏɴ ʜɪꜱ side next to Otto's feet, his tail thumping the floor and his eyes half-closed with pleasure. He moaned while Otto kneaded the muscles in his neck and patted his back. "Good boy," Otto told him. They'd spent the evening indoors where Otto worked on tightening a few loose kitchen cabinet hinges and rewiring a box fan. Rex had supervised the projects, following Otto from the basement workshop to the kitchen and back down the stairs several times. Now they sat contentedly after eating a snack of crackers with slices of cheese provided by Otto's wife, who had just left the back porch to answer the phone. Otto nursed his can of Old Style while listening to the Brewers game on the radio. A perfect summer night.

"Otto? Phone."

He squinted up at her in confusion. "What time is it?"

"Nine o'clock."

"Pretty late for somebody to call," he groused and got up to answer it.

"Otto, Jay Hodge here. How's everything with you tonight?"

"Fine," Otto said, an edge of suspicion hardening his voice.

"Beautiful out, isn't it? The grandkids are spending the night and we just came inside from catching fireflies. You ever do that as a kid?"

"I suppose so."

"Fun to watch them do those things. You have kids, Otto?"

"Two girls, both grown."

"Grandkids?"

"Not yet."

"Let me tell you, they're a joy. Make everything you go through as a parent worth the hassle."

Otto waited for Jay to get to the point. He knew it wasn't a social phone call. He heard the ballgame announcer's voice rise with excitement and he bit back his irritation at having his peace and quiet interrupted.

"Our spot on the local news really got the conversation rolling for the No Wake movement. A few of us got an idea to take things up a notch by demonstrating just how crazy things can get out there on the water. Any chance you plan to go fishing Saturday?"

"Yes," Otto said. He strained to hear if the Brewers had scored.

"Can I persuade you to take an hour or so and help me out—you can stay on your boat. In fact, you can keep fishing."

"How's that?" Otto asked.

"Well, we want to film how just a few boats can create congestion in some of the narrow channels can handle at any given time. Sure, the buoys mark them so people know where to go, but there's no limit on speed. It's up to the drivers to decide, and that doesn't make much sense."

"Go on."

"Can you drop anchor and fish near the buoy just west of the stretch past Tamarack Bayou at about eleven? Just fish in that channel for an hour?"

"That's crazy!" Otto blurted out. "The channel will be packed that time of day. Why the hell would I want to fish there?"

"Exactly. You'd help demonstrate how unreasonable the traffic has become. Think of it this way: why should heavy traffic prevent you from fishing wherever you damn well want? It's as much your right as it is anyone else's."

Jay's words needled Otto. He had a point. It was his right to fish in the channel if he wanted. Or anywhere else for that matter. Why was he letting other people infringe on his right to fish?

"There's a little something called international maritime law. One of the rules is that nobody can own waterways. That means no matter who owns the shoreline, everyone gets equal access to bodies of water. Essentially, you can fish anyplace you want to."

"I don't know how good it will be to fish at eleven, though. Boaters will scare all the fish away. And it's pretty hot by then. Fish don't bite when it's hot."

"Catching fish isn't the point of this exercise. All I need is you to drop your anchor there for one hour," Jay said. "Tell you what, I'll buy your gas. I just need you to stay in that spot for an hour. A few friends and I will be nearby filming how busy the traffic gets and if we're lucky some kid on a jet ski will even blow through there and we'll have visual proof of how dangerous the high speeds are."

"Just an hour?"

"Maybe less if we can get a good shot of the traffic. Might only take twenty minutes."

"And I get a full tank of gas?"

"Yes, sir. Next trip to the marina, you put it on my tab. I'll let them know."

"What if it's quiet?"

"A deal's a deal, Otto. One hour of fishing at eleven near the channel and you get a tank of gas."

"I think you're nuts, but I'm in." Otto calculated the payment in both dollars and time.

"We'll see you out there Saturday."

Otto hung up and rejoined his wife and dog on the porch.

"Who was that?" she asked.

"Just some No Wake business. All taken care of." He settled back in his chair and reached down towards Rex. "What did I miss?"

"Moliter just hit a home run. We're up three-zip."

"Feels good to win," Otto remarked as he took a sip of beer.

TWENTY-THREE

Wednesday morning peg shuffled through the paperwork sitting by the cash register at the bait shop. Dave LaMay would arrive after lunchtime and she was covering for Maw while he took the crew fishing—about the only activity he could do outdoors since he broke his leg Monday afternoon. She hoped Dave's new manager was as decent as Will had been. Over the years Peg had developed a tolerance for the hard-partying Chicago DJ, but she'd developed a fondness for Will. She'd been both heartbroken and happy when he announced he was taking a new job at a public relations company after marrying Judi. She'd miss the polite, easygoing guy, but he'd be back to visit his new mother-in-law in Bassville.

Her fingers were crossed that Dave's new guy was as good. It didn't take much to steer Maw or Dave off the rails, and they needed a steady person at the wheel.

"Maw? Are there more spinner baits anywhere?" she asked as she picked through a display of lures near the empty rack. "It looks like you need a new box of cinnamon Trident gum by the register, too."

"Coming!" Maw's muffled voice floated down the hall from the former storage rooms. After accepting that people were not interested in touring a fake minnow lab, Maw had agreed to tear down the façade and repurpose the empty rooms.

"But not all for storage," Peg had argued. "Keeping rooms full of inventory is a waste of money. You have to leave it all on the floor." Her husband had a terrible tendency to hoard. He'd sniff a deal and buy more than he could sell, his head full of inflated sales figures and discounts from buying in bulk. Peg was more pragmatic. It wasn't a bargain if you spent money on stock that collected dust. And if you couldn't sell stock, that was money down the drain, no two ways about it. It took a lot of badgering, but Peg ultimately convinced him to convert the larger of the two rooms into office space and lease it out.

"We've got a parking lot, all you gotta do is make a separate entrance. That's the opposite side of the building from the minnow tanks, and it faces the road, so it could work for somebody."

Bit by bit Maw was dismantling the "minnow breeding lab" and building shelving in its place. Peg had also insisted on that. "Ridiculous to keep boxes of things all over the floor, you bury half your stuff and can't find it when you do need it. The room's empty anyway, might as well organize it."

The kids had (for a small price) moved all the boxes of T-shirts and can coolers, rods and lures to the future office space and would move it back when the shelving was finished. Peg had talked to Scotty about installing an additional exterior door and a couple more electrical outlets, but they'd recover the cost in two months' rent. After that, all profit.

Maw had earned his play time with Dave, but Peg wasn't stupid.

Somehow or another Maw's getting together with Dave LaMay always ended up being expensive. She didn't know the details, but she had a hunch that the rap video would cost a lot, too. Maw's schemes never panned out.

That wasn't completely true. They had done better than expected with the minnows, and they sold cases of the bizarre Bikini Fishing Team calendars. But setting aside the overhead of the minnow lab, the weekends in Chicago promoting the store, and the mail-order bait fiasco, they probably only broke even.

Maw emerged from the back storage area with a crutch under his left arm and a couple of boxes tucked beneath his right arm. "Here's your spinners and your gum." He dropped the boxes on the counter and smacked his wife on the cheek with his lips. "Dave's staying at the Hotel with his crew. You joining us later for dinner at the Pub?"

"I should—if only to keep an eye on your wallet."

"No faith in me, woman! After all these years." Maw shook his head sadly. "Where's your fidelity?"

"What are you wearing?" Peg asked and wrapped her fingers in the long gold chain around his neck. "You look ridiculous." She tweaked his beard.

He adjusted his baseball cap so the bill was sideways and struck his gangster pose—arms crossed with his hands tucked under his armpits. "I look tough. Maw Cooper, rap god."

"Please." She laughed and pulled the bill of his cap forward again. "Don't be an idiot."

"Peg! I'm affronted!"

"Well, now you are," she nodded to his adjusted baseball cap.

"Want to hear my latest song?" He reached for the notebook beside the cash register.

"Save it for later. I've got a load of wash to hang out and we need to eat lunch before you take off. How does tuna salad sound?"

"Healthy."

She patted his round stomach affectionately. "Never say I don't care about you, sweetie."

On her way back to the house she could hear Maw chanting his latest rhyme. *I'm a man with moxie, the ladies call me foxy, my lyrics stick like they're made of epoxy.* She and Dave both had their work cut out for them this weekend.

Dave LaMay oozed out of his yellow Corvette convertible and smoothed his receding hairline with his left hand. The woman at the hair salon told him the widow's peak was sexy, Bruce Willis had one, but he'd grown self-conscious of it. His mirrored sunglasses reflected the gravel parking lot. Things had changed since his first visit to Bassville six years ago. Gone were the kids' toys scattered all over the yard and driveway. But the rusted Buick, the motorboat and trailer for sale (was it the same one or a different one?) and the marquee sign advertising Maw's Bait and Tackle: Home of the Belligerent Minnow! never seemed to change. He nearly tripped over a bicycle blocking the path to the shop door. Dave paused to wipe the dirt off his new white leather Air Jordans. Then he pushed open the screen door and yelled for Maw.

The metallic click of Maw's crutch accompanied the thud of his foot hitting the ground and Maw dropped the dip net he was using to scoop minnows for a customer. "Hey, hey, it's Dave LaMay!" Maw sang and lurched towards him.

"Whoa, what happened, man?" Dave took a step back and whipped off his sunglasses. "Tell me you're still down to party this weekend."

"One minute," Maw called over his shoulder to the man waiting for his bait. "I'm good to go, can do almost anything with my crutch except speak Japanese, but I couldn't do that before, either."

"What happened, man?"

"I was shooting my music video." Maw shrugged and knocked the rubber tip of his crutch gently against the plaster cast on his leg. "I was ready for the dance moves, but the dance wasn't ready for me. Took a bad turn. It's a high ankle break." It sounded better to have hurt it actually performing instead of practicing. "Delayed the shoot, but we're working around it."

"You have demo tapes, though."

"Yeah, yeah." Maw nodded and waved towards the register where a poster advertised his cassette tapes for sale. His fisherman-gangster pose in front of the graffiti-covered bridge turned out tough, he thought. And Ed Lyons had been right about developing the photos in black and white. The red lettering reading *Anglin' Gangster* really popped against it. "Sales should take off once you get it on the Chicago airwaves. And you said you can get these in some stores down there, too, right?"

"Sure," Dave said. He picked up one of the cassettes and tapped it on his palm. "Can I give it a listen?"

"Let me check this guy out first." Maw hobbled back to the tank to finish up as Dave strolled up and down the aisles of the store.

Finally Maw switched his boom box from radio to tape and hit play. The down beat filled Dave's ears and a synthesizer played a simple melody before Maw's gravelly voice rasped out a series of rhyming lines. A grin spread his lips wide over his teeth and Dave nodded along to the song. "It's great stuff, man."

"Thanks. Turns out writing songs is something I'm good at. My expansive vocabulary really helps."

"When do we roll?" Dave asked.

"Are you it? No manager? No entourage?"

"I'm a solo act this weekend." Dave flipped over the cassette and read the song titles printed on the insert. They'd work as novelty bits during the morning show, but Maw was crazy if he thought his songs had wider appeal than that. He probably heard Weird Al and imagined that act could be replicated. The trouble with oddities is that they're only popular because they're odd. Most odd things could not be successfully repeated with the same effect. Dave considered trying to explain this to Maw.

Will's departure and his failing health had forced Dave to grow up. Recently he'd gotten really sick, bad enough to end up in the hospital. During that time he'd actually started to pay attention to booking guests on his show and discovered he had a nose for music and fads on the cusp of becoming popular. His new manager didn't need to keep him on a leash as he suspected Will had done; in fact, he barely saw the guy outside of the radio station and scheduled guest appearances. Against all odds, Dave LaMay evolved into a responsible human. He'd even given up cigarettes and started eating vegetables other than French fries.

"You're not a solo act," Maw laughed. "We're a duet. Like Loggins and Messina. Slash and Axl."

"Just don't say Hall and Oates," Dave joked. "What's the plan?"

"Fish the cutout first. The panfish and crappies are biting like crazy. Then we'll head to the Pub for dinner, drinks, go from there. You check in at the Hotel already?"

"Yeah." It had been wild. Sue had greeted him like a long-lost relative. Homesick for her daughter, probably, but she'd never *hugged* him before. Or offered him the room with a private bathroom, either. Come to think of it, she'd always insisted there was no such room and he'd previously been forced to use the communal bathroom at the end of the second-floor hallway. "Sue gave me the good room."

Maw raised his eyebrows and whistled. "Holy shit."

"I know. I had to double-check I was in the right place when I saw I had my own bathroom."

206

Peg bumped the door open with her hip, her arms wrapped around a full laundry basket. "Okay, you two bozos can hit the road now. Hello, Dave. We already ate, but I can whip together a sandwich if you're hungry."

"No thanks, Peg. Do you need a hand with that?" He gestured to the basket in her arms.

Peg stopped moving to give Dave a puzzled look. "What? No, but thanks." She waved them both towards the door. "I'll see you later. Six-thirty, right?"

"Six-thirty." Maw kissed her cheek, flung a life jacket towards Dave and crutched his way behind him towards the parking lot. "Okay if you drive us to the dock? I had the kids load up the boat earlier with everything."

"Sure thing, brother."

Peg watched them through the window and marveled at Dave's transformation from self-absorbed creep to actual *human. Did he just offer to help her with laundry?* She must have misunderstood.

The summer day grew dim as the sun fell behind the tree line. Dave cast his line out into the water and took a deep breath. How had he not appreciated the beauty of the river before? He slowly reeled in his line, feeling the drag of his bait through the water. They'd had to adjust the length of the hooks right away, a log kept snagging them, then they caught bluegills and white crappies. Surprised and pleased by his sudden interest this trip, Maw taught him how to tie a slip bobber and promised to teach him how to fillet the fish once they got to shore.

"Nothing to it, but it's better to clean them by the river, then you can throw the carcasses in the water. The gulls love 'em. Of course, lots of people like the fish guts for their gardens. They're great fertilizer, especially for tomatoes."

"Wouldn't that smell disgusting—rotten fish carcasses in your yard?" Dave asked.

"What? No, you dig a hole and put them *in* the ground."

"Can we have fish tonight?"

"Instead of burgers?" Maw asked. "Sure, if you want to. We can go to the Pub later for drinks."

"I do," Dave said. "Let's cook them ourselves."

"Really?" Maw cracked open another beer and tossed his empty can into the cooler before shutting the lid. "You want to fry them or what?"

"Whatever you suggest," Dave told him. He pulled up his empty hook and positioned his thumb on the release to cast again. Dragonflies hovered overhead before swooping to feed on small bugs. The drone of a motor further down the river momentarily drowned out the sound of crickets and birds before fading. "How far down the river can you go by boat?"

"Geez, pretty far I guess."

"How long is it? In miles," Dave said.

"'Bout two hundred from one end to the other." Maw scratched at his jaw and squinted. "It starts way up north off the Flambeau River, and curves back and forth across six counties until it spills into Lake Winnebago."

"You ever travel the whole thing? Can you?"

Maw realized that even though it felt like he was repeating himself in this conversation, he wasn't. Five years ago, he'd told *Will* all about the river while Dave had napped in the bow of the boat, hungover and uninterested. The Bikini Fishing Team was the only thing on the river that really perked his interest, until today. "I've boated all the way from Loon Lake to Lake Winnebago, and I remember fishing a stretch of the Wissipaw up north one summer when I was a kid. But no, I've never gone the whole distance."

Dave gazed across the water and said softly, "It would be cool." He looked over at Maw, "If I was young, I'd do it. In a canoe. Camp along the way. How long do you suppose it would take?"

"Probably a week or two, maybe a little more. It's pretty narrow, a lot of rapids in the northern stretch." Maw watched Dave's expression grow wistful. The man was actually considering it.

"How dangerous do you think it is?"

"No worse than driving in rush hour traffic." Maw started laughing at the memory of his first experience on Chicago's toll ways and the panic attack that landed him in a hospital.

Dave smirked. "Well, that almost killed you the first time you tried it."

"Hell, I was never so scared in my whole life and I've been in some scrapes. If you hang with the Dohills long enough, your life flashes before your eyes pretty regularly."

"When you showed up at the radio station wearing only a hospital gown," Dave slapped his hand on the side of the boat and bent double, laughing harder. "I can't remember—did you even have shoes on?"

"You brought me to Marshall Fields," Maw said. "You made me ride up the damn escalator with my ass hanging out the back of that gown."

"Dude, it was so funny. There were clothes at the station—you could've worn a custodian jumpsuit. We were fucking with you so hard."

"And I fell for it. You better hope I don't pay you back someday. Probably shouldn't ask me to outfit you for your next fishing trip. I might put you in a leaky rowboat and leave you in the river twenty miles upstream."

"Well, now I know better. I'd ask Peg to set me up."

"Shit!" Maw held up his wrist and pointed to his watch. "She's expecting us for dinner. If we want her to fry this fish for us, we gotta haul!"

Steve was cracking wise behind the bar later that evening when Maw, Peg and Dave rolled in and sat down beside the locals. "Hey, Dave!" Steve reached out to shake the DJ's hand. "I didn't know you were coming to town."

"Taking a little fishing vacation. Catch the next round on me."

"Martini?" Steve lifted the shaker from its spot by the sink.

Dave held up a hand and shook his head. "I'm sticking to cranberry juice. On a health kick," he explained. He had learned that most people accepted his not drinking if he used health as an excuse. If he told them he was an alcoholic, people tried to talk him into drinking again. "Can you have a beer then?" they'd ask, as if having a drinking problem wasn't actually a problem. Saying he was on a health kick kept people off his back without any further questions. Weirdest thing.

"Beer for me," Maw said. "Peg?"

"Beer."

"What's new in town?" Dave asked Steve.

The bar owner flipped the bottle in his hand into the trash barrel and thought for a moment. "Some new people moved in since you were last around. Couple new houses built. You remember Jake Paulick? Tall blonde guy, used to date Mona, my old bartender?"

"Yeah."

"He's in Atlanta, Georgia, working on building stadiums or something for the 1996 Summer Olympics. That's a long time off, but I suppose it takes eight years to get everything ready."

"That's pretty cool. So, your old bartender's single?" He hadn't quit *all* of his bad habits.

210

Steve grinned. "Married to her farm."

Dave cocked an eyebrow. He remembered Mona. Pretty, but not a knockout. "Farm?"

"Dirty Girl Veggies, she's a vegetable farmer. I designed her logo," Maw said. "Should get you one of her T-shirts, they're funny."

"How do you like your new neighbors?" Dave asked Maw.

"They're good," Maw said. "What?" He scowled at Peg.

"The one woman, Tammy, she's pretty bossy. But the other one seems okay."

Maw leaned in conspiratorially and said in a low voice, "We only like new people if they don't ask any questions and do exactly as we say."

"Ah." Dave nodded.

By ten, Dave was yawning. Another side effect of sobriety: he got bored and tired faster. It turned out that drunk people were really irritating. And loud. Especially after midnight. He edged out the back door of the Pub to stand on the dock away from the noise. Maw was getting sloppy, Peg had holed up in a corner with some other women, and Dave found himself in the odd position of wanting to head to bed. Alone. To sleep. He rubbed his hands over his face and sighed. In Chicago there was live music at the good clubs. And women to dance with. The nightlife in Bassville was pretty lame by comparison.

Still, fishing was fun and the meal they'd eaten was delicious. He'd never had pan-fried fish before. Peg had served them green beans from their garden, early sweet corn and some dinner rolls popped out of a cardboard tube she'd gotten from the fridge. He hoped they'd have the same thing tomorrow for dinner.

Dave glanced behind at the scene playing out on the other side of the windows. Groups of people laughed, shot pool, drank. He strolled up the dock and climbed over the fence to the road to avoid walking back through the bar. The street was quiet except for the jukebox music floating through the open windows at Grumpy's. He passed dark shop windows and reached the Hotel. Sue was behind the bar ignoring her few customers by reading a paperback. Dave waved at her and headed to his room. The good room, he reminded himself. Maybe he'd enjoy a long soak in the tub before going to sleep.

"Where the hell did Dave go?" Jenny shrieked at Maw over the noise at the Pub. Since they'd arrived a couple hours ago Steve had cranked up the volume and now everyone had to yell to be heard over the jukebox.

Maw glanced around and shrugged. "He's staying at the Hotel. Maybe he didn't feel good and left."

"He used to be fun," Jenny pouted.

Maw agreed with her. Not that fishing hadn't been good, and dinner was nice, but he was totally opposite from other visits. Before he'd always endured the fishing and eating, excelled at the drinking and partying end of things. "Where's Beau?"

"Who gives a shit?" Jenny narrowed her eyes.

"Are you two off again?"

"I'm so done with that son of a bitch."

Some things, Maw thought, never changed. He patted Jenny's shoulder and looked past her at Spade. "Are you ready to deal me in yet?"

Spade squared up the deck of cards and tapped the small pile of bills in front of him. "Money up, my friend."

"Deal me in, too," Jenny said and dug in her purse.

Maw shook his head at Spade, eyes wide.

"Easy money," Spade told him and gestured to Jenny to take a seat. "You kids are in luck. Scotty's leaving his paycheck on the table tonight."

Scotty snorted. "When I'm out, I'm out. And I'm not like Spade here, going up to ask Steve for a loan."

"It was only for fifty dollars," Spade argued.

"That's the reason you've got a problem, Spade." Scotty took the cards dealt to him and discarded one on the table. "When you can't quit, it's a problem."

"Well, then I got a lot of problems."

"We all do, buddy," Maw said and grinned. "But can you call drinking and smoking and gambling problems? They're fun!"

"Men are a problem," Jenny grumbled.

"Hey, feel free to leave," Maw told her.

Jenny shook her head. "I'm betting on cards, not love."

"Someday you'll meet someone who'll deserve your love," Scotty said to Jenny. "Beau's one of my best friends, but I wouldn't want him for my boyfriend."

"I hope not!" Spade said. "That would be sick."

"You know what I mean," Scotty reached across the table and slid a new card off the deck. "He's a great guy, but no offense, Jenny, he's just not interested in settling down. Definitely not the marrying type."

"Says another confirmed bachelor," Dob teased. "You're one to talk."

"Oh, I'd be a better boyfriend than Beau." Scotty's cheeks flushed. "Just have to find the right woman."

"Or maybe," Jenny leaned in close to Scotty and examined his face, "the right woman hasn't found you."

"Sure," Scotty said. "Look, we playing cards here or playing *Love Connection*?"

"Hey, I'm not the one bringing up love and marriage," Dob pointed out. "Hell, I already got those problems, right?"

"Did you hear that?" Maw yelled to Dob's wife, who sat with Peg at a table by the window. "He just called you a problem."

"Baby, you have no idea what a problem I can be," she called over to Dob and raised her glass to him.

"She's a problem all right," Dob muttered. "All women are."

"I'm right here, Dob," Jenny said through gritted teeth.

"So you are, my dear. One of the best women. Beau just can't see it because he's blind and stupid. Okay, I'm in for ten," Dob said.

"Ten," Spade said.

"Yep."

"Yep."

"I'm in."

The Pub's loyal, local customers continued to swap gossip, money and cards until Steve turned off the jukebox at midnight and turned up the lights. "Last call!"

The thinning crowd groaned and a few people headed for the door. Peg jangled the car keys at Maw. "If you want a ride, you better come now."

Dob pushed his stool back and gathered his winnings into his pocket. "Until next time."

"I can't afford to hang out with you people," Scotty said. "You okay to drive, Jenny?" Jenny slid off her stool and took a couple stumbling steps. Scotty sighed and gave Spade a pleading look.

"She's all yours. I gotta work in the morning."

Scotty sighed and grabbed Jenny's arm. "Come on."

"Let's go to the Luau Lounge," Jenny said.

"No way," Scotty led her towards his truck and boosted her into the seat. He had no interest in getting involved in any argument between her and Beau. And if he had to choose, he'd always pick Beau over Jenny. Bros before hoes, right? By the time he'd turned on to the highway, Jenny's eyes were closed and her head lolled against the window. Really, he never had to choose between them because eventually one of them would pass out and he'd just leave them to sleep it off until the next day anyway.

TWENTY-FOUR

THE NEXT MORNING DAVE rolled over and stretched. He hadn't slept this late in ages, but the peace and quiet of the Hotel combined with the day out on the water kept him down for the count. Eleven hours. Damn.

After enjoying a long shower in his private bathroom, he shaved and dressed. Then he grabbed his keys and wallet and headed for the restaurant downstairs. He'd never traveled alone like this before and it was nice. He didn't have to answer to anybody, he didn't have to worry about anybody. And going to bed sober usually meant he went to bed alone these days, which was nice, too. No more awkward conversations while trying to get rid of some woman the next morning. No more lies, fake phone numbers for staying in touch, room service breakfasts purchased out of guilt. He missed the sex a little, but not as much as he'd expected.

Sue met him in the dining room with a pot of coffee. "Good

morning, sunshine."

"Good morning." He pulled up to a table and turned the coffee mug right side up on the paper placemat.

She poured him a cup while examining him closely. "Your face has some color. Your eyes aren't bloodshot. What's going on? Where's the real Dave LaMay?"

"I'll have the number three, scrambled, sausage, toast." Dave snapped the menu closed and handed it to her. "And orange juice, please."

Sue crossed her arms and frowned. Dave smiled. She pushed her glasses up her nose and took the menu. "It's called clean living, Sue. You should try it. It's great."

After she disappeared through the swinging doors to the kitchen, Dave pulled out his pill bottles and portioned out his morning dose before jamming the bottles back into his pocket. When Sue returned with his juice, he cheerfully thanked her and snuck the pills down his throat after she turned her back. Then he grabbed the abandoned newspaper on the table next to his and started scanning the sports scores. He'd finished the business section when his breakfast arrived and neatly refolded and replaced the paper before digging in.

"What gives?" Sue slid into the chair across from him before pouring herself a cup of coffee. "Don't tell me Will leaving you made you become a better man, because he just married my daughter. If that's the case, her life's about to spiral out of control. So either you got religion or you're in love, but you didn't say grace before you started eating and you're here alone, so what's really going on? Why are you acting ... *normal*?"

Dave swallowed a forkful of eggs and looked up at the older woman. Her expression was as plain and frank as the rest of her appearance: no makeup, no hair dye, no mask for Sue. She was as authentic as they came. "Can you keep a secret?"

217

She pointedly glanced around the nearly empty dining room. "What do you think?"

"No one knows this except for my doctor, and maybe a nurse or two. I don't even know why I'm telling you. But we've grown close over the years."

Sue snorted and shook her head.

"I mean it. From the first day I walked into your bar and you refused to take shit from me, I kind of looked at you like a mean grandma. A loving one, but mean."

"Grandma? You *are* a charmer." She smirked. "I bet you say that to all the women."

"Only the good ones. Seriously, Sue. You and Peg refused to roll over when I acted like an asshole, which usually never happens. The only other woman who does that is my accountant at the station, but I don't think she's completely human."

"You've grown on me, too, Dave." Sue suddenly reached across and grabbed his hand.

He took a deep breath and looked her in the eye. "A month ago, I tested positive for HIV."

Sue didn't flinch. She tightened her grip on Dave's hand.

"I don't feel ready to talk about it and I don't really have anyone to talk to. The upshot is I had two choices: clean up my act and live or keep partying hard and die sooner."

"So you cleaned up your act."

"Yeah."

"Good for you."

"It's been weird. I've had to change everything, but it's not as awful as you'd expect."

"What's the doctor telling you?"

"So far, so good. Keep taking my meds, don't get sick and I'll be around for a long time." Dave inhaled again, his breath shaky, and he wiped his eyes. "Shit. I don't know why I get so emotional over this."

"It's scary, that's why." Sue gave his hand a squeeze and they sat quietly for a long time after Dave finished his breakfast. When he headed out to find Maw, Sue hugged him again, her arms wrapped tight around his arms and back. It felt good being hugged that way, not a sexy hug but a supportive embrace that gave him a sense of strength.

Getting into his car to drive to Maw's, Dave remembered the demo tape and opened the cassette case. Punching it into the console, he turned up the volume and started his car. Seconds into the first song Dave was cringing. He pressed fast-forward and discovered the next song was just as terrible. So was the next, then the next. His chuckling evolved into a belly laugh, his chest heaving. "My God, this is the worst!"

Maw's gravelly voice recited his rhymed lyrics in a redundant sing-song voice. The vocals had no punch, no expression. It sounded like drunk karaoke singing, flat and off-key in a few parts. But the lyrics were definitely inventive. Dave dialed down the sound and considered his next move. Maw would expect him to play this on the radio, but Maw didn't live in Chicago, so he wouldn't know how much airtime his songs would get, which was a good thing. All he had to do, Dave decided, was mix them in with other songs and just play a few bits. He'd have the guys down at the station fix Maw's recordings with some fades and sync in some fresh beats to cover up the crap tempo.

He pulled into the bait shop parking lot and remembered something else. Maw's music video. Dave groaned. Colossal flop ahead, he knew it.

"Hey, hey! Dave LaMay!" Maw hobbled around the counter and thumped Dave on the shoulder. "Where did you disappear to last night?"

"Aw, man, didn't you see me leave? With the hot little filly in the tight jeans? No? We rolled back to my room and, well, a gentleman never tells, does he?" Dave winked.

"No, plus the kid's here, so save the details for later." Maw grinned at his youngest, who was reading a comic book by the register. "You got this under control, right buddy?"

"Yep," he muttered. The boy reached for his can of soda without taking his eyes off the page.

"I only leave the store in the hands of trained professionals," Maw joked. "You ready to hit the river?"

"Absolutely."

"Don't know if I mentioned, but a bunch of us are heading out for dinner tonight. Kind of a celebration after the chicken barbeque last weekend. You're welcome to join us if you'd like. We're going to Pine Tree—fabulous steaks. Not sure if I ever took you there before."

"Thanks, man. Let me see how I feel after fishing all day."

"Sure." Maw propped the door open with the end of his crutch and gestured for Dave to lead the way. "Did you have a chance to listen to my tape?"

Dave felt glad he left his sunglasses in place so Maw couldn't see his expression. "Man, you laid down some cool tracks," he lied smoothly. "I never heard anything like it before."

"I did, didn't I? Did you like that third song, *Minnow Report*? You catch the tribute to Run DMC?"

Dave held up his hand to high five Maw. "Killer."

"Think it'll sell? How will it work, distribution-wise? Will you play it and then other radio stations pick it up or do you have some pull with other DJs? I have no idea how this process works."

"Music is like fire," Dave said. It was a vague enough metaphor that Maw could interpret it however he chose. He'd heard Tom Petty say that line in an interview and was impressed how the guy could say so little yet people took his words to mean so much. He appropriated that particular line frequently.

"Yeah," Maw nodded. "I get it. The good music will become a conflagration. Burn up the charts."

"Exactly."

"Well, I should keep fishing while I have the time then. Before my music career takes over and I'm touring and stuff." Maw grabbed a cooler and pulled a hat on his head. "Let's roll."

Thursday afternoon Kelly dabbed blue eye shadow onto her lids and hummed under her breath. As much as she'd initially resisted the invitation, she found herself growing excited about the evening ahead. Since they'd moved to Bassville a month ago, she'd barely left the house, mainly because there was nothing to do. Her yard was half mud, she hated bugs, which seemed to crawl and fly across every square inch of their new country life, and she didn't know anybody other than Tammy. She'd left Northport with ideas of how charming living in a small town would be. She imagined drinking lemonade with a neighbor and embracing the free time and solitude to craft, paint and create. Instead she was stranded with two kids who had at least become friendly with Tammy's son and daughter, but only one neighbor within walking distance and a town that looked more and more weather-beaten every time she drove through it. What had attracted her the first time they'd driven out here?

It had been fall when they'd decided to buy lot number sixteen in Traysons Acres. The rich colors of the leaves and fields, the heady scent of cinnamon and the snug comfort of her new wool scarf (from Eddie Bauer, a green and navy plaid) made the empty lot seem romantic and full of possibility. They broke ground the following spring and now it was July. Bassville smelled like rotting fish and manure. The humid and hot air made her skin itch. Kelly realized that "town" really consisted of bars, a couple of churches, the grocery store, two gas stations, bait shops and the river, which hummed with more activity than the roads surrounding it. The library was a room no larger than her new bedroom and most of the books were old. Other than the Ladies' Auxiliary, she had no idea what the women in Bassville actually *did*. They were, it seemed, invisible.

Northport had clubs and organizations. Tom had enthused with her how great it would be to leave that behind, free up their busy schedules and spend meaningful time with each other. Well, Tom now worked longer hours since his company's merger and the added commute meant he didn't get home until after 6:30 every night. She was stranded in a social desert with no oasis in sight. Had she imagined she'd discover a community of potters and poets—they'd drink tea and run craft fairs?

Kelly sprayed her curls into place and carefully pulled on her shirt, stretching the neck wide to avoid messing up her bangs. Maybe tonight she'd talk to a kindred spirit. Any place seemed lonely at first, she rationalized. Once she got to know people, had some phone numbers and made contacts, life would become less isolated. She selected one of her favorite necklaces, amber and teal beads triple-wrapped on a long chain. Jewelry making had been one of her favorite hobbies. Maybe she'd take it up again.

"You about ready?" her husband called up the stairs.

"Yes." She doused her wrists and neck with Exclamation and slid her feet into sandals. At the bottom of the stairs she paused to speak to her sons, who were slouched deep in the couch cushions on either side of a huge bowl of popcorn. "Nobody in, nobody out. We'll be at Pine Tree. It's a restaurant. I left the number on the kitchen counter if you need anything. Be good, okay?" She leaned in to kiss their foreheads. Their eyes barely flickered from the screen where Mel Gibson stood in a warehouse aiming a gun at bad guys.

"Okay?" she asked in a louder voice.

"Mnh-hmm," came the mumbled reply.

"Let's head, honey. They'll be fine." Tom reached for her elbow.

Kelly let him guide her to the garage and into the car. She leaned back and exhaled. *Let it be fun*, she prayed silently.

Pine Tree was a log-cabin style supper club on the Wissipaw, halfway between Bassville and the next town to the south. Kelly's dad was a truck driver and he'd advised her years ago that the best way to find a good place to eat was to find a parking lot full of local license plates. His wisdom had proven true so far and Pine Tree looked promising by that measure. Kelly heard the sound of people talking, dishes clinking and music playing when she stepped out of the cool, air-conditioned car.

They could barely wedge through the door since people stood four and five deep around the horseshoe-shaped bar. The dining room must be full, Kelly guessed, if the crowd for tables was this big. She stretched up on her tiptoes to try and find Tammy or some other familiar face.

A hand waved and Tammy's huge smile popped up briefly before disappearing behind a man's shoulder. Kelly leaned to peer around it and saw Tammy waving at her. She'd been looking for them and that made Kelly feel better.

Tom led her back to a corner where the Parkers sat with several other couples. "We put in for a table right away, but it's going to be a while," Tammy told her in a loud voice.

The stout woman with curly hair who Kelly recognized from the barbeque nodded and added, "It's how they do things here. They keep you at the bar for a minimum of three drinks—the brandy Old-Fashioneds are excellent, by the way, get them sweet with mushrooms—then whatever they serve you to eat will taste great because you're drunk and starving. I don't recommend three drinks. They pour them pretty stiff." She held out her hand. "I'm Dottie Trayson. I don't think we've been formally introduced."

"Kelly Ogden." She grasped the woman's meaty hand and felt the strength in her squeeze. "We built on your old farm?"

Dottie nodded. "Long story," she glanced around the packed bar area. "But I think we've got time if you want to hear it."

Kelly nodded and leaned in to hear her better. She noticed Tammy give an approving look before returning to a conversation with two other women. The tall and skinny one Kelly recognized as the waitress from the Pub. The other had a softer look about her and wore her hair in a stylish blonde bob.

"I met your son at the picnic last weekend." She tried to remember his name.

"Scotty. He's our oldest. We have a daughter, too. Actually, it was because of Angie that you got to buy your property. It was my husband's family's farm, three generations. We had dairy cattle, but it started out as a pig and crop operation with his father. Anyway, six years ago our daughter was really sick, she was diagnosed with leukemia. She was only eleven at the time."

"How awful. I'm so sorry," Kelly said.

Dottie's lips tightened with a quick acceptance of her words. "She needed a bone marrow transplant, brand new procedure at the time, and the only way we could afford treatment was to sell the place. It was a real fiasco. We needed to get new zoning and it turned into a huge fight. I don't think Otto Zimm ever got over it entirely."

"Who was fighting you?" Kelly wanted to know.

"Bassville's a small town. Close. Traditional. Sure, we have tourists and fishermen, but the locals are local and that's that. Nobody's looking to buy a family farm, milk prices are too low—they were worse six years ago. But land's another story. If we sold the farm for development like we did, then it had much more value. But selling our land meant changing the town. New people would move here." Dottie gave Kelly a gentle smile. "Like you. And new people means change. There's people here who never change and they hated the idea. So when we went to the town board to ask for rezoning, people took sides. Some, like the Dohills, love it." She gestured to two barrel-chested men and their wives, jolly-looking people enjoying their drinks. "They make money building things, so more people means more business. Others like Otto want the peace and quiet to stay the same forever."

Dottie lifted her shoulders and took a sip from her drink.

"So you had to sell your land. How's your daughter? Did she … ?" Kelly trailed off, uncertain of what to say just in case.

"Angie's fine," Dottie's bigger smile revealed a dimple that matched her son's. "Her older brother, my Scotty, was the donor and the treatment was a success. She's perfect now. Going to be a junior this year and you'd never know she'd gone through all of that to look at her. Her hair grew back—curly if you can believe it, used to be stick-straight. Curls are wasted on a boy. Now life is normal. Well, as normal as you can get when everything else has changed." A small quiver entered Dottie's voice

"How did everything else change? Not your son … ?" From what Kelly had seen, he seemed healthy and pretty normal.

Dottie brushed aside this question with her hand. "Scotty needs to change. He's twenty-six years old and still sleeping in the same twin bed he's had since he was four. Good boy, but hasn't found his direction yet. I wish he would." Her eyes grew thoughtful. "No, selling the farm saved Angie, but farming was what we did. Without a farm, what are we? We haven't figured that out yet. It's not that we need money, but we sure as hell need something to do."

"Wow." Kelly realized she had no idea the lot they'd bought had come at such a price. Not just saving a girl's life, but disrupting a town and taking away this family's business—and purpose. What would it be like to have your job disappear like that? "You said some people never got over it?"

Dottie chuckled. "Never did and never will."

The tall, skinny woman nudged Dottie aside and asked Kelly what she was drinking. Her dangly earrings swung wildly from her earlobes while she leaned forward to hear Kelly's answer.

"Nothing yet."

"What do you *want*?" Her tone made Kelly feel stupid.

"Um, an Old-Fashioned."

"Brandy or whiskey?"

"Whiskey."

"Sweet or sour? Or press?"

"What's press?" Kelly asked.

"Half and half."

"Sweet."

"Olives, cherries or mushrooms?"

"Olives."

"Got it." She turned away.

"That's Arlyce Shanski, she and her husband own the Pub. You probably recognize her from there."

"Did she not want you to sell your land?" Kelly asked.

Dottie laughed again. "No, that's just Arlyce. She comes off as crabby but her heart's bigger than a double-wide trailer. She's no-

226

nonsense, but you would be, too, if you had four kids plus Steve and a business to run."

Kelly thanked Arlyce for the drink and reflected on Dottie's story while she tasted the sweet and bitter cocktail. She ate the olives, thankful for something to chew while her stomach growled. A glimpse of the dining room revealed a long wait until tables opened up. The hostile attitude of the farmer behind her had a history. This knowledge changed everything.

"Who owns the farm behind our house?" she asked Dottie.

"I'm June Butterfield." The woman with the stylish blonde bob elbowed her way into the conversation and reached out a hand with blush-colored fingernails.

"Kelly Ogden." She shook June's hand.

"Welcome to Bassville, though I'm sure you've heard that enough already. I meant to get over and introduce myself at the picnic last weekend, but it never slowed down. How do you like your new house so far?"

"It's been a transition," Kelly confessed. "We've had to adjust from living in the city."

June gave her a sympathetic smile. "Slower pace and more smells?"

"A little of both."

"Kelly was just asking about Ezra Pike," Dottie told June.

The edge of June's mouth twitched and she exchanged a look with Dottie. "Ah, yes."

"What?" Kelly glanced from one woman to the other, her curiosity growing.

"Definitely was *not* in favor of us selling our land. How much has he been harassing you?" Dottie asked Kelly.

"Well, let's just say he hasn't rolled out the welcome mat," Kelly said.

"Dish," June leaned towards her and swirled the straw in her vodka tonic. "Tell us every detail." She glanced over her shoulder at the men. "I bet nothing will surprise us."

"Ezra's a piece of work. Some might go so far as to call him a son of a bitch," Dottie said. "In all fairness, he mostly keeps to himself. But when he gets riled up, look out."

"Some of the most contentious town meetings involve the Pikes. Remember the culvert?" June asked Dottie. "When they first started cutting the ditches that man went nuts." She turned to Kelly. "The county decided to start cutting back the roadside weeds about ten years ago. It was a safety thing, to give people a better view at the intersections. So they hired Glen Barlow and he gets to Ezra's lot line and sure enough, Ezra has dragged these huge boulders right up to the side of the road. Glen can't mow because the boulders will bust up his blade, and technically the boulders are on Ezra's property so he can't do anything about it."

"They went round and round at those town meetings," Dottie chimed in. "It took months and finally the board gave up. You can still drive down the county highway—that area of tall grass right up to the shoulder? That's Ezra's farm."

"He argued that mowing back would cost him a quarter acre of field," June said. "It was incredible, all that fuss over a quarter of an acre."

"That's nothing," Dottie waved her arm and her drink sloshed a bit over the side. "His farm is almost two thousand acres. The production he claimed he'd lose was so insignificant."

"He'd cut off his nose to spite his face," June said. "Didn't care that he was the only landowner not allowing the town to mow. Didn't care about the safety—that's why the intersection by his fields is the only four-way stop in the entire county highway system. You've probably noticed every other road only has a two-way stop because you can see the traffic. But not by Ezra's land."

"Even back in high school he was an ass. He'd pick fights about the most ridiculous issues and dig in. Remember how he tried getting Miss Schmidt fired for breaking up a fight in the hall? He argued that she was interfering in his personal problems. Had his dad call the principal."

June nodded. "And remember how the principal responded? He said, 'You'd be suspended for three days for fighting if Miss Schmidt hadn't broken it up, so you best thank her.'"

Dottie laid her hand on Kelly's forearm. "So what's he done to you?"

Kelly explained to the ladies about the electric fence and then the hay cutting.

"You brought him *lemonade*?" June looked impressed. "Kill him with kindness sort of thing?"

"Something like that."

"He's awful, honey. Don't take it personal if he keeps being a jerk. It's his way," Dottie said.

"Does he have a family? There was a teenaged boy with him," Kelly said.

"Probably his nephew. Ezra's a confirmed bachelor. We have quite a few of those around here." June started ticking off names on her fingers. "Ezra, Spade, Beau, Scotty ... "

"Scotty's going to find someone. He's not a *confirmed* bachelor," Dottie argued.

"Okay, he's a late bloomer." June gave Dottie a squeeze around her shoulders. Kelly decided she liked these two women and the obvious affection they showed each other. Friendships like theirs encouraged her to think she could develop the same closeness with her new neighbors.

"I love your necklace," June said suddenly. "Isn't that a pretty color combination!"

"Thank you." Kelly pressed her hand against the beads. "Sort of a hobby of mine."

"You *made* that?" Dottie asked. "It's beautiful. Do you sell them, too?"

"I've given away a few pieces," Kelly told them.

"Well, I'd buy one from you if you're ever selling any of your work. My favorite colors are yellow and blue, by the way."

"So, Tammy's your neighbor," June said. "Next door for now, until other houses get built?"

Kelly nodded and glanced over at Tammy, who deep in conversation with a couple of women at the other end of the bar area. *She* seemed to have no trouble finding her place in town, but people like Tammy always made themselves comfortable no matter what their situation. It was an enviable trait.

"My daughter mentioned her coming to a council meeting. My husband and my daughter are both on the town council." June said this with pride.

"Oh?"

"She was pretty angry about the weeds growing up in the fields out there. Sounds like it worked out though."

"At first she thought we should mow it," Dottie said. "How crazy was that? Why would we mow land we don't own anymore?"

"She probably thought you did because of the name on the sign," June pointed out.

"I know, but she was just so huffy about it. Rubbed me the wrong way."

"My father," Kelly said, "taught me you catch more flies with honey."

"Which is why you served Ezra lemonade. Well, maybe that will work out for you." Dottie gestured to her husband that her glass was empty and he reached for his wallet.

230

"And if it doesn't, you should sic Tammy on him!" June giggled. "Okay, I'm starving. I know it's a three-drink minimum at the bar, but I can't drink at this pace on an empty stomach."

"How long for a table?" Dottie asked her husband when he handed her a full cocktail and took her empty glass from her hand.

"They're saying ten minutes." He gave Kelly a friendly nod before drifting back to the circle of men nearby. Their laughter had grown louder since the last round of drinks and Kelly noticed that Tom's face had grown flushed, a sign that he was reaching his limit. He seemed to be enjoying himself, though.

"Have you ever eaten here completely sober?" June asked Dottie.

"Can you? I've never tried."

"Kelly!" Tammy wrapped her arms around Kelly. Kelly suspected she was a hugger when she drank. "Did you leave your kids home alone, too? I never did that before we moved here, but it didn't make sense for us to call my mom and have her drive all the way out here. She'd have to spend the night. She wouldn't want to drive back in the dark. And we don't know anyone to call to babysit, plus they're at that age when they sort of don't need one anyway. I mean, twelve? That's old enough to take the babysitting safety course, so yes they're old enough to stay home for a few hours, right?"

Tammy could talk the paint off a barn, Kelly thought again. Maybe she was lonely and thirsty for human interaction or maybe Tammy was starting to grow on her. Either way, she noticed the woman didn't annoy her like she had previously. "I left ours parked in front of movies with a big bowl of popcorn," she said.

June nodded approval at this. "Totally safe to do here. Probably safe to do anywhere, but your kids will be fine."

"Besides," Dottie added, "if you bring them along, they cost an arm and a leg. Remember how much our kids used to tap us for quarters for the jukebox and the pool table? It's much cheaper to leave them behind at home. They probably have more fun parked at home, too."

Kelly finished her drink and surveyed the crowded bar. Her stomach rumbled and she was feeling tipsy from the drink. A second cocktail would have to wait until she'd eaten something besides a few olives. "How old are your children?" she asked June.

"Mona's twenty-six and Sean just turned thirty. Sean works in Connecticut as a researcher. My scientist," June added with pride. "It broke his dad's heart when he decided to leave the farm, but he really loves his work."

"But Mona's home," Dottie pointed out. "She's a farmer, just not cows. She's a veggie girl. You've seen her farm stand? Dirty Girl Veggies?"

"I have! That's your daughter?" Kelly asked June. "She had a stand at the weekend farm market in Northport, right?"

"That's her. Mona used to work for Arlyce and Steve," June pointed to the tall skinny woman who busy waving them over to the in the dining room.

"Looks like they're ready for us," Dottie said. "I recommend the prime rib or the ribeye. The fish is fine, but their steaks are fantastic."

Back at the Hotel, Dave finished his dinner and he and Sue sat together on the deck looking over the water. Music from the bar down the street mixed with the low hum of a boat heading up the river. Little waves gently slapped against the seawall below and a wisp of clouds floated past the crescent moon above. Sue sipped her whiskey and water while Dave chewed on a plastic straw.

"You sure I can't get you something to drink? Tea? Water?"

"No. I'm perfect right now." He rested his feet on the railing and tilted his head back to admire the stars. "I never learned any constellations besides the Dippers. You know any?"

Sue pointed out the few she'd learned as a child. "The north star is the last star on the Little Dipper—Polaris."

"Got it. That's the one people follow to get home, right?"

"I suppose sailors did." They sat quietly for a moment. "Do you plan to stay in Chicago? Keep up the DJ act?"

"For now. I'm close to my doctor, but I think I might hang it up in another year or two, depending on my health."

Sue cleared her throat and kept her gaze on the shimmering surface of the Wissipaw. "You're welcome to come here, Dave. I have a spare room now that Judi left and if you need someone to take care of you, you know … well, I don't know if you have family or anything but I want you to know I'm here. I know Bassville's pretty tame compared to Chicago, but I have a feeling you'd keep it lively."

"That's kind of you." Dave felt his throat grow thick with tears. He took a deep breath and smelled the pine trees and someone's cigarette smoke. "I might do that. It's good to have a place to call home."

"I'd put you to work, you know," Sue said. "You'd have to earn your keep."

Dave chuckled. "All right. What's the price of room and board?"

"How are you at doing dishes?"

"Terrible."

"Laundry?"

"Atrocious."

"What can you do?"

"Play music and talk shit."

"Fair enough. You come up here and play me some music and talk shit and I'll take care of you."

Dave reached out and grabbed hold of her callused hand. "Deal."

The couples had been seated at two long tables, men at one, women at the other. After the waitress took their orders, Arlyce stood and clanged her spoon on the side of her water glass. When everyone stopped talking, she dramatically cleared her throat before launching into a speech.

"You should all feel proud of this year's barbeque. We had a few changes," she gave Tammy a brief nod, "and managed to earn the most money ever for the fire department. As you all know, the profits from our event will go towards a new pump truck and thanks to everyone's hard work we're one-third of the way there. I want to especially thank Maw for announcing, Tammy for organizing and Dale for his generous donation of the 50-50 winnings. So, good work and if anyone has ideas for next year, you know where to reach me."

"Here here!" Dob called out and the group burst into applause.

Arlyce sat down and June gave her a quick hug, whispering in her ear, "Nice work, you're a class act, honey."

The evening grew looser after another round of drinks and soon all of the couples were loading into cars. "Let's head to Grumpy's!" someone suggested.

"Great idea," Arlyce agreed. She fell into Kelly's back seat and scooted over to make room for Dob and his wife.

"Guess I'm driving?" Kelly asked her husband. She'd only had two drinks before dinner.

"We're having fun," he said. "Yes, you are."

Back in Bassville, Kelly parked on the street outside the rundown bar. She could hear Stevie Ray Vaughan playing on the juke box and the lights glowed red behind the screen door. The place was shadowy and even the windows looked crooked, all strange angles and warped. As she followed the crowd through the door she stumbled, aware of how the torn linoleum floor sloped beneath her feet. A handful of tough-looking men dressed in black leather biker jackets sat hunched over their drinks and a large, shaggy-haired man with a bulbous nose yelled a greeting in their direction.

"I forgot about Snuffy!" Dottie said to Kelly while waving to the bartender. "He's a bachelor, too!"

"Confirmed?" Kelly asked.

"Probably not if he could help it." June said.

"Snuffy, you old son of a bitch." Dob wrapped his arm around the man and kissed his smudged cheek. "What's going on?"

A door swung open in the corner and a woman teetered across to the pool table on high heels. Her long hair flopped in her eyes and she wiped at her lips with the back of her hand. "Snuffy? I need a shot."

Snuffy gave Dob a light punch on the shoulder and winked. "Be right with ya. Star's having a rough night." He lowered his voice. "Word of warning: Butch took off again and she's on the prowl."

Kelly felt her eyes grow wider while she watched the man pick up a dishcloth and toss it to Star. "Told you you'd feel better after throwing up. Better stick to beer."

"Tequila. To kill ya." She stumbled to an empty bar stool and slapped her hand on it. "Hit me, baby. You're too good to me, Snuff."

Snuffy poured her a glass of beer and slid it over. "Let's do a shot later. I gotta take care of these new customers who just walked in." He wiped his fingers on a grubby Lynyrd Skynyrd T-shirt and then spread his arms wide to welcome the couples who stood around the empty end of the bar.

"Jim, what's the word?" Loyal asked one of the bikers while he leaned his forearms against the bar.

"What brings you out tonight, farm boy?" the grizzled man asked, giving Loyal a good-natured grin.

"Celebrating a successful chicken barbeque weekend. How's your family?" Dottie asked him.

"Same as always. The wife never lets me have any fun." The man reached for his wallet. "Let me catch you one."

"No, we've got a kitty, you're on us."

"A kitty?" Kelly asked June in a low voice.

"Everyone pitched in twenty dollars at the start of the night. Pays for all the drinks. Don't worry, your husband took care of it," June told her. "Oh, and careful what you order. This place never passes the health inspection, so you don't want to drink out of a glass. Get something in a bottle or a can."

"You should tell Tammy," Kelly said, pointing at her neighbor who was seated at the bar watching Snuffy mix a shaker full of something bright red and pour it into shot glasses.

"Alabama Slammers?" June asked and considered for a moment. "She'll be fine … there's enough alcohol in those to kill any germs. Besides, I bet she's going to feel worse for wear tomorrow anyway."

Kelly silently agreed. Tammy was keeping pace with the men, drink for drink all night long. She watched Tammy grab the edge of the bar railing for support while she swayed. Balance recovered, she stretched out her hand towards the bartender. "I'm Tammy Parker, my husband and I just built a house here this spring."

"You call me Snuffy, pretty lady," the bartender reached out a beefy hand to shake hers. "Welcome to Bassville."

The men gathered around the pool table, while the women stayed at the bar. "Does Star have a ride home?" Kelly heard June asking Snuffy. "We can drop her off if you need us to."

"There's an extra sleeping bag under the pool table. She can shack up here for the night." He raised his hand in response to June's protest. "Butch won't care. Sometimes a girl's gotta run off a little steam, too, ya know."

"Geez," Kelly muttered under her breath. She checked the time and saw it would be at least another two hours until the bars closed.

She wondered how to encourage the group to move to a different location, politely of course. "Will this be our last stop?" she asked Arlyce.

"Good question." Arlyce raised her eyebrows at the ladies. "Death March?"

"Aren't we too old for that?" Dottie asked. Then she cackled at her own joke.

"Age is only a number. Hey guys," Arlyce hollered. "Pace yourselves. We're headed to Riverside next."

"Death March!" the men cheered.

"I know I've asked a lot of questions tonight," Kelly said to June, "and I'm afraid to ask one more. What's a Death March?"

TWENTY-FIVE

WHEN KELLY ROLLED OVER Saturday morning and looked at her alarm clock she groaned. Almost noon. She sat up and remembered what time they'd gotten home. She'd played taxi driver for what seemed like half the town. Tom snored loudly at her side and she eased her feet to the floor.

Downstairs she found the boys watching TV and eating chips. They barely glanced at her when she passed them.

Fragments of the previous night flickered through her mind while she gulped a glass of water. She recalled standing with her arms wrapped around Peg and Maw singing a Johnny Cash song at top volume. Tammy eating a pickled egg. As Kelly had herded her drunk husband and neighbors into the car, Tammy got lifted up by her husband and carried over his shoulder. Her arms had dangled limply down his back, she'd fallen asleep at some point along the way.

Welcome to Bassville, indeed. There was no way she would keep up with the locals, she decided.

Fresh air would help her wake up. Kelly opened the patio door and the stench of fresh, wet manure made her eyes water. Across her yard, just on the edge of the electric fence, was a huge pile of steaming shit.

"Your friend," was how Scotty greeted Mona Saturday morning. She shoved a Styrofoam cooler filled with baby greens into his arms and lifted another to carry to the truck. It did please her to see him wearing the T-shirt she'd given him.

"Don't even start. I don't want to hear it," she answered.

"Oh, no. Let me tell you all about how I had to babysit Jenny Wednesday night." Scotty followed Mona to the truck. "Why weren't you out?"

Wordlessly, Mona pointed to the crate of carrots.

"Yeah. Carrots. Don't you pick them by Thursday anyway?"

"Look how clean they are, you idiot." Mona grabbed a bunch by their leafy tops and shook them in his face. "Do you remember last weekend when I came back to the stand and I told you how I wanted to compete with the best sellers and I'd noticed how they displayed their produce?"

His expression was blank.

She exhaled loudly and retraced her steps back to the barn to grab a flat of peppers. "Everything at the best stands looks table-ready. Scrubbed and polished. I was up until ten o'clock buffing out the shine on these peppers." She tilted the crate of purple, yellow and green peppers with glossy skins so he could admire them.

"Really?"

"No, but I scrubbed the carrots and potatoes, rinsed the dirt off the rest."

They silently continued to load the truck until Scotty spoke. "You didn't miss much. Dave LaMay's in town, bunch of us played cards, Dob won the pot."

"So the same old, same old happened in Bassville."

Scotty slammed the back of the truck shut and leaned his elbows on the metal edge. "Dave cut out early. Seemed like he wasn't drinking. That's something new."

"That is new. And odd," Mona added.

"Yeah, I thought so, too. He's different this visit."

"Maybe he grew up after Will left."

"Maybe."

Mona climbed in the truck cab beside Scotty and reached over to turn on the radio. She didn't feel like talking, her mood sour. Maybe it was irritation that she wanted things to change but felt trapped. That couldn't be right, though. She loved the farm and her work. Was it Jake? Missing him? She adjusted the volume and smiled an apology at Scotty before saying, "I'm not in a talking mood this morning."

"Sure," he said and kept his eyes on the road.

The farmers market crowd was bigger than usual in July. Usually Mona kept track of time by how quickly they sold out of various things. The raspberries were first to go by nine-thirty, then the beans and peppers disappeared by eleven, and when nothing was left but potatoes it was close to noon. The sun was still at an angle when she closed the cash box and lifted the half-full box of Early Ohio potatoes. "That's a wrap."

"It's not even eleven."

"I know. All my scrubbing paid off."

"You do realize there's an art fair on the other side of the park, right? We had twice the traffic."

It slowly dawned on Mona that they had seen a lot of people carrying metal sculptures, cardboard tubes and paper bags. "Oh. Do you want to check it out?"

"If you want to," Scotty flipped an empty table on its end and folded in the legs. "I have to get back kind of early today. Mom's having the whole family over for Angie's birthday supper."

"Let's go for a little while. We can leave this until later—heck, if anyone wants these potatoes, they can take them."

"Sounds good to me."

After locking the cash box, scale and the bags she used to wrap up the vegetables in Scotty's truck, she grabbed her purse. "Maybe you can find something pretty for yourself," Mona teased.

"What I want to find is something edible. Like lunch," Scotty patted his stomach.

Across the park, aisles of stalls had been set up and a string quartet was playing in the gazebo near the fountain. Jewelry, pottery, paintings, sculptures and all sorts of wood carvings were on display. Mona lingered near a stall selling pottery. She studied the whimsical bowls, mugs and teapots. "These are so cute" she told the man sitting at a table with a contented beagle by his feet.

"Thanks. I get a lot of inspiration from my pets," he told her. He reached up to tighten the bandana on his head, dark brown hair curled over his shoulders. "I like to make things cheerful."

"I love the little birds on the top of this teapot. Do you sculpt those animals yourself?"

"That's right. I use my scrap clay to make all kinds of creatures." He pointed to a row of pencils with cats, pigs, dragons and dogs covering the erasers before sliding a business card towards her.

"Gary Rith Pottery. I'm guess you're Gary." Mona said.

He held out his hand to shake hers. "I am he."

"I'm Mona Butterfield." She fingered the price tag from one of the serving bowls, delicate brushstrokes of dark green contrasted with brighter shades of blue, the interior of the bowl was as lovely, with a flower painted in the very center of the bottom. She could imagine her mother serving salads out of it at family suppers. Mona picked it up and held it out to Gary. "I'll take it."

"Nice choice. I've made some vases that are similar if you're interested." He started covering the bowl in bubble wrap. "This piece was inspired by the beads in my grandma's craft stash."

"I use my grandma's old stuff, too," Mona told him.

"Are you an artist?"

"I'm a farmer." She laughed at his double-take. "I found my grandma's heirloom seeds from her garden and now I grow produce for a living. Dirty Girl Veggies."

"She must be proud."

"She's dead, but I imagine she is."

Mona found Scotty sitting on a bench near the gazebo eating a sandwich. "There you are," he mumbled around a mouthful of roast beef. He pointed to the package and she told him about the pottery and the man who was inspired by his pets and his grandmother's bead stash. "It was interesting to talk to him—I always love hearing people when they're excited about their work."

Scotty's eyes narrowed and he ripped off another chunk of sandwich with his teeth with a grunt.

"I passed a booth with earrings you should check out. They make good presents."

"I'm hungry. Can't a guy eat lunch? You know I get crabby when I need to eat."

"You can't eat and walk at the same time?"

Scotty wadded up the sandwich wrapper and tossed it in a trash barrel. "Fine." He trailed her with a confused expression while she paused to admire wind chimes, some coffee mugs, and stained glass Christmas ornaments.

At a jewelry booth, Mona held a pair of earrings up to her ears and jiggled them. "What do you think?"

"Pretty."

She pressed them into his hand. "Get them."

"My ears aren't pierced, but if you insist." He curled his fingers around the silver and amber earrings and walked towards the jolly looking woman standing behind a table of beaded bracelets. "How much for these?"

"Fifteen." The woman held them up so the sunlight glinted through the beads. "Nice choice." She leaned in closer and whispered, "They bring out the color of her eyes, don't they?" Her eyes twinkled while she smiled at him.

Scotty flushed and shuffled his feet. "How much for—" he scanned the bracelets and grabbed the nearest one.

"Also fifteen."

"Okay."

"This crystal is beautiful. She'll love them," the woman said, "but how about this one instead?" She selected a bracelet with amber and brown beads. "It'll match the earrings so she can wear them as a set." The woman wrapped the pieces in tissue paper and tucked her business card into the fold—KC Beading Creations. "I'm Karen, by the way."

"Thanks, Karen."

After paying for the pieces Scotty turned and handed the small bag to Mona. "Here." He leaned toward her, his mouth close to her cheek.

"What?" Mona took a step away from him. "What are you doing?"

"Don't you want your earrings and your bracelet?" Scotty asked.

"What are you talking about?"

"The earrings and bracelet you wanted me buy you at that booth," he explained patiently.

Mona frowned slightly and then started to laugh. "You moron, those are for your sister. You said her birthday's today."

Scotty's cheeks turned scarlet. "Oh, right. That makes more sense."

The full realization of what happened dawned on Mona and she felt terrible. Scotty kept talking. "I thought it was weird, you expecting me to buy you earrings."

"I mean if you want to buy me jewelry, feel free … " She forced out a laugh to ease the tension between them.

"No! I mean, thanks. For Angie. Yeah, that's a good idea." He folded the edge of the bag over and shuffled his feet. "Well, we should get going back. Gotta get home for that birthday dinner."

Kelly spent the afternoon stewing. She periodically moved from couch to window to glare at the pile of manure. *What the hell is that guy's problem? I brought him lemonade. I played nice. He ramps up his attack?*

When Tom came downstairs and went to pull open the patio door, Kelly jumped to her feet with a shriek. "Don't!"

"It's beautiful outside—we moved here for the fresh air. Why do you have the air conditioner on? Besides, I feel awful, I need—" Tom stopped talking, gagged and slammed the door shut. "What the hell?"

"Our neighbor, asserting his domain."

"Jackass." Tom peered through the glass door at the pile on the other side of the fence. "What did you say to him? He must have done this for a reason. *I've* never met the guy," he pointed out while tugging up the waistband of his sweatpants.

"I told you already. I brought him lemonade and introduced myself.

That was it."

"Baloney. You must've said something to piss him off. I know how you can get, not that you didn't have every right to be mad after the electric fence."

"I brought him lemonade."

"Did it taste okay?"

Kelly responded by chucking a throw pillow at Tom's head.

"All right, all right," he walked to the coffee maker with his hands raised above his head. "Just asking questions. What are you going to do?"

"What am *I* going to do? Why is this *my* problem? You live here, too."

"Yeah, but I'm at work all day. This is sort of your area."

"I don't know yet."

Tom sat across from her and took a drink of his coffee. "Oh, that's the stuff. I feel terrible."

"Me, too. I can't keep up with the natives here."

"They do like to run wild. I got pretty drunk last night."

"I tried pacing myself, but I guess when you drink for six hours it catches up to you." Kelly walked back to the window and studied the pile again. It seemed bigger, if that was possible. But there was no way he could've added to it. She'd have heard the tractor. *When did he do this? Had to have been last night after we left, I'd have noticed otherwise.* "Do you think he's stalking us?" she asked suddenly.

"Who?"

"Ezra Pike. The farmer. He dumped that while we were gone last night. And he put up that electric fence when no one was here—us or the builders. He must have a way of knowing we're gone."

"The kids were home," Tom pointed out. "And the lights were on."

"I feel like there's no way he'd have done this if we were around. We'd have heard him."

Tom joined her at the window and rubbed the back of her neck with his hand, kneading away the tension. "Coincidence. That's all it is. But obviously we have to get him to move his shit."

"But how? I was nice to him and this happens." She blinked back tears of frustration.

"Hey, it's okay. We'll figure it out. And besides," Tom turned her around to face him and lifted her chin with his fingertips. "You are smarter than any dumb-ass farmer. You're one of the smartest women I know. And even shit loses its stink over time."

Kelly knew her husband was speaking the truth, but it didn't stop the burning rage in her gut. She had one resource in the neighborhood and it was time to use it.

"Tammy? Kelly here. How's it going?"

"Super. Just got done setting up some storage shelves in the basement and now I can organize my holiday decorations. We're finishing the rest of the space as a rec room, but I wanted to get stuff out of the way first, especially if the sump pump fails. Nothing's worse than everything getting soaked because you left boxes on the floor during a bad storm. That happened once … "

Did the woman not experience hangovers? She distinctly remembered Tammy getting lifted out of the bar by her husband and carried over his shoulder to their car. What kind of superpowers did she possess? Or was it all an act? "Have you looked outside?" Kelly interrupted her story.

"Today? Yes, I saw it's beautiful out. Might go for a walk later. Why?"

Kelly explained the manure pile situation. "I was wondering if you had any ideas on how to get rid of it." When Tammy didn't immediately reply, Kelly wondered if she'd hung up. "Tammy?"

"Still here, just looking out the window. I see what you're talking about. We turned our air conditioning on so I didn't notice it until now."

"It's kind of hard to ignore if you step outside."

"I imagine. It's on his property, we can't move it, and he has a legal right to do this. Does it count as air pollution? Is there some kind of easement law about where you can legally pile stuff on your property? That seems like it might be a thing. Or we can prove it runs into water, which is a possibility. We'll have to watch when it rains. It's a mean thing to do, horrible, really. You said you tried to be nice and this was the response?"

"Uh-huh." Kelly sat down on the couch again and massaged her forehead with her left hand, clutching the phone receiver with her right.

"Maybe this man only understands nasty. Some people are like that. They don't pay attention until you start screaming. So we have to figure out a nastier move."

"What can I possibly do to him that's nastier than a pile of shit on the edge of our property line? And an electric fence one foot off our property line? I don't believe in escalating things, but this cannot go on."

"Hold on. I'm thinking."

"Nasty. Nasty nasty nasty," Kelly murmured. "What can I do on my side of the fence that would disrupt him as much? This guy's diabolical."

"Got it!" Tammy chirped. "Remember how he had all his tractors and stuff in the street last week?"

"Yeah."

"Obviously he needs to get past us to get into his field, so we make it impossible for him to use the street."

"How do we do that?"

"Weight limits."

"Weight limits?"

"Yeah, random information to most people, but my dad works for a truss company—Valley Truss? They have to move the trusses using these big trucks … "

"What's a truss?" Kelly wanted to know.

"Those wooden triangle shaped things that go into roofs. They weigh a lot, so every year my dad's company would have to wait until the weight limits came off the roads before they could haul the trusses to the construction sites."

"Go on."

"We can get a weight limit or truck ordinance passed in the subdivision. Not all roads are created equal, some are built to bear all kinds of weight, but streets in neighborhoods are not. All we have to do is get a weight limit posted and that jerk can't bring his tractors through."

"Love it! Except there's one problem … "

"What's that?"

"What if he doesn't *need* to use our street? What if he just brought his tractors through this way to annoy us? And believe me when I tell you it worked, there's still big chunks of mud I have to drive around. He made a real mess."

"If he went that much out of his way to get to his fields, he does have issues. But it's something. We'll come up with other ideas, this is just a start."

"All right. So how do we do this weight limit thing?"

"I'll go to the town hall tomorrow. It can't be complicated."

"If there's one thing I learned after moving to Bassville, Tammy? This place is complicated."

The argument in the Pub's kitchen was escalating. "Squares."

"Triangles."

"Squares."

"Triangles. Dad?" Hunter turned towards his dad who was coming in from the bar. "Pizzas get cut into triangles, right? Because they're pies and that's how you cut a pie."

"What's your mom say, buddy? Arlyce, I've got a table by the window ready to order."

"I told him squares," Arlyce said to Steve and ground out her cigarette. "Cut into triangles wastes pizza. People never finish an even number of slices. Cut it smaller, it's easier to take home leftovers or eat what you really want." She steamed past her husband to take care of their customers.

"You know better than to fight your mother," Steve chided his son.

Hunter sliced the pizza in half with the cutter with a challenging expression on his face.

"Watch yourself, son. Mom rules the roost back here and don't you forget it."

"Stupid rule," Hunter muttered and cut the pizza again with two parallel swipes before turning it ninety degrees and repeating the process.

"You're lucky that's a large. You'd be shit out of luck if you tried that move on a smaller pizza."

Hunter slid the pizza pan towards his dad. "Now what?"

Steve nodded towards the sink. "If you're caught up on pizzas, get moving on the dishes. There's an old saying in this business: you got time to lean, you've got time to clean."

"This place was a lot more fun before I started working here." Hunter slid the pizza towards his father.

"I've thought the same thing myself," Steve said and took the pizza towards the bar.

"He's awful," Arlyce complained to Steve after taking the customers' order and coming behind the bar to get their drinks. "June was right, we should've gotten his lazy carcass back here sooner. Spoiled brat."

"Aw, he'll figure it out. Give him a week or so. Once he gets that first paycheck he'll be singing a different tune."

"Right now the tune he sings is 'Wha wha wha.'" Arlyce mimicked a baby's cry.

"Maybe we should get his brothers on the schedule, too, if you think we waited too long with Hunter."

"That's not a terrible idea," Arlyce said. She glanced over her shoulder at Hunter, who was elbow deep in soapy water. His Walkman headphones covered his ears and his head bobbed rhythmically while he scrubbed a pan clean.

"We could make him wait tables," Steve suggested.

"Quit while you're ahead." Arlyce carried the drink order to her table on the deck.

"People always tell me to do that," Spade chimed in from where he sat nursing a soda and watching the weather on TV. "I never listen."

"Which is why we like you coming around, ya big loser." Steve chuckled.

"I've never told you that," Dob told Spade.

"I wonder why?" Spade mused.

"By the way, my kids said to thank you for the new shoes. I took them shopping and told them to get whatever they wanted because my good pal Spade left me a big ol' gift on the table Thursday night."

"Maybe I should start working here," Spade said. "Hanging around the Dohills is really bad on my budget."

"You'd probably get in less trouble if we kept you back in the kitchen, too," Steve chuckled. He glanced up at the TV and frowned. "There's that damn ad again," he said.

The others craned their necks to see the screen. Jay Hodge was talking about the dangers of the river. Beneath his face was the caption "No Wake: Take Back the Lake President Jay Hodge." His voice echoed through the bar. "It's about safety and doing the right thing. Simply slowing down the traffic from the boat landing to the lake will make life better for everyone." The screen changed to show a group of small children jumping off a raft while a canoe paddled past them.

"I gotta turn this off before Arlyce flips her wig." Steve hitched up the back of his khaki shorts and moved around the edge of the bar to change the channel. "Why does this jerk want to mess with our town? I wish he'd bought a place somewhere else."

Arlyce returned to the bar and slapped her hand on the cooler to get Steve's attention just as he switched stations. "I need two more Pepsis. Why'd you turn off the weather?"

"Looking for a baseball game," Steve said.

"My fault," Dob said while raising a calloused hand. "I'm sorry, but I wanted to see if the Brewers were playing."

Arlyce gave Dob a brisk nod. "S'all right. Two Pepsis, hon," she said to her husband.

TWENTY-SIX

After an early lunch Saturday, Maw and Dave cruised down the straight stretch of river before hitting the bend by Tamarack Bayou. They'd just slowed down to make the turn when they noticed a cluster of eight boats farther upstream in the narrow passage towards Pine Tree Supper Club.

"Looks like we're missing a party!" Dave yelled over the motor.

"Let's check it out," Maw suggested.

Dave shrugged and Maw changed course. He dropped speed about fifty yards upriver and drifted closer. Three pontoon boats were anchored near the shore and four speed boats were lined up trying to pass. In two of the boats, men stood shouting at a fishing boat that had dropped anchor right in the middle of the river. Maw groaned.

"What's going on?" Dave asked.

"That nimrod Otto," Maw told him. "Half the reason people fight on the river lately is because of the speed boats kicking up their wake and the jet skis zipping through making it dangerous. The other half of the fighting comes from that." Maw pointed to the middle-aged man seated in his fishing boat, ignoring the boaters telling him to move out of the way. The man expertly cast out his line near the shore and tipped his hat forward to better block the sun—and the view of the line of boats. "Stupid son of a bitch drops anchor right in the middle of the busiest and narrowest spot just because he can. Ain't no law against it, but it's a goddamn stupid thing to do. No fish through here, that's for certain. All he's catching is grief and you can bet he's doing it on purpose. He thinks if he makes life difficult enough, people won't come through here."

Dave noticed the three pontoon boats didn't seem to be engaged in the outrage and pointed at them. "So what's their deal?"

Maw squinted and tried to see if he recognized the people on board. "No clue. Looks like they're just parked there for no reason—not going through but not arguing with Otto, either. Only person I recognize out there is Otto."

"Should we do something?"

"Like what?" Maw asked.

"I don't know. Maybe direct traffic or ask Otto to move?"

"Here's the thing, Dave." Maw fanned his hand at a mosquito pestering his right ear. "Otto hates me and anyone who tries to make a living off the river. And none of those people as far as I can tell are here to fish, so they're not potential customers. I don't win if I get in the middle of this and I don't like to play if I can't win." Maw pushed the throttle forward and steered his boat away from the fracas. "Let's head to the bayou like we planned."

They'd started to pull away from the scene when a loud crashing sound made them turn around. Otto was on his feet, shouting and waving his arms. A man on one of the pontoons had joined whatever argument was taking place and two of the speed boat drivers were pulling closer to the pontoon boats.

"Jeez, it's getting pretty feisty."

"All right, all right," Maw said. "We'll distract them with our good looks and fame." He steered back towards the channel.

"Move your damn boat!"

"I have every right to go where I want. International maritime law! Nobody owns the water!"

"Hey, Otto!" Maw called over and waved in a friendly fashion. "What's going on here?"

"I'll tell ya what's going on," snarled a hairy bare-chested man wearing swim trunks. "This moron's blocking the channel."

"I see that," Maw said in a mild voice. "Seems like an inconvenient spot to fish, pal," he told Otto.

Otto slowly turned the handle of his fishing pole and pursed his lips.

"How about we head towards the Tamarack—a lot quieter back there and more fish biting, too." Maw didn't want Otto anywhere near where they planned to fish, but maybe he'd take the bait. "Got plenty of minnows," he said and patted the top of the cooler on the seat behind him.

"You don't have to go anywhere, Otto," called a man from one of the pontoon boats. "Nobody owns the river."

"Stay out of it, grandpa," the hairy man yelled. His party, two other couples and their kids looked uncomfortable as they avoided eye contact with Otto or the pontoon boats. "I have a right to get through the channel," he told Otto.

"Go ahead. No one's stopping you."

"You are!" shouted an older woman from one of the other speed boats while raising her fist at Otto.

"There's room," Otto said. He raised the tip of his pole and the bait wiggled in the air for a moment until he cast it back into the river.

"Screw him, just go," another man said. He flipped his boat's bumpers over the side of his vessel and turned on his engine. "Use this," he told the woman riding with him and handed her an oar. "Just push off the side of his boat if we get too close." The man started to drive through the congested channel.

Otto kept nervously glancing over his shoulder at the boat coming closer and closer. "Stay calm, Otto," the man on the pontoon said. "I'm taping everything."

"Ahhhh," Maw murmured.

"What?" Dave asked in a hushed voice.

"That's Jay Hodge over there," Maw told him quietly. "Big shot lawyer from Northport who's trying to change the wake rule through town. He's declared a war between the speed boats and everyone else. Funny thing," Maw cranked on his steering wheel and turned away from the chaos, "he used to own one of those cigarette boats and would come tearing down the river at full throttle. Now he's retired and owns a cottage down the river. He wants it all quiet and calm because it suits him. Hodge never cared about the wake he threw up when he drove a speed boat, but now he's a grandpa and a property owner and suddenly the traffic is a destructive nuisance. Constantly complaining about the damage to his seawall, his dock, the stuff he's got tied up to his dock, like he didn't damage anyone's stuff with *his* big wake. Looks to me like he's got Otto staged there so he can record the fallout. And trust me, he'll make it look like Otto's some kind of victim." Maw pushed his throttle forward. "I love excitement, but I won't touch that drama with a ten-foot pole. It's bad publicity no matter how you slice it."

Maw steered them into the bayou and they glided far back into the still water. When he cut the engine, Dave noticed that the silence became loud in his ears—the buzz and hum of insect life paired with birds chattering. A flapping sound drew his attention to tree branches overhead and he watched a hawk lift into the air before it soared in lazy circles, hunting for lunch. He had to agree with Maw. Otto was an idiot to pick a fight in the busiest spot on the Wissipaw when there were plenty of tucked-away places to enjoy.

"Wonder when we'll see that on the news," Maw mused while he passed Dave a pole. He unwound his own line and adjusted the bobber before grabbing a golden shiner out of the bucket. "If Jay's taping it, bet ya ten dollars we'll see it on the news by tomorrow night. That guy's got pull."

"You should give him a copy of your music video," Dave suggested. "He could get you some airtime around here."

"That's a good idea! And I've been thinking about making another video, once I'm fully mobile again." Maw rapped his knuckles against his cast. "That Wisconsin song? The one that goes 'We love our brats and our schnapps, our barley and our hops, growing alfalfa crops, the winter snow never stops?'"

Dave nodded. He remembered it included an entire verse about cheeses where Maw extolled the virtues of a rich cheddar spread and a melted brick that was 'sick.'

"I want to film in different locations, in a field of cows, at a cheese factory, maybe even head over to Green Bay and get a shot of Lambeau."

"Just be careful, the NFL's really strict about their trademark."

Maw slowly reeled in his line and Dave watched the tip bend and jerk with the weight of a fish. "Here we go!"

"That's a fighter!"

Maw kept the line taut and pulled the fish in a few feet at a time before relaxing some slack. He gave another quick tug and kept cranking the fish towards the boat. Whatever he'd hooked was fighting hard. A silvery flash of fins broke the surface and Dave grinned while watching the creature try to get loose. A moment later Maw yanked the fish free of the river with a hoot. "Look at her!"

"Nice!" Dave reached over the side of the boat for the stringer. "Looks like we'll have another fish dinner tonight. One last hurrah before I head back to Chicago."

"You do know we caught fish like crazy every time you came up, right?" Maw asked. He lifted an eyebrow at the DJ. "Why the dramatic change? You spent your fishing trips napping on that front seat."

Dave took the sharp metal end of the stringer and poked a little hole in the bottom of the fish's mouth like Maw had taught him. He retied the end of the rope and dropped it back into the water. "Guess I grew up, Maw. I'm the same but different now. I used to party pretty hard and those days are over. Turns out clean living agrees with me."

Maw nodded. "Did something happen? You join AA or something?"

"No," Dave chuckled. "I'm just staying high on life for a while, that's all."

Maw studied the other man's face for a moment and shrugged. "Well, good for you."

Dave grinned and cast his line perfectly into the deepest part of the bayou. "It is good for me."

From the living room window Dottie watched the unfamiliar station wagon pull into her driveway and wondered who had gotten lost. She climbed down from the chair where she was balanced to hang crepe paper across the ceiling for Angie's party and moved to answer the door. She hoped whoever it was wouldn't take long. The party was supposed to start at two. Tammy stood on the gravel driveway squinting to see through the screen.

"Hello!" Dottie waved and trotted towards her, letting the screen door slap closed behind her.

"Hi! I wasn't sure I had the right address. The three is kind of rubbed off on your mailbox. But then I drove further up the road and the next number was in the four hundreds, so I figured this had to be you." Tammy took in the two-story white farmhouse with new red shutters and carefully tended flower boxes. "Do you want to come in? I can put on a pot of coffee."

"No, I don't want to bother you, I just need some advice."

"Have a seat," Dottie invited her onto the front porch. The space was cozy with rag rugs, a swing and two rocking chairs catching the breeze from the west. A few old milking tins from the barn now held white geraniums.

"Your porch is so pretty," Tammy said, sitting in one of the rocking chairs. "It's like a picture."

"Thank you. What's the trouble?"

Tammy explained the manure pile and how it had come on the tail of the electric fence and farm equipment blocking the road. "Kelly has tried to be nice, she brought the guy lemonade, but he won't quit the nasty behavior. I can't imagine what's worse than a pile of poop on the edge of your yard, but this guy will figure it out."

Dottie stifled a smile. Ezra Pike was diabolical, no two ways about it. But she'd also suspected he would be ashamed if called out on his actions. Apparently not. "Hm. This is a sticky spot. A *stinky* spot. He's perfectly within his rights to pile things wherever he wants, but if he keeps being a jerk, you're within your rights to make him stop. There's this law called right to farm, which means farmers can do what they need to on their property. It's meant to protect the industry from complaints from other landowners."

"But he can't dump his crap anywhere and not expect people to complain!"

"Correct. When we zoned our land residential and commercial, that meant farm laws don't apply to it anymore. But Ezra's land is zoned agricultural, which means he can do what he wants on his property, as long as it doesn't affect water supply."

"Will manure get into our water?" Tammy's eyes grew big with horror at the thought.

"No," Dottie said and patted her arm to reassure her. "I think this problem is easily solved."

"How? Can we find somebody to haul it away?"

"Actually," Dottie pressed her lips together and considered the idea, "that's one option. Though he could claim it was theft if his property gets moved off his land, but we could do that."

"What's the other option?" Tammy wanted to know.

"Loyal Butterfield is on the town council. He can talk to Ezra and point out that if he keeps acting like a jerk, the town will push for an easement."

"What's that?"

"It's a rule that limits what he can do on the land adjacent to yours, usually up to two hundred feet."

"That sounds good!"

Dottie pushed her glasses up her nose and chuckled, "Ezra will not want an easement in place. They're a pain to work around and could limit more than just where he piles his cow manure. If Loyal can convince him to play nice, then everyone wins."

"Why can't we convince him to play nice?" Tammy asked. "Kelly's the one affected, she's talked to him once before. She could tell him about the easement … "

"Ezra's a man's man. He's a bachelor with little time or patience for women. And he resents anybody telling him what to do. Trust me when I tell you he'll take a conversation with Loyal, a council member and fellow farmer, much better than he will from a woman, let alone someone new in town who doesn't know anything about farming."

"I see your point. Okay, when can Loyal talk to him?"

"I'll give him a call this evening. Meanwhile, you might send your kids over with a wheelbarrow and sneak some of that manure over to your own yard. It makes good fertilizer, and hardly smells once it dries out. Spread over your lawn, the smell will disappear in a few days. Plus your grass will grow better."

"That so?"

"See for yourself." Dottie held out her arm to her own yard, which Tammy had to agree was lush and green and hardly had a weed in sight. "And if you have a garden, even better."

"I don't garden."

"You might try it. Nothing like a tomato fresh off the vine. It'll make you wonder why you ever wasted money on a store-bought one. But if you don't care to do it yourself, I recommend Mona Butterfield's farm stand. Of course, if you wait another month and forget to lock your doors people will leave their excess zucchini and cucumbers right on your kitchen counter for you."

"You're joking!" Tammy looked skeptical.

"Sort of. Not entirely." Dottie stood, a polite way to let her visitor know it was time to go. Angie would be home soon with her friends and Dottie still needed to pull her birthday presents out of hiding.

TWENTY-SEVEN

Monday morning after cleaning up from breakfast, Tammy headed straight to Kelly's house feeling satisfied that she'd solved her problem. Some people painted, others sewed, but Tammy found her joy in helping people. Creating solutions where problems existed. Fixing situations. Her face glowed with pride while she rapped on the Parkers' front door.

Kelly opened the door and ushered her inside. The house smelled like cinnamon. "I've been baking and boiling oranges and cloves on the stove to combat the smell outside."

"Your electrical bill will be insane!" Tammy remarked. "Baking *and* running your air conditioner at the same time?"

"I don't care. Baking is therapy for me."

Tammy trailed behind her to the kitchen where on the countertop loaves of quick bread and cooling racks of cookies sat waiting for hungry mouths. Kelly's kitchen sink was full of bowls and mixing cups. The house did smell wonderful. She reached over and helped herself to a Snickerdoodle. She chewed, swallowed, and announced, "Problem solved."

"Really?" Kelly's face lit up.

"Well, nearly." Tammy took another bite. "These are incredible. You need to kick in some baked goods at next year's chicken barbeque. I'd have come by sooner but we had church yesterday and then went to visit Rawley's aunt in the afternoon. But I got some advice from Dottie Trayson." She finished chewing and swallowed before continuing. "So there's this farm law that says Ezra can do what he wants on his land, but Loyal Butterfield is going to talk to him. It sounds like if he doesn't play nice, then the town can force him to by making something called an easement—two hundred feet of limited activity. The way Dottie explained it, Ezra will rather behave than have someone tell him what he can and can't do on his own land. She made it sound like an easement is no big thing to pass."

"That's great! How long do you think it'll take?" Kelly glanced out her kitchen window at the large pile of manure. The steam had settled some, but the heap of cow dung still reeked.

"That I don't know, but if it's anything like getting somebody to mow a vacant lot, at least a month. Nothing moves fast around here. Dottie also said manure stops smelling when it dries out and suggested we might steal it to spread on our yards as fertilizer."

Kelly laughed. "Is that a fact? It doesn't smell when it dries? I guess that's true." She tapped her index finger contemplatively on her chin. "Now that's a great idea. Not only will it kill that jerk to discover his manure pile is missing, but for us to use it for something good would really get his goat."

"I kind of thought she was joking," Tammy said, her brow furrowed. She didn't really want to mess around with that smelly pile. "I don't know if it will really work."

262

"Actually, I think it's a brilliant idea. And we can take care of it today." Kelly turned off her oven and pulled out a tray of cookies. She threw aside the potholders and shouted, "Boys! Come in here!"

Kelly's sons stumbled through the doorway, jostling each other in their haste to stuff cookies in their mouths. Their hair was tousled and they wore pajama bottoms.

"Fill up and then I need you to get dressed, put on your old shoes and grab shovels from the garage. And the wheelbarrow. Grab that old wagon you never play with, too."

"Okay. But why?" the oldest mumbled around a mouthful of cookie.

"We've got a yard project. You know the big pile of cow poop out there?" She pointed outside and her kids nodded. "Well, we're going to spread it all over our yard and the Parkers' yard. They're going to help us. And if there's still poop left over, we'll spread it all over the field between our houses."

"Why would we do that?" the younger son asked.

"Two reasons. First, it'll help our grass grow really nice. Second, Mrs. Parker told me that poop stops smelling when it dries out. If it's spread out in a thin layer, it'll dry fast in the sun. And if we can make this problem disappear while vexing Mr. Ezra Pike, I'd say it's worth trying." Kelly turned to Tammy. "Get your kids and your own wheelbarrow. We'll meet you outside in a half hour. Oh, and I'll pay your kids with cookies, too."

As Tammy hurried home to change her clothes and rally her children, she realized her neighbor might have the same can-do attitude she prided herself for having.

A half hour later Kelly was directing the children while she carefully maneuvered her body through the wires of Ezra's electric fence.

The heap loomed a few steps from the fence line and she could see undigested clumps of straw and grass. The rich odor filled her nostrils and made her eyes water. "You stay on your side of the fence so you don't get shocked. I'll pitch the poop over to your wagons and you carry it away and dump it out in piles around our yards. Tammy, you rake it flat so it works into the ground and can dry fast."

Tammy nodded and adjusted the bandana she'd tied over her face to keep the smell out of her nose. She'd doused the fabric with perfume. Raking didn't sound too difficult, she thought, and she grabbed the wooden-handled tool and headed to the far corner of her backyard. "Let's work our way out first," she called.

Kelly speared the pointed edge of the shovel into the side of the pile and lifted a soggy clump free. It weighed more than she'd expected. She heaved the end of the shovel into the waiting wheelbarrow, careful to avoid making contact with the fence, and repeated the motion. Her back and shoulders would ache within an hour, but she figured this would count as exercise, right? Then she could skip her *Buns of Steel* workout tape later.

"Ew!" The kids giggled when the first shovelful landed with a plopping sound. "Major Doo Doo!" her youngest exclaimed.

"No, no, it's General Doody! Get it? Duty-doo-dy?"

Kelly was glad they were finding the humor in the situation while she dug in again. She kept looking over across the field to make sure Ezra didn't appear and catch them in the act of stealing his shit pile. The thought of his outrage and confusion when he discovered it missing kept her motivated to work steadily over the next hour. He'd be confounded and there'd be no way for him to know what happened to it. The kids trundled their wagon and wheelbarrows back and forth, keeping a stream of toilet-themed jokes in play the entire time. Tammy raked each smaller pile across the ground, hiding the evidence of their theft. Between the six of them a steady and productive rhythm of loading, hauling, tipping and raking took shape.

When she guessed they were halfway through spreading out the pile, Kelly tossed her shovel over the fence and climbed back through to join the others. "I'm pooped," she declared and collapsed on the grass. The kids giggled and flopped on the ground next to her. Tammy wandered over and looked down at her. "I need a break. Twenty minutes."

"But we're almost done!"

"There's still half the pile to go!" Kelly protested. "My arms are killing me. My shoulders are burning."

"We can't quit now," Tammy put her hands on her hips. "Look at how much progress we've made. And the kids haven't even started whining yet."

"Just twenty minutes. Then we'll finish. I am dying." Kelly closed her eyes and peeled down her own bandana, letting the sun dry the sweat off her face. She felt the tension recede while she melted into the ground, her limbs heavy and tired.

"Then I'm taking a break indoors away from the smell." Tammy turned to the kids. "Who wants lemonade?" They clamored behind her while she led the way to her place. "I'll bring you a glass if you want—or you can join us," Tammy said.

Kelly lay still while the kids followed Tammy and after a moment she began to isolate the sounds of different birds and insects. A soft flapping noise caused her to open her eyes and see a blue jay land on a fence post nearby. In the distance an engine hummed. A fly landed on her shin and she swiped at it with her fingers. With enormous effort, she rolled to her stomach and pushed herself up. A glass of lemonade would taste good.

Inside Tammy's immaculate kitchen the kids sat around the table drinking from tall glasses with straws. A half-finished bowl of popcorn was on the table surrounded by wadded up napkins. Kelly gratefully accepted a glass. She chugged three-quarters of it without taking a breath and felt the cool relief move from her throat down her chest. "Ah, that's good."

"Do you want a bandana for your face, too?" Tammy offered. She held up a square of yellow fabric and a bottle of Jean Naté.

"You know, I will. That's a good idea." Kelly tied it around her neck and adjusted the knot so the bandana fit tight over her nose when she pulled it up. "Though you do get used to the smell after a while."

Tammy scrunched up her nose. "I can't. I mean, I know they say you do, but I don't stop noticing it. Same with noise. When we lived near O'Hare in Chicago for a year, I heard every plane overhead. There was no getting used to it no matter what I did."

"Chicago to here, that's a move," Kelly remarked.

"We were just there for two years while Rawley worked on his MBA at the university. I'm a Milwaukee girl; Chicago was too big for me."

"I've never lived anyplace bigger than Northport. I went to college at Ripon."

"My favorite city is Madison, but Rawley can't get a transfer there. And he doesn't want to start at the bottom at some other company, so here we are."

"But why here? Why not stay in Northport if you like a city?"

"Space. Safety." Tammy rolled her eyes. "Bigger house, bigger yard, more room for toys."

Kelly finished her lemonade, rinsed the glass and set it upside-down in the sink. "Thanks. You were right, this did hit the spot."

"Ready to finish this thing?" Tammy clapped her hands.

"No," the kids protested.

"Okay," Kelly pretended to think. "How about if we sweeten the deal to include a movie?"

"At the theater?" Miles asked. "And we get to go to the arcade after."

"Sounds like we're going to the mall," Tammy said.

"With candy?" Hannah asked. "Skittles and Dots!"

"You drive a hard bargain," Kelly told her.

"Can-dy! Can-dy!" the kids chanted. Kelly raised her eyebrows at Tammy.

"They have worked really hard," Tammy pointed out.

"Okay. One box *each*," Kelly said. She retied her ponytail and stood up.

Grabbing handfuls of popcorn, the kids raced outside to their wagon and wheelbarrows.

"They really have been good sports," Kelly said.

"I think they've bonded through this, too." Tammy pulled up her bandana.

Kelly steeled herself and followed them outside, her shoulders tingling with pain and her jaw clenched. She mustered up another image of Ezra driving along the fence line to discover his shit pile gone. Her lips curled into a smile beneath the yellow bandana and she eased her way back through the electric fence.

The pile was rapidly diminishing when a low rumble in the distance caused Kelly to look up from shoveling. A farm tractor kicked up clouds of dust as it rolled through the dirt towards them and its driver was leaning forward as if urging it to go faster. "Go! Hurry! He's coming!" Kelly shouted to the others. She tossed her shovel over to her side of the fence and followed, catching her elbow against the wire and getting a sharp jolt up her arm in her rush to escape. The kids were running towards Tammy who was motioning them into her garage. Three full wagons of shit headed her way and she didn't tell them to stop and dump it. The tractor drew closer and Kelly realized there was no point in running away now. Ezra saw her, maybe not the others but he definitely could see her standing near the back edge of her yard, bandana over her mouth and nose, shovel in her hands. Her mind raced while she speculated on his reaction. What had started as a shoulder-high pile ten feet across was now knee-high and four feet across. He'd demand an explanation, possibly accuse her of moving it. Kelly glanced over her shoulder and noticed that there was no trace of it in their yard or Tammy's. They'd raked out the smaller piles, so unless you stood directly over the ground and looked down, you'd never see the yellowish chunks of cow dung mixed in with the dirt and weeds and spikes of new grass.

The tractor stopped about twenty feet from the property line and the engine rumbled for a moment before the air fell silent. Kelly couldn't hear the kids or Tammy, she'd probably pulled them inside. She took a deep breath and considered how she'd play her next move. Ezra climbed down and strode towards her, his eyes narrow.

"Hi!" Kelly waved at him in a friendly way. Her hands were trembling while she pulled the bandana down below her chin and she tried to keep her voice steady. She had to believe Tammy was watching from her window and would call for help if Ezra started to attack her.

"What's this?" he demanded. He held his hands out palms up and scowled. His face looked as dark as the stains on his jeans.

"What's what?" she asked in a cheerful voice. Playing dumb was the route to go.

"Where's my pile?"

She cocked her head and frowned, arranging her expression into a mask of innocent confusion. "Pile? Pile of what?" she repeated.

"Pile. My manure pile."

"You mean that?" Kelly pointed helpfully to the much smaller heap of manure. "That's a pile of something. Looks like manure."

"It was bigger." Ezra whipped his head around as if looking for the rest of it somewhere.

"Wait a sec. You mean you *put* manure in a *pile* right *there* on *purpose*? It's supposed to be an even *bigger* pile?" Kelly acted astonished by this revelation.

The furrows on Ezra's face grew even deeper. He crossed his arms across his dirt-streaked undershirt.

Kelly shrugged. "I have no idea where your manure might be. Seems like it would be pretty rude to store actual cow poop right on our property line, though."

"I have to put it somewhere," Ezra said with a defiant snarl.

"Huh. Well, it looks like that must be your pile then."

"It was bigger. Way bigger. What did you do with it?"

"What did I do with it? You're not seriously accusing me of stealing a pile of cow poop," Kelly said.

"You moved it then."

"Maybe you moved it. Maybe you forgot where you put it."

"What are you doing out here with that shovel?" Ezra asked, pointing at the tool in her hand.

"Deciding where I want to put in a vegetable garden. I'm really excited to have room to grow my own tomatoes and corn now that we live out here in the country. You farm," Kelly said, as if this information had just occurred to her. "Maybe you could suggest the best spot to put it!" She smiled at him expectantly.

"For God's sake." He spat on the ground and narrowed his eyes at the house. It was like he knew Tammy and the kids were inside.

"No? I'm pretty new at this country life, so I'd love any pointers. I mean, you seem really skilled at farming from what I've seen."

Ezra cleared his throat and met her gaze. They stared at each other for a long moment while Kelly thought of all the staring contests she'd won as a child. The trick was to not think about actually looking at the person but to just keep your eyes open. This jerk thought he could push her around, but he was wrong. She was not having it. She focused her stare and watched him blink.

"Maybe," she paused while she waited an extra few seconds before blinking her own eyes. "Maybe if something is important to you, you shouldn't leave it out at the edge of your property. I'm not certain how one calculates the value of manure—by the square foot or by the pound? Maybe it depends on where it came from. Like is horse manure worth as much as cow manure? I don't know. But if you think I took it, feel free to come on over and look around. Take it back if you can find it."

Ezra's glare cut across her yard to her garage and house and back to Kelly. She stood a little taller. He kicked his foot out at the pile and stomped back to his tractor.

"You don't want to give me some advice on where to plant a garden?" she hollered after him. Her voice shook and Kelly realized she'd been holding her breath. Her head felt light and her right arm still tingled from where she'd hit the electric fence. Curling her fingers tighter around the shovel, she watched him climb up on the seat, start the engine and drive away. "Yeah, fuck you, Ezra," she said in a low voice. She believed they could freely move the rest of the pile because there was no way that jerk would come back. Not if it meant he'd have to face her. He was a scared bully and she knew it.

Later that evening when Tom came home from work, he found his wife and kids on the couch watching TV and eating snack food out of bags. "No dinner?" he asked.

"There's brownies, cookies and bread on the kitchen counter." Kelly crumpled up an empty Doritos bag and passed it to him. "Do you mind throwing this away when you go in the kitchen?"

"Is there a bake sale coming up or something?" Tom asked from the kitchen.

"Not yet." Kelly waited a moment and then she heard his exclamation.

"How did you do it? And don't tell me you had nothing to do with it—you got him to move his poop pile!"

Kelly groaned and rolled off the couch to the floor. Her shoulders, back and for some reason even her butt muscles screamed with the effort and she limped into the kitchen so the kids could watch their program uninterrupted. "Tammy actually gave me the idea."

Tom was midbite over the sink, moaning with pleasure. "I love when you bake. So where did it go?"

"Closer than you'd think. It's actually in our yard, but spread out it's not so horrible." She shook ice cubes into a plastic baggie and sealed the top before slapping it against her right shoulder. "Ahhhh."

"What?"

Kelly explained how they snuck the manure pile, load by load, through the electric fence and spread it over their yards and the field between their houses.

"All six of you."

She nodded.

"How long did it take you? That was a big pile."

"Most of the day. But I imagine it'll smell normal around here in a day or two. Once it dries out."

"I know you hear it all the time, but you are brilliant."

"Well, I do owe some credit to Tammy. I didn't tell you the best part yet."

"What's that?"

"We took a break and had just started up again when Ezra came across the field on his tractor, mad as anything that his pile was gone. Of course he couldn't really say anything when I asked him why he piled it next to our yard, and he felt stupid accusing me of stealing the manure when he couldn't actually see where it was."

Tom laughed. "Did you tell him what you did with it?"

"No, I asked him to show me where he thought it went and of course he had no idea. I suppose he'll figure it out eventually, he's not stupid." Kelly grinned. "He caught me red-handed with a shovel and I played it off like I was digging out an area for a garden. I actually asked him advice on where I should plant it. He was speechless. Not that he talks much anyway."

"I'm afraid to ask, but do you think this is the end of the Farm Wars or will he attack again?"

Kelly shrugged, but the painful movement made her wince and she adjusted the ice pack. "I hope not. I guess Loyal Butterfield's going to talk to him. If that doesn't work, Tammy's going to the town board to ask for an easement. That will create a two-hundred-foot buffer between our properties to limit what he can do on it. He can still grow crops or graze cows, but not much else."

"And here I thought my day was productive. I've got nothing on you."

"We did all right." Kelly took a peanut butter cookie off the cooling rack and nibbled at it. "It felt really good to confront Ezra. But you know what felt better?"

"What's that?" He opened the fridge and pulled out the carton of milk. He held it up to her inquiringly and after she nodded, he poured two glasses and joined her.

"Working with Tammy. We really bonded over this experience. She's not so bad. Pushy, but her heart's in the right place and when you want to get something accomplished, she's your girl." Kelly took another bite. "We're bringing the kids to Northport tomorrow to see a movie at the mall and hang out."

"So the new neighborhood's off to a good start. To friends and neighbors." Tom tipped the edge of his glass against hers.

"I'll drink to that," Kelly agreed.

TWENTY-EIGHT

TUESDAY AFTERNOON MAW AND his crew started shooting the first music video at Butterfield's pasture. Maw step-hopped towards the cluster of cows, ignoring the crutch that he'd dropped next to the Buick. "C'mon girls, we're wasting daylight!"

The Bikini Fishing Team, including Jenny and Sheila, followed Maw amid complaints about the weeds scratching their legs and the gnats buzzing around their faces. Ed Lyons trailed behind and started giving directions on how they should pose. "All right, when the music plays, I want you to start dancing. I'm going to get shots from different angles. Maw, you need to move your lips like it's live. We'll sync up the sound in the studio later, but you have to act like you're singing." Ed swung his video camera to his shoulder and pushed the play button on the boom box he'd set on the ground.

Maw unleashed a series of dance moves while trying to keep weight off his right leg. The girls churned around him in a semicircle, wiggling their hips and shoulders. Ed walked the perimeter of the scene with his camera hoisted on his shoulder and tried to avoid stepping in cow patties. After filming the scene once, Ed paused his recording, rewound Maw's cassette tape and the song began again. This time Ed crawled closer on his knees, getting shots of Maw and the girls from below, capturing a heifer rhythmically chewing her cud and directing Jenny to mime milking with her hands. Anyone driving by would think they'd gone crackers.

"Is that a wrap, Ed? We've gotta get over to the cheese factory and do the tailgating scene." Maw wiped sweat from his brow and limped over to the car to retrieve his crutch.

"Yeah, we're good. Let's go."

On Sunday Dave had gone back to Chicago with promises to help distribute Maw's music. After covering for Maw in the bait shop while he spent Monday in the recording studio down in Milwaukee, Peg had agreed to give Maw one more day—only one—to wrap up this "rap music nonsense" as she called it. Whatever didn't happen wasn't going to, because the vital combination of Peg's patience and Maw's money was running out. Ed had agreed to the job on the condition that Maw allow him free use of storage space for the next year. Ed planned to move to Boston to pursue his dreams of becoming a photographer for a magazine and needed to pare down his belongings. The spare room at the bait shop would let him avoid throwing away his extensive record collection among other possessions without having to pay for a storage garage. A year would give him time to find a permanent place to live. Maw was determined to keep this latest development a secret from Peg for as long as possible. The way he figured it, money would be pouring in from album sales so she wouldn't even care if they didn't collect rent on the spare room.

The odd assortment of people—Maw wearing his gold chains and using his crutch, Ed wearing his trademark black beret and holding a handheld video camera, and the Bikini Fishing Team wearing cut-off jean shorts and bikini tops, hauling fishing nets and poles—climbed into the Buick. Since Ed and Jenny were the shortest of the group, they got jostled into the middle spots in the front and back seats. "Let's get the tailgate shots next while there's enough daylight." Maw planned to use the parking lot by Bud's Supermarket where cars were usually parked. He'd add their vehicles and Steve would pull his truck over from the Pub to make it seem like a party was happening.

Three hours later they finally made their way to the Sweet Clover Cheese Factory still wearing their Green Bay Packers fan gear. The girls were rowdy after drinking their way through a twelve-pack of beer during the last part of the shoot. The tailgate scene had taken longer on account of people from town stopping by thinking an actual party was under way. Frank and Nancy had rolled up, as had Snuffy, Spade, a group of teenagers and T.C. Barlow. Maw had to admit they did get carried away when he'd gone into Bud's for packages of hot dogs to put on the grill. But additional people had the effect of making the crowd seem more authentic and exciting.

"I'm sorry, but you cannot go in there, it's a sterile environment," the cheese factory manager explained to Maw after stopping him at the door. "We're making food. Everyone walking through the plant has to wear appropriate protective clothing. If a single hair made its way into a batch of cheddar … "

Frustrated, Maw scratched his neck and looked around the cheese shop. Ed and the girls stood nearby with a range of bored and exhausted expressions on their faces. Sheila nibbled away at samples of brick cheese while the others watched the factory workers through the window that separated the production from the storefront. "Can you suit us up and let us stand in the doorway like we're going in?" Maw asked.

"Absolutely not."

His mind raced through possible solutions. Maw refused to give up his vision. They had to include cheese somehow. He had pictured them in front of a vat of milky white liquid, wearing the white coats and maybe Sheila stirring a huge wooden spoon. Admittedly, his concept of cheese making was limited to a program he'd seen one night on public television. He really had no idea what happened behind the doors of the factory. All he knew was that the guys who worked here wore white and were very clean. And that the result of combining milk, enzymes and sometimes bacteria was creamy and delicious.

"I wish you'd have called ahead. Then you wouldn't be wasting your time." The manager shrugged his shoulders and moved to take away the tray of cheese samples from Sheila.

Maw scratched his head. He was hooked on his very specific vision for his music video debut. All of the important parts of Wisconsin had to be represented—the Packers, beer, the dairy industry and fishing. "Look, how would you feel if I used a reproduction of your factory but included your name on it?"

"I'm not sure I understand what you mean," the manager said. A wrinkle appeared between his eyebrows.

"We don't actually go inside your factory, but we use your name and your cheese in the video."

"Well, I don't see how that could do any harm … "

Maw kept talking over the manager's hesitation. "I want to promote the great things about Wisconsin, you get free exposure for your brand—it's win-win. Picture it," Maw draped his arm around the manager's shoulders, "everything that makes Wisconsin great featured in shot after shot—snowmobiles, tailgating at Lambeau, dairy farmers and Bassville's very own Sweet Clover cheese. What's not to love about this opportunity? Your brand featured in my video."

The manager started to imagine it. Suddenly a picture of Green

Bay Packer Sterling Sharpe eating a slice of Sweet Clover colby entered his mind. He'd be crazy to say no to this sort of publicity. "Well, I could give you a few blocks of cheese to feature in your video. But there's no feasible way I can let you film inside the factory. I'd lose a week of production by shutting down to clean and sterilize all of our equipment. You can use the store front, but I can't let you back inside the factory area."

Maw nodded. His mind had leapt to the solution. The big vat of creamy white stuff would still be his centerpiece; Plan B was not a problem. *Creative people have the advantage of being resourceful,* he thought while accepting the manager's donation of three blocks of cheese—colby, brick and medium cheddar stacked in a brown paper bag. "Come on, girls." Maw bustled towards the door. "We're burning daylight!"

"You want to *what?*" Ed asked while Maw parked the Buick back outside Bud's Supermarket.

"We're going to stage our own cheese factory scene. C'mon Sheila, I need your help."

Inside the store Maw grabbed a cart and headed to the baked goods aisle where he grabbed every box of powdered milk. "Probably can use flour, too. That'll make it thicker." He pointed the end of his crutch at the bags of flour.

"What's going on, Maw?" Sheila asked while she lifted a ten-pound bag of flour off the bottom shelf and loaded it in the cart.

"Grab five bags."

"Hi, Maw. Can I help you with anything?" Bud rounded the corner carrying a flat of canned corn.

"Yeah. Got any more powdered milk?"

"There's a half a case in the stock room. I'll bring it up to the register for you."

At the check-out aisle, Sheila thumbed through a tabloid magazine

277

while Maw passed across twenty-dollar bills to the cashier. "I need a receipt," he told her.

"What on earth are you up to?" Arlyce asked when she walked in the store and saw the cart full of flour and powdered milk. "I never saw a recipe that called for more than five cups of powdered milk."

"Just a little prop-building for my music video," Maw explained with a wink.

"I know I shouldn't ask, but does Peg know about this?" Arlyce made a note of the total sale on the cash register. She could hardly wait to pass *this* nugget on during the weekly Stitch n' Bitch.

"I'm offended by your insinuation." Maw shook his head sadly before leading Sheila pushing the shopping cart outside to the Buick.

Back at the bait shop Maw directed the girls to relocate all of the minnows from the back tank. "Try not to get too much water on the floor," he warned them. "It'll get really slippery." The girls, armed with nets and buckets, got after their task. Maw turned to Ed. "We gotta clear that wall." He indicated the back wall of the bait shop, which was covered with posters for fishing tournaments and poker runs. "You move the display racks over there and I'll start peeling this clean."

"I'm not sure I follow where this is headed, Maw," Ed said. He set his camera and gear bag next to the register.

"Trust me."

More dangerous words were rarely spoken.

An hour later Maw stood next to the empty minnow tank. The wall behind him was dingy with age and scuff marks, but otherwise clean. "Should we paint it?" he mused.

"You cannot be serious," Jenny said.

"I am." Maw pointed to his son who was manning the cash register. "Go get that gallon of white paint from the basement. Be quick about it!" He turned to the girls. "Just a quick coat to clean it up, that's all. Sheila, help him find some brushes. Hurry!"

Ed stroked his goatee. If he understood Maw's vision, it would require a different lens. He dug through his camera bag and started sorting through equipment. They'd need a little more lighting, too.

Rubbing his hands together, Maw's eyes gleamed with excitement. This would be better than an actual cheese factory, he decided. He tore open the first box of powdered milk and dumped it into the tank. The white flakes dissipated quickly into a milky film. Maw repeated the process, fifteen total boxes and the water had turned pearly white.

"Should you leave all of the filters running?" Ed asked. He walked over to the output valve where the water was recirculating back into the tank. The liquid bubbled up gently—there didn't appear to be any issue with the filtration system.

Maw ignored him. "We've got to get this thickened up. Can you picture it? We'll get one of the girls to stir it around using a canoe paddle. It'll look like an actual vat of cream! The others can hold up the blocks of cheese. We'll figure it out as we go." He lifted one of the bags of flour and gently tipped it towards the tank. The fine powder rose in the air, coating the front of Maw's shirt and causing him to sneeze.

"Bless you," Sheila said. She handed each of the girls a paint brush while Maw's son opened the can of paint.

"How do you want me to stir this?" he asked Maw.

"Use that yardstick behind the cash register," Maw directed him.

"Won't it ruin your ruler?" the boy asked. "You'll paint over the numbers and it won't be any good."

"Well then find a stick in the yard. Can't you see I'm busy?"

"You sure you don't want me to unplug your filters and stuff?" Ed asked.

"Goddamn it, Ed. It's fine!" Maw snapped.

Ed refrained from commenting on the possible damage caused by adding flour and powdered milk to a filtration system. He wasn't paid to talk, he reasoned to himself. He was paid to take pictures and make videos. And even if Maw's business dried up, he'd still have storage space available, so what was it to him anyway?

While the girls quickly slapped a fresh coat of white paint over the cinderblock wall at the back of the store, Maw grabbed a wooden oar and stirred the liquid in the vat. The flour had sunk to the bottom in a muddy sort of glob. He tried breaking it apart, but it was hard to get any leverage from where he stood. Muttering a chain of curses under his breath, he headed for the garage to grab a rake. What he needed was teeth, not a flat edge.

"Honey?" Peg's voice through the kitchen window made him jump. He'd forgotten she was home.

"Yeah?"

"You want frozen pizza or leftover casserole for dinner?"

"Think I'm gonna skip dinner tonight, sweetie. We're kind of busy wrapping up this video shoot."

"Things going okay?" Peg appeared at the door, her expression shifting from amusement to concern.

"Oh yeah, yeah. Great. Just a little hiccup that we have to handle in-house. We'll be done in about an hour. No need to feed us."

"You sure?" She opened the door and leaned outside. "Are Ed and the girls still with you?"

"Yeah. We ate a late lunch. Hot dogs," he added, to make things sound cheaper. He left out the part about buying hot dogs for a small party in Bud's parking lot. But they got free cheese. And then he bought a cart of powdered milk and flour. Maw steered his brain in a more positive direction. *This video will be a hit. I'm going to sell so many tapes I might even quit selling bait.*

"All right. Send the boys in if you see them. I'll just throw in a pizza."

"Thanks, sweetie." Maw continued towards the garage, relieved that Peg didn't show more interest or follow him. The sooner he got the final shots filmed for this video, the better.

After adding all of the flour Maw still wasn't satisfied with the consistency of the "cream" in the vat. "I should've drained out some of the water," he said. "Let's try it anyway. Act like it's harder to stir than it really is, Sheila." He passed her the oar and she thrust it in the minnow tank, slowly dragging it in a circle. "Okay, a bit much. You don't need to act like it's concrete. Think of it like stirring pudding. That thickness."

Sheila adjusted her grip on the oar's handle and swished the paddle through the water. The white liquid flowed gently in its wake and Maw nodded. "What do you think, Ed?"

"It'll work," he said, thinking at this point it didn't matter what Maw would add to the vat. Flushing it clean would be a real chore. Maw had finally turned off the filtration system, but the flour had already made its way through the pipes. Maybe it would be easy to clean out with an air compressor, but Ed wouldn't stick around to find out.

"Sheila, put on that lab coat and let's do this thing!" Maw clapped his hands twice and adjusted the boom box he'd plugged in nearby. "Okay, girls, you know the drill. Act like this cheese is the best thing you've ever seen. It's Jon Bon Jovi covered in chocolate."

"Cripes, Maw, you wreck everything," Jenny said. She lifted her block of cheese and kissed it. "That good?"

"Let's see you give it a little tongue," Maw joked. He pressed play to get the music started and nodded to Ed.

Ed zoomed in on Maw's face while he sang along with the tape. He kept a tight frame around the girls with the tank, including enough to suggest it was an actual stainless steel vat designed for cheese making and not for keeping golden shiners alive. Sheila stirred the oar around with a goofy grin on her face and the others crowded around her so they wouldn't get cut out of the video. Ed felt certain none of them would be discovered and made famous by virtue of being in Maw's video, but they had absorbed his enthusiasm and confidence. They were each convinced this was a steppingstone to something bigger.

Maw rewound the tape while Ed adjusted the lighting, then they shot three more takes of the song. "That's a wrap!" Maw crowed when Ed twisted the lens cap on his camera. Maw grabbed his crutch and hobbled to the back cooler to break out a six-pack. Passing it around the group, he took a can for himself, cracked it open and raised it in the air. "To the best bunch of rap video artists around— besides that Ice-T guy."

"Hear-hear!" they chorused and tipped back their own cans. Sheila turned on a radio station and within another beer the girls had climbed into the minnow tank upon Jenny's suggestion that milk baths were good for people's skin.

"Maw, you should convert these into hot tubs," Jenny told him. She'd found a five-gallon bucket and was sitting on it, the milky water covering her shoulder and the bottom of her jaw. The ends of her hair were stiff and frosted white with drying flour. "You could be a bait shop-spa and market to fishermen *and* their wives."

"I don't think they're supposed to handle too much temperature." It began to dawn on Maw exactly what he'd done to his minnow tanks and the familiar sense of dread crept into his gut. He'd be able to clean it up, he thought. How hard would it be?

"Plus now the back wall is painted and clean," Sheila added. "It looks nice."

The back door swung open and a loud voice hollered a greeting. "We heard you were having a party!" T.C. thumped Maw's shoulder and he held up a case of beer. "I told Beau to grab Chex mix, but instead he brought this."

Beau hung over the edge of the minnow tank and wiggled his fingers in the water. "This doesn't look like minnows to me, Maw. And if you don't mind me saying, something's wrong with your water." He tugged at Jenny's bikini strap.

While the carousing reached another level, Ed packed up his equipment. Hefting his bags onto his shoulder, he waved to the group.

"You're not leaving, Ed!" Maw cried. "We have to celebrate!"

"I've got a lot of editing to do before we send the video along to your guy in Milwaukee. See you all later." Outside, Ed emptied his nearly full can of beer onto a bed of marigolds and loaded up his car. No good would come from letting drunk people near his very expensive cameras and tripods. A peal of laughter rang out through the screen door and Ed shook his head, thankful it wasn't his mess to clean up. Although he'd never be so impulsive to make that much of a mess.

TWENTY-NINE

Steve was leaning on his elbows watching TV when Arlyce passed through the bar with a box full of plastic garland she planned to hang around the windows to make the place feel more tropical. "What're you watching?"

"Our local idiot, Otto Zimm."

Arlyce peered above her bifocals at the screen to see a speed boat bumping into the side of Otto's fishing boat. The boaters were pointing and yelling at Otto. Their fury, however, had no effect on the fisherman, who silently sat with his head down and line in the water.

"Is that what happened Saturday? I heard some people on the deck complaining about some jerk blocking the channel. They said the guy dropped anchor to fish right by the buoy, but I was skeptical that anyone would be that stupid. Shows what I know."

"Keep watching," Steve murmured.

The newscaster came on the screen then and stood next to Jay Hodge who wore a serious expression and a T-shirt from Maw's bait shop. "You were an eyewitness to these events on Saturday. What can you tell us?" the reporter asked.

"The river's too crowded and the only fix is to slow down the traffic so everyone can enjoy it safely. What happened was tragic." Jay paused to let his words take effect.

"Tragic." Arlyce sniffed with contempt. She began to unravel the garland of bright orange lilies and green leaves. "This stuff looks so real you half-expect to smell it."

"We're all very fortunate no one was seriously injured. The fisherman involved is a local man from Bassville who has fished the Wissipaw his entire life. He deserves to enjoy his river as much as anyone bringing in their watercraft on a trailer to enjoy it for a day or a weekend."

"You were nearby when this happened," the newscaster pressed. "What made you decide to videotape the incident?"

"My family and friends were together celebrating a birthday. I always have a video recorder to capture special moments with the grandkids." Jay gave an indulgent smile before continuing. "Guess we were in the right place at the right time to catch the true nature of how dangerous the Wissipaw has become."

"Dangerous! What's dangerous is his vendetta against people using the river!" Arlyce cried out. Steve shushed her again.

"You're also spearheading a group that wants to pass a no-wake ordinance through Bassville."

"I believe good rules help keep everyone safe and this problem needs a solution. So, yes, I have been active in trying to make the river safer for everyone."

While the newscaster wrapped up Jay's self-righteous segment, Arlyce sputtered her frustration. "Who the hell does this jackass think

285

he is? The whole thing smells fishy. When has Otto *ever* dropped anchor to fish in the channel? Even on a weekday? He's a crank, but he knows better than to try to catch fish where it's busy with traffic. It doesn't make any sense."

Steve shrugged and peeled back the flaps on a case of Old Style so he could stock the cooler. "You saw him on TV, though. He was in the channel fishing."

"I don't believe it."

"He was there, you saw it with your own eyes."

"I know what I saw, but I don't believe it was normal. You want my opinion, the whole scene was staged just to give this No Wake business more legs than it's actually got."

"Could be. Seems like a lot of work, though."

Arlyce scowled at her husband and began hammering a string of fake flowers above one of the windows. While she pounded each nail, she imagined she was hitting Jay and Otto with her hammer.

Mona and Loyal were stooped over their hoes, working up the weeds between the rows of potatoes in the field. Mona paused to tighten her ponytail and tuck the loose tendrils of hair away from her sweaty forehead. "One acre doesn't seem as big when it's just cows grazing on it."

"Or when you're in a tractor," Loyal grunted. He eyed the distance they had yet to go and reckoned it would take them another forty minutes at least. Cows didn't break his back like vegetables seemed to.

"You see that news story about Otto this morning?" Mona asked.

"Your mother called me down. She likes to watch the news before she leaves for work at the women's shelter. I was getting cleaned up for breakfast when it was on."

286

"What the heck was Otto thinking, fishing in the channel like that?"

"Don't know that he was."

"What do you mean?"

"No one's going to catch fish in the channel on a weekend, too much boat traffic. On busy weekends the fish swim to the quiet spots like the bayous, far away from the humans. Otto knows that. No, I think he staged the whole thing with that lawyer."

"That's illegal!"

"It's not entirely *ethical*, but dropping anchor like that isn't illegal. Inconsiderate? Yes. But not against the law."

"Do you think it's a good idea to pass a no-wake zone all the way through town?" Mona asked. Her hoe clanged off a large stone and she knelt to dig it loose and toss it towards the edge of the field before continuing down the row.

"I think it makes sense to slow down the traffic when it's heavy, but not all the way through town. The stretch from the bridge to where it opens up in the lake is wide and straight. Makes more sense to slow things down by the boat landing and the narrow spots."

"I think a weekend rule makes more sense than all the time."

"Look at you," Loyal said with a teasing note in his voice. "Thinking of a solution different than the two choices put in front of you."

"I learned from the best, Dad."

"Well, I don't know about that."

"Good government is about solving problems, you say that all the time. You've taught me to be suspicious whenever someone tells me there are only two choices. Gotta walk things back to ID the real problem and then figure out how to fix it. It's not rocket science."

"Tell that to the men in Washington."

"Ah, I'd tell you that they're the problem. They're men! And the solution is to replace them with *women* in Washington," Mona teased.

"You are your mother's daughter," Loyal chuckled. "Let's talk about your other problem. How do you plan to fix your manpower shortage with your business? Or should I call it *people* power? You won't have me around in a week when it's time to cut hay."

Mona's expression grew serious. "I am getting behind. I should've planted second crops of peas and greens by now. I asked Scotty, but he doesn't want to work for me. You know how proud he is, he wants to be his own boss."

"That is a problem," Loyal observed. They worked along in silence for a minute and then Loyal cleared his throat. "The question becomes, do you want a partner or an employee?"

"I don't want to give someone half of my stake in the business. I've worked really hard to get it going. I want someone to work for me. Maybe I'll have to find a high school kid and just settle for summertime and weekend help."

"Well, if that's what you want, then Scotty's not your man. Maybe a high school student is the way to go." Loyal gently untangled an earthworm from the roots of a clump of grass before setting it beneath the shade of a potato plant.

But I want Scotty here, a little voice in Mona's head said. She'd heard that voice before. There was no good answer to that. Unless she hadn't fully identified the problem, she realized. *What was the problem, then?* She stabbed the pointy edge of the hoe into the soil and unearthed the short snarl of roots feeding a clump of pigweed. Using the flat edge, she broke apart the dirt so the weed would shrivel and die in the sun. "You ever think about offering Scotty a share of the dairy side of things?" Mona asked her father with some hesitation. He was the third generation. Suggesting someone outside of the family to run Butterfield's was no small thing.

He gave her a funny look and stabbed his hoe into the ground, lifting out the long tuberous root of a dandelion. "You really think we could separate them at this point?" Loyal used the sleeve of his T-shirt to mop sweat off his forehead and cheeks. "We share the fields—no, don't give me that face. We're going to rotate crops and that includes your stuff, too. We share the barn, the outbuildings and machinery. No, sweetie, I think it's a package deal at this point."

She scowled, not believing this was completely true. But his name was on all the paperwork, so he had a point. "Would someone I hire automatically work for both of us, then?"

"In a sense. You know, I wouldn't mind having some time off once in a while. Your mother's pretty adamant that we take a trip to visit Sean this fall. And I do owe her some vacation time. She'd like to see the fall colors in New England, though I can't see how leaves look any different there than they do here. Anyhow, an extra pair of hands would give both of us some freedom."

Mona mulled this over while they worked their way to the end of the potatoes. "Guess I'll have to use some of *our* hay bales to mulch this and keep the weeds down."

"Probably want to use *our* tractor to haul it out here," Loyal told her and handed over his hoe. "I've got a fence to check before I head in for lunch. See you later."

The July sun formed a warm cap on Mona's head while she walked to the barn. She didn't feel capable of running both businesses solo, and they'd grown to rely on each other in so many ways. The vegetables were doing great, until they ran into bad weather. Then the dairy side would pull them through. Likewise, the revenue from the vegetables could help out when milk prices dropped too low. It had become complicated, but there was no way she'd pick one part over the other. To do so would put both businesses at risk and break her father's heart. The Butterfield name had hung over the barn for eighty-five years. She was determined to keep it that way, so the compromise had been struck. But running two businesses had resulted in more work than she and Loyal could handle. She needed to do something.

Scotty discovered that happy hour at the Pub was pretty sour Tuesday afternoon. After seeing the news, people gathered to hash it out. "What the hell was that son of a bitch thinking?" Dob repeated. He shook his head in disbelief that anyone would act so dumb.

"He figured he could force the town's hand on the no-wake rule," Steve said. He was in constant motion behind the bar trying to go through his cleaning list while waiting on his customers. The good thing about scandal in a small town was it brought people out to gossip and all of the bar stools were full on a weekday, which was rare. "Arlyce thinks the whole thing was staged."

"I'd believe that," Snuffy wheezed. His dirty T-shirt clung damply to his large belly. "No fisherman with Otto's experience would fish the channel. Not even in the dead of fall."

"That's crazy. That Hodge guy seems like a sleaze, but asking Otto to drop anchor like that in the channel is a spectacularly bad idea. Somebody could've been hurt." Beau shuffled the deck of cards in his hands and started dealing them out to Spade, Dob and Dale. "Anyone else want in?" he asked.

"You folks are too rich for my blood," Snuffy said. He had three grubby dollar bills in his pocket and he knew Steve would spot him one beer, maybe two. Then he'd have to return to Grumpy's.

"Deal me in." T.C. dug in his pocket for a five-dollar bill.

"I don't know that Otto would risk damage to his own boat unless someone promised him something," Scotty said.

"That's what I think," Steve agreed. "At first I didn't believe Arlyce, but the more I think about it, the more it makes sense."

"Were the angry boaters in on the act, too?" Gene asked.

"I wouldn't be surprised, but that one man looked really mad on the video." Scotty swirled the beer in the bottom of his glass. "The way Otto kept his head down, that was strange." None of what he saw on TV added up. Otto would never try to fish in that spot, even on a quiet day.

"He was really shook up from that accident with the jet ski. I don't think he'd put himself out there like that on purpose," Spade said. "I never saw anyone so scared as he was that day. When we went back to bring those skis to the marina, he looked white as a ghost. His hands were shaking and he barely talked."

"Otto doesn't talk much anyway," Gene remarked.

"That's true," Steve agreed, "but Spade brings up a good point. Otto's hardly out looking for trouble after that experience."

"Don't be too sure. That guy loves fishing more than he loves his wife." Dob swapped out a card and scowled. "Though he is really faithful to Rex."

"How do you think you'll vote on this no-wake business, Gene?" Beau asked.

"We'll strike a balance," Gene said mildly and gave Steve a nod. "There's a balance between getting business here and keeping the traffic safe."

Scotty grinned at his dad. Between him and Mona and Loyal, the right decisions would get made.

"See?" Beau said and played the ten of hearts. "I told you not to get worked up. Our town council makes good decisions. Have a little faith, people."

"What's your stake in it, mouth?" Spade retorted. "You work down the river away from all the fuss, you rent your property, you're not a business owner, and you have every intention of leaving as soon as you figure out how to permanently unleash yourself from Jenny." He ticked off the reasons on his fingers and the rest of the men laughed.

291

Beau's face flushed. "Doesn't mean I don't care about Steve or Maw or even Snuffy here."

"Thank you, Beau," Snuffy muttered in a low voice.

"My money spends the same even if I don't own a business."

"That's true," Gene said. "And he does pay sales tax."

"Geez, you all act like I'm not a contributing member of society or something," Beau grouched.

Another ripple of laughter echoed through the bar. "No, no, no. You are a giver." Steve refilled a pitcher of beer and chuckled harder. "Probably gave at least five girls the clap last year." The men laughed harder.

"I don't have to take this, you know. Plenty of other places to drink in this town."

"That is true," T.C. said. "Bassville has no shortage of watering holes."

"C'mon with me," Snuffy offered. "I'll spot you one at Grumpy's." He stood to leave, having finished his free beer.

"I will," declared Beau. He dropped his cards on the bar and followed Snuffy out.

"Wow," Spade said after the door slammed shut behind them. "What's his problem today?"

Scotty shrugged. "No clue. Deal me in the next game," he told Dob. Beau was acting touchy, but a guy could just be cranky some days.

"Whatever you end up deciding," Steve told Gene, "I appreciate that you're thinking of the local businesses."

THIRTY

Mona's bike was coated by a film of dust when she went to get it out of her garage. She'd been so busy with pulling weeds, transplanting seedlings, harvesting and preparing for the farmers market that she hadn't ridden it in weeks. It was time for a break— she had a dozen chores to take care of but she needed to clear her head. How had she ever made time for her girls' night out with Judi? She'd gone out with her friends only once since the bachelorette party. There was no time for any fun anymore. Wiping her hand across the seat so she wouldn't end up with a grey patch on her butt, she reached down to test the tire pressure and the chain. All looked good. She snapped on her helmet and wheeled down the street.

A breeze from the west made the weather feel perfect. Mona waved at her grandparents, who sat side by side beneath the awning on the front of their apartment. Bassville was quiet on a Wednesday morning. A few boats were tethered to the docks by the Pub. Snuffy was fixing the screen door on Grumpy's. She pedaled past and turned up the road towards Bunker Hill. When she reached the rutted dirt trail that wound around the wooded and hilly spot popular with kids on dirt bikes and young men with ATVs, Mona braked hard and studied the new sign posted. "No Trespassing." On the corner another sign read "For Sale: 53 acres wooded by owner (715) 258-5551." For sale? It never occurred to her that anyone owned the land, it was just called Bunker Hill and people always rode on the trails. Who owned it? And what was their sudden interest in selling it—and keeping people off the trails?

She glanced up the road and seeing no traffic, Mona decided to ignore the warning. The tree branches overhead made the air feel cool while she worked her way up the trail. It had been a dry summer, so the trails were hard and packed down. By the time she reached the highest point, a sheen of sweat covered her forehead. She stopped to look across the fields towards Traysons Acres. The two houses looked tidy and Mona could see some kids running around the backyard of one. On three lots basements had been dug and foundations poured. The framed house on the far end of the subdivision—the one that all the vandalism seemed to happen to—looked like it was starting to come together. Nothing had been reported lately, so hopefully whoever was behind the trouble had stopped. Cows were grazing in the adjacent pasture and she could spot the roof of the Traysons' farmhouse and their silo. The old fields of corn and cows had definitely changed, with the road winding through the houses, but it didn't look awful. The new people seemed all right to her. Funny to think how scared she'd felt four years ago after the Council voted to allow the Traysons to develop their property. So much had changed.

Four years ago, she was confident about a future in Bassville with Jake, and now their lives had taken such different paths. He'd be gone for years building Olympic stadiums and a whole village for the athletes. Her heart belonged to the farm. It made her feel good to walk the familiar route through the barn and fields every day, to keep her dad's legacy alive even though it wasn't exactly the way he'd done it.

A monarch butterfly careened past and she watched its orange and black wings navigate the breeze. The faint aroma of spread manure filled her nostrils and a movement on the road caught her eye. She spotted a black truck and her heart lifted when she thought for a flash that it was Scotty's truck. Scotty. She kept having the same reaction around him, ever since he started helping her with the market. She depended on him, but more than that, she looked forward to being around him. It made sense the more she thought about it; he was the partner she wanted. How had she not seen him this way before?

Mona unhooked her leg from the frame of her bike and with both thumbs on the hand brakes, she started down the hill. Loose gravel caused her tires to skid, but she kept her balance and rolled to the bottom without falling. There was time for one more go on the hill before she'd ride back to town.

Tammy marched over to Kelly's front door and rang the doorbell with a flourish. "Come in," came a muffled voice from the back of the house. Tammy followed the noise to the kitchen where she discovered Kelly's backside sticking out of a kitchen cupboard. "Just a sec."

Tammy pulled up a seat and tapped her nails impatiently on the table while Kelly clanged a few more pans and emerged holding a large enamel kettle. "I finished the proposal. I want you to read it before I present it at next week's town Council meeting."

Kelly set the kettle in the sink before taking a seat across from her neighbor. "Let's take a look."

"Kind of hot for making chili," Tammy remarked. "I got sweaty just walking over here."

Kelly glanced over her shoulder at the kettle. "I'm making jam."

"Jam?"

"Raspberry. I bought a couple gallons from Mona's farm stand. I never tried it before, but how difficult can it be?"

"What's a jar cost at the store?" Tammy asked. "About a dollar, right?"

"Homemade jam is better." Kelly read the sheet of paper. "This looks wonderful."

"Really? I didn't leave anything out, did I?" Tammy pulled back the paper and ran down the bulleted list of reasons why a buffer between the houses and the farm would make everyone's lives better. "Do you think this part about safety and liability with children and farm equipment is clear?"

"It looks great." Kelly said. "I can't think of anything to add."

"The meeting starts at six-thirty, so we'll pick you up at six."

"I'm sorry?"

"You have to come. That's how these things work, you know. The more people show up, that's pressure on the Council to take our side. I already talked to June and Peg and a few of the other people in town. Plus, this Ezra guy doesn't even know what we're doing, so he won't be there to oppose us. Oh, and bring your kids. It's really hard for people to say no when they look at little children and think of their well-being."

"Won't it look pushy to have a bunch of people there?"

"It will look *supported*," Tammy said. "Do things well and you only have to do them once, that's what my mom always taught me." She pushed her chair back and headed for the door. "I'll see you later," she called over her shoulder.

296

Back at the farm Mona stabbed her weeding fork deep alongside the long root of a dandelion. The bales of hay she'd strewn between the rows had made a huge difference, but she still had to tend to the carrots, beets and onions so they'd have room to grow without competition. Fewer weeds, better soil moisture and it even seemed like the heat-loving peppers thrived. The insulation kept the ground warmer through the night and stimulated their growth. With a grunt she pulled the dandelion loose from the ground and tossed it into a wheelbarrow. She'd ask Scotty out for a date, she decided. Then she almost felt sick to her stomach thinking about it. What if Scotty said no? It was a huge risk—could they even stay friends if that happened? She squeezed her eyes shut to push the idea out of her head. What would Judy tell her? She imagined her friend telling her if he said no, then nothing changed. She was already by herself. Inhaling the sweet smell of the hay, she tried instead to think about how he'd say yes. "You gotta stay optimistic," she whispered softly. "Otherwise no one would ever get together, right?"

A crow cried out sharply over her head and she watched it float down and walk toward her between the rows of beets. It prodded at something in the ground and turned its glittering stare at her, cocking its head.

"We'd work," she told the crow, and felt foolish for talking to a bird. "He's cute. He's sweet. I know we make each other happy."

The crow flew away. Mona stood and trudged back to the wheelbarrow heaped with weeds. Judi would give her sound advice. She'd call her tonight.

Arlyce repeated the list so she wouldn't forget anything on her way next door to Bud's Supermarket. Her earrings jangled while she recited "Celery salt, box of lemon Jell-O, stainless steel scrub pad, limes." It felt good to get in the fresh air outside of the bar. The sunshine made her smile. After she got done with work at three, she'd take the kids down to play on the river, she decided.

"Hello, Arlyce!" the cashier greeted her.

"Too nice of a day to be working." Arlyce grabbed a shopping basket. She started down the second aisle of the tiny supermarket past the beady gaze of the taxidermied wildlife displayed overhead. The store's aisles carried the basics, but the front window was dominated by cases of beer and soda as it catered to Bassville's tourists. Bud's specialty was the back of the store where he hand cut any kind of meat they needed. The quality made the locals loyal enough to ignore lower prices at the larger grocery stores in Northport. Arlyce found the first two items in the baked goods aisle and was about to ask the cashier where to find a scrub pad when Otto walked through the door. She narrowed her eyes at him.

"Afternoon, ladies," he muttered, moving past them without making eye contact.

"Otto, what was that stunt you pulled this weekend in the channel?" Arlyce demanded.

"Don't know what you're talking about."

"Baloney. Everyone in town saw it on TV—you sitting there acting like you're fishing right at that narrow spot before Pigeon Lake. What are you up to?"

"I was fishing like I always do." Otto checked his watch. "I have to keep moving."

"You're conspiring with that Jay Hodge. You old fool, you're gonna ruin this town with your crazy no-wake rules. Nobody's gonna come here if we make the whole river a no-wake zone. Is that what you want?"

"I want to be left alone."

"You're selfish," Arlyce followed him to the coolers along the wall. "You think Bud's will be here for you if their business dries up? Where you gonna take your wife out for dinner when we don't have boaters keeping money in our till? You want to live like a hermit, that's your right but you have no right to chase everybody else away!" Arlyce poked him in the chest with her index finger.

"I just need to buy a gallon of milk. Leave me alone, Arlyce."

"I'm asking you to leave *us* alone. You keep pushing for less traffic on the river, you'll end up the most hated man in Bassville—if you haven't earned that name already. And as for that rich jackass you're working for … "

Otto stepped past her and flung open the glass cooler door. He pulled out a gallon of 2% milk.

"You're in for a rude awakening with him, too. Won't be long until all of Jay Hodge's rich friends start buying up the river and making it their playground. You can't really believe he's on your side. If you do, you're a bigger fool than I believed possible."

Otto paid the cashier and kept his back turned towards Arlyce.

"He's using you, Otto. Don't be his pawn."

Otto left Bud's and Arlyce inhaled deeply. Her hands shook with anger. "Where do I find a scrub pad?" she said to the cashier. "Sorry about the scene."

"No problem. Between you and me? You're absolutely right. Worst thing we could do to this town is a no-wake zone. It would kill everyone's business and I need my job."

"We'll fight this." Arlyce pursed her lips and nodded. "We need to form our own alliance to protect our town."

While Judi described the details of her Las Vegas wedding and honeymoon, Mona rolled onto her back and kicked her legs over the edge of her living room couch. She adjusted the phone receiver more comfortably. "We came back to the room and there was a bottle of champagne in a bucket of ice and a plate with chocolate-covered strawberries. I'm telling you, The Tropicana knows how to make a honeymoon special!"

"Did you win any money?" Mona asked.

"We went to the casino the next day. Will likes to play roulette. The first slot machine I walked over to was filthy. Someone had left behind a full ashtray and an empty glass. So I sat at the next machine over and started dropping in my quarters. Couple minutes later this old lady walks up to the disgusting slot machine and fifty cents later she hits the jackpot! She won eight hundred dollars!"

"No way!"

"Yeah, and I ended up losing twenty dollars before I got bored and found my husband—can I say that again? *My husband* still playing at the table. He won enough to take us out to dinner, so it wasn't all bad. I really don't think many people win big there, but it was fun walking around and looking at the different buildings and all the crazy people."

"I'm glad you had a good time. You deserve it."

"What's going on in Bassville? Anything new? I bet you never find time to leave the farm."

"Business is booming and Scotty's been my right hand for the last month. Actually, that's why I'm calling."

"You're planning to open a farm stand here in Chicago?"

"No, but that was a good guess." Mona took a deep breath before confessing it. "I think I might have different feelings about Scotty. I don't know why I didn't see it before—he's been right in front of me the whole time."

"Mona!" Judi exclaimed. "When did you finally figure it out?"

"You mean you knew?"

"He's *always* had a thing for you. Every time we'd go out, he'd look for you. His face totally lights up when he sees you walk in the bar. Everyone sees it—except you, I guess."

"Why didn't you say anything?"

"Because you were with Jake. So when did this start?"

"That's the thing—it hasn't really."

"How are you going to tell him? Will you ask him out? What's your plan?"

"That's why I'm calling you."

"Okay, you need to ask him out. And I have the perfect first date idea for you … "

Later that night Mona climbed into bed and tried to think of when or how she could kiss Scotty. Things like kissing a guy were always easier after a few drinks, but she wanted an honest response. Jenny always called alcohol "truth serum." She swore people were more honest when they were drinking, but that wasn't Mona's experience. Mona felt sure that drinking made people stupid and do silly things. Jenny believed this because Beau was always drunk when he was vowing his love for her, so of course that's what she wanted to believe. She'd have to kiss Scotty another way. Maybe she'd take him to dinner to thank him for all his help and then at the end of the evening she'd lean in and go for it. That seemed like a good plan.

THIRTY-ONE

OTTO POURED COFFEE INTO his thermos and twisted the cap tight. After kissing his wife and giving Rex a brief scratch on the head, he gathered his lunchbox and headed out the door to work. All night Arlyce's words replayed in his head, and Otto had begun to question Jay's position on the no-wake zone. No wake all the time would slow down traffic and hurt the businesses down the river. Otto believed in people's freedom to do what they wanted, but he also recognized the value in a little give and take for the good of the group. During his lunch break he dug a quarter out of his pocket and called Jay from the pay phone at the edge of the mill's parking lot.

"Jay Hodge speaking."

"Listen, Jay, this is Otto."

"What can I do for you, Otto? You got your tank of gas all right, didn't you?"

"I did, thanks. I have a question for you."

"What's on your mind, friend?"

"This whole no-wake thing. I'm wondering, do you plan to compromise on no wake all the way from boat landing to lake? Is that a starting point for your group or the only plan?"

"Not sure what you're asking me, Otto."

"Well, I've been thinking how it could hurt the businesses in Bassville because if the traffic slows down too much, they'll lose customers. People won't want to spend extra time to crawl down the river, they'll just get as far as Gala and turn around."

"That's a fair point. But let me as you something, Otto. Where's your wife's favorite restaurant?"

"She really likes Pine Tree."

"And how long does it take you to drive to that restaurant on a Friday night when you take her there?"

"About twenty minutes, I suppose."

"Let's say there was a road construction project that created a detour and added ten minutes to your driving time. Would you be willing to drive an extra ten minutes to bring your wife to her favorite restaurant?"

"I guess so, but … "

"Otto," Jay interrupted him, "Bassville has wonderful restaurants and places to visit. A no-wake rule would make it safer for people to get there and add to the value of the trip. It's like when I fire up the grill on the weekend—sure it takes a little time to get the coals just right, but I enjoy that time standing by the flames, smelling the charcoal, drinking a beer. Frankly, the extra time adds to my anticipation and makes the moment when I take the first bite that much better. So to answer your question, No Wake: Take Back the Lake *is* the best thing for Bassville. Sure, it might take a little longer for a few people to get here, but that doesn't change the fact that Bassville is a great place to go. A no-wake rule preserves everything that's beautiful about the river."

"I'm not sure I… "

"Otto, I have another call coming in. I hope I'll see you at the next meeting. Have a great day."

Otto listened to the dial tone in his ear for a moment before hanging up and walking back to the entrance to Plant 3. Jay's arguments made sense, kind of. But ten minutes more in a car wasn't the same as thirty minutes by boat. Still, Disneyland only had one location and from what he'd heard, hundreds of thousands of people made the trip to visit it. But Bassville was only one of several spots along the river where people could pull up to the dock and grab a pizza or a burger. As much as he wanted peace and quiet, it would be bad to hurt people like the Shanskis and Maw. The whole business was becoming more complicated the more he thought about it.

Mona felt silly walking into the Hotel to find Scotty, but she was also making good on a promise to Judi. "Good morning, Sue!"

Sue let her glasses fall to her chest. "Mona! I don't suppose you're here to rent a room?"

"No, just thought I'd stop by and check in on you."

"Aren't you sweet. Pull up a seat. Can I get you anything?"

"No thanks." Mona sat on a chair in the lobby and Sue joined her. "How's everything going since Judi left?"

"Busy. I wish she'd have left in the fall when things slow down."

"Did you find some help?"

"I hired a girl to clean and help with breakfast. She's still learning so it's hard to say how she'll work out."

"I talked to Judi last night. She sounded good. Happy."

Sue nodded. "I think she is. I plan to visit after Labor Day. Close this place down for a week and spend some time down there."

"That will be nice—she'll be all settled in by then and ready to take you on the town."

"It's funny." Sue gazed out the window towards Main Street. "I knew I'd miss her, but it turns out it's the little things I notice more than anything. Like how we'd chat a little every morning while getting breakfast ready, or how she'd leave a cup of tea for me in the afternoon on her way upstairs to clean rooms."

Mona thought about Scotty, how he brought her the raspberries and had tightened the loose door on her greenhouse last week. "You're right. It is the little things."

After a few more minutes of small talk, Mona stood. "Is Scotty on the deck? I need to catch up with him about something."

Sue waved her towards the dining room where the patio doors led to the deck.

Scotty was crouched in the corner twisting a screw in place. His arms flexed with the effort. Sawdust flecked his T-shirt and his hair clung against the back of his neck. *How have I looked at him my whole life but now he looks new to me?* Mona cleared her throat to get his attention.

"Hold on," Scotty torqued on the handle one more time and squatted back on his heels to look over his shoulder. "Mona!" His face lit into a grin and gave her confidence.

"Do you have plans tonight?"

"No." He set down his tools and stood. "You need help with something? I think the raspberries are done for the season."

"Actually, I wanted to take you out to dinner."

Scotty raised his eyebrows, curious. "Okay. I never say no to free food. Where do you want to go?"

"A place in Northport. Pick you up at five-thirty?"

"I can drive, it's no problem. I'll come get you at five-thirty."

"Awesome." Mona felt silly standing there with a goofy smile on her face. "So, I'll see you at five-thirty."

"It's a date."

It's a date. Mona replayed his words in her head while she left the Hotel, weeded between the rows of onions and carrots, checked the raccoon traps near the sweet corn and picked beans. *It's a date.* Tonight she would find out if he felt the same way about her. Judi said he'd always loved her. Was it true? How did the old song go? *It's in his kiss, that's where it is.* She hummed while she worked. They'd go to Northport to an Italian restaurant she'd eaten at once with Judi on a girls' night out. It was romantic, dark and quiet with candles on the tables and what guy didn't like Italian food? Too bad she didn't want Jenny to know about her plans, or she'd be tapping her for advice on what to wear. But Jenny was terrible at keeping secrets and Mona knew if Jenny knew, Beau would find out and that would be the end of everything.

Mona grabbed the handles of a wheelbarrow and headed back towards the field to check on the squash vines.

Otto pulled into Maw's Bait and Tackle on his way home from work. He'd hashed Arlyce and Jay's arguments over and over but doubt niggled at his brain. Something didn't completely add up.

"I gotta ask you something," he announced inside the store. He noticed Maw had hung some of the No Wake posters on the walls, but they were partly covered up with other signs.

Maw was sitting on the floor behind a minnow tank surrounded by machine parts and tools. He set down a wrench and frowned up at Otto.

"What's your thinking on the no-wake business. You for it or against it?"

306

"Mostly against it." Maw tapped the side of his leg with a flathead screwdriver. "You probably knew that."

"Tell me why."

Maw's lips twisted into a smirk. "Really? Seems obvious, doesn't it?"

Otto crossed his arms over his chest and waited. Maw grew serious and gave him a curt nod. "Okay then. You slow down traffic and nobody will come upriver past the boat landing. Maybe they'll stop at the Pub, but it isn't likely they'll go much further. I understand the need to slow things down and I agree it makes sense, but only in the two channels where the river gets narrow and only when the traffic is heavy, on the weekends and holidays. Think about how wide the river is through town. There's no reason why people can't go as fast as they want through there."

"What about the other traffic with those jet skis?"

"They're a problem, but I bet they'll have regulations on them after a point. It's like anything new. People will figure it out and the laws will catch up to make them safer."

"Jay says people will still come through no matter what the rules are."

"You know where his place is, right?" Maw asked Otto.

"Yeah."

"Ever consider how a no-wake rule really benefits him more than anybody else?" Maw leaned back against the wall and waited for Otto to connect the dots.

"How so?"

"His house is in the wide stretch. That son of a bitch didn't care about big boats and big wakes when he had his big boat. He didn't give a shit until he bought a house here. Before that he and his wife tore through here in a cigarette boat better suited for Lake Michigan than the Wissipaw. Bet you any money he'd have opposed any wake regulations five years ago before he had waterfront property and his own dock to protect. Now he lives by the water and he wants it nice and quiet."

Otto considered this. "That's probably true."

"And there's another thing," Maw gestured with his notebook. "I'm surprised you're taking the side of someone who wants more rules. Hodge's a bully, he wants things only his way to suit him. Is that what you're about, Otto? I had you pegged for more of a 'live and let live' kind of guy." Maw pointed the end of his pen at him and shook his head. "Now unless you need to buy some bait, I've got to finish fixing this filtration system. It's all clogged up and I might've burned out the motor."

Mona had curled her hair, applied eyeliner and changed her shirt four times before settling on a turquoise blouse with a deep neckline that showed the top of her cleavage. Tonight she'd make sure Scotty saw her as somebody besides his mom's best friend's daughter—his playmate since nursery school and his drinking buddy. She sprayed perfume generously on her neck and wrists and then blotted it off with a cotton ball soaked in rubbing alcohol. Overkill was another story, she decided.

The doorbell rang and she skipped down the hall to answer it. Scotty stood there with his hair slicked down, still wet from a shower, wearing a button-down shirt with his nicest jeans. A dress shirt. He'd dressed like he was going on a date, Mona noticed with satisfaction.

"You clean up nice," he said. "After you." He swung out his arm with a flourish and followed her down her front sidewalk to his truck. Mona felt a twinge of disappointment when he didn't stop to open the passenger side door for her, but she blamed it on the buddy factor.

"Where to?" he asked her with a happy grin.

308

"It's called Genova's, just off 4th Street downtown Northport. Judi and I ate there once."

On the way they talked as usual, discussing Otto and the no-wake business, the logistics of building a hoop house at the farm and Maw's rap video. "He's got a whole tank out of commission," Scotty told her. "I don't know what he was thinking, dumping it full of flour and powdered milk, but the motor on his filtration system blew out and he's down to two tanks. Lucky for him it's not the white bass run, so he's keeping up with only two minnow tanks, but still." Scotty shook his head. "That guy gets some pretty wild ideas."

"Jenny told me they had a blast, though. I bet Peg went ballistic when she found out."

"I guess he did clean off one entire wall and had the girls repaint it, so that made her happy. Peg was getting mad about all the clutter in the shop. She's been after him to clean the place up now that they want to rent out part of the building."

"I wonder who would move in there," Mona mused. She discreetly checked her hair in the side view mirror while Scotty turned the corner.

"This the place you want to go?" he asked. Genova's was a low brick building on the corner of a line of shops and apartments. The restaurant's name painted on the glass door and an "Open" sign hanging from a window were the only indicators that it was a restaurant.

"Wait until we get inside," Mona promised. The exterior was not a selling point. They walked through the door and Scotty let out a low whistle. Murals of a Venetian courtyard and distant mountains covered the walls and in the center of the tables a small fountain bubbled.

"Just two of you?" asked a young man wearing a white apron over his slacks and polo shirt.

"Yes," Scotty told him and followed Mona to a corner table. The restaurant was half full. Soft violin music played against the clink of dishes and people's conversations. Mona unfolded the white linen napkin across her lap and reached for the wine list propped up in the center of the table.

"What do you say? Should we get a bottle?" she asked.

"Of Bud Light?"

"Wine."

"Oh. I guess so. I never tried it before, so you're gonna have to pick what kind."

After ordering Mona watched Scotty hesitate before sipping his glass of house red. He scrunched up his nose and grimaced. "Delicious?" Mona asked him.

"Kinda sour. I'll get used to it." He reached for a breadstick and took a bite. "Pretty fancy place."

"Do you like it?"

"It's nice. I had no idea it was here. But when I come to Northport it's either a lumberyard for supplies or working at a job site."

"How are your parents doing?"

"They're figuring it out. Mom started delivering a couple times a week for Meals on Wheels, so that gets her out of the house. Dad's still climbing the walls. I told him I need help with some of my jobs. I really don't but I thought it would give him something to do. He keeps turning me down, though, so I don't know what he's looking for."

"They're pretty young to be retired," Mona remarked.

"Yeah. And Dad's got no interest in anything besides fishing and town politics. Maybe he could start teaching some agriculture classes or something. That would be cool."

"I could connect him with some of my instructors at the technical college if you want."

"That would be nice. Maybe if he can't actually farm, he'd be happy to talk about it all day."

Mona fidgeted with her necklace, sliding the pendant back and forth on the chain. "Maybe he could check out consulting. I know the county extension has experts who answer people's questions and such. That might be something to consider, too. What about you? Have you given any thought to your future?"

He sighed. "Every day. But I'm making good money and I don't need a lot, so it's crazy to worry about it."

"You should be happy, though. Content with what you're doing. For me, tending bar didn't feel fulfilling. Now that I have my greenhouse business, I love it. I mean, it's hard work, but I feel different about my work compared to when I worked at the Pub. It's more purposeful."

"I know what you mean," Scotty agreed. "I don't think I want to own my own business and boss people around, but I do get a little of that good feeling when I finish building something."

"Maybe carpentry is your thing."

"Maybe." Scotty gazed over at the restaurant fountain. "Think people throw coins in that and make wishes?"

"I bet they do. Want to make a wish?"

"Naw, that's for kids."

After they finished eating the waiter set the check beside Scotty. Mona reached for it but he gripped the other end of the bill. "I got this."

"I asked you out."

"Your money's no good here. That's what the sign says."

"What sign?" She looked over her shoulder where he'd pointed and felt the check slide out from her fingertips.

"You didn't see it?" Scotty stood and dug into his pocket. He handed Mona a quarter. "Go make your wish while I settle up."

It was a hopeful sign that he paid for dinner. Mona walked across the tiled floor and closed her eyes tightly while she flipped the quarter into the water. The coin sunk to the bottom, bright against the dark pennies that others had dropped in. *I hope Scotty loves me.* She joined him at the door. "Thank you."

"No, thank *you*. This was fun." He looked at her sideways. "Did you want to go straight home?"

"You want to do something else?"

"Let's walk around a little. Been sitting too long and it's a nice night."

The streets were quiet and the sky was still light when they turned up the block. They took turns commenting on cars that drove by, window displays and the noise, so different than evening in Bassville.

"Especially on the farm, though," Mona said. "When there's a little breeze, like tonight, to keep the bugs away, I love to sit on the porch and look at the stars."

Scotty tilted his head back. "Hard to see as many stars here. Too many lights."

"Can't hear the nature sounds either."

"What's your favorite?" he asked.

"Crickets. My second favorite is a robin because that means winter's over."

"Frogs. I like the racket they make when there's a pond full of them."

"Favorite smell?" Mona asked.

"Fresh cut hay. Yours?"

"Lilacs."

They reached an intersection with four lanes of traffic and no sidewalk on the other side of the street. Scotty said. "I don't get why they make it so darn hard to walk around here." He turned to head back the way they came.

"We do at least have sidewalks on Main Street," Mona said.

"And the street's paved now, too, thanks to some progressive leadership on the town council."

"We aim to please, private citizen."

Mona kept waiting for a still moment when she could lean forward to kiss his cheek, or maybe even reach for his hand, but they never stopped moving and Scotty kept his hands balled in his jeans pockets. Her courage was fading even while she reminded herself that the real chance would present itself back at her front door. Her heart pounded while she tried to act composed.

When they returned to Genova's, Scotty did unlock her side of the truck first *and* opened the door before heading around to the driver's side. Maybe, she thought, he was starting to feel it, too.

His whole life, Otto opposed big government telling people what to do. He didn't appreciate red tape, excessive regulations or wasted money on bureaucracy. He resented paying taxes for stuff he didn't use, like schools and libraries and national parks. Living in the "land of the free" meant not having obligations or rules to follow, but Otto did believe something had to be done about the noise and speed on the river. A dangerous river would be as bad for Bassville's businesses as a no-wake rule. People wouldn't want to navigate the traffic or risk damaging their boats if things stayed crazy.

He loathed a rich guy pushing his weight around, too, which was the same as the government. Jay wasn't truly part of Bassville like everyone else. He owned property here, but he didn't volunteer around the community or invest in it. In fact, Otto realized, Jay was a lot like him. He wanted his own peace and quiet when it suited him and really didn't give a damn about anybody else's problems. Otto thought of all the times he'd dragged a fallen tree to block off part of the river or ignored the boat launch fee boxes when unloading his boat into the water. He'd never compared his behavior to another person before, but suddenly it became clear. He closed his eyes while recalling his opposition to the Traysons selling their property. They had the right to sell what they owned, but he'd pounded a "No Grow" sign into his front yard and voted against rezoning because he didn't want the town to change. Essentially, he wanted a rule to limit someone else's activity for his own benefit.

Rex nuzzled Otto's hand and whined gently. "Need to go out?" Otto opened the back door. Rex paused and licked his owner's hand a few times before trotting outside. "The only reason you do not hate me," Otto told his dog, "is because you don't understand the big picture."

"What's that, honey?" his wife asked from the other room where she was reading the paper.

"Nothing. Just talking to Rex." He moved to the living room and stood in front of his wife who looked up from the word search puzzle she was finishing. "Do you think I'm a selfish person?"

"That's a strange question. Why would you ask such a thing?"

Otto sat in the armchair next to her and folded his hands. "You know how I just want to be alone on the river to fish, right?"

"It's fair to say that fishing's a pretty solitary sport. And I really don't mind you going without me." She pushed her glasses up her nose and tucked her feet beneath her seat.

"I'm talking about how I don't want anyone else on the river with me. Which is why I was against the Traysons selling their land and Maw making his bait shop bigger ... and now I'm supporting that no-wake rule."

"Are you changing your mind about it?"

"I think so. At least I'm starting to think Jay Hodge is too far to one side anyway. I'm all for less regulation and no wake feels pretty restrictive."

"Maybe some rules can be good?"

Otto nodded. He felt weak and unsure of his position anymore.

His wife continued talking. "Think about those times when you're in a hurry to come home off the water because it's cold, or the weather turned nasty. Maybe slowing down's a good idea when there's other traffic, but when you're all alone with no one in sight?"

"There usually aren't too many other boats on the water. I can't see the point in puttering along when nobody else is around. It's not a safety issue most of the time, really."

"What about the damage from the waves?"

"I think that depends on the boat. My fishing boat doesn't kick up the same amount of water as those big power boats. A johnboat is less damaging than a jet ski."

"And a canoe or a rowboat is the gold standard," his wife joked. "Let's face it, the best rules benefit everyone, they protect people from hurting each other. That's why we have them in the first place, right?"

Otto rubbed his palms together and stood. He knew what needed to happen. First a phone call, then a vote next month—he'd suggest a compromise rule for weekends only, and just in the narrow spots on the river. "I think I'll call Hodge tomorrow and tell him not to include me in his group anymore."

"I thought they had a stupid name anyway," his wife told him. "Take Back the Lake—their no-wake proposal ended at the lake anyway, so what was that even about? Didn't make any sense. Just a stupid rhyme is all."

Scotty shifted his truck into park in front of Mona's house. She took a deep breath. She would not wait awkwardly to find out if he planned to walk her to the door or not. *This is it. Here I go.* She leaned across the black leather seat and aimed her puckered lips at his cheek. Scotty turned his head and his eyes grew wide. There was no turning back, she thought, so she stayed the course and planted her lips on his. She'd laugh it off as trying to be friendly if he backed away.

"Jesus, Mona," Scotty murmured. He pulled back with a surprised expression.

Mona felt her heart thud harder inside of her chest. Nausea swept over her. "I was just ... "

"I'm sorry," he said and held up his hands. "I thought you ... I mean I turned my head and you ... "

"It's okay. I was only trying to give you a kiss on the cheek," she explained to cover up her embarrassment.

"Oh. Right."

Mona caught the slight slump of his shoulders and how his expression shifted and discomfort moved to disappointment. Encouraged, she quickly leaned in again and kissed him on the lips, on purpose. He was not rejecting her. When she felt him kiss her back elation burned through her entire body, from her toes through the top of her head. She'd never forget any detail about the moment—the way his knees brushed the edge of the steering wheel while he turned toward her, the way his skin smelled like Dial soap, Bob Uecker's voice on the radio telling them that Paul Molitor had caught a pop up fly ball. She memorized the way Scotty's hair curled around his ears and the nape of his neck, how he reached his callused hand across to cup her cheek and his voice, husky and quiet, telling her, "Me too."

THIRTY-TWO

Mona felt giddy waking up the next morning. Giddy and silly. Humming to herself, she started the coffee maker and poured a bowl of cereal. When Scotty had driven away, she'd laughed out loud, partly relieved and partly thrilled. By the time she left the cab of his truck, everything between them was fully understood. Everything she'd been feeling, he felt, too, but for far longer than she'd even known.

The phone's metallic ring startled her enough that she knocked over the quart of milk. Grinning, she answered it, expecting to hear Scotty's voice on the line. "Good morning!"

"Good morning. Is this Mona Butterfield?"

"Yes."

"Larry Meiller here, from Garden Talk. I'm looking to get you on the schedule a couple times before fall if you're available."

"Absolutely!" Mona pulled the free calendar from the credit union off the wall and grabbed a pen. "I'm pretty free except for Saturdays, so you tell me what you're looking for."

After agreeing on the dates and discussing possible topics for upcoming fall and winter programs, Mona hung up with a satisfied sigh. She reached for a dish cloth to wipe up the milk and contemplated the sweet turn her life had taken.

Her kitchen back in order, she tied her hair into a ponytail and changed into shorts and a Dirty Girl T-shirt. Today she'd drive to Clearwater to teach a seminar on collecting seeds at the public library. She knew she'd feel distracted thinking about last night. Getting to spend her whole life with Scotty by her side was the only thing that mattered in the end. People might talk, but there was no rule about how long to date somebody before you got engaged or married. She would not waste time when she knew what she wanted.

The bell on the door jingled and Maw looked up from his Word of the Day calendar to see Mona step into the bait shop. "Hello! This is a surprise—I can't think of the last time I saw you in my store."

Mona approached the counter. "I need your help."

"Okay." He placed the calendar back on the shelf and leaned forward on his elbows. "Whatever you need."

"First you need to swear to keep your mouth shut. I'm only here because you're the most creative person I know, but you gab more than the whole Stitch n' Bitch combined." Her expression was so serious that Maw frowned. "Promise me."

"On my father's grave," Maw vowed. He was itching to use his new word but couldn't figure out how to work it in yet. "What's your conundrum?"

Mona glanced around the store to make sure they were alone before continuing. "I need help planning a marriage proposal."

"Ho-lee shit. You're gonna head to Atlanta."

"What?" Mona shook her head. "No, you fool." She sighed and hesitated. "Scotty," she confessed in a low voice. A blush covered her cheeks.

Maw's eyes widened. They both farmed. They both loved Bassville. They'd been two peas in a pod for as long as he could remember. Their parents were best of friends. Mona and Scotty made sense. In fact, he was a bit put out he hadn't considered this sooner—it made perfect sense. If two crazy kids belonged together, well, not two crazy kids. Two sensible, hardworking, decent kids—and he always suspected Scotty hung around her wanting more than just her friendship. "Congratulations! I always thought he was in love you with you," he told her.

"Really?" Mona's voice and head lifted.

Maw nodded. "Thought he was moonin' around you after T.C. left for Alaska. But then you and Jake got together and … Hell, let's not quibble over the history of it." *There it was. He got it in play.* "If you've got amorous intentions for the boy, then let's precipitate the proposal." He tugged at his beard while he thought.

"I want to do this in style. But not in front of anybody. The memory of Jake's proposal at the Pub in front of everybody still makes me cringe. If Scotty's going to turn me down, I'd just as soon nobody witness it."

"Private," Maw mused aloud. "Let's start with two things that boy loves, cows and the river."

Mona nibbled at a hangnail while Maw worked an idea around in his mind. She walked a nervous lap around the store. It had been a while since she'd last stopped in. He'd added more racks and displays, including a stand full of hats, can coolers, cigarette lighters and other stuff branded with his minnow logo. One of the minnow tanks was drained, its filtration system parts lay on the concrete floor next to an operation manual and a toolbox.

Finally, Maw grabbed a pad of paper, ripped off the top sheet and started jotting a list with a pencil. "Okay, kid. Here's what you're gonna do."

Mona returned to the counter and listened.

Kelly called through Tammy's screen door, "I've got a present for you, neighbor!"

Tammy dodged through her children's toys strewn across the living room floor and let Kelly inside. "Homemade jam!"

"I think it turned out pretty good for my first try. We ate it this morning on toast. Enjoy."

"Thank you!"

"Nice to have our windows open again, isn't it?" Kelly admired the view and the fresh manure-free aroma of the day.

"I can't get over how fast the stench left once we got that pile spread out. I honestly didn't believe it until today, I thought I was just getting used to the smell."

"The only thing worrying me is what that whacko will think up next." Kelly looked towards Ezra's farm, half expecting tractors or a stampede of cattle to rush across the field at them.

"Loyal Butterfield's probably already talked to him by now. I don't think he'll bother us anymore."

"I hope you're right. Are you ready to go?"

Tammy grabbed a laundry basket full of beach towels, sunscreen and sand toys while calling for her children. "They'll be so excited when they see what I did."

Ten minutes later they reached the empty lot in Bassville where a small crowd of children had already gathered to play in the water. A slope of sand stretched from shore to the water's edge and, according to Tammy, some distance beyond. "A beach!" Tammy flung out her hands like Vanna White showing off the grand prize on *Wheel of Fortune.*

"I can't get over it!" Kelly marveled. "How did you do it?"

Tammy commanded her children to "make a T" while she smeared sunscreen across their shoulders and backs before cutting them loose to race towards the water. She capped the bottle and rubbed her hands dry on her own shoulders before sitting in one of the lawn chairs Kelly had carried to the side of the water for them. "After that awful day before the picnic I did a little thinking. How can this town not have a proper spot for kids to play in the water? And do you have any idea how cheap it is to buy a truckload of sand? I didn't know either, but I called around. Turns out sand's ridiculously inexpensive. A little corporate sponsorship and voila!" She waved her arms out to where the kids splashed and swam.

"What did it cost?"

"Me? Nothing but my time making a few phone calls. And the whole thing's tax-deductible because it's a donation to the town. The grand total was less than two hundred dollars for sand and labor."

"You just called in a dump truck to unload sand at the water's edge," Kelly said in disbelief.

"Two trucks, but yes. That's what I don't understand," Tammy tucked her frosted blonde hair into a clip and popped open a can of Tab. "You have a dangerous but open area for kids to play and people just let them without giving it a second thought. Leeches, clam shells, goodness knows what else is lurking on the shoreline there and without hardly any effort you can make it a nice beach. Problem solved. It's like people have no imagination or something."

"Or motivation," Kelly murmured, again in awe of Tammy's resourcefulness. She wasn't much for joining clubs, but if Bassville had a PTA she was signing up just to watch Tammy in action.

The seed-saving event in Clearwater was a bust. Only four people had showed up, a grandma and her two grandkids and the librarian who'd hung around to be polite. Mona had kept a smile pasted on the entire time and wrapped up earlier than planned. But the grandma had been very sweet and mentioned hearing Mona on Garden Talk, so that took the sting out of the low turnout. Back at the farm, she grabbed bushel baskets and trudged out to the rows of beans she had to pick. She should've come out in the early part of the day when it was cooler. Now it was hot and she'd be a sweating mess by the time she finished.

Mona squatted on an upturned bucket and began brushing the leafy cover back with her left hand and snapping beans free from the plants with her right. She'd nearly reached the end of the row when Loyal joined her. "Thanks, Dad."

"How'd it go in Clearwater?" He swatted at a mosquito before picking beans across from Mona.

"Not so good. Only one person showed up if you don't count grandkids and paid employees."

"I'm sorry."

"It's no big deal. The lady was really nice anyway. Where were you this morning?"

"I had to have a little chat with Ezra Pike."

"That sounds dreadful. How'd it go?"

"About as you'd expect." Loyal's eyes crinkled when he grinned at his daughter. "He's one ornery son of a bitch."

"Why'd you have to talk to him?"

"He's been hassling the new people over in Traysons Acres."

"What? He hates people. I can't picture him going out of his way to talk to them."

"Oh, he's been bothering them in more passive-aggressive ways. He strung an electric fence right along the property line."

"Jesus." Mona's eyes widened. "That's expensive."

"And pretty mean when you consider both of those families have kids."

"What else'd he do?"

"Dumped a pile of manure right on the edge of the Ogden's backyard. Like two feet from their property line, a huge load of it."

"What a jerk!"

"There's some concern that he's responsible for the damage to the building sites out there, too, though of course he denies it."

Mona dumped a handful of beans into the basket and shuffled further down the row. "I've seen the police reports. The damage was considerable. I mean, he didn't ruin anything, but he's definitely caused them problems. But that seems to have stopped now, right?"

"We don't know it was Ezra, though."

"We also don't know it wasn't. The guy's a real creep."

"Being a creep doesn't make you a criminal, but I agree someone should keep an eye on things out there."

"So, what'd he say when you talked to him?"

"Not much, really. He thanked me for coming by and listened to what I had to say, but he didn't admit or deny anything." Loyal twisted around to stretch his back. "I'd rather not mess around with an easement, but we'll see how he behaves going forward."

"Do you know what time it is, Dad?"

Loyal glanced at his wristwatch. "About three. Why?"

Mona leaped up from her bucket. "Can you finish up here? I have to get someplace and I don't want to be late. I'll bring this stuff up, though." She dumped Loyal's basket of beans on top of hers and paused to thank him.

"Everything okay?" he asked with concern.

"Yes." She bent down to kiss his cheek and jogged up to the barn. She had less than an hour to get ready and she needed to clean up first.

THIRTY-TWO

Maw held his breath while the receptionist put him on hold. He had crossed his fingers, legs, arms and the toes on his left foot for luck.

"Hey, man. How's it going?" Dave's voice crooned over the phone line.

"Good, Dave. Great. Finished shooting my video last week and Ed's working on pulling it all together. I should be able to send it to you by Monday. I was wondering if you had a chance to get my songs on the air yet."

"Well, I took the weekend off, so I left it with the guy covering the airwaves. I think he gave it good play."

"Did you send it anywhere?"

Dave chuckled. "Maw, you gave me a little stick. It's gonna take a while to get a bonfire going."

"Right, right."

"Everything okay, man?"

"Yeah." Maw folded the bill from the recording studio in half so he didn't have to look at the final balance "due in full." "Just want to keep an eye on everything."

"I'll let you know when anything happens, man. Keep rockin'!'"

Maw got off the phone and closed his eyes. He needed a break. A big break. Waiting to get lucky was not going to be enough. Suddenly the radio station became a buzz of static and Maw fiddled with the dial until he tuned in a pop music station. Then the solution hit him. Maw reached into the drawer below his cash register and pulled out a legal pad to begin writing his request. Why hadn't he thought of this earlier? Dave LaMay had a big radio audience, but someone else had a bigger one.

The sky had clouded over a little and the river looked dark where it gently slid past the fallen logs and grassy banks on either side. The sharp aroma of ozone was in the air, rain would fall by evening. Mona brushed a spider off her forearm and watched the bayou intently from her spot on a fallen log. He'd be back here anytime now if he took Maw's advice this afternoon when he bought bait. Mona inhaled deeply to calm the nervous feeling in her stomach. Her plan had too many moving parts, but Maw insisted and if anyone knew how to make an event special, Maw did. She had to trust him.

She listened hard for a motor in the distance but all she heard were birds and the occasional buzz of a dragonfly swooping past her spot in the woods. At her feet were the corked bottles, ready to toss into the water when she heard Scotty's boat. The plan was clever but private. Mona peeled the bark off a long stick just for something to keep her hands occupied while she waited. *What if he didn't come? What if something came up? Or he chose a different fishing spot?* No, that was crazy, everyone listened to Maw.

Mona was nearly ready to head back to where she'd parked her car when a faint hum reached her ears. She leaned forward and concentrated, a smile spreading across her face when the hum grew more distinct. She reached for the first bottle and balanced on a log at the water's edge to throw it in. The bottle flew out of her hand and landed too far away in the tall weeds on the other side of the bayou. "Shit." But they'd planned for mistakes, so she took another bottle and threw it more easily this time. It landed with a quiet splash near the center of the river, disappearing for a second before popping up and bobbing half-submerged. Using the same soft underhand toss, three more bottles followed the first. Then Mona ducked behind a tamarack bush and waited.

Scotty's boat came around the bend and slowed down. Mona watched the bottles, nervous that they'd get pushed to the shore with the waves while he approached. They moved, but floated far enough from the shore that Mona knew he'd see them.

Scotty turned off the motor and dropped his anchor over the side before lifting his tackle box and digging around in it. He prepared his pole, baited the hook and threw it out across the bayou before sitting back—and facing away from the bottles Mona had tossed into the water. "Damn it," she whispered. If she had superpowers, she'd turn the idiot around, turn the boat around, command a fish to nudge the bottles to a spot where he'd notice them. Instead she concentrated on him while nervously chewing at a hangnail.

He reeled in his line and cast it back out a few more times before finally turning around to look further into the bayou. Scotty noticed the bottles after two more casts. First, he attempted to drag a bottle in by leading his fishing line around it, but the bottle kept sliding past the wet nylon line. Eventually, Scotty gave up and sat with a net ready in his lap. He'd wait for the bottles to drift closer and catch them.

Mona wished she could stand up and yell at him. *Move your boat closer and pull them in, idiot! Open and see what's inside!* Patience in growing plants was one thing, but in this case she felt anxious.

Finally, Scotty stood and leaned over the side of the boat and scooped up the first bottle with his net. He lifted the bottle and held it with one hand while he used his teeth to remove the cork. Mona held her breath and sweat beaded on her face. He worked the paper out with his finger and held it up. After looking around the bayou, Scotty dipped the net into the water again. And again. And again.

Birds chirped, a turtle crawled off a log into the river and Scotty let out a single "Whoop!" before starting to laugh.

Laughing was a good sign, Mona decided. She wiped the sweat off her face with the edge of her shirt and snuck back down the shoreline to the canoe she'd hidden in a stand of cattails. Slipping through the water, the canoe glided towards Scotty's boat. He was pulling up his anchor with his back to her and she called out.

"There's a lot of fish in this river, but you're the catch I want, Scott Allan Trayson."

He let go of the rope and turned to face her. "That a fact?"

She paddled closer. "That's a fact. You taking the bait?" She dragged the paddle on the right side of her canoe so she was facing him.

Scotty crossed his arms and looked down at her. "I'm checking it out." He glanced over his shoulder and smirked. "I might drop my hook over there."

"Don't make me keep fishing, Scotty." Mona pulled in her paddle and rested it on her thighs.

He knelt down and reached for her hands. "Hook, line and sinker, Mona. I'm all yours."

The hardest decision was who to tell first, until Mona remembered her father's advice: think of more than just two choices. The following evening June and Loyal greeted the Traysons while they took a seat at the bar to wait for Mona to join them. "What brings you out on this fine summer night?" June asked them.

"Scotty asked us to join him for supper," Dottie said. "I've been after him to pitch in around the house more, so maybe this is his way of making a meal."

"Mona asked us to meet her here, too. Maybe we can all get a table together." June sat beside her friend and ordered a vodka tonic from the bartender.

"Where's Steve?" Gene asked the bartender.

"He and Arlyce took the night off. Their oldest is waiting tables."

June and Dottie looked at each other and laughed. "About damn time," June said. She raised her drink and tapped against Dottie's glass.

Mona and Scotty walked in a moment later and waved to their parents. "You started without us," Mona said.

"We're waiting," June said blithely and nodded towards Dottie. "The Traysons were here so we pulled up a chair—what did you just say? Us?" June tilted her head to one side.

Loyal and Gene paused, their cans of beer held mid-air while Scotty and Mona exchanged a sly smile with each other. "Us," Scotty announced and reached for Mona's left hand to raise it overhead.

"We," Mona paused for emphasis, "have something we'd like to tell you. All of you," she looked at Dottie and her grin grew bigger.

Dottie reached down and squeezed June's knee. "Are they—?"

June's hands flew to her chest and she gasped.

"We're making a permanent partnership," Scotty told them.

"We're getting married!" Mona burst out. She'd never been hugged so many times in her life. Dottie burst into happy tears and Gene thumped Scotty so hard on the back he nearly knocked him over.

"I think you'll make a perfect pair," Loyal said.

"It's just too bad Arlyce and Steve aren't here to celebrate with us," June said later while they sat at a table on the deck. "After all those years of talking to her about our unsettled children. I can't wait to tell her."

"Not much makes her happy," Dottie added. "But I think this news will do the trick."

Loyal cleared his throat. "Does this mean we have help now?" he asked Scotty.

"Yes, sir. I still plan to work construction and side jobs, but you can count on me to pitch in on the farm."

"I can't think of a finer pair of hands to put in charge." Loyal raised his drink. "To a Trayson-Butterfield union."

THIRTY-THREE

Sunday evening the Shanskis were out on the deck clearing away debris from the boaters who were steering their sunburned and worn out parties back towards home. Arlyce lugged a bus tub full of dishes and glasses into the kitchen when she heard it. "Turn that up!" she commanded her sons. Hunter pulled his hands out of the soapy dishwater and twisted the volume knob on the kitchen radio. She lit a cigarette and leaned towards the speaker.

Mona and Scotty were studying a catalog of wedding invitations when her phone rang. "Turn on your radio—now!" Jenny's voice squealed in her ear. "You will not believe it!" Mona looked wide-eyed at Scotty and stood to grab the transistor radio off the kitchen windowsill.

"What station?" she asked.

"One-oh-one. OH MY GOD!"

Tammy and Rawley were curled beside each other on their living room couch watching a movie on TV when their son called down from his bedroom. "Dad? What's the name of that guy from the bait shop? The one who took us fishing?"

"Maw Cooper. Why do you ask?"

"He's on the radio right now. You should listen."

Maw and Peg sat at the picnic table behind their house with their kids and listened to the program on their daughter's boom box. She had a blank tape waiting to record the big moment when it happened.

"You know you're crazy. This might not happen, you realize that," Peg repeated for the hundredth time.

"I know, but I have to try. I can't just go back to being normal. It isn't me."

The DJ's smooth voice broke through the last refrain of the song. "And moving up the charts this week, the Fine Young Cannibals with 'Good Thing.' Now it's time for a letter from a long-time listener."

Maw gestured to his daughter to start recording.

"'Dear Casey, I live in a small fishing town in northern Wisconsin. Bassville is known for a lot of great things, but mostly for the Wissipaw River that runs through it. Casey, my dream is to put Bassville on the map so people can learn about this special town and maybe even pay us a visit someday. I started making Bassville famous five years ago when Dave LaMay, Chicago's DJ on WLUP, called for a fishing report. Since then my shop, Maw's Bait and Tackle, became world famous for my unique breed of minnows, the Cantankerous, Belligerent, Passive-Aggressive and our brand-new Pugnacious minnows. These minnows actually go after the fish for people. This summer I started writing music about fishing and Bassville and what makes the Wissipaw great. If you'd play one of the songs I produced, I'd appreciate it. Every week I hear you give the advice to 'keep your feet on the ground and keep reaching for the stars.' Can you play my song about Bassville so the world can hear what makes this place so wonderful? Sincerely, Maw Cooper.' Maw, listening to your song really did make me want to visit Bassville and I'm sure my listeners will want to come fishing after they hear your song. Here's your very unique request and dedication to Bassville, Wisconsin."

Maw held his breath while the first notes played. A few chords later his gravelly voice started rapping.

While Casey Kasem took a commercial break after the song was over, Maw leaned back in his lawn chair and gazed up at the night sky. The clouds covered most of the stars but he could pick out Polaris and he delivered a silent thanks for the divine intervention.

"That was a sweet tribute, honey." Peg leaned over to peck his cheek.

"You were on national radio, Dad," his son said. "That's really world famous."

"Did you get it?" Maw asked his daughter.

She rewound the tape for a few seconds and hit play. Maw's voice came over the speakers and she nodded. "This might not be the dorkiest thing you ever did."

Maw laughed and wrapped his arm around his wife's shoulders. "If I have my teenaged daughter's approval, then I think it's a hit."

The river flowed silently past the grassy banks, its dark glassy surface reflecting the gleaming night sky. An owl hooted, its lonely call echoing down the bayou, magnified by the water. The chirping notes of newly hatched crickets grated against the whine of mosquitoes.

A pair of wings flapped and a quiet splash announced a fish rising to the surface to snag an insect. The water, colder near the murky bottom, pushed a few empty snail shells along towards the channel where they'd spin and twist faster before getting tangled in some seaweed in Pigeon Lake. A catfish bobbled its head back and forth, its barbels skimming the river bottom for food. Several feet above, a turtle swam towards a mossy log that had lodged between a boulder and the shoreline. Beneath the log, the first bloom of algae appeared and the leaves at the farthest span of the maple trees were tinged with orange.

Acknowledgements

Appreciation for the production team of Mitch Miskoviak, who created gorgeous cover art; Becky Brown, who performed phenomenal copy editing; and Beth Cole, who developed the lovely book design.

A shout-out to the experts: Janelle Westemeier, my sister-in-law who silently corrects my grammar while reading proofs for me, and Paul Hermsen who offered electrical advice.

Gratitude to my writers group: Marni Graff, Lauren Small and Mariana Damon, three women who make my work better with their expertise and give me so much encouragement. Writing can be a tough, solitary grind and their help keeps me from quitting.

If the Kapitzkes had not hired me off the street one slushy day in March to work in the Bridge Bar I would not have these stories to tell. Bartending taught me many lessons, one being that people are generous, especially with stories. Thank you, reader, for spending time with mine. I remain especially thankful for the people who sat at the bar and shared their lives and stories with me.

Finally, I am grateful to Doug for supporting my work and bragging on me.

About the Author

Melissa Westemeier lives with her husband and sons in northeastern Wisconsin where she teaches high school English, writes, reads and messes around in her garden. Learn more at melwestemeier.com

The author, age 6, serving up drinks with a smile behind her grandparents' basement bar.